MOSS-SIDE.

BY MARION HARLAND,

AUTHOR OF "ALONE," AND "THE HIDDEN PATH.

> "Love took up the harp of Life, and smote
> On all the chords with might,—
> Smote the chord of Self, that trembling passed
> In music out of sight."

NEW YORK:
DERBY & JACKSON, 119 NASSAU STREET.
1857.

W. H. TINSON Stereotyper.

GEO. RUSSELL, & Co., Printers.

TO

J. C. DERBY, ESQ.

AS A TOKEN OF GRATEFUL ESTEEM AND PERSONAL FRIENDSHIP,

This Volume

IS AFFECTIONATELY INSCRIBED,

MARION HARLAND,

MOSS-SIDE.

CHAPTER I.

"ARE you aware, Louise, that in all our correspondence about this important affair, and in our lengthy conversation this afternoon there has been signal neglect of the happy man of your choice—that I am ignorant even of his name?"

"Ah! that was rather a careless omission on my part. See! this is May Seaton's present, the work of her own fingers—the dear little creature! Does it not remind you of her? She is to be one of our travelling party; I wrote to you to that effect, I believe?"

"You did."

I admired the exquisite embroidery of the satin mouchoir-case, the quilted lining of blue silk; inhaled the verbena perfume that lingered within its depths; wondering, all the while, at the bride's forgetfulness of my question.

We had been school-fellows—Louise Wynne and I; had passed two happy, busy years at Mrs. W——'s celebrated seminary, and being room-mates, must, of necessity, have learned to love or hate each other with our whole hearts. We preferred the more amiable course, and although we had never met until now, since the day of our graduation, the intimacy had sustained no rupture. Our letters, long and frequent, had kept each advised of the other's movements and undiminished affection. It is true I knew nothing of her attachment to her successful suitor, or indeed that such a being existed, previous to her announcement of the anticipated marriage ; but this was an offence easily pardoned—the more easily, since she had not forgotten our ancient compact concerning the bridesmaid's office ; one which is invariably entered into by "inseparable" school-girls, and very rarely respected in the time of trial. Louise never overlooked a friend or broke an engagement, and this is the explanation of my presence in her chamber on this summer day, far away from my southern country home, the roar of a thronged city coming in at our windows, and immediately about us, tokens of the near approach of some gala occasion.

"Herbert and myself planned our route," continued Louise. "I sent you the programme ; the White Mountains and Niagara —not an original one, by any means, but we could think of no other that promised equal gratification to all of us ; Herbert being the only person who has been over the ground before. We concluded, however, to confer with yourself and your brother, before making an irreversible decision. If you can propose any novelty in such an excursion, or if you prefer a visit to Saratoga or Newport, we will cheerfully alter our course."

I assured her of our perfect satisfaction in the existing arrangement.

"I hope you like large parties, in or out of season," was her next remark, as she drew from the wardrobe the bridal dress and veil. "Herbert does not favor this one of my whims. His taste would be for a morning ceremony, travelling-dresses and a family breakfast ; but these hum-drum, economical proceedings do not tally with my notions."

It certainly was not suggested by her lively tone, or anything in her behavior and countenance ; yet as she stood brushing lightly the flounces of her wedding-robe, the veil, with its chaplet of orange blossoms placed upon her head, that I might better observe its length and the beauty of its texture, I thought how pagan priests decked the choicest of their flock with ribbons and garlands, and then led her to the sacrificial altar.

"The ceremony will be a bore—it always is," said Louise, still busy with the lace and flowers. "A large assembly is the only thing that effectually relieves its tedious formality. There are not enough people in town to crowd the rooms, so we shall be comfortable, hot as the weather is."

"Who will compose your travelling-party ?" asked I.

"We shall number six in all. You and Herbert, May and that handsome brother of yours—by the way, how *very* handsome he is !"

"Yourself and Mr. Blank," I interrupted, laughing. "You did not finish your answer to my inquiry."

She colored, but not with the unbidden, rapid rose-tint I had expected to see.

"Have I not told you his name yet ? The truth is we have had so much else to talk about. There is nothing particularly euphonious or aristocratic, either in the prænomen or patronymic of the gentleman in question. He answers to the address of David Wilson."

It was not a patrician title ; I would have chosen Mordaunt or Howard in preference for the high-bred girl who was to assume it, yet it was not this trifling disappointment that embarrassed me into saying, as if trying the effect of the sound upon my ears, "Louise Wilson."

"For Heaven's sake none of that !" broke impatiently from her ; the next second, she bent down and kissed me. "Don't think me cross, dear ; but to you I would be forever the Louise of our other days. You can remember even the dead with love —can you not, Grace ?"

"I can never forget what you have been—what you are now to me," I answered. "Do not hint that you must cease to be my dearest friend, although you love another more."

She kissed me again, because I proffered the pledge of constancy, but her lips were cold and hard, and she went to the table, bestrewed with her bridal gifts.

"I have forgotten whether you ever saw my eldest brother," she said interrogatively.

"I have never met him, I am sorry to say. He was in South America most of the time we spent together at school."

"O, yes! I recollect! He is living here now. We speak of you so often and familiarly, that he feels well acquainted with you, so you must not be shy to him. You will like him, I am sure. He is only my adopted brother, you know?"

"Yes—he is a cousin, I believe?"

"Not even that—but the nephew of my father's first wife. He was a widower when he married my mother. Herbert was orphaned in his infancy, and his aunt promised her dying sister to rear him as her own son, an engagement which my father, after her death, still felt himself bound to fulfill. He has had a collegiate education, and chose the mercantile profession of his own will. They say he is doing well."

She said all this, as if reciting a lesson learned by rote; a very different tone from that in which she generally alluded to her favorite brother. I noticed, moreover, that confusion, instead of order, marked the progress of her hands over the glittering silver, the jewel-caskets, and the hundred nameless articles of bijouterie she pretended to arrange. Suddenly, her arms fell to her side. Some strained cord had snapped asunder.

"I am tired!" she said, fretfully. "May I sit here, Grace, as I used to in the times of study-headaches?"

She dragged a cushion to my feet, as she spoke, and throwing herself upon it, laid her head in my lap. The strange aching at my heart would not let me speak, but from the force of an old and almost forgotten habit, I unbound her hair and passed my fingers through and through the heavy locks, a kind of loving mesmerism, that of yore had always proved efficacious in quelling pain and nervousness. We sat thus for a silent half-hour. Louise might have been supposed to slumber, except that no healthy sleep was ever so motionless, so fearfully still. For myself, I lapsed into my inveterate practice of dreaming. All my surroundings were unfamiliar. The furniture of the apartment was splendid in comparison with that of my simple room at home, and scattered everywhere were garments, that to my eyes, were fit for the wear of royalty itself; silks, that re-produced the shifting hues of the rainbow and the sunset clouds; other and lighter fabrics, whose folds blossomed into bouquets of imperial exotics, or were overrun with graceful vines; muslins, fleecy and sheer as morning mists. Even the friend at my feet was not a reality. I saw not an inch below the surface upon which the world might gaze; whereas *my* Louise was a frank, affectionate child, who had slept in my bosom and wept away every grief in my embrace. In my bewildered musings now, I seemed to see her attempting to lift a ponderous iron gate to bar my entrance to her heart, the threshold worn by my footprints. This thought had come to me during her labored recital of Herbert Wynne's story, and when her arms gave way, I could imagine that I saw the fall and heard the crash. The dull, heavy roar without, never waxing louder or more faint, like the incessant roar of a cataract through a stagnant atmosphere, made my mind wander still more. I knew little then of the bending backs and breaking hearts; the toiling arms and tortured brains; of the battles for life, the groans of the vanquished, the shouts of the victorious that make up that tumult, mighty, yet monotonous—a sound that must reach Heaven's high gate as a sigh from the grieving earth ; but as I listened, it almost stifled me.

"Grace !"

The voice was hollow and broken, but it was her own at last, and my heart leaped to hear it.

"My own Louise !"

"I am very miserable ! Pity me !"

"I *love* you, dearest !"

I drew her nearer to me, and calling her by all the winning names our affection had taught me, assured her of my sympathy in every sorrow, my willingness—my anxiety to aid her by every means this affection could invent.

"I need no help—I ask none ! I ask nothing of any human being besides yourself. I do say to you—pity me !"

"And why, dear Louise ?"

She said nothing for a time, and when the words came, they were not a reply to mine.

"Grace ! do you believe in a God ?"

I could scarcely answer, so great was my astonishment.

"Certainly ! Who can doubt this ?"

"I !"

"Louise ! you are mad !"

"I am sane ! If I believed there was an All-seeing Eye, which would witness and cause to be recorded the tremendous sin I shall coolly commit in three days more, do you think that I, daring as I am, would risk the consequences of such an act ? My father and my mother are members of a Christian church. The God of the one is Gold, that of the other, Society. I disdain hypocrisy—therefore I declare that I have none !"

"Yet there was a time"— I commenced.

"I know ! I know ! I am changed in everything since then, Grace. O, darling ! those happy golden hours !"

I was glad to see the tears—a fiery deluge though they

were. She checked them with a suddenness that surprised me.

"I left school and came home with a mind full of undefined yet enchanting pictures of the free, joyous life in store for me. Society, as seen in chance glimpses from the nursery and in my vacations was a flashing, noisy—merrily noisy stream, upon which my barque would bound without fear of wreck or danger. My début was a 'sensation,' so my mother informed me with natural pride, and from that moment began the development of her plans. Do you suppose that the Circassian slave likes the ring of her gilded fetters better than the wretch in the galleys does the grating of his rusty irons?"

"Both servitudes are galling," I said. "His is no worse than hers, I should think."

"That is because you are unsophisticated. My mother would say that the seraglio fetters are to be coveted; that in this civilized land, in this Bible-reading, God-fearing age, woman's ears should desire no more acceptable music than the clank of the manacles that confine her to the prescribed pace upon the turf of fashionable life. But hear of my heinous transgression—my outrageous sedition! I was involved in an imprudent love-scrape—thus my mother termed it—before I had been 'out' a month, and to the holy horror of the virtuous Mrs. Grundys of our set—with one who was not 'eligible' in the first, second, or even third degree—a poor medical student. At the termination of this, his last session, he had nothing that man had bestowed to rely upon except the diploma his diligence had earned. Heaven's endowment of genius and a brave, true heart were naught in their eyes—blind, besotted bats that they are!"

"Louise! dearest!"

"Don't interrupt me!"

She was sitting upright on the floor, her black hair streaming down her shoulders, her brow knit, her face growing white instead of flushing, as her speech increased in vehemence.

"My mother is never violent. There she had the advantage of me when the outbreak arrived—which, thanks to her diplomacy, was not until weeks of absence and estrangement had driven me well-nigh to doubt of his love, while they forced me to confess mine, for the first time, to myself. His visits having been discontinued, our casual meetings were those of apparent strangers, or slight acquaintances. The truth was revealed one day, when, through singular negligence on her part, we found ourselves together at the house of a friend, in circumstances where an interview could not be avoided. From him I learned that my mother had insinuated her disapprobation of the attentions my duller sight had not considered marked, and his proud nature required no more to exclude him from our dwelling. He was ready for departure for the far West, but this conversation decided him to postpone the journey. A formal declaration, sanctioned by myself, was presented to my father, and met, as I had forewarned him it would do, with a peremptory refusal. I joined my pleadings to his. They were not offered to my mother—I knew her too well—but to the parent who had hitherto indulged my every caprice, although I had never thought of seeking sympathy from him. Like most other men, he made a business matter of our petition. Could the drops that were falling from my heart have been coined into guineas for my lover's purse, how gracious would have been his reception into our family—with what a flourish our plighting been proclaimed! But they were only life-blood, whose flow must leave that heart a dead, worthless thing, and for all practical purposes, I would be better off. Then I vowed that no mortal power should hinder me from becoming his wife; that I would follow him through poverty, toil, banishment, to the world's end. I met opposition here for which I was not prepared. I shall never forget the sad but resolute words that answered my offer to do this, and more, if he would permit it.

"'No, Louise! I cannot—I ought not to avail myself of your

generosity. Mine you cannot be now. All that I ask of you is to remember and to wait. If I live, I will claim you when your friends shall feel honored, not disgraced by the alliance.'

"'Remember and wait!' This was my watchword, my talisman for six months, and then I had a letter from a brother physician in a distant city, who had seen *him* die!"

The brow did not relax; the lips were still rigid. She bowed her head again to my knee.

Twilight was gathering in the corners; the gleam of the silver was dim, and the vari-colored robes were sobered into one dun hue. The bridal dress had been hung upon the foot of the bed, and the veil spread over it. Through my tears, the streaming white flow of its drapery took the form of a living presence—an angel, whose garments of light were the one spot of brightness in the room, bending towards the grief-smitten girl in an attitude of love and compassion. Without, the roar of the Fall was heavy, ceaseless, and I began to discern some meaning in its voice.

"His zeal in his profession," continued Louise, "so said the writer, 'had led him into the midst of a dangerous epidemic, then prevailing in that place, and he had fallen, an honorable sacrifice.' I told no one of the tidings I had received. The letter reached me in the forenoon. That evening I appeared at a large party, and danced, and laughed, and coquetted until daybreak. A week later, my mother saw the announcement of his death in a Western paper, and sent it up to my room. When we met, not a syllable was exchanged on the subject, nor has his name ever passed my lips or pierced my ears since. But, Grace!" and her voice sank to a whisper—"deep in my heart there is a grave—sealed fast! for I trampled down the earth myself—beat it hard! No grass grows there; no tear ever wets it; no sunbeam ever strays through the darkness to light it. My former self is buried there with *his* memory!"

A spell was on my tongue and senses. I saw the lonely grave; shuddered in the frosty night that enveloped it. Once a fear crossed my mind that we were going mad together, for a maniac I believed her to be at that moment.

The angel seemed to draw nearer—to bend lower.

Louise resumed: "I am to be married in three days—and to man for whom I have no more respect than I would feel for a love-sick schoolboy; one whose society I barely tolerate; just such a commonplace puppet as you might pick up by the dozen in any modern drawing-room well furnished with guests. But my sagacious mamma has consulted confidentially with each of the five hundred oracles of 'Society,' and this is unanimously voted a suitable match—by the same rule that a grovelling barn-yard fowl, if his wings were tipped with shining yellow, might be considered a 'suitable match' for the soaring falcon!"

"But, Louise, you had a right to protest—to rebel against this sale of yourself!"

"Why should I be refractory, my dear Innocent? I prefer an establishment of my own to my present residence—a purse, whose strings are entirely at my command, to dependence upon a father whom my unruly spirit has displeased. Marry I must, or my younger sisters will push me off the stage before the bloom of my youth has departed. Could I remain here to fade and shrivel into a scarecrow-warning to Misses Amelia, Marcia, and Julia Wynne to shun the calamitous crime of a 'romantic attachment?' My mother blandly 'supposed I would treat Mr. Wilson's proposal with the respect it deserved,' and congratulated me after the most highly approved style, when I informed her that I had returned a favorable reply. I have had other wealthy suitors, but none of them were quite so rich as he, and he possesses the additional virtue of good-nature, so I trust he will not incommode me seriously. He is foolish enough to adore me, and I, as I have said, do not esteem him of sufficient importance to dislike him—so we shall be a pattern couple, and happy—yes, quite happy !"

She was raising the gate again—no longer with spasmodic uncertain energy, but with the efficient, continuous power of will—a will, which in her earlier, and I was obliged to say to myself, her better days, was invincible when excited to exert its full vigor.

It was only a puff of wind that fluttered the veil, but the angel seemed preparing for flight. Steps and voices were heard upon the stair-case. Louise sprang to her feet, folded me in a convulsive embrace, pressed a last kiss upon my mouth—and the grim door clashed to—never more to yield to the touch of a mortal's hand.

Amelia, a pert girl of fourteen, and Louise's maid were the intruders. The latter brought a pair of lamps that drove gloom and apparitions from the chamber.

"Bless me, Louise !" exclaimed her sister, "don't you mean to dress for tea ? And Mr. Wilson is the soul of punctuality."

"There is the less need then of my embodying the quality," retorted Louise, carelessly. "Miss Leigh and myself have been making work for you, Margaret," to her maid, who was surveying the disordered room in manifest dismay. "I will help you put these dresses away ;" and without even smoothing her hair, she proceeded to fold some and replace others in their several repositories.

"It does provoke me to see you so unconcerned and collected," said Amelia. "Did you ever see another bride behave as she does, Miss Leigh ? Even Herbert complains that you are disrespectful to Mr. Wilson, Louise, in always consulting your own convenience, taking your own time, without caring whether it suits him or not. It is too bad !"

As her sister did not notice this reprimand, delivered with the asperity of a dictatorial duenna, the flippant miss addressed herself poutingly to me, and tendered her assistance to expedite my toilette. She doubtless animadverted mentally upon my stupidity, as she had done upon Louise's indifference, for my maze was not ended, nor was the new aching at my heart removed. I was under the necessity, more than once, of pausing in the task of dressing, and holding myself up by the table, so strong was the impression that the vast, rushing river, booming without, was bearing me with it—that I had become one of its many moaning waves.

CHAPTER II.

Amelia had erred in her statement of the habits of her future brother, or something had caused him to deviate from them this evening, for when we descended to the parlor, three-quarters of an hour after the time to which that young lady had declared him to be "as true as the clock," we found no one there excepting Mrs. Wynne. I had been rather inclined to like her in my childish days, but the revelations of this afternoon had effected a revulsion of sentiment, and I was conscious of replying very distantly to her overtures, as she gave me the seat at her right hand on the sofa, and reiterated the ceremonial of welcome to her house. She was rather a handsome woman, not yet past the meridian of life; for not a strand of grey was mixed with her blonde hair, and the fashionable cap was worn more because it was becoming, and imparted to her the requisite matronly appearance, than to conceal time's ravages. Her face expressed the very superlative of placidity. Had it been more frequently, or, I might say, had it ever been disturbed, I could sooner have believed this the equanimity of a bland nature, and not an adroitly adjusted mask. She was an endless talker, yet nobody was so unrefined, as to style her even, subdued, melting speech, dissolving in the ear, as butter does in the mouth—volubility. I was never able to account for the queer association of ideas, but whenever she opened a conversation with me, I fancied myself a babe in a cradle, which she kept moving to and fro—a gentle oscillation that lulled whether I willed to be quiet or not. Louise sat down to tune her harp just within the folding-doors, too far off, I thought, to hear much that we said.

"After all," said Mrs. Wynne, in her soft undertone, "I am perhaps the person most obliged by your visit, Grace—or am I to do violence to my feelings and custom by saying 'Miss Leigh?'"

"By no means, madam," I rejoined.

"Thank you! I cannot divest myself of the notion that I have a proprietorship in you. You have been a kind, faithful friend to our dear Louise, and it is one of my weak points—an amiable weakness some people are so good as to call it—that I cannot refrain from extending something of a mother's love to those who are beloved by my children. When our sweet girl here asked my permission to write for you, she commenced a statement of her reasons for wishing your attendance upon this interesting occasion, when I checked her—'My love,' said I, 'I am ready to scold you, for imagining for one single moment that I could forget the charming intimacy that has existed between yourself and Grace for four or five years. You know that I have fostered it, have commended your selection of a bosom friend, and incited you to fidelity. Moreover, I shall be happy to see her for my own sake. Her agreeable society and buoyant spirits will beguile me of much of the sadness a mother inevitably feels at such an event as the marriage of a dutiful and cherished daughter. I shall depend upon her to help me bear the trying scene.' So, my dear Grace, you see how selfish I am, and how much you are expected to perform."

The cradle was in full swing, and I answered precisely as she meant I should, that I was honored by the responsibility, and would do my best.

"Mr. Wilson is a superior young man," continued Mrs. Wynne. "Our Louise has made a judicious choice, one seconded with satisfaction by Mr. Wynne and myself. His affection for her recalls some of the most delightful passages of my own experience, for, my little Grace, I was once young, and had my suitors. I must be permitted to observe, as I am speaking to you, that the conduct of Mr. Wilson's *fiancée* is entirely *comme il faut*. A young lady owes it to herself and her sex to conduct herself with great circumspection under these circumstances —my love!"

This was a mild reproof to her daughter for the breaking of a harp-string that twanged loudly at this instant. The placid blue eyes returned to me:

"I suppose our bride has informed you of Mr. Wilson's generosity in purchasing a house on the next block to ours. It is in keeping with his taste and wealth, and I have solaced myself in some poor measure for the loss of my child by superintending the arrangements for her future comfort. Mr. Wilson has consulted me in everything of this sort, and exhibited such an ardent desire to do all in his power to promote his idol's happiness that he has quite won my forgiveness for the robbery he intends committing. I shall soon love him as a son. We have already one adopted child who has never felt the loss of his natural parents; and if it were possible to repay the care we have bestowed upon him, his exemplary conduct would recompense us. He has his faults, it is true."

Louise looked over at us, and although the blue eyes did not stir from mine, her mother evidently substituted another for the sentence on her tongue.

"But there are volumes to be said in his praise. I, of all women, have reason to be proud of my children."

This maternal devotion was, in the language of Society, "a beautiful trait in Mrs. Wynne's character." If so forcible an expression had been admissible in its vocabulary, it would have been termed her most remarkable characteristic. I was made aware, by her rising with a benignant smile towards the door that two gentlemen were entering. Both were young; both well-dressed; but one was taller, and had a finer face and figure than the other. This was my hasty observation as they advanced to pay their respects to the lady of the mansion.

"Mr. Wilson," she said to me; "my son, Mr. Herbert Wynne."

Mr. Wilson bowed; Mr. Wynne shook hands with me cordially as his sister's friend and guest, and took the place his mother vacated for him at my side. I answered his preliminary remarks with attention unequally divided between him and his companion, who had gone from us to Louise. Her description of him was correct, so far as outward appearance was concerned. His bearing was quiet and gentlemanly. There was nothing in it or his face to distinguish him in a crowd. He was not homely; yet his features were not perfectly regular, and whether he was speaking or they were at rest, they were lacking in mobility; forming one of those unfortunate countenances which always lead us to wonder if Nature, in an absent-minded fit, forgot to establish the telegraph between them and the souls of their owners, yet do not tell the unmistakable tale that idiocy reports, of wires severed and destroyed.

Mrs. Wynne approached him after he had spoken some words to his affianced. He arose respectfully and remained standing while he heard and replied to her. His tone was deferential; it was plain that all connected with Louise were objects of peculiar reverence in his sight.

"We have been tempted to quarrel with you for your unheard-of remissness this evening," said the prospective mother-in-law, by a smiling glance, skillfully including her daughter in the plural pronoun.

"My delay was unintentional, I assure you, Mrs. Wynne. It was caused by a circumstance over which I had no control, and displeased me more than it did anybody else."

The lady shook her head. "It is all very well for you to say so ; but I am inclined to suspect a ruse on your part to excite our anxiety, or stimulate our desire for your company."

"No, indeed, madam ! I had no such thought. Miss Louise will acquit me, I am certain."

"Of course," was her reply.

Her mind seemed to be intent upon the instrument now nearly ready for her performance. Her deportment to her lover was uniformly the same ; never rude, yet never exactly respectful. He was unremitting in his homage, craving, as his reward, only the privilege of being near her as the most faithful of her slaves. He had no taste for music, yet when she played, he was contentedly happy to stand a listener to strains as meaningless to him as they would have been to a deaf man ; to hold the gloves or handkerchief she would have tossed on the carpet or table, in the absence of an obsequious beau. My brother was one of our evening visitors, and conversed much with Louise. He was a gay youth of two-and-twenty, chivalric and intelligent, qualities that were not likely to be overlooked or undervalued by her. She had never been more beautiful, more fascinating, than during the hour he remained at her side. So real appeared her enjoyment that I was more than ever disposed to consider the scene of the afternoon as a fever-dream and forget it entirely. I could see that Frederic made various polite efforts to engage Mr. Wilson in their discussions. That these were abortive seemed to be a matter of small consequence to the bride-elect ; nor did her betrothed betray any symptoms of mortification or jealousy at his inability to play any part except that of a looker-on in a dialogue she enjoyed with such gusto. The most patient of automatons, he maintained his post at her left hand ; and when, in a moment of unusual animation, she wheeled quite away from him to face her new acquaintance, he consoled himself by a prolonged study of the bouquet she had intrusted to his care when her fingers were needed for the harp-strings, and which she had not thought to reclaim. He was very fond of flowers, and had brought her this that very evening. She had held it negligently for a few minutes, and observed casually that it was "rather pretty," but her touch had rendered it a sacred thing, enhanced its beauty and fragrance.

May Seaton and myself occupied the same divan, and Herbert Wynne was enacting the agreeable host in his best style. May knew him well, and I soon found myself on the way to like him as much as she did. He was very tall—more than six feet—but as straight as a young pine, and so symmetrical in every proportion that his height was rarely remarked, unless by comparing him with men of ordinary stature, and then one was apt to regard them as dwarfed, and him as the right standard of manly growth. May, tiny sprite! would have been obliged to stand on tiptoe to take his arm, and glanced up at him as the anemone might at the laurel. Opposite as they were in appearance, and, in many respects as to character, they were fast friends—friends in this, the clear, early morning of their lives—truer, when the thunder-cloud swept over the noon-day sun. But memory is anticipating the pen.

Mr. Wynne, a taciturn, abstracted-looking man, who seldom brushed the dust of the counting-room from his coat, and never from his brain, had, with the briefest of excuses, gone out to fulfill a business engagement. His lady-wife left the parlor at the same time, but came back after a while to see how matters were going on. Her eye rested first upon our group, and bespoke amiable approval; then, with a stealthy, cat-like motion, passed over to the other trio. I cannot relate the exact manœuvre by which she accomplished the change, which I saw was decreed the instant she entered. It was apparently a voluntary act of the parties concerned that they were shifted like the pieces on a chess-board; that I was presently seated at the piano, singing with Herbert; Frederic chatting with May, and Louise the circumspect auditor of Mr. Wilson's discourse; while the incomparable mamma gazed benedictions upon us from her chair of state. If I had marvelled at Louise's absolute resignation of soul and body to her mother's control, as I heard her passionate plaint over her lost love; the fierce, bitter denunciations of the code that had murdered her all of earthly joy, this wonder was now merged in the greater admiration of the resolution that had dared, even for a season, to contend with this woman of smooth tongue and iron heart.

The drama was played through bravely by all actors, excepting my "unsophisticated" self. It required my utmost power of self-command to restrain the utterance of emotions that held high, alternate sway within me. There were times when I could have knelt to Louise and wept out my prayer that she would have mercy upon herself; others, in which I was sorely tempted to divulge the truth to the cruelly-deceived dupe of Mrs. Wynne's ambition; or, grown yet more desperate, revolved the probable result of an appeal to this feminine autocrat—a half-resolve, that faded into air when those undisturbed eyes encountered mine. Then I was indignant—ready to brand the whole family, Louise not excepted—with shameless duplicity, abominable fraud. Could Herbert, in whom I hourly discovered more to like and esteem, be ignorant that this marriage would seal the misery of the sister he loved so well, or was he as culpably heartless as the rest? I asked myself this again and again, averse to admit the truth of the reply my mind was forced to give.

The evening came. I was dressed, and awaiting the summons to take my place in the procession. I had dismissed my maid, and the night being sultry, stood leaning out of the window in the vain hope of catching a breath of air fresh enough to bring ease to my laboring lungs. The hoarse murmur of the unquiet river found an answer in my breast; for my thoughts were of human sin and human woe. I longed for, yet dreaded the arrival of, the fatal hour. How much the latter feeling exceeded the other, I discovered when a tap at my door startled me as though it had been the herald of doom.

"Come in !" I said, faintly, and Mrs. Wynne appeared.

"Forgive me for interrupting you, love, but if I recollect rightly, you borrowed my vinaigrette yesterday when your head ached. If you do not need it yourself this evening, may I trouble you for it ?"

I hastened to obey her, and expressed my regret that my thoughtlessness had obliged her to ask for it.

"It is not of the least importance, my sweet child. I seldom have any use for it ; but I find myself a little nervous—nothing very strange, you will say. But I deem it my duty to struggle with my feelings for the sakes and good of those around me. You deserve credit for your punctuality—a very uncommon virtue on these occasions. Let me see whether you are as charming as usual"—throwing a blaze of lamp-light over my figure. "The most chaste taste could propose no alteration. But these pale cheeks, my little Grace ! they are not altogether to my liking. What say you to a touch of artificial bloom, to be kept a profound secret between us two ? No ? then I will not insist. When that modest-looking head is shaken in the negative, nobody who knows you will urge you further. And, indeed, upon second thought, an interesting pallor is preferable. Only, we must bear up, and not distress our dear Louise by our selfish sorrow ; must endeavor to remember, in the midst of our bereavement, that our loss is her gain."

The repressed tide broke from eyes and lips together.

"Oh, Mrs. Wynne ! if I could believe that this is so ! That she will be the happier for this marriage—that her heart goes with her hand !" I sobbed.

She did not tremble in a single nerve. The fall of my hot tears was upon glassy ice. I knew this by instinct before the steady hand she laid upon mine confirmed it; and if I still wept, it was in utter hopelessness. She obliged me, against my will, to hear her; yet her modulations were low and persuasive as ever.

"My darling girl! you are grieving yourself needlessly—spoiling your eyes and complexion, injuring the tone of your spirits at a time when you most need to be cheerful—and afflicting me—for nothing! I have but a minute to stay with you: I ought to be down stairs even now; but I cannot desert you in your trouble. Trouble it is, although imaginary. Look at me, Grace!"

The infallible lullaby motion was beginning to be felt. She smiled as I wiped away the remaining drops, and with one heart-breaking sigh, submitted to the dominion of the look that had quelled storms yet more violent.

"Now, I can talk to you. Have you ever seen in me any proof of slight affection for my children? Have not their interests been mine from their birth up to this hour? Do I not know the peculiar temperament, the disposition, the need of each one of my flock? Is not their welfare the study of life? Am I a very unnatural mother, dear Grace?"

"No madam," she rocked me into saying.

She continued: "I do not chide you for your fears, for I do not doubt that their spring is love, but I appeal to your judgment to decide which of us is the more likely to consult Louise's real good. You have a warm, tender heart, and a head which will become as reliable in its way, by and by. Just now, it is apt to be hasty. If, at your age of discretion, you make as admirable a choice of a husband as your old school-fellow has done, the tears shed at your wedding will be as uncalled-for as these. I have faith in your excellent sense to believe that I shall see the day when our views on this important subject will correspond more nearly than they do at present."

"Heaven forbid!" said my grief-swollen heart; but I essayed a sickly smile as she kissed my forehead and bade me "Be of good cheer—trust and hope!"

Nothing but her presence and watchfulness carried me through the heartless rôle of that evening. Louise was magnificent in dress and carriage; the praise and pride of the assembly; while the groom had never appeared to less advantage. There was, in him a happy flurry and a levity of behavior unbecoming the dignity of his position; nor was this more excusable to the company because it was the evident effect of his intoxicating bliss. According to the Agrarian law of society, he had no right to indulge in more raptures than his neighbors; nor I to be more miserable than the bridesmaid next me in order—a lively rattle who had "run up from the sea-shore, at this barbarously shocking season to see Louise married—not without some hope," she archly confessed, "that so commendable an example might prove contagious."

Mr. Wilson's extremely comfortable frame of mind disposed him to play the entertaining; and although he was not to be inveigled three paces from his wife's elbow, he was bountiful, superfluous in his attentions to every one who approached her. His forte did not lie in the direction of saying the brilliant nothings for which Louise had acquired a reputation, but he had the temerity to stray into this dangerous field; doubtless, with the laudable aim of gratifying her and proving a congeniality of talent and taste. I had avoided his vicinity as much as I could, consistently with my duties as one of the attendants, for the simple reason that I could not endure the incessant allusions made by those who addressed either him or Louise, to their new relation, so I knew nothing of his adventurous spirit until I was the chance listener to a conversation behind me.

"Wilson is coming out alarmingly," said a young man to a lady acquaintance. "I never suspected him of being a wit before, but his scintillations have set the room in a blaze this evening. They are attributable, I suppose, to the inspiration of the occasion. What was his reply to your congratulations?"

"Decidedly a unique one," answered the lady. "He told me that I was the most tastefully-dressed lady in the room—except his wife!"

"And mine was as original. He slapped me on the shoulder, inquired how business was to-day, and complimented the cut of my whiskers."

"No! now, is it possible?"

Their laughter subsided as Mrs. Wynne passed by them, and the subject was resumed when she was at a convenient distance. I did not linger to gather more of their refined criticism, but similar remarks were current wherever I moved. Then occurred to me another and an agonizing element in the unhappiness of Louise's lot—the thought that she was wedded to a man of whom she must often be ashamed! I felt that this must brim her cup of humiliating anguish. Already, ere she had been two hours a wife, one of her main strongholds had been proved untenable. She had never questioned her ability to preserve her individuality; never dreamed that his weakness could detract from her strength. To me, she had declared that she could not despise one to whom she was perfectly indifferent, that "he would not be much in her way;" but she was now to learn that the undiscriminating public will identify the wife, however gifted, with the husband, however inferior; will persist in ignoring the possible duality of their existence. Thanks to her mother's precautionary application of "a touch of artificial bloom," no casual observer would have suspected any emotion at war with those the time and place were presumed to excite; but I was persuaded that I interpreted truly indications of her disgust at his proximity, mortification at his conduct, hatred of the bonds scarcely riveted.

One gesture and look I have never forgotten. I stopped to speak with her at a turn in the promenade, when Mr. Wilson interrupted me with a vapid compliment, not a whit more sensible or appropriate than were those I had heard accredited to him awhile before. Mrs. Wynne happened to be by, and covered the lame attempt dexterously, as she alone had the tact to do. Louise was toying with her bracelet, the bridal present of the enamored groom. The clasp was entangled in her veil; an impatient movement to release it, loosened the spring, and the superb bauble fell to the floor. As Mr. Wilson stooped to regain it, his bride set her foot upon it. Hardly one of the rich cluster of pearls escaped fracture.

A sad accident!" said her mother. "She is a heedless creature, Mr. Wilson, but she will learn care in time, I hope."

I had no thought or observation for the mischief done, for I had seen the glance that went from child to parent. It was present with me for hours and days—stamped indelibly upon my recollection by a horrible nightmare that visited me in the troubled sleep of that, and more than one succeeding night; the apparition of this, my dearly-loved friend, decked in her bridal attire; that scorching gleam in her eyes—crying in sepulchral accents that chilled my blood—"Woe unto them that call evil good, and good evil; that put darkness for light, and light for darkness; that put bitter for sweet, and sweet for bitter! Woe to *myself*—woe!"

CHAPTER III.

We had a fatiguing day's journey, but one full of pleasant excitement; and at even, the sun went down behind Mount Washington, quenching its burning life in an ocean of crimson glory, whose waves bathed many a pure cloud-islet.

The driver of our vehicle—a large, open wagon, mounted upon springs, and furnished with cushioned seats—was a weather-beaten mountaineer, proud of his native hills; and in the course of our ride, he had become imbued with a thorough respect for a party whose admiration was so constantly and energetically expressed. We, on our part, were inclined to cultivate the good-will of a man who knew the history of every rock and tree on the route, and whose traditionary lore was varied and extensive enough to put to shame a library of "Traveller's Guides." He answered every query; humored every caprice, and had found it convenient to halt in the prettiest, most romantic glen on the way, to allow us to eat our luncheon, because May cried out, "What a lovely spot for a pic-nic!"

"The horses are as ready for their feed as human creturs, I guess," was his excuse for declining our united thanks for the favor, and others were as ready when we were seized with a fancy to walk down a mountain, or to feast upon the wild raspberries that reddened whole acres of tangled vines.

We had just emerged from a wooded defile into a cleared plain as the day-god disappeared, and the general exclamation of delight acted instantaneously upon the reins. He said nothing this time of tired horses or steep roads. The scene was ample apology for the pause. With one consent, acknowledged but unuttered, we arose, Herbert and Frederic removing their hats. Right before us was the venerable patriarch of the chain, his iron-grey head bold and stern against the flaming background, undaunted by the storms of thousands of winters, and ready, in his majestic might, to battle with thousands more. Now, for the first time, I realized the sublimity of the expression, "the everlasting hills." It was less difficult to believe that the changeful sky hung above them could "be rolled together like a scroll," the "heavens pass away with a great noise," than that their granite fronts should tremble and bow, their foundations, rooted in the very bowels of the earth, be moved.

How vividly arises to my remembrance the countenance and posture of each of our select company! May Seaton, standing upon the seat where Frederic had placed her that she might have an unobstructed view, a solemnity that verged upon awe stilling her breath and chastening her smile; my brother, with eager eye and dilated nostril, taking in every object with the ardor of one whose love for Nature was unsated and unrestrained: Herbert's lofty figure, statue-like in its quiet, towering above us all, his features eloquent of calm delight, and in his eyes a gleam of glad recognition, and an upward look that was almost adoration. Louise's seat was directly back of mine, and the rapid glance that daguerreotyped the rest, showed me a marble visage; but never through sculptured stone shone such a light as beamed from her awakening soul. If the heart were dead, the intellect, with all its exquisite susceptibility to beauty, its grand capacities, its undying desires, lived still, and its expansion, its longings in this hour were painful in their intensity.

Mr. Wilson approved of the landscape, for he smiled at me, and inquired if I "did not think it very fine?"

Even the uneducated driver comprehended that the magic silence was at an end.

"I guess you've seen it 'most long enough," he said, rather curtly, as he flourished the whip about his leaders' ears.

"How far are we from our stopping-place?" asked Mr. Wilson, yawningly.

"Fifteen miles, over a rough road," was the reply. "It will come on moonlight though, presently; and there's *some* of you won't think the ride too long. Be you hungry, sir?"

"Not yet; but as I have had no dinner, and only a light luncheon, I shall be ravenous by supper-time."

"I shouldn't wonder," said the shrewd Yankee, with an emphasis more significant than polite.

The moon was round and bright in the East before the West was grey, and our four gallant horses bore us on surely and steadily, if not fleetly.

"There's good singing-ground at the bottom of this hill," observed the driver, looking over his shoulder.

We laughed, for we understood the hint. He had lent a pleased ear to several songs and glees with which we had made the mountains echo from time to time in the earlier part of the day, and this was his flattering "encore." As the wheels touched the level road, May's voice began that most familiar and dear of evening lyrics—"Twilight dews." Louise and her husband did not join in our chorus. The one was silent through choice, the other from necessity. The horses trotted softly, and their master's hands were relaxed. The nearest heights took up the rising melody, and repeated it to others more remote, until, in broken snatches, it came back to us, like messages from the far-off summits which were the goal of our journeyings.

"Hallo, there! turn out!"

The call sounded from a gloomy pass, whose descent we had commenced. For a second, a host of absurd fears rushed over me: nursery tales of banditti, and highwaymen, and haunted glens—terrors that fled as precipitately at our driver's assured tone of reply.

"Hallo, there, yourself! what's broke?"

A more pertinent query could not have been constructed. In the middle of the road lay a wagon upon its side, upset by the breaking of a wheel. Its master had untackled his team, and was now engaged in gathering the scattered baggage and cushions. On the other side of the wreck, at the elevation of half a dozen feet from the ground, twinkled something like a small red star, which never moved while the colloquy between the drivers made known to us the cause and extent of the disaster. A Will-o'-the-wisp would not have remained stationary so near to us, nor does that naughty imp regale himself with such choice incense as crept to our olfactories from the meteöric phenomenon aforesaid.

"Well, now!" said our guide, at last; "What do you calculate to do? You are in considerable of a fix."

"Well, I guess, if you can find room for my passenger and his contrivances, or for him without 'em, we will haul the wagon up into the bushes, and I can take the horses back home to-night. Some of the boys will come over with me betimes in the morning and fix up things. Maybe, though, you don't fancy such a heavy load."

"I aint afraid of my team and wagon, without my passengers object," remarked the other, in a louder voice.

"By no means!" responded Herbert, springing to the ground and approaching the luminous point, which was instantly changed to a falling star, and lay flashing its last sparks in the dust.

"We consider ourselves very fortunate, sir, in having arrived in time to offer you a seat in our conveyance," pursued Herbert. "We have room for your trunks also, our baggage having been sent on in the stage. It might inconvenience you to leave them here, as your driver proposes."

"A little, I grant, sir," said a voice, that in spite of its slight foreign accent, did not seem strange to me; and there advanced into the moonlight, a figure nearly as tall as Herbert's own.

"But, although deeply grateful for your kindness, I cannot think of burdening your carriage with what my worthy conductor here calls my 'contrivances.' I dare say he can forward them to-morrow, and for the night, they will be safe where they are. I accept a seat for myself with great pleasure."

In this speech, I could not but note the incongruity of his easy use of English idioms and the accent I have mentioned. He yielded gracefully to Herbert's reiteration of both clauses of his offer, and his assurance that we would not suffer by his compliance with them. The trunks were stowed away under the seats, and with the stranger on the bench with Herbert and myself, we began climbing another ridge.

In the glimpses of light that fell through the trees I could see that our guest was wrapped from head to foot in a furred cloak, as a protection from the chill night air, from which precaution I concluded that he had been accustomed to a more salubrious climate. His travelling cap was slouched and brought forward over his brow and eyes; but now and then I caught a glance that startled me by its brightness. Few Americans, at that day, had adopted the transatlantic fashion of beard-disguise; and his visible contempt for the tonsorial art proclaimed his un-Republican principles upon this head. The conversation, commenced by Herbert out of politeness, was soon a source of lively pleasure to all who could hear it. May and Frederic were so far back that the noise of the wheels drowned what was said by those on the front seat before it reached them; but from the tones that greeted our ears when our road was smooth or our progress slow, we were led to believe them in blissful ignorance of their deprivation, and did not make any useless expenditure of our sympathy. I was glad to perceive that Louise was an interested listener, also that Mr. Wilson's heavy breathing in the slumber that overtook him, did not appear to be observed by the entertaining Frenchman. That this was his nationality, and his breeding Parisian, I speedily determined to my own satisfaction. In learning, the arts and light literature, he was cosmopolitan. Herbert, as has been said, had received a classical education, to which travel and reading had added much that was valuable and ornamental. The stranger proved himself an adept in ordinary surface conversation, before, with inimitable address, he applied the touchstone flint, and struck fire from the steel whose existence his discerning mind had suspected.

For myself, although I said very little, and that only in reply to the courteous attentions of my companions, that three hours' ride in the mountain moonlight was a season of the purest intellectual gratification. The wild variety of scenery ; the virgin forest, in whose impenetrable jungles the owl and whip-poor-will held dismal concert ; the giant hemlocks, clasping arms over us, as if they grudged the usurper, Man, the narrow pass he had hewed through the wilderness ; the brawling streams that leaped and lashed over our way, and laughed, in mocking defiance, from rocky beds no human foot had ever trodden ; the open valleys, flooded with moonbeams and girt with Alpine heights—all were accessories to my enjoyment. It was with a sigh of regret that I looked up at the frowning walls of the Notch, and passed through the stupendous gateway, for I was told that our stopping-place for the night was just beyond.

The tired horses quickened their gait ; Mr. Wilson shook himself and stood up to survey the hotel, with a fervent ejaculation of thankfulness ; and we drew up before a well-lighted house, whose dimensions, although respectable in reality, were woefully insignificant to eyes that had gazed so long upon objects measured by miles instead of feet.

"I am as hungry as a wolf," said Mr. Wilson, stretching his cramped limbs after alighting. "I have been dreaming of eating for the last hour. I thought we had venison and claret for supper—not a bad idea—hey, Wynne?"

Our wayside windfall did not appear at the table to which we presently sat down; therefore he formed the principal topic of discussion. Mr. Wilson had his say in this matter, and deserved the more credit for his communicativeness since he was, as he protested, "amazingly sharp-set." He had found the gentleman's name inscribed directly beneath those of our party. It was "H. Dumont." We saw no more of him that evening; but when Herbert knocked at the door the next morning, to call May and myself to breakfast, he told us that Mr. Dumont had exchanged cards with him, and, at his request, was now awaiting the ladies in the parlor.

I did not like our nocturnal acquaintance so well by daylight, without being able to assign a satisfactory reason for my disappointment. He was older than I had supposed when I saw him by the moon and lamplight, for the frost had not quite spared his curling auburn beard, and I was sure that the abundant head of hair was not his by right of original growth. There was something in the protracted look, with which he honored me at our introduction, that did not please me; and I imagined, moreover, that his manner was less affable to Frederic than to Herbert, being tinctured with a sort of hauteur, amounting, I should have said, to dislike, had not the idea been too ridiculous. The high-spirited youth received a like impression, and formed a prejudice against him before breakfast was dispatched. But, apart from these fanciful censures of ours, we could not but concede to him the title of a finished gentleman. Herbert and Louise seemed particularly drawn towards him. He escorted the latter back to the parlor; and while Mr. Wilson puffed his Havana in the piazza, and watched the uncouth gambols of a bear, chained to a pole upon what was denominated, by courtesy, the lawn, the courtly Parisian charmed his wife into forgetfulness of his very existence by his dazzling play of wit and sentiment.

I was looking out of the window in the direction of the Notch, when Herbert joined me.

"We have accidentally procured a valuable addition to our number," he remarked. "There is a species of fascination about the man that tempts me to profess a belief in his theory of animal magnetism. Do you not like him?"

"I admire him," I said, hesitatingly.

He smiled. "You are cautious of allowing strangers a place in your affections; you do not permit them to pass within the outer court without strict examination of their credentials, and personal knowledge of their merits. Am I right?"

"You commend me for more discretion than I possess," I replied. "Those who are worldly-wise warn me that the gates of my heart are too readily opened. But the case in question is not one of the affections—hardly of acquaintanceship. I want a word to express the relation which this Mr. Dumont, to whom I was introduced an hour ago, bears to me"——

An admonitory sign advised me to bridle my tongue. May and Frederic, equipped for a ramble, were talking with Louise, and Mr. Dumont was crossing the room towards us. Herbert did not allow me to be embarrassed.

"Miss Leigh is saying, Mr. Dumont, that our language is barren of words to signify the many degrees of acquaintanceship, liking and friendship. She thinks, and justly, that the mere pronunciation of the name and style of Mr. Smith to Mr. Jenkins, and *vice versâ*, cannot be said, in fact, to make these gentlemen 'acquainted,' a term which our lexicons define as 'known—familiarly known.'"

"I concur in her criticism and yours," said Mr. Dumont; "and its justice becomes more apparent if we follow up the intercourse of the aforementioned worthies, until they deserve the appellation bestowed upon them at first sight. They shake hands now, when they meet, instead of exchanging formal bows. Jenkins thinks Smith 'a clever fellow,' and asks him to dinner to-day at his hotel; a courtesy which Smith considers himself under obligations to reciprocate, by inviting him to a supper of champagne and oysters to-morrow night, in a note beginning, 'Dear Sir,' and signed, 'Truly yours.' The liking, of which Miss Leigh speaks as the second grade of initiation into the brotherhood of soul and heart, has now begun, as both are ready to attest when they arise from the convivial board. The next billet will commence, 'My dear Friend'—'and my friend, Mr. Smith,' comes naturally and frequently from Jenkins' lips. Some fine morning he reads in the day's Journal or Herald of 'the untimely and lamented decease of Alphonso Smith, Esq. 'Ah, poor fellow! who would have thought it?' and if he be very tender-hearted, he breathes a sigh to his faithful cigar, as he turns the sheet to inspect the list of 'prices current.' You, Mr. Wynne, are young and fortunate enough to believe friendship something more than a name. You may have a soul-brother, in whose joys you rejoice, in whose woes you are afflicted; your time, your fortune, your life, if need be, are his. You would mourn his death as the greatest calamity that could befall you —yet you have no single word to describe this other self, except the identical one used by the bereaved Jenkins."

"I dispute his right to employ it," said Herbert. "Smith was his companion"——

"Which is in common use as a synonym for husband or wife," interrupted Mr. Dumont. "In French, he was '*un bon camarade;*' in Latin, his *socius*—the English is wanting. Associate, crony, chum—neither of these is precisely what you need."

"But abused and weakened though it is, by indiscriminate use, 'Friend' is a grand, a glorious name," replied Herbert, "and I, for one, never speak it unless when my heart goes forth in its utterance."

"Take, then, the advice of one who has seen more of the evil in mankind than you ever dreamed of, and speak it as rarely as possible," said the stranger in a tone of melancholy sweetness. "This counsel is distasteful to you, I see, but my word for it, if you and Miss Leigh live twenty years longer, you will revere my memory as that of a prophet."

One of those sudden clouds that often surprise the traveller in mountainous regions rolled over the sun, and the air became cold and damp.

"You shiver!" observed Mr. Dumont to me. "Allow me to lower this window, and set your chair out of the draught. This climate is as fickle as Fortune."

He closed the sash, and took a stand nearer to me. I seemed to grow colder in his shadow than in that of the cloud. There was a general movement of shutting doors and windows, for the mist was thickening fast, and penetrated everywhere. Herbert, always thoughtful, left the room to get my shawl.

"You find the changes of weather here more trying than in your city, Miss Leigh?" Mr. Dumont said, turning a large seal-ring he wore upon his third finger, a trick of his, when listless or abstracted.

"I certainly feel them more sensibly than do my New York friends," I rejoined, "for my home is in the South."

"Ah! I beg your pardon! I understood from Mr. Wynne that his entire party was from that city. I have travelled in the Southern States, and have many most agreeable recollections of my visits to New Orleans, Savannah and Charleston."

"Did you pass through Virginia?" I inquired.

"I passed through it literally, for I did not stop in any place within its precincts. I regret this the more, since I infer from your question that it is your home. You bear a name which no student of American history can hear unmoved. The Revolutionary era produced few more accomplished orators or braver men than Richard Henry Lee."

"I can claim only a patriotic pride in his fame," said I "Not only does the different orthography of my name put to rest the subject of relationship, but my father's birth-place, and that of his whole family, excepting myself, is in another State --in Alabama."

"He reversed the common order of emigration"—with a civil feint of interest. "The tide sets most strongly Westward and Southward."

"My mother's health required the change, I believe, sir, and after her death, my father saw no reason why he should remove to his former location, the social institutions of the States being the same, and the climate of Virginia the more healthy of the two."

"Did he accompany you North? I have some valued acquaintances"—he smiled as he pronounced the word—"in Alabama, who may likewise be his."

"He remained at home, unfortunately—that is, for my brother and myself, who, being the youngest children, still reside with him."

I was ashamed of having been betrayed by my selfish pleasure at the mention of a home and father so beloved, into this tale of family affairs. I would stop here, I determined, and not disgrace myself by further egotism. He must think me very transparent, not to say silly. Yet, when he asked another question with respect and growing interest that began to seem genuine, I answered him with the same frankness.

"Then you left him alone?"

"No, sir. An aunt, who has lived with us for many years, is his companion."

Herbert brought the shawl and disposed it about my shoulders As. I thanked him, I met Mr. Dumont's gaze, and again I felt as if he were the cloud that had changed the warm, bright day into a drizzling twilight.

"Miss Leigh and myself have been speaking of Alabama," he said to Herbert, "you have heard the circumstance from which, it is said, it derived its name?"

"Not that I know of," was the reply. "What was it?"

Mr. Dumont turned his ring, thoughtfully. "According to tradition, a tribe of Indians, driven Southward by the advance of civilization, after many weeks of toilsome march, one day at sunsetting, reached a lovely country, a sanctuary unviolated by the remorseless white man. On the banks of a broad, calmly-flowing river where their canoes might ply as they hoped, unmolested for ages; in the skirts of a forest where the deer were sporting like tame kids, the chief struck the pole of his tent into the earth, exclaiming, 'Alabama! Alabama! (Here we rest)!'"

"Beautiful!" said Louise, who had come up at the commencement of the legend.

"Beautiful, and very touching," replied Mr. Dumont, "when we reflect how fatally blighted were the anticipations of the doomed people. They were in their autumn then, fading away, but trusting that spring would visit and revive them in that distant, sunny land. Their winter is hopeless. The withered leaves that rustle now across the Western prairies will not be succeeded by others of living green."

The rain forbade any sight-seeing that forenoon, but we were far from disconsolate in our imprisonment. May and Frederic—a phrase which is becoming stereotyped to the reader's sight, as it is upon my heart—two merry children, talked, and danced, and sang away the hours; Mr. Wilson roamed from piazza to parlor (the bear having been pelted to his kennel by the showers), took a siesta after luncheon, and consecrated the remainder of his leisure to complacent adoration of his wife, who, gay and earnest alternately, indulged in a sprightly ramble of fancy, or held metaphysical converse with the singularly attractive being whom Fortune appeared to have sent to preserve her from ennui. Herbert was, of course, my most constant attendant, and we were the reconciling elements of the party, for May, undesignedly taking her cue from Frederic, shunned Mr. Dumont, and had we not formed the connecting links, our circle would have been broken into separate, perhaps antagonistic parts.

By dinner-time the vapory curtain was lifted as rapidly as it had descended. From gorge and hill-side and mountain-brow arose fantastic columns and wreaths of mist; some becoming entangled in the tree-tops, and after a struggle breaking away with torn edges, to soar with the rest to another place of meeting, or to lose visible form and substance in the fervid beams of the July sun.

A visit to the Willey house was proposed for our afternoon excursion, and we were so favored as to obtain for teamster our friend of the preceding day. We rattled down the slope of the mountain in exuberant spirits, with scarcely a thought of what we were going to see, until Mr. Dumont asked the driver the date of the event that has clothed the spot with mournful interest.

"Eighteen years ago next month," was his answer. "I remember it as well as if it had been yesterday."

"Was the situation considered unsafe before the slide occurred, or was it entirely unexpected?" questioned Frederic.

"Unsafe, sir, as unsafe could be! The Willeys knew, and everybody around here knew, that they were in danger. Every hard rain brought down rocks and earth, and sometimes little trees, and there were big cracks in the side of the mountain back of the house; but, ah me! its human nater' for folks to get venturesome when they've lived in dangerous places for awhile, nothing has happened to scare 'em more than common. We see enough of that every day in the world, to tell us not to be hard upon these poor wretches who paid for their mistake with their lives."

We were very quiet when we reached the house, whose aspect

of mysterious desolation struck home to our hearts. We stepped lightly through the dismantled rooms, and talked in whispers of the midnight tragedy.

"The avalanche was divided by that rock," said Herbert, pointing from the rear casement to a perpendicular mass of grey stone; "and sweeping to the right and left, overwhelmed the unhappy creatures who sought for safety in the open air. If they had remained in the house all would have been well; but who could have foreseen that?"

"There were nine of 'em in all," our guide was saying to May. "Two were never dug out. The mother and the youngest child were carried a smart piece down the valley, and were afterwards buried where they were found—down there—yonder, where you see that pile of stones. It was an awful time! She had an awful death, but, woman-like, she held her baby tight to her bosom to the last. I have heard say that they could hardly separate them, dead as she was. That's a feeling never wears out!"

We walked down the road to the sepulchre, and added each the customary offering of passers-by to the monument thus gradually raised in commemoration of a love faithful unto death. Reverent hands laid those stones, and pitying tears were dropped at the rude tomb of the humble cottager, whose terrible fate and maternal affection have made her resting-place a shrine to the pilgrim of pleasure, as to the chance traveller in that lonely wild. That this incident in the story affected all minds most powerfully was shown by Herbert's remark after our return to the vehicle.

"How universal is the testimony to the unchangeable might of a mother's love!" he said; "and how admirable the economy of that Providence, which makes man, in his most helpless state, dependent for life itself upon such an unfailing stay!"

"What do you say to the universality of this sentiment when you hear that hundreds, thousands of children are sacrificed annually to heathen gods; that the regular tribute—fixed by government—of certain provinces to the Ganges that enriches their lands, is a specified number of infants? Or, to bring the matter home, when you read in the police reports of your moral Gotham of babes deserted, maimed, murdered by their mothers? When in the very circle in which you live, girls are sold as publicly and unblushingly as was ever an Eastern slave, to gratify the passion of their parents for wealth and distinction?" inquired Mr. Dumont.

The driver's honest face was a picture at that moment. His stare of wonderment and distrust of the speaker and his auditory, his abhorrence of the community which tolerated such enormities, would have excited the risibles of Mr. Dumont himself, had not his regards been fixed upon his ring, while he waited for Herbert's reply.

"The fanatical Hindoo is moved by the same frenzy that afterwards leads her to cast herself under the wheels of the idol-car, or upon the blazing suttee. Reason and natural instinct are dethroned by superstition. Nor do I deny that every spark of humanity may be extinguished by a career of vice; that crime and want may urge to infanticide, as well as drive the God-forsaken wretch to falsify a proverb as old as the world itself—'All that a man hath, will he give for his life.' As to your last example, moral perception and feeling are perverted by a heartless, worldly code, to which you will see the daughters bowing with as eager servility as do their unnatural mothers."

I did not dare to look at Louise, convinced as I was that her brother's severity had no intentional reference to her.

He went on: "Argument upon this subject seems to me absurd. Almost every dwelling in the land will afford you proofs that the instances you enumerate are exceptions to—I repeat it—the universal rule, besides the more conclusive one of what divines call 'internal evidence.' Excuse me for citing an egotistical illustration. I, perhaps, of all here present, have known least, personally, of a parent's love. My father died before my recollection; my mother, when I was in my fourth year. Her place was supplied by the kindest guardians that Heaven ever sent to orphan; but I cherish her memory with more fondness than I do that of all the friends of my youth and manhood. In childhood's trials, in the struggles of boyhood, I felt an irresistible consciousness that the only being who could have entered fully into every feeling, consoled me in every grief, loved me through weal and woe—the better as I lost my hold upon other hearts—was the gentle, loving woman who had gone to her God so many years before. She taught me to pray, and man that I am, I am not ashamed this night, before I lay my head upon my pillow, to fold my hands, and upon my bended knees, repeat, 'Our Father who art in Heaven.' If, as some teach, and I love to believe, the spirits of the departed are permitted to minister to the loved ones of earth, I know that the benignant genius who has guarded me from evil when the waves of temptation rar highest, is my blessed angel mother."

Mr. Dumont turned his ring in silence. The upper part of his face was expressionless, but his moustache lay more heavily upon the beard below, as if his lips were compressed.

Our sturdy teamster drew the back of his hand across his eyes, and chirruped to his horses.

"Good for you, sir!" he said, exercising the freedom of speech arrogated as his birth-right, by every free-born, independent American. "These women are wonderful creatures, take 'em as you will."

Mr. Dumont glanced from him to Herbert disdainfully, as to say, "A fitting advocate of your side!"

Mr. Wynne encouraged the blunt New Hampshire man.

"Wonderfully good—most of them—are they not?"

"Accordin' to my way of thinking, sir, they are too good—the worst of 'em—for men; yet we don't often treat them as they deserve. I've got an old woman 'mong the hills, back of us here, that's worth ten of me, and my old mother that's been in Heaven this twenty-odd years, was just sich another. The best of 'em will get worried sometimes—but then, sez I, 'let 'em fly round and have their own way.' They'll get over it sooner, and live the longer for bein' let alone. Depend upon it too, sir, when a woman frets, a man would swear and take to drink, if he was in her place. My wife jest worries enough to let me know she ain't a saint. She is a little the worse for weather and wear in the face—none of your fancy goods, you understand—but a patienter, harder-working, cheerfuller cretur ain't to be raised in the country round ; and if I was to fall sick, or be laid up with a broken leg or arm, some day—bless your soul, sir ! there's nothin' she would not do for me. She's a prime wife—that's what my old woman is !"

" And she has a prime husband, I'll warrant," said Frederic.

" We can't be too good to 'em, sir. Remember that, young gentlemen, if you are ever so lucky as to get married, as is more than likely. I know that on my death-bed, every cross word and look I've ever give my wife will be a pound of lead on my conscience. I had 'most as lief have a man's blood upon my soul as a woman's broken heart ; 'specially if she was the one I'd promised to 'love and cherish.' That's how *I* feel in the matter !"

CHAPTER IV.

It was the morning after our arrival at Niagara, and I was awakened by May's voice, as she lightly warbled a roundelay at her dressing-table. I lay still, watching the movements of the little sylph, as, unconscious of my observation, she combed out her hair in rippling waves to her waist, and looked at the rosy face in the mirror, with more indifference than others were wont to exhibit in its survey. One of her greatest charms was her ignorance that she possessed any worthy of note. I had subjected her to the closest scrutiny for hours, when, surrounded by admirers, she laughed and chatted with the joyous freshness of a nature, unpolluted by the breath of the world that had done its best to spoil her, yet never detected the least symptom of personal vanity. I had loved her when we were at school together, but my engrossing affection for my then inseparable friend had prevented my doing justice to the character, which our daily association was now unveiling to me. As Louise retired into herself, grew unapproachable behind the iron-gate of resolute reserve, locked up the heart-treasures she once lavished upon me, the gentle May glided into the vacant space, healed the soreness of my spirit. There was no flaw or cloudy mixture in this pearl, and, as my eyes followed her this morning, I thought, with sisterly pride, of one who would seek—would, I hoped, wear it in his bosom.

A magnetic sympathy may have influenced her to look towards me as this idea was in my mind, for we both blushed at the meeting of our glances.

"I have been amusing myself with your profound sleep," she said, offering her ripe, cherry lips for a matutinal kiss. "Sleeping, while the thunder of Niagara is shaking your very bed, and the spray damping your pillow! And yesterday you were in a tremor of impatience to get the earliest glimpse of the mist that rises from it! How will this story do to tell?"

"The truth is, May," I said, arranging myself in a more comfortably indolent position, and making of my arms a cushion for my head, "it is uncertainty, suspense, that renders us impatient. I feasted my eyes in part last evening; took off the edge of my optic appetite, so to speak, and some measure of delay is necessary to restore its tone. The Falls will be here, and so will we, for several days to come. I am an epicurean."

"I thought that Mr. Wilson was the most conscientious disciple of the old heathen gourmand in our company," she replied, "but it appears you do not despise his philosophy."

"I apply it more intellectually—do me the favor to add," rejoined I, pretending to be offended.

"Grace," pursued May, her small hands running over with the wealth of brown tresses she endeavored to bind up, while the glass showed me a very grave countenance, "some things trouble me grievously."

"Such as what, my lady-bird?"

"Why did Louise marry Mr. Wilson?"

"Why do most people marry, May?"

"Because they love one another, or imagine they do," she said, confidently.

"And may not Louise imagine she loves her husband?"

"Hardly; I think her indifference is unfeigned, although how any one, a woman especially, can be indifferent in such a relation is a greater puzzle to me than wedding through absolute spite to accomplish the misery of the other party by one's own unhappiness. Love or hatred would be the alternatives with me."

Cordially as I endorsed this remark, I laughed at the thought of May's hating any creature or thing in creation.

"It is a pity," she said, finding that I made no rejoinder, "that they were ever 'joined together.' Louise has qualities that would make her the joy and glory of a congenial mate, and Mr. Wilson would be an excellent husband for a woman of a lower grade of talent and less refinement. He is good-natured, easy-tempered to a fault, and generous, besides having really a deep, rich heart, if he only knew how to speak of its abundance."

She was in the mood for talking seriously, and I would not stop her, wondering, as I did, when she gained this insight into a subject never broached until now by either of us, without my suspecting that she was on the watch.

"They say that similarity of temper and taste is requisite as a foundation for enduring friendship," she said, "and that love seeks contrasts; but I do not listen to this. Unless there is a wide field of kindred sentiments and harmonious traits, there can be no true soul-union—only the mockery of a name, acknowledged as legal by man, disallowed by their own hearts and Him who sees their secrets."

"I rejoice that you feel thus, May; married or single, you will be none the worse for right views upon this point," I added, sagely, seeing the quick crimson she turned from me to conceal, and guessing that the earnestness of my first sentence had created the flow. "It is not for us to judge of the motives that impelled Louise to a step that is, to us, unaccountable. To neither of us would the position we think she occupies be endurable, but we may hope for the best, that we have erred in our conclusion, or that matters may mend with her. Mr. Wilson is, as you say, a man of deep affections, which are undividedly hers, and his moral worth is undisputed. He may yet win her love."

"I trust it may be so," returned May, reflectively, pausing in her toilette, and tapping the table with her hair-brush. Her mind was not yet unladen.

"Grace," she resumed at length, in a lower key, "Do you know that I wish Mr. Dumont had never crossed our path?"

"My dear! how can he annoy you now, when he left us three days ago, and all the chances are that you will never behold him again? What harm has he done?"

"I do not like the influence he acquired over Louise," she said, positively. "Do not look so shocked! I do not mean over her heart, but her head. The man is utterly heartless, Grace, and although wiser people may sneer at my notion, I *feel* that such an one is necessarily a dangerous associate. Then, when I attended, as we all did sometimes, to his novel theories, many of which, Herbert says, were stated as the hypotheses of others, and sustained by him for the sake of argument, I could not comprehend half that he said, doubted and disliked what sense I gleaned. He seemed to me to talk transcendentalism, as your brother called it, when Herbert was by, and infidelity, when he was away. I accounted for this upon the ground that he feared contradiction from no one else, since your brother never noticed his lectures by a reply, and Louise most frequently sided with him. You nor Herbert heard the most wicked of his scoffs at the 'superstition of the pietists,' under which class, as well as I could judge, he included everything we honor as religious truth; nor how eloquently he discoursed upon the 'religion of nature,' and the 'emancipation of mind.' Louise has a stronger intellect than mine, and she may have seen through his sophistry, while she listened for the entertainment of her idle hours. I hope she did, that no evil fruit will spring from this seed, but I would not subject my principles of thought and action to the test of association with the accomplished foreigner for worlds."

"May! dearest! how you talk!" I said, surprised at the energy and heat with which she spoke.

"I should be an infidel or a maniac in a week!" she affirmed. "I am afraid of him, Grace, and I wish Louise shared in this fear!"

The breakfast broke in upon her speech, and in the hurried preparations that ensued, we could not pursue a matter that had provoked unprecedented uneasiness on her part, which infection had attacked me during this conversation.

Another bridal couple sat opposite to us at table; both very young, very shy, and very happy. The girl-wife looked askance at us under her drooping eye-lashes, when her husband referred to her decision the question of "steak or chicken," as if she feared his tone might reveal to us what they, simple souls! fancied they were guarding so well from the surrounding strangers; and as the waiter replied to an inquiry touching the same steak, "yes, sir, rare and tender, sir," loud enough to be heard half-a-dozen chairs off, their guilty blushes would have convicted them of the offences of love and recent matrimony in any court of gossip, and suggested to any imagination a resemblance in some particulars to the vaunted surloin. In the plenitude of their bliss, they neglected the breakfast when it was brought. Frederic said they would never have known of its coming, but for the officious waiter's repetition of the laudation previously bestowed upon the beef, with the equally felicitous supplement, "Pair young spring chickens, sir!" as he slapped the dishes down before them.

I am never moved to laughter when I witness these evidences of mutual, all-absorbing attachment in those who have just entered the estate connubial. No haven has quicksands or sunken reefs, and destructive indeed must be the hurricane that wrecks the boat so lately embarked upon these halcyon waters. It is meet that the early hours of the voyage be consecrated wholly to love and joy; that the youthful mariners turn a deaf ear to the croakings of tempest and rocks from those on shore;

cautious or disappointed sages, whom, nothing, they aver, could induce to tempt the treacherous wave ; meet that the eyes of each should pierce no further than to the glad face of the other; for what need that the boiling surf, the tossing, broken craft upon the horizon should mar their rapture by ill-timed bodings? It may be that favoring winds and tranquil seas will be mercifully vouchsafed to them to the end. There are many to whom the heaven of love has continued changeless through life ; or, if it changed, its variations were like those the Southern tropical traveller hails in the natural skies, when every day's journey brings to his sight new constellations of more brilliant and tender lustre. Blessed, thrice blessed they who, peacefully moored in the evening of their existence, behold, most glorious of all the matchless array, the Cross, starry emblem of their faith, beaming down upon them with a brightness the morning never knew !

Louise and Mr. Wilson were seldom suspected to be the wedded ones in whose honor our tour was made. Mistakes, diverting to the gentlemen and confusing to May and myself, were of frequent occurrence wherever we stopped. The very pair whose late coupling was so manifest, and whose perceptions were sensitive by virtue thereof, would, if called upon, have singled out, as the least likely to sympathize in their happiness, the cold, proud-looking lady, who did not once during the meal, bestow a smile or a voluntary word upon the gentleman next to her. Mr. Wilson's skill in table and kitchen mysteries had constituted him, par excellence, our taster, an office which he performed with a due sense of its responsibility.

"Don't eat that egg, Miss Leigh!" he pleaded with me. "It is a trifle too hard, and as indigestible, of course, as a paving-stone. It must have boiled four minutes at the very least—perhaps five. It is disgraceful to any decent hotel to have such a thing upon the table."

"I am very well satisfied with it," said I, dropping it into the glass, but he looked so much concerned that I forbore, and let him remove the obnoxious object.

"Here, waiter, another egg! and see that it does not stay in the water more than three minutes and a half, provided it is boiling when you put the egg in. Three minutes and a half—do you hear? then whip it out in a twinkling! And, waiter! are these the largest glasses you have?"

"The largest for eggs—yes, sir."

"They are too small. I can't mix the egg properly. But they must do, I suppose. You can go," laying his watch upon the table. "In four minutes I shall begin to look for you back. It is a remarkable fact, Miss Leigh, that an egg cooks so much in the shell after it is taken from the water. Hence, the necessity of opening it instantly. I have seen many a one ruined by standing a second too long before it is emptied into the glass. Tough steak, soaked, waxy potatoes, and hard-boiled eggs give me the horrors."

"Mr. Wynne and myself were abroad at sunrise," remarked Frederic to me. "Some morning, while we are here, we must induce you ladies, and you, also, Mr. Wilson, to follow our example. You will be amply compensated for the exertion, and the sacrifice of your second nap."

"I suppose the Falls look very fine at that time," said Mr. Wilson. "I think I have heard or read that they do. And you two gentlemen felt quite poetical, I dare say?"

"We kept it to ourselves if we did," replied Herbert, who received the flattest commonplaces of his friend with the utmost good-nature. "Our pockets were guiltless of sonnets or impromptu blank verse when we returned. The poetaster who could scribble on the brink of Niagara ought to be thrown into the rapids without a form of trial."

"Table-rock would be another Tarpeian precipice under this

ıaw," observed Frederic. "The *cacoethes scribendi,* like the hydrophobia, grows violent at the sight of water; and the greater the quantity, the more serious is the paroxysm."

"Grenville Mellen has not desecrated his subject," said Louise.

"Because he was a true worshipper in Nature's temple," answered her brother. "He did not seat himself at a convenient distance from the 'ocean leaping from the cloud,' and protected against the chance jets of spray by an umbrella—as we saw a gentleman this morning—fill the prepared clean leaf of his journal with 'First impressions,' 'Jottings of thought,' or 'Stanzas upon beholding Niagara.' He was content to wonder and adore in silence. His lines, grand in their truthful simplicity, were the echoes of the thunders that uttered their voices to him there."

"I wish this hotel was a little further off from them," complained Mr. Wilson. "The noise is enough to deafen one. Doesn't it make your head ache, Louise?"

"No," she said, briefly.

"That is queer, when you are so subject to nervous headaches. Do you know, Miss Seaton, that she cannot bear, at times, to have me step across the room or to come near her, so much is she suffering from these attacks? You must eat heartily, Louise, for we shall be riding all the forenoon, and nothing gives me a headache sooner than fasting. It would be a capital notion to take a luncheon with us. It strikes me that a pic-nic among the rocks would be what you call picturesque—really romantic—hey, Wynne?"

"The tailor made a single note—
Heavens! what a place to sponge a coat!"

whispered Frederic to me, as we arose.

Louise showed no signs of mortification at the harmless peculiarities of her liege lord. If we walked, she took his arm ; if we rode, accepted his escort, as she would have done that of a lackey that knew his place. Once, that morning, we came upon them when no one else was by. Louise sat on a stone, not far from the brink of the cliff, looking down into the abyss ; Mr. Wilson, near by, lolled upon the grass, and smoked at his ease. There was a faint play of enthusiasm over his countenance ; and he accosted us animatedly—

"How I wish I had my gun ! Did you ever see a more magnificent chance for a shot ?" pointing to a dove, perched upon a bough that hung directly over the cataract. "I could knock him down with a pistol, even !"

"It would be a shame to kill her," said Herbert, admiring the pretty, fearless creature, swinging with the twig rocked by the rushing waters ; her plumage glistening with mist from the caldron seething whitely, hundreds of feet beneath her. "Innocence should be safe everywhere."

"It is a male bird—why do you say *her* ?" corrected Mr. Wilson. "Are you afraid of fire-arms, Miss Leigh ?"

"Not in the least," I replied.

"Are you tired ?" he then asked.

Again I responded in the negative.

"It is surprising—one of the most surprising things in the world, what powers of endurance you ladies have," he pursued. "There's my wife, now, whom I used to think, in our courting days, could not walk three blocks to save her life. She has broken me down, scrambling up and down these rocks, and frightened me out of my senses by venturing into all manner of dangerous places. Lend me that spy-glass, if you please, Wynne."

He examined something upon the other shore with grave attention.

"They are putting up a handsome building over there. I wonder what it is for—a hotel or dwelling-house ?"

"It is probably a factory," said Frederic, joining us. "There is a sufficient head of water in the Horse Shoe Fall to keep the machinery going in the dryest weather."

"It is hardly near enough to the bank for that," returned the literal bridegroom, not noticing the general smile. "And now, I look again, it is too elegant an affair to be used as a factory. I should like very much to know who intends to live there. He must be a millionaire, but his taste is not mine. Rather a damp situation, I should say. The very table-cloths and napkins here are never dry, and the sheets are wet enough to give one the rheumatism—I would not stay here through the summer for five hundred dollars a week, and in winter—ugh !"

I passed on to Louise's side. Her eyes were moist, yet flashing, and her face wore the excited pallor I had marked the evening of the sunset behind Mount Washington. She did not stir as I approached, and I sat down by her without a word of interruption. Thus the others left us for a long while. The spray dashed up to us, every now and then ; and to our brows it was the baptism of Holy Mother Nature, purifying us for devotion in this, her most wondrous of cathedrals, from which volumes of incense arise unceasingly to heaven, and deep, mighty organ tones swell the sublime anthem—"The Lord God Omnipotent reigneth forever and ever—Hallelujah !"

I repeated it aloud almost unconsciously.

Louise laid her hand on mine. "Thank you !" was all she said, while her face was yet more radiantly beautiful.

I love to think of that last soul-communion, although the black, iron bars over her heart were stern as ever.

"Louise," said her husband's voice, "are you not tired of this one prospect ? I am afraid you are catching your death of cold, sitting here. Why, your dress is heavy with the dampness ! I shall never forgive myself for not looking after you sooner.

She drew her shoulder from under his hand, and remained still as before.

"My dear," he urged, anxiously, "this is awfully imprudent. Had not you better go back to the hotel at once for dry clothing? You can come here again some other time. Dinner will be ready in half an hour."

She broke from him, and darted forward to the very edge of the precipice. For an instant, I expected to see her disappear over the dizzy height, for I had seen her look—the same that had haunted me on her wedding night.

Mr. Wilson stood paralyzed—pale as death—too much terrified to move, even to snatch her from the perilous spot.

"Louise!" said her brother's voice, in an accent of command; and he walked very slowly towards her.

She met him half-way to us.

"She needs a keeper," he said, laughingly, as he brought her back. "See that you prove a more watchful one in future, Wilson. Some heads are not to be trusted in high places."

I could see that this jesting was forced; nor was he quite himself for the rest of the day.

Louise's room was more desirable than mine; being a large apartment in the same story with the parlors; its windows opening down to the floor, and out upon the piazza that formed the principal promenade of visitors. That evening, I slipped away from the company to write a home-letter, and, by Louise's permission, took my desk into this chamber. I had nearly concluded the task, leisurely accomplished, and interrupted by sundry fits of dreaminess—for I was thoughtful as well as happy—when Louise entered. She "had been dancing," she said, with unequal breath and heightened color, and "had torn one of the flounces of her dress from the skirt." I made her sit quietly, to rest, while I mended it. She talked incessantly.

"You are a sober mope!" she said. "Why could you not wait until to-morrow to pen that important document?"

"The mail is closed at nine o'clock," I answered. "If I happened to oversleep myself, I should miss it."

"I thought you said you were going to write to your father! There are six pages!"

"They are all for his reading. I should not presume so much upon the patience of any other correspondent."

"Is this done from a sense of duty, or do you wish to per suade me that you prefer the occupation to the amusements we frivolous butterflies are carrying on in the ball-room?"

"What a question! I love to write to him, and his answers are more acceptable to me than any other gift I could receive in my absence."

"Is he kind to you?"

"He is the best, most affectionate parent that child ever had. I love as much as I respect him."

"And you are hoping, perhaps, that you will never quit him unless to marry some one whom you hold dearer yet? Did it ever occur to you that this loving father may controvert your designs in that respect? that, although your happiness now seems to be his chief aim in life, when an issue of that nature is raised, he will not scruple to overthrow your air-castles—to teach you that this is a world of realities, unsuited to the growth of romance? What will you do then? what *can* you do?

Was this *my* Louise who questioned me so mockingly—so cruelly? Infinitely preferable would have been the bitter scorn, the vehemence that so distressed me in the narration of her heart-history. And, as I looked up reproachfully into her face, she repeated with a frozen, worldly smile—"What will you do?"

"I trust that such a trial will never visit me. I cannot stretch my imagination to the extent of believing that it will, therefor I cannot settle upon my probable line of conduct."

"Why should you be exempt?" she said. "Every gir has some love-cross."

"Mine will take some other form then. My father would not

oppose my choice, if it were a wise one. I confide not in his affection alone, but in his justice. If he could forget both, it would still be my duty to submit to his will."

"Wherever it forced you to go?"

"No!" I said, firmly. "It should not force me to marry a man for whom I could not feel a wife's love."

She laughed at this. "You are candid with me, I see."

"I have never been otherwise, Louise."

"I own it. You would not shrink from telling me, for instance, if pressed to declare your real sentiments—that there never was a more incongruous match upon earth, one in which Heaven had less share, than this most 'proper' alliance of Mr. Wilson and myself; that it is a moral impossibility for me to love or respect him; that my mother's pride of wealth urged me to accept him; that, but for the handsome fortune inherited from his father, the rich grocer, who began life selling fish and molasses in a small retail way, and ended it in a palace, possessed of his million—but for this, his son never would have entered our parlor, much less aspired to my hand. Answer me, like the straightforward, fearless girl you are—do you not envy me my conjugal felicity? You have had a tolerable opportunity for studying the character of my lovable spouse. What do you say of him?"

"That he *is* your husband, Louise!" I retorted, outraged by her total want of delicacy.

"You are mistaken, my dear—you are speaking now after the manner of men—particularly of discreet women. I, Louise, say to you, Grace, that he is not, that he never was—that he never will be my husband. Love him, I do not, honor him I cannot, obey him I *will* not! My bonds do not trammel me much. I shall be a faithful wife in the letter of the law—in the spirit of the managing, prudent dames I mentioned just now. Mr. Wilson asked me to marry him, and I have done it. He ought to be satisfied with, grateful for my amiable complaisance."

"Oh, Louise! when you are deceiving him continually! He loves you as his own life, and believes that your heart is his!"

"The error is his—not mine. I have not told him that I regarded him with any especial favor; nor do I apprehend any inconvenient disclosures as to this section of the compact usual in these affairs. We are a fashionable couple, and the acme of refinement in this relation is a polite indifference. I flatter myself that in study and practice I am perfect in my lesson."

She thanked me for my assistance in repairing her robe, said it was done with neatness and dispatch, and "would not detain me longer from my delightful employment."

I was relieved by her departure, for my heart seemed bursting. She had not only ceased to be my friend, but she was fast learning to spurn her womanhood; treading down all tender and gentle feelings belonging to her sex; putting out of sight every thing that could remind her of what she once was, and striving after that false and abominable system of opinion and argument which would finally enable her to glory in her shame. I was too much excited to weep. I could not go on with my letter; but, with my forehead resting upon the desk, let the flood of troubled thought have its way.

A sound like a sigh or a groan caused me to lift my head and listen. After a short interval, I heard it again. It came from the portico. Timidity in my loneliness would have been most natural; but, without a thought of fear, I cautiously undid one of the blinds and peeped out. Lamps were hung against the pillars of the piazza, and one opposite to me displayed the figure of a man crouched in a chair, leaning over the balustrade. He started up at the slight noise I made in unclosing the shutter, and I perceived that it was Mr. Wilson.

"I beg your pardon!" he said, confusedly; and after some inarticulate murmurings, he appeared about to leave the spot, but his limbs failed him, and he sank again into his seat.

"Are you ill?" I inquired; "cannot I do something for you?" I hardly knew what I was saying, such was the turmoil in heart and head. Had any presence of mind remained, I would not have spoken the next sentence—"Let me send for Louise or Mr. Wynne!"

"Louise! O, Miss Leigh! have mercy!"

My worst suspicions were then correct; yet the removal of suspense restored me to some degree of reason. I brought him a glass of water, and implored him to go into his room and lie down until he felt better.

"I shall never feel better!" he said. "Oh! if I had never been born! Louise! Louise!"

It was a heart-wail of love and sorrow. Never, in all my life, before or since, have I heard any other sound so inexpressibly mournful as the repetition of that name.

"Miss Leigh," he said, presently, with a dignity that surprised me, "I have heard a part of your conversation, but without intending it. I was about to go into that chamber, in search of her, having missed her from the ball-room. I had my hand upon the window to open it, when she mentioned my name."

He stopped and battled with the recollection until he overcame it so far that he could go on. "May I trust you to conceal from her that I know her feelings towards me, and to hide them from others as much as you can?"

"You may," I said. "Fear nothing from me. I would do anything to save you further pain."

"You are very kind;" his voice faltering again. "Poor Louise! She can never be happy with me. It is my fault that she is what she is—yet I would lay down my life for her. You told her so, did you not? Perhaps that would be the best way."

"Mr. Wilson!" I exclaimed. "You wrong yourself by this language. Your intentions were—are good."

"They are! I never meant to make her miserable Miss Leigh. I hoped that she could be happy with me, or, believe me, I would never have asked her to marry me. Yet this hope was blind and selfish. I should have seen that long ago. It is too late now—yet I *do* love her with all the soul I have!"

A step resounded through the piazza, and a gentleman came rapidly in our direction.

"Both found, and together!" said Herbert, laying his hand upon Mr. Wilson's arm. "I arrest you upon the charge of unlawful monopoly. But, what is the matter?" he asked, excited by our awkward silence to a suspicion that all was not right.

"I have been writing a letter, and—and happening to step out here, found Mr. Wilson," I said, blunderingly, my tell-tale features contradicting the careless statement I would have given.

He was not deceived, but, in compassion, withdrew his searching gaze.

"Will you go to your room, or return to the parlor?" inquired he. He spoke kindly, but the most authoritative mandate would have left me equal space for choice. To one or the other, I must depart—and now. This was what he intended, and I was not inclined to be refractory.

"To my room, if you please," I answered, catching at the thought of its quiet solitude.

As he parted from me at the chamber-door, he said, "If you do not object to a walk before you retire, I will call for you, by and by. May will not leave off dancing for two hours yet."

I acquiesced in this, likewise, for in his mind it too was a fixed purpose.

By the time I was tranquillized—able to think and talk, he knocked for me to come forth. He was very grave; and my prescient heart began to tremble. Nothing was said that verified its foreboding until we had taken several turns in the portico. I noticed that he kept close to the outer railing, and spoke softly, and wondered whether this did not prove his knowledge of the unfortunate accident above related.

At length I was assured. "I had a talk with Mr. Wilson after I took you to your room, and gathered from him what he was very unwilling I should learn—what you know better than either of us. Had he been less grieved, or I less positive, I should have been none the wiser for the conversation. There are one or two questions I wish you to answer."

"Oh, no! I cannot!" I cried in alarm. "Indeed I have no right to say anything; I have pledged my word to be silent."

"You promised Mr. Wilson to keep his secret, which is now mine as well. I shall not tempt you to a violation of your word. I wish to inquire if Louise expressed her repugnance to this marriage before it took place."

"Once, and once only—to me," I responded.

"Is it your belief, then, that she has ever done so to any other person?" he interrogated.

"I think it very doubtful. My impression is that she has not—even to her mother."

"Since her marriage, has she been in the habit of speaking to you in the strain she adopted to-night?"

"She has not opened her mouth on the subject before. She is too proud to hint these things to any one but myself. We have been intimate for so long!"

"You have. I wish your friendship had saved her from this fatal step. My misguided sister!"

I could feel his chest heave with the sigh that followed the words.

"Why did you permit her to take the step, then?" was in my heart to say. Something impeded its utterance.

He replied as if I had spoken:

"I was astonished at her acceptance of Wilson's addresses; for he is her inferior in many respects; but she repulsed my expostulations so ungraciously; was so decided in her declaration of her intention, that I, ignorant of the undercurrent operating upon her will, concluded, absurdly enough, that she was willing to overlook his weaknesses for the sake of his noble traits. You do him flagrant injustice if you despise him. His sterling integrity; his industry; his freedom from every appearance of ostentation, and his generous heart endear him to those who look deeper than the outside show. I had not an idea that Louise did violence to her inclination when she wedded him. True, I was, at the outset of the engagement, unfriendly to the match, for much as I esteemed Wilson, I had hoped to see her marry a man of more sprightly intellect; whose tastes and pursuits were more in consonance with hers, but I had no right to interfere—no ground for opposing her will. I would have torn her from him at the very altar, if I had suspected with what motives she went thither."

I felt that he would have acted thus; and it was no longer a mystery why Louise, in her mad resolve of self-immolation, had misled him to believe her a voluntary offering.

"It is hard to say what is best to be done," he said. "I would have informed Louise that her wicked false-dealing—forgive me—but that is just the phrase I designed to use, and you must not dissent—I say, my earliest impulse was to tell her that her wicked false-dealing had been discovered by the man she has injured, but he would not hear of this. You would have respected him, if you could have listened to his pleading in her behalf. The hope that she would ever love him had forsaken him, he said; but he would not court her hatred, nor render her lot less endurable. Blaming himself for his folly in taking her love for granted, he contended that his punishment was just. He represented that she had never deluded him by language or act of fondness. All the demonstration had been on his side, she being only a passive recipient ; conduct he had hitherto ascribed to womanly reserve, and for which he had honored her the more. Not a single reproach must light upon her, either from her family or the world. She was his wife, and while she bore his name, he would protect and cherish her. He commissioned me to thank you for your goodness."

"I did nothing," I interposed.

"You gave him sympathy, and I, with him, bless you for it. He wishes, moreover, that everything shall go on in seeming as before ; that you meet him to-morrow, and always in future, as if nothing had happened. For your own comfort, Grace, you had better forget that there is one sorely-bruised spirit among us to-night, which, this morning, was perhaps the most buoyant of our number."

"I cannot forget his sorrow ; I must feel for him, although forbidden even to look my compassion. Nor ought you to judge Louise too severely ; she is not deliberately heartless."

"I will hear no excuses of her course. Do not *you* attempt to justify it !"

He said this so sternly—it was so unlike himself—that it brought tears to my eyes.

"I did not mean to wound you," he continued. "My mood is not so charitable as you may think that it should be. I am chafed, disappointed—angry ! I may as well out with the whole truth at once !"

"Angry with me ?" said I, fearfully.

"Never !"

His hand touched mine, and my eyes were clear again.

We walked up and down the dim colonnade.

"Hear the Falls, Grace ! What do they say to you ?"

"They calm me," I said.

"As they do me. The sound is not dissimilar to the roar of

the ocean, but its effect upon me, at least, is entirely different. There is no restless moaning here over an undying, mysterious grief, but a strong, exultant shout, the united voice of many waters. We will let it drown the strife of human passions for this hour, will we not?"

We could not be cheerful all at once, nor was our converse gay at last, yet we paced the porch until the rising moon apprised us of the lateness of the hour.

"Are you still sad?" he asked at my door, and I smiled my reply.

May was sleeping soundly, and I lay down beside her. I would have been very light-hearted if I could have lost the recollection of one event of the evening. I thought of my summer, and the black midnight of him, the innocent sufferer; of my full, joyous heart, and hers—the erring woman's—an empty grave-yard, and marvelled vainly why these things were so, in a world that could afford so much of delight.

Then, as a breeze brought the voice of the cataract, louder and more jubilant, to my ear, there was a strange, unspeakable comfort in recognizing the burden of the anthem—in whispering it over in the darkness—strange, because I know now that I did not appreciate the beauty and comprehensiveness of its meaning. The sacred words alone could interpret its language, and they arose unbidden to my lips. Yet I remember that there was a sense of security, of trust in an overruling, all-reconciling Power, induced by the Hallelujah chorus, pealing through the solemn watches of the night, when it only rendered audible praise to the Omnipotent.

CHAPTER V.

My Virginia home had no pretensions to architectural elegance, nor was it imposing in size. A frame farm-house, a story and a half high, with peaked dormer windows in the roof; its walls owed their coat to the whitewash brush, and the casements had no blinds except running roses, virgin's bower and jessamine. Mrs. Wynne's placid orbs would have widened, and her aristocratic shoulders executed the meaning shrug, learned from the most stylish French modiste of the day, at the sight of the humble abode of her daughter's intimate companion; but this benign lady was as far from our minds as we were from her patrician presence, on the evening of our arrival at Moss-side.

If there were little porcelain, and less silver upon our tea-board, loving hearts and smiling faces surrounded it, and the master of the house could not have done the honors of the feast with more graceful hospitality had he been a prince, and we his titled guests. Frederic was his youngest son, and resembled him most in personal appearance; but the fire in the eye, the electric play of expression, were chastened in the elder by age or care. I had often, since I had been old enough to read physiognomies, seen in his, melancholy approximating to gloom; but his ordinary aspect was one of winning benevolence and a mildness nothing could disturb. My aunt sat at the head of the table. She was the sister of our father, and my memory went not back to the date of her entrance into our household. My most infantile recollection was of a tall, pale lady, whose black eyes rarely shone with pleasure, never with mirth; who spoke almost as seldom, unless compelled to it by politeness, which was with her, like every other observance of her daily life, a duty; and who always wore a mourning dress, severely simple as were her manners. She had not altered, to me, since the hour in which my dying mother committed me, a child who had scarcely seen her sixth summer, into her charge. "I give my youngest darling to you, Agnes,"—so the legacy was worded. After that I slept in her room, not in her bosom, but in a crib or cot beside her bed. If I awoke in fright or sickness, she required no other call than my uneasy tossing; she had taught me, patiently and well, until I went from home to school; I had never had an unkind admonition or corporeal correction from her; she was exemplary in every capacity; yet I did not love her with the ardor with which my soul went out to my father. To him I was wont to carry my childish secrets of joy or grief, for fondling and tenderness were necessaries of my nature, and I understood intuitively, before I could well speak his name, where these were to be found. Not that my aunt was repulsive. Her features were fine; her bearing bespoke the lady in birth and breeding; but there was an indescribable chilliness experienced upon a near approach to her, that never failed to deter the boldest from further and familiar advances. She was taciturn now in the midst of our rejoicings, while Frederic's burlesques, and my gossipping stories, did not allow the smile to die away upon my father's face during the repast, and frequently moved him to hearty laughter.

The only satire upon an individual acquaintance was pronounced by Frederic upon Mr. Dumont. The instinctive dislike had been mutual, and I was obliged to qualify the impetuous youth's strictures by some tempering praise of the conversational talents and scholarship of the personage so roughly handled.

"Yes, his pedantry was unequalled, except by his puppyism, and both were set off to the best advantage by his impertinence," returned Frederic, contemptuously.

"But," said I, "we must not measure him, a foreigner, by our standard of etiquette, which is, no doubt, as strange to him as his philosophy is to us."

"I don't believe a syllable of his French origin," was the reply. "He was too much at home in our vernacular, which, but for his finical aspirations, broad *as* and rolling *r-r-r*s might be his too. I'll wager my head that wherever he may have learned these, he was born and raised on this other side of the Atlantic, and that the colors he sails under, are as false as his Macassared hair."

My father bestowed upon him a glance of mingled amusement and warning, and prudently changed the channel of the conversation.

"You did not meet our neighbor, Townley, in your travels, I suppose?"

"No, sir. How far did he go, and when?"

"Not further northward than New York city, I think. He was absent but a fortnight. Had he made the tour of Europe, and consumed a year in the work, his budget could not have been richer and more varied. Do not plume yourselves upon the pitiful scraps you have collected. You will be humble enough to learn of him when he begins to uncover his stock of information.

"How are the sisters three?" I inquired.

"Very well, and brisk as ever. Miss Judy was over yesterday to ask my advice about purchasing a pair of Berkshire pigs Mr. Jones has for sale, and to ascertain if I were averse to joining fences with her in separating our wood-lots. She alleges that the negroes do not pay neighborly respect to our boundary lines; that mine cut down trees on her side, and hers are not slow to return the favor. She is a singular, but an upright woman."

"And Manufactures and my favorite Fine-Arts—are they flourishing?" asked Frederic.

"They are not dull, I fancy ; although I have heard nothing new in the line of either, if I except a 'gem of a picture,' which Mr. Townley brought home for Miss Malvina. She introduced me to it the other day, when I was there. The subject is not striking in elegance or originality—a peasant girl, washing her feet in a brook ; but Mr. Townley informed me that his sister considered it a *pick-toe-rial* treasure."

"Atrocious !" exclaimed Frederic ; "more nauseating than the general run of what, by an odd flight of fancy, he calls puns. He would attempt these horrors at his last gasp, I believe."

"So some one once told him," said my father—upon which he rejoined—"and you, I presume, would deem that a *di-er* misdeed."

Before noon, the ensuing day, as I was standing upon the back porch, exchanging some last words with Frederic, who was equipped for hunting, we heard the rattle of wheels that stopped at our gate.

"Who is it, Joe ?" questioned Frederic of a negro boy, who had run around to the front of the house to reconnoitre.

"Mr. Townley's carriage, sir."

"All three ladies, Joe ?" questioned my brother, dropping his voice, and withdrawing to the corner of the porch best screened from observation.

"Yes, sir—all on 'em !" showing his teeth in lively glee.

"I will be back to supper, sis," was the sportsman's farewell, as he vaulted over the railing, and under cover of a cedar hedge that ran across the yard, made good his retreat to the woods.

I was vexed with him for leaving me to encounter, single-tongued, the force before which he had fled ; yet I was glad, for his sake, that the long, tedious hours of conversation, and the almost as heavy season of dinner was spared to one of us. This act behind the scenes passed so quickly that I was enabled, after seeing Frederic leap the fence into a corn-field—to meet the visitors at the door. I ushered them into the parlor; went into minute inquiries as to the health of each, and in the proper time, invited them to remove their bonnets.

Miss Judy had already loosened the strings of hers, never tied too tightly.

"I should like to speak to my driver," she said, stepping towards the door.

I would have offered to send for him, but she was too brisk for me. I heard her loud tones, ordering that the horses should be unhitched and taken home again, for the purpose of completing a certain job of farm work.

"Bring them back by sunset—do you hear?" she finished the command.

Meanwhile, Miss Susan removed, with much care, a Leghorn hat, trimmed by herself with green ribbon and yellow flowers; and Miss Malvina waited for a second petition before laying aside her more stylish head-piece of pink silk and French lace.

"I do not know that it is advisable, Sister Susan," she said, deferentially. "We came over to make a morning call."

"I am going to stay all day!" put in Miss Judy, reëntering. "I want to have a nice neighborly talk with Mr. Leigh, and look at Miss Agnes' garden. They tell me it beats mine out-and-out," shaking hands with my father and aunt as they came in.

She was a tall, gaunt woman of forty-five; hard, yet not ill-favored, the honest frankness of her sunburnt features redeeming them from homeliness. Her dress was scrupulously neat, but of a make and fit that defies description. She abhorred "furbelows," and a redundance of drapery would have been a sore inconvenience in her walks over the plantation; so her apparel was destitute of ornament, and except in the waist and arm-holes, where she "liked to have a plenty of room," was cut out of the smallest possible quantity of material, the skirt barely reaching her ankles. She wore thick-soled Morocco shoes, and no gloves or cap ; her hair being arranged with the same view as was her attire, "to get it out of the way." Yet, Miss Judy, eccentric and ungainly though she was, masculine in manner and pursuits, was my favorite of the triad.

Miss Susan was thirty ; an inch shorter than her elder sister, pale, with high cheek-bones, and an aquiline nose, a sour expression about the mouth, compressed to a mere line in the lower part of her face, except when it curled to speak ; and a cold, virago stare in the eye. She never moved without her work ; and now drew from her hand-basket several squares of a bed-quilt. I took up one by way of beginning a conversation. The ground-work was white, upon which was sewed a bouquet, consisting of a blue tulip, a purple rose, and an orange pink, cut from glazed, highly-colored furniture chintz, and all mounted upon stalks that might have supported mammoth cabbages.

"After the flowers are transferred, each piece is to be wadded and lined, and then quilted in imitation of a Marseilles counterpane," explained the needlewoman. "Afterwards, the squares are to be stitched together."

"How tedious!" I remarked. "You are courageous to undertake the task."

"It might be tedious to *some* people," pointedly—"I was brought up not to mind work."

"Sister Susan is the most wonderful woman I know," said Miss Malvina; "the most industrious and ingenious person I ever saw. She shames me, but I have no taste—not the slightest, for these occupations. You should see a rug Sister Susan has just finished. It is really superb, very handsome, indeed! The colors are so artistically assorted!"

"We must not expect Grace to look at home manufactures *now*," and the vinegar settled still more sharply about Miss Susan's thin lips. "How plain and mean everything must be to you, after all the finery you have been used to lately! I quite pity you."

"You needn't," Miss Judy answered for me. "Grace has too much good sense to have her head easily turned."

"Thank you, Miss Judy," said my father. "I believe you only do her justice."

This almost made a child of me. The blood rushed to my face and the water to my eyes. I tried to smile and turn the matter off with a jesting speech, which was very imperfectly spoken. Miss Susan had a remarkable faculty of saying unpleasant things; an intuitive perception of one's tender point, and I felt that she had struck her hard hand directly upon one of mine, perhaps the sorest I then had. I was not ashamed of my home; for all that pertained to the unpretending establishment seemed to share in the self-respect of its inmates; and there was such perfect harmony, such genuine good taste and neatness throughout the whole, that even Mrs. Wynne would have found nothing to offend her sense of propriety and general fitness, while she would have sneered at the extreme simplicity of country life. But this morning, I was "ennuyéed"—a word caught from Louise. The excitement of the past month, the scenes and society in which it had been spent, had induced a sort of fretful reaction, which I was ready enough to ascribe to boredom by the present company. I was shocked by Miss Judy's stentorian tones and inelegant attire; Miss Susan was the most uninteresting of cross old maids, and Miss Malvina's mincing and languishing were odious, unbearable affectation. This inopportune visit, while I was still suffering from the fatigue of travelling, and my exchequer of rare and curious news for the loved ones at home almost untouched, was of a piece with their usual disregard of others' feelings and convenience. Yet, there sat my aunt, knitting a worsted stocking, and listening with grave politeness to Miss Judy's vegetable catalogue; how one beet had measured three feet in circumference, and a single tomato weighed a pound ; of how many bushels of butter beans and black-eyed peas she expected to gather for winter, varied by receipts for pickles, sauces, and catsups, and infallible remedies for the gapes in young poultry, and all ills that fowls of a larger growth are heir to.

My father, with the grace of a Chesterfield, lent an attentive ear to Miss Malvina's platitudes and sentimentalisms. I needed only an affectionate smile from him to rally my spirits, and I recommenced the dialogue with the tart spinster. She cross-examined me as to the newest patterns for French embroidery, netting, tetting, tapestry, and especially bed-quilts. It is an unexplained fact, that the industry of amateur seamstresses almost invariably turns in the direction of these nondescript abominations. Miss Susan had, in her own private storeroom, a pile of not less than twenty-five of such *useful* articles—from the irregularly-joined patch-work that testified, by its gaping stitches and puckered corners, to the infantine fingers that drove the needle into the motley spread, up through every variety of circle, hexagon, star, and block work, to the "rising sun," her glory, until it was eclipsed by this latest burlesque upon nature's handiwork ; its improbable flowers, impossible birds, and impracticable baskets of floral and fruity treasures. The truth was, that I had not seen a single quilt during my absence, and after several dexterous evasions to avoid the rudeness of hinting that her hobbies were not quite *à la mode,* I achieved a master-stroke, by assuring her that hers were superior in pattern and workmanship to any foreign ones that I had examined. The vinegar was sensibly diluted, and she proceeded, more graciously than was her habit in speaking to one whom she regarded as a "chit of a girl," to expatiate upon her branch of domestic economy.

It was a sultry September day. The crickets sang in the crisp grass, and the locusts piped their drought prophecy from

4

among the dying leaves of the poplars. The parlor was a large, square room, with four windows draped with white dimity, fringed and starched, looped up in stiff curves by blue ribbons. The clean floor had no covering except a rug laid before the hearth, where stood a jar of asparagus boughs. There were two ponderous sofas, supported by spindle legs and overgrown claw-feet, upon opposite sides of the apartment; a dozen chairs of similar style and age, in prim file against the chair-board; a round candle-stand, its top turned up perpendicularly, set well back into one corner; a book-case with sliding doors in another, and in the exact centre of the floor—exact, according to my aunt's eye, more just than any foot and inch rule—a circular table spread its ample circumference over three claws, as disproportionate to the stem they upbore as were those of the sofas. The piano was as much out of place as a city belle, in flounces and crinoline, would be at a tea-party of country Quaker cousins. My father had surprised me with it on my return home from school. It was shut to-day, and the music tucked away out of sight in the drawer of the book-case appropriated to it. Frederic and I had sung and played duets for an hour immediately after breakfast, and left loose sheets lying about; but my aunt had visited the room since. As I have said, there was no disorder, no tawdriness to offend the most fastidious eye; but there was, on the other hand, as little to divert; an absence of suggestive objects to stimulate or maintain conversation.

I had found in my work-box an interminable strip of cambric, which I hemmed to keep my fingers in motion, and my eyes steady. Miss Susan talked and talked—her accents unmusical and monotonous as the locust's cry. I heard both with like apprehension of their meaning.

"And this is your life!" said Discontent. "These are your associates! Stirring—is it not? And are they entirely congenial? There is wide scope for the play of Imagination; fine opportunity for the exercise of conversational powers! Your glimpse of the world has only begotten in you a longing for a different sphere. Feast as you will, upon your garnered memories of that bright view, they will not cheat the Present of its tedium. Herbert and May could give wings to even these weary, hot hours, you plead: but that is not at all apropos to the subject now under review. You are required to accept the spinster sisterhood of three, this fascinating triangle, to be squared presently by their witling of a brother, as substitutes for your late companions. What do you say?"

"That I will not do it!" I answered obstinately.

"Are you dreaming about your sweetheart?" asked Miss Susan, coarsely.

Miss Malvina tittered. "Just what I was going to inquire. You do look *so* interesting and lack-a-daisical, Grace! Come, make a confession. We are all friends, you know."

Again I reddened, and more fierily than before; but the half-formed retort was fortunately prevented by a cheery voice in the hall, and the appearance of the runaway Nimrod. He brought, moreover, a most acceptable visitor, although there was nothing at the first glance that would have interested a stranger in the very quiet-looking personage whose greeting lighted up even Miss Susan's crab-apple visage.

He was our nearest, and certainly our best neighbor. A widower at thirty, he had now lived ten years alone in the house which had been the scene of his wedded happiness. Unsoured by sorrow or his solitary existence, he was, without question, the most popular man in the county, that *rara avis* of humankind—one of whom no one knew or spoke any evil. He was groomsman at every wedding, uncle to all the children, cousin to all the girls, confidant in every love-scrape, and arbiter in every quarrel. Mr. Townley, a lawyer of sharp and not over-scrupulous practice, pretended to cherish a grudge against him for having spoiled more law-suits than he had ever gained. The thermometer of my blood fell, and that of my spirits mounted, as I held out my hand :

"Mr. Peyton ! I am very glad to see you !"

"And I to see you back, Grace !"

Volumes of protestations could not have conveyed more to my heart.

My pleasure did not, however, blind me to Miss Malvina's flattering reception of my fun-loving brother. He was at the age when the prospect of a flirtation with a willing damsel is irresistible to a Southern youth. Miss Malvina was four years his senior, but as she was condescendingly anxious to overlook this trifling disparity, he was too gallant to remember it. The whole family courted him most sedulously, and he allowed them the privilege. Mr. Peyton and I fell into a friendly chat, marked by something of paternal interest on his part, and much communicativeness on mine. Mr. Townley's comings were never a cause of special gratification to me, and I had seldom been less happy to see him than when he bowed himself in, half an hour before dinner.

He was a small man, with a very white face and sandy hair, parted down the middle, a mode of coiffure which imparts an air of effeminacy or affected saintliness to the most manly set of features. His politeness was extreme. Few of his acquaintances had ever known his suavity to be disturbed ; in the social circle, his smiling ease was imperturbable. He entered now, sliding his feet over the floor, with the air of a true carpet-knight, in the direction of my aunt, whose stateliness he reverenced by a bow of deep respectfulness ; then I had a benefit :

"Accept my congratulations upon your return in safety, and, as I am rejoiced to behold, in health."

"Thank you. I am well, and have had a very pleasant journey and visit."

"You will not, then, be grieved to receive a *post*-visit reminder of your Northern friends?" approaching his hand to his pocket.

I had the presence of mind to smile at the pun (?) before I inquired,

"Have you, then, a letter for me?"

"Give me credit for for a spice of Yankee cunning in ensuring a welcome;" and he proceeded to distribute his dispatches. "I took the liberty of bringing your papers from the office, as I was coming directly hither," he apologized to my father.

There was a letter for Frederic, and another for me. We glanced, each at the superscription of that which the other held, and both looked foolish as our eyes met.

Mr. Townley chuckled a little, low laugh, his most boisterous exhibition of amusement.

"Really, Fred, one would imagine that I had given you the wrong epistle. I strongly suspect what, in one sense, my eyes assure me is true, that the more feminine—I may say the very feminine packet—was intended, *under color* of your sister, for you."

Frederic laughed gaily. It required no effort in his then state of mind. Mr. Townley was complacent that his brilliant effort had not escaped notice, and we chose this moment to withdraw. We read our precious missives in "father's room," the usual gathering-place of the family. As I finished mine, I saw that Frederic was watching me in some impatience.

"Will you exchange?" he said.

I complied silently.

He took the perfumed satin sheet caressingly.

"There is a breath of her presence about it," and he raised it to his lips.

There was no mockery in this, and neither of us smiled at the action, extravagant as it might have appeared to a third party. I had never seen Herbert Wynne's handwriting until I read this,

his letter to my brother. It was as characteristic in its way as was May's. But it was no scented Bath post for which I had bartered her dainty note. The paper was large, clear white, and a firm, manly hand had guided the pen. I could hear him speak each sentence as I read it, and I dwelt upon its perusal to enjoy this fancy. There was a message to me in the conclusion, a mere phrase of friendly remembrance, but I turned back to look at it again, lest I had not perhaps quite understood it.

The dinner-bell interrupted me. In our haste, Frederic retained my letter, thrusting it into his bosom ; and I did not stay to return him his. He was back in the parlor in time to offer his arm to Miss Malvina, whose pink cheeks took a more vivid hue as she accepted it. I could have quarrelled with this best-beloved brother for his show of devotion to a girl for whom he felt neither respect nor affection, while his heart was yet warm with thoughts of, and words from its ruling angel. I marvelled if he did not contrast the round, fat face she vainly attempted to coax into intellectuality; the half-sigh, half-smirk which responded to his attentions ; the Dutch figure that waddled, when it would have tripped along, with the lovely fay, whose mirth and gravity were alike unaffected ; whose heart and soul spoke in eye and expression ere the tongue could syllable their meaning. I grew wiser in after days ; understood why Love should never think of comparing refined gold with pewter metal ; the sun with a farthing taper. I doubt if it occurred to Frederic that May belonged to the same sex as the buxom creature by whom he ostentatiously manœuvred to obtain a seat at table—a feat, that, to Miss Malvina's notion, warranted the application of her handkerchief to her mouth. I expected a renewal of Mr. Townley's raillery ; but while we were out of the parlor, another subject of interest had been started by a paragraph in one of the papers he had brought. Affairs of honor at that day were less susceptible of amicable adjustment than in the age of accommodation we now enjoy. Shots were occasionally exchanged, and blood drawn even by M.C.s ; and of such an encounter the mail brought us tidings. The result had not proved fatal to either party ; therefore, in the discussion that sprang up, opinions were not suppressed by respect for death or bereavement.

The subject, in itself, was neither agreeable nor interesting to me ; so for a while I did not mark what was going on, except that Mr. Peyton and Mr. Townley were upon opposite sides—the one as severe as his nature permitted him to become, in denunciation of the code of honor, stigmatizing it as "sanguinary and heathenish ;" while the lawyer, in conciliatory tones, defended or palliated it.

"How can you talk so, James?" I, at last, heard Miss Judy speak up in her independent way. "I am like you, Mr. Peyton. I hold that a duellist is as much a murderer as a midnight assassin."

"More!" said Miss Susan, shortly, opening and shutting her mouth as with a spring.

Miss Malvina always seconded her senior sisters ; "Sister Susan" in particular. Sentimental though she was, her forte in conversation, if she had one, was in echoing the sentiments of others. For herself, she had none, except upon "Fine Arts"—courtship included. She sighed a slight scream here, and said that "they were indeed dreadful creatures—so cold-blooded, so heartless—so—why, in short, such wicked, horrid wretches! Now, there is something romantic in a Corsair, or a Giaour, or a Bandit!"

"There *is* a difference," responded Frederic. "Your Pirate follows his trade of blood from deliberate choice, and its object is plunder, rather than vengeance or glory. He unites the characters of thief and murderer. The duellist flies to the field in the heat of anger—often of righteous indignation at wrongs done to the defenceless objects of his best affections. To avenge them, to cleanse his own fame from blots more hateful than death, he meets his foe like a brave man, and grants him a fair chance for life."

"The same chance which the beast of prey grants his antagonist—precisely the same, Fred," replied Mr. Peyton. "If the Creator had intended that brute force should decide on which side lies moral right, we would have been supplied with fangs and claws instead of brains and consciences."

"So I—so all of us would argue, seated peacefully in our homes; good friends with the world and ourselves. I do not hold my honor dearer than you do yours, Mr. Peyton, and I know that to-morrow—to-day—were your character assailed, if calumny menaced the downfall of your reputation, and with it, all your hopes of earthly happiness, you could not rest upon your bed until you had tracked the serpent to his den, and destroyed him."

"Maybe so, Fred—maybe so! My temper might get the upper hand of me and drive me to forget that I was a man and a Christian; and so might it be with you in a similar temptation; but two wrongs would not make a right. The laws of God and man should be respected."

"I should transgress none of the Divine commands in preserving my life, if I were attacked; why then have I not equal liberty to save that which is better than mere animal existence?" returned Frederic. "As to human law, the pretended guardian of society, since it cannot protect my best treasure, am I bound to remain without a safe-guard when I can establish one for myself?"

Mr. Townley's voice fell upon the ear in an oily flow as the excited youth ceased.

"Let me suppose a case, gentlemen. You have a sister, Mr. Peyton—lovely and beloved, the idol of your heart and home. Gentle, pure, helpless, she appeals to every feeling of nature and manliness. She is insulted, defamed—it may be, is crushed to earth by the perfidy or abuse of him whose duty it is to cherish and protect her—what course shall the brother take?"

Volcanic fire was in Frederic's glance—lava in his impetuous outbreak—"I would have his heart's blood for hers—and so would you, Mr. Peyton! I would not sit at this table—would not remain under the same roof with you, if I did not believe this!"

"My son!"

The unfamiliar accents drew the attention of all to the foot of the board. My father supported his head upon his hand; his gaze still lingered rebukingly upon the hot-spirited boy, but his countenance was so agitated, so pale, that a terrible idea of a death-stroke of illness flashed into my mind.

Frederic passed to his side with the speed of this thought. "You are not well, sir!"

"Yes—yes!" subduing the pain, whatever it was. "That is—I am better. I had a spasm, I think. I know it of old, but it is passing. It seldom lasts long. Forgive me for alarming you all. I assure you that your anxiety is needless."

His natural manner was returning. He even smiled along the double row of frightened faces; his eye resting longest upon my aunt, whose self-possession was more shaken than I had ever seen it before. She had arisen at Frederic's exclamation, but the power to stand was wanting, and only the wild, earnest eye and pallid cheek told the fullness of sisterly sympathy. The look her brother bestowed upon her was angelic in its beautiful tenderness. What evil chance made me pass from its contemplation to the smooth face of Mr. Townley, who sat at his right hand? He had light-grey eyes—not remarkable in color or expression. I had hitherto thought them rather vacant and shallow. Was it my excited fancy which eliminated the blue lightning that played through them now? It was but a single flash—keen, forked, triumphant—then, quicker than the passing of electric fire from the clouds, the orbs were quiet and depthless again, with their ordinary greenish tinge, as if a blind had been shot across them, just below the surface.

"I think this seizure is nothing serious, sir," he said; and butter and honey were a harsh mixture compared with his modulations. "A slight megrim, probably—and a *grim* one it looked to us, for a few seconds."

With real tact, he succeeded in raising a laugh by some further jocose observation, and the incident, startling for the moment, seemed to be forgotten by the time the meal was over. I wore a careless outside show also, for there was no apparent cause for solicitude. The object about which it gathered, by his manner, put to flight any suspicion of its need. He was the cheerful, urbane host all the afternoon; attended his fair guests to their carriage, and detained them a moment after the door was closed, to invite a renewal of the visitation, which he did not call by this name, and promise Miss Judy some choice seed-wheat which Frederic had procured in his travels. My brother and myself stood with him at the gate. We watched the carriage roll away, and Frederic kissed his hand to the farewell wave of Miss Malvina's handkerchief.

"Ah, Fred! you are a sad flirt, my boy! Take care you do not go so far as to produce mischief," said his father, but smiling fondly into his roguish face.

"Trust me, sir; I will guarantee the safety of both hearts. The danger to her is no greater than to me—and I could not say more for the perfect security of either of us."

We did not go directly into the house; but strolled through the yard into the great, old-fashioned garden, where venerable trees grew yearly more decrepid under the unmerciful weight of fruit, laid upon their aged limbs; where were giant lilacs and "snow-balls," and conical mountains of box-wood; and tangled thickets of rose-bushes, their stems hoary with time; and long borders of lavender, sage, thyme and sweet Basil; more fragrant in the twilight than would be the much-prized exotics of modern conservatories, whose perfumes chill in their cups as the sun goes down.

We paced up and down the main walk, my father's arm clasping my waist, and his other hand laid upon Frederic's shoulder. Our recent visitors were not mentioned. We were too happy to be able to talk of matters of more interest. Conversation with the good who have passed the meridian of life, is to me like the enjoyment of rare old wine—and a fair crown is the almond-blossom for such a draught. The joy is rare, I say—at least it has been so to me. Experience only too soon enlightened me as to the fallacy of a doctrine inculcated in my childhood as carefully as was religious truth ; viz :—that increase of years ever brings wisdom in their train ; tempers passion, and perfects virtue. If years had not wrought this effect upon my father, affliction and heavenly grace had accomplished the work. He had never lectured us, and since we had arrived at man's and woman's estate, a word or a glance sufficed to hold us in check, while we never dreaded to avow an opinion or confess a fault to him. So, we had not walked very long when I was made aware that my heart was not the only one from which the alarm at dinner-time was not wholly effaced. Frederic's repeated surveys of the mild countenance, so serene in the rosy light, emboldened him to ask a plain question.

"Father, was I too hasty in argument with our excellent friend, Mr. Peyton, to-day ?"

"It was hardly an argument, my son," was the pleasantly spoken rejoinder.

"Our dispute then, sir. I allow that to be the better word. I imagined that you were on the point of reproving my heat, when you were taken ill."

My father's face was a shade more grave, but his answer was prompt and calm.

"My censure, if it had been spoken, would have borne upon the matter, more than the manner of your speech, Fred."

Frederic bit his lip. "I am sorry, sir, that I have been so imprudent as to incur your displeasure"—

"Not 'displeasure,' my boy; say that I disapproved of your remarks upon one subject—remarks, too, which were actuated by impulse more than deliberate thought and conviction."

"I regret, then, that I have failed to meet your wishes upon every point. I spoke too warmly, I own. My reason tells me that mine was the anti-Christian—anti-human, if you choose to style it—side of the question, and yet," his mouth and chin becoming stern, "I am sure that, if put to the test, I would act out what I then declared would be my part; I could take no other conscientiously."

My father's arm tightened upon my form.

"May the trial never come, my son!"

We were at the lower end of the walk, where stood a summer-house, roofed with creepers, looking towards the west. My father sat down in the rustic chair at the entrance. Our promenade had wearied him, for his breath was short; and as I passed my fingers over his forehead, I brushed off thick beads of perspiration.

"I trust I should meet it like a man, sir, not as a coward," Frederic said decidedly, yet with respect.

"If one of the alternatives must be met, there is certainly need of more hardihood to enable one to live for years with the brand of blood-guiltiness upon his soul, than to encounter speedy death from the hand of another," answered his father, composedly. "The breath of slander can never stain so darkly, corrode so deeply, as the blood of your fellow-man. No more of this now, my boy. Shake hands, Fred! We are too good friends to quarrel about what is, thank Heaven! an abstract principle."

We sat at his feet, and the very balm of peace descended upon our spirits as he talked with and to us. I sighed no more for gayer scenes, for a wider orbit of sight and action, for I felt how truly great one could be in simple goodness, how the most obscure sphere could be dignified by such as he ; and in the flush and fragrance of that autumnal sunset were born other and purer aspirations, views and hopes more humble, yet more exalting than the vague longings of the noon.

CHAPTER VI.

October fruits, vermilion and gold, strewed the orchard grass; nor had liberal autumn been chary with these precious dyes in field and forest. The woods were one vast kaleidoscope of daily increasing gorgeousness. In our upland rambles, our feet were entangled in crimson vine-wreaths, and rustled to breaking, the brittle broom-straw, scaring up from its roots bevies of partridges, fond loiterers about the nests that now yawned bare and empty; the streams, shrunken by the drought, were traceable by bright borders of the golden rod, glittering chains upon the sere bosom of the meadow.

And in such a season, upon a faultless day, when clouds and rain were to be found nowhere, save in our hearts and eyes, Frederic went away. In the vicinity of his Alma Mater resided an eminent physician, who was in the habit of directing the medical studies of a small class of young men, residents in his own family, and, alternately, the companions of his professional excursions. Under his care, my brother designed placing himself for a few months, prior to his entrance upon a regular course of lectures in a northern college. Session after session he had left us for the same journey, and the same time, but I could not look upon this in the light of his former absences. It was a decisive step; the seal of his choice of a profession that would oblige him to seek another home, for he would never be content to bury his talents in an interior country neighborhood, too well stocked now with professors of the healing art.

A visit from Mr. Townley the evening before the departure,

afforded some diversion to my sad thoughts. He was profuse in his sympathies and good wishes ; predicted early consolation to me, and a most successful career to Frederic, and with the portentous gravity that always warned us to watch narrowly, lest we should miss the point of a pun, stated as " a singular fact that the ills of patients are in a conspiracy to make physicians *weal*-thy."

At parting, he brought in a box from his gig.

" A farewell token from the girls," he said ; " whether you *fare well* in getting it is another thing, Frederic."

" I have no misgivings," laughed the recipient, and the sleek man of law took a final leave.

In the box were a dozen juicy pippins, and a fruit-cake from Miss Judy ; a worsted comforter, wrought by Miss Susan ; and a portfolio of card-board, bound and lined with cherry silk. One side bore a water-color drawing of an anchor suspended to a wreath of forget-me-nots, beneath which was written in mimmeny-pimmeny characters, the name of the flower. The reverse was more elaborate in design and execution, and was, I suspected, purely original. In the centre of the board a yellow serpent made frantic, but useless, attempts to swallow himself, his spine being too stiff to suffer him to do more than seize the extreme tip of his tail with his teeth. This interesting reptile was supported on the right by an inverted cornucopia, in favor of whose contents the laws of gravitation were suspended, and upon the left by a scrub-oak, almost hidden in ivy branches ; above, two doves flew in opposite directions, tying a true-lover's knot in an azure ribbon ; and at the bottom of the whole array was penned with a crow-quill and India-ink, " *Amor vincit omnia.*"

I seem now to see Frederic throw back his handsome head and laugh until tears, real tears, clear and large, coursed over his cheeks, as a dim sense of the meaning of the worse than Egyptian hieroglyphics dawned upon him, and the look of perplexed amusement in my father's face while he studied this fresh triumph of "Fine Art." I managed to stow away all of the gifts in trunk and portmanteau, Miss Malvina's chef-d'œuvre scenting a pile of handkerchiefs in the tray of the former. A note of thanks to the three was left in my charge.

Our beloved one was gone ; and for days, the desolation and stillness of the grave reigned in our home. Gradually a seeming of cheerfulness came back, invoked, I shame to say, more by my father than by me. He appeared to think only of my sorrow, as if the strongest prop of his advancing age were not removed. He encouraged me to walk, to ride, to visit, and used every means to tempt company to the house. I could not be ungrateful for such kindness, and throwing off despondency, I endeavored to look courageously at the comparatively lonely winter in prospect, and prepare for it as best I could. My life was uneventful, yet I learned a certain negative satisfaction in it. Like most other young ladies who are raised above the absolute necessity of labor, I never dreamed of any duties obligatory upon me beyond a little needle-work ; a little housekeeping, ornamental and gratuitous ; a little music, and making myself agreeable at home and abroad. I read without system or fixed purpose ; sewed when I felt like it ; practised an hour a day or less ; ate, slept, received and returned visits.

My happiest hours were those of reverie, a practice that was strengthening into inveteracy. My aunt and myself sat together at work much of the morning, and when my father was not present, our conversation was limited to a few queries and replies, uttered at long intervals. My seat was near a window, commanding an extensive stretch of rolling fields, bounded afar off, by the variegated forest. Bare as were these hills at this season, my eye acquired the power of distinguishing numerous different shades of coloring ; and when the clouds left their sides in purple shade, while the sun slept in golden rest upon the summits, or the light and darkness chased each other over ridge and glen, I watched the scene with a delight I had never felt in the survey of a summer landscape. I have often sat for hours, my hands laid idly in my lap, gazing into the mellow sunlight, or into the dim atmosphere of a cloudy day, revelling, as I deluded myself by saying, in the beauties of Nature ; in truth, wandering through the Elf-land of my own imaginings. We come in time, to smile at the Chinese paintings upon the walls of our now disused, out-of-date dream-chambers—pictures unrelieved by shading, without perspective, and tinted with the most gaudy colors of Fancy's palette ; but when did real joys, actual and present delights, ever thrill the soul as did those early visions. I never asked myself—"will the awakening come at last ?" never reflected upon the consequences most likely to ensue from this droning musing. It was a pleasure that did not pall ; my chief solace, and I gave the reins up to Imagination.

Now and then, I was aroused as by a jostle, to some sense of the sterner, harder life which others led. Mr. Peyton has been introduced as our nearest neighbor. A mile from us, in another direction, was the cottage of the widow Bell, a highly respectable matron, whose fortunes had not always been so lowly as now. Extravagance, dissipation, sickness—strong fiends, armed—had visited her home since her marriage with one who was remembered by many of the older inhabitants as a promising young man, kind-hearted, and possessed of fine talents, but "inclined to be wild." He died when Annie, the only surviving child, was a mere infant ; and the widow invested the remnant of the once noble property in the purchase of the small brown house under the hill, to which was attached a farm of proportionate size. Two negroes, a man past his prime, and his wife, remained to her, and their labor, with her own, had supported the family, kept up the place, and educated Annie as thoroughly, if not as showily as any other girl in the surrounding country. Most people expected that she would make the most of this advantage by applying for a situation as governess or teacher of a private school ; but the independent, affectionate daughter preferred pursuing the profession of a seamstress with her mother. She received the encouragement her honest pride merited. Mr. Peyton was their staunch friend, their benefactor in every way in which they would permit him to confer a favor. He was my frequent and most brotherly escort, and three-fourths of our rides and strolls were in the direction of Mrs. Bell's.

One mild afternoon in the Indian Summer, we set out to make a call, partly of friendship, partly because I had business with Annie. A quarter of a mile from the house we met old Zack, Mrs. Bell's factotum, trudging on sturdily, in no wise embarrassed by the weight of a large wooden bucket on his head, and a basket on his arm. He pulled his forelock and scraped his foot in salutation, and Mr. Peyton reined up his horse to parley with him.

"What now, Zack ? Eggs, I hope."

"Yes, Mars' Robert, and honey, sir."

He lowered his bucket and vouchsafed us a peep, under the clean cloth, of piled-up comb, almost as white, which dripped with amber nectar.

"Aunt Agnes would like some of that, I know," I said. "Go directly to our house with it, Uncle Zack."

"What she does not take, I will," added Mr. Peyton. "How many eggs ?"

"Four dozen, sir," opening the basket. "Dere's some Guineas, too."

Mrs. Bell's hens laid the fairest, plumpest eggs that ever filled the measure of a housewife's desire ; and the brownish-yellow of the smaller and richer "Guineas," as Zack called them, made the rest look like so many balls of snow.

"All right !" was Mr. Peyton's comment. "Take them to

old Nancy, and tell her I sent you. Are you getting on pretty well, now-a-days, Zack ?"

"Farly—Mars' Robert—farly ! Mis' and Miss Annie's mighty well, and my ole woman don't complain much of her rheumatics. As to me and Sultan"—touching a tawny and black Newfoundland beside him—"we's as peart as young folks—aint we, Sultan ? I'se 'mazing thankful for all dis, Mars' Robert !"

"So am I, Zack. Good bye. A faithful old fellow," he said to me, as we rode on. "He is Mrs. Bell's mainstay. She had better part with her right hand than with him."

"She is a wonderful woman," I remarked, "and most surprising in her cheerfulness under misfortune."

"Misfortune is often the best teacher of cheerfulness," replied he. "She has learned it in a hard school, Grace ! I cannot but think that the rest of her stay in this world will be tranquil."

Very tranquil was the aspect of the cottage as we now saw it, nestled in the shelter of the hill ; the trees, that made it cool in hot weather, letting in the sun freely upon the roof and porch. The pleasing confusion of a poultry-yard and the hum of bees came successively to our ears on our way to the door ; and Annie's flower-garden was gay with chrysanthemums. She answered our knock. I had time to perceive a troubled look foreign to her face, before she saw who we were. Then she smiled most cordially, and stood by to let us enter.

Mrs. Bell had other company. A very glossy hat, which would have served as its master's card to any one who was familiar with his appearance, stood on the good lady's work-table, and a dapper riding-whip was set within it. Mr. Townley was, as usual, overjoyed to see us, and further evidenced his pleasure by monopolizing our conversation. Mrs. Bell's deportment had in it nothing of the disquietude it cost Annie a constant struggle to hide. She stitched the fine linen bosom of a shirt, while we were there ; never pausing to rest her fingers or wipe her spectacles. Annie sat a little behind her, her needle almost invisible in its swift course, one minute, to slide from her hold the next. The work required much fixing, for she often stooped low over it, and twice took it to a stand, where she remained for some moments with her back to us. The last time she did this, I followed her.

"Annie !" I whispered, hastily.

She started and turned her head away, while her hand went up to her face, I saw, to dash away a tear.

"Let me go up to your room," I continued, "I want to speak with you in private."

Mr. Townley arose, as we passed him, and bowing to my ear, murmured, "Linger not long !"

"Annie," said I, when a flight of stairs and two doors separated us from him, "before I talk about anything else, tell me what ails you. Are you in trouble ?"

The poor girl burst into tears, and flung herself upon my neck. I crowded inquiries upon conjectures, and hap-hazard consolations upon all, until she could articulate, for I was not prepared for this extreme distress. At last she sat down by me on the bed, her head against mine, and still sobbing, like a grief-weary child, gave me the substance of the sad story.

Mr. Townley, who had a magpie zeal in exploring dark pigeonholes, and law records, whose must and mould would have sickened most stomachs, had discovered in the settlement of an old estate, involved in a Chancery suit, a bond of the deceased Mr. Bell's for the sum of three hundred dollars, given fifteen years previous to the owner of said estate. It had never been cancelled, very probably had never been paid, and of course the heirs of the original creditor had a right to look to the widow for the money.

"The debt must be discharged at once," sobbed Annie. "Mr.

Townley says his orders are imperative to levy an execution upon the property. Is it not hard that we must give up our home to satisfy a demand we were ignorant of until to-day ?"

"Must it come to that ?" I asked. "After waiting so long, I should think they could afford to make some accommodation with you—let you pay as you can raise the means."

"Mr. Townley recommended another way," her voice trembling yet more. "He advises that we keep the house, and sell"——

She broke down in a rain of tears.

The blood boiled in my veins. "The inhuman wretch !" I ejaculated, as the picture of Uncle Zack and his wife—sundered in their old age, toiling in the service of another than the mistress they had followed with such heroic constancy from her very babyhood ; with whom they had grown grey ; for whom they would have shed their blood as they had spent their fresher energies—arose to my sight. "The inhuman, unnatural monster !"

"It is his duty, I suppose," answered Annie. "He professes to perform it with reluctance, and we have no right to doubt his word. But this will not help the matter, Grace. Forgive me for grieving you so selfishly. I must bear up for mamma's sake. She is the greater sufferer, but she has more fortitude than I. You said you had something to say to me. It is about work, I hope, for I must keep busy, and forget this trouble as far as I can."

While I delivered a message from my aunt touching some sewing she wished to have done, Annie bathed her eyes and face in cold water, and opened the window that the air might help to banish the redness that would betray her recent agitation. I tried to cheer her up by indefinite allusions to the numerous friends of herself and mother, who would not see them oppressed.

She interrupted me with a sudden blush and an involuntary tone of haughtiness.

"From none of these—from no man or woman living would we accept charity! We must meet the storm."

After a pause, she added, "I thank you, Grace, and love you. Your sympathy has done me good."

"You will not refuse, then, to let me help you whenever I can, Annie? I have no pecuniary aid to offer."

But I was inwardly resolving to lay the matter before my father so soon as I reached home. I would have broken forth with it by the time we were out of hearing of the cottage, but Mr. Townley rode with us most of the way. I was as discourteous as a lady could have shown herself to be under the circumstances; conduct that had no effect whatever upon his civil small-talk. I rejoiced when we arrived at the cross-road leading to his house, and shook in impatience as he delayed a reply to Mr. Peyton's ill-timed and very unnecessary politeness in inviting him to accompany him home. I was relieved, at length, by his resolve to part from us, and while the subdued clatter of his horse's hoofs still mingled with ours, I began the narration.

Mr. Peyton was not demonstrative. My cheeks glowed with excitement, and to the incidents of the discovery and presentation of the bond, I subjoined a description of Annie's emotion, dwelling upon her proud scorn of dependence—and stopping in sheer breathlessness, after a vituperative commentary upon the suave barrister. My companion listened, his eyes bent upon the neck of his steed, with no exclamation, no change of complexion or expression.

"You are harsh upon Townley," he said sententiously.

"He deserves it all—and more!" I returned.

"Perhaps so, Grace—perhaps so! but we ought not to judge him. We have no warrant for doing so—no warrant."

He had an absent way of speaking when his mind was intent

upon any important subject ; a state betrayed by a short, dry tone and tautological sentences. He rambled on, his gaze fixed as before.

"Townley is a lawyer, you know, and must do his duty to his clients ; that's certain—certain ! He *must* do his duty to them —no help for it, Grace. I have nothing to say against him—nothing at all. He is a kind neighbor—kind and hospitable ; a very polite man—*the* most polite man I ever saw—and I have seen many a French dancing-master. He seems good-hearted, too ; is fond of his sisters, and they dote on him. I cannot believe that he would have chosen a job like this, but"— and here he looked at me, and brought down his whip upon his knee with an energy under which the flesh must have tingled to the bone —"I'll be shot if I would have soiled my fingers in such an affair for anybody, alive or dead !"

The fury evaporated in the lash of whip and tongue. He did not reply to my next question, and I repeated it.

"But what is to be done, Mr. Peyton ?"

I spoke hurriedly, for we were at the Moss-side gate.

"Ah ! here we are at home," was all the answer I got.

We dismounted.

"Walk in, Mr. Peyton. I cannot let you go yet," I urged.

"Not to-night, Grace—not to-night. I will see you again soon."

He was in the saddle, and had wheeled his horse from me, when the echo of my earnest query seemed to reach his wandering brain.

"O, Grace ! one thing ! Say not a word about this business before day after to-morrow, and never breathe to any one that you have told me of it. Good night."

I obeyed most unwillingly. I did not relish my occupation of picture-making that night or the next day. I had seen a new phase of Life-trial—hard and unromantic—something that would affect the outward estate, while it wrung the heart. Poverty, as it had appeared to me in Mrs. Bell's situation, was very comely, totally unlike the grim goblin known to me in print. This bond, trifling as its amount sounded, had stripped off the mask, and I shrank from the sight. It terrified me in dreams, and ceased not to torment my eyes in the daylight. I could not be quiet as the hours wore into noon, afternoon—and the stretching shadows lazily told of coming night. At sunset I went into the porch to strain my vision once more along the road to Linden—Mr. Peyton's place.

"Miss Grace !" spoke some one beside the steps.

I had overlooked old Zack, who pulled off his hat with the double purpose of bowing, and of presenting me with a note pinned to its lining.

"Dear Grace," wrote Annie, "you were so kind to me in our sorrow, that I must tell you now of our joy. Mr. Townley has been here again, but with what different tidings! Only think, Grace, the creditors have withdrawn their claims; so Mr. Townley learned to-day. He could give no particulars, but I surmise from something which escaped him that this generous treatment is the result of his remonstrances, offered when the bond first came to light. If so, what injustice we did him yesterday! The thought pierces me with remorse in the midst of my happiness. My heart is light and grateful—grateful to heaven and to our benefactor, whoever he may be. Come very soon and see us in the home that is still *ours*.

"Annie Bell."

Mr. Peyton supped with us. I found an opportunity to show him Annie's billet.

He nodded at the close—a non-committal gesture that by no means suited my humor.

"Well," I demanded, "have you nothing to say ?"

"Yes ; I am glad our friends are delivered from their difficulty —very much pleased, indeed !"

I searched his countenance for some twinkle of self-complacency, some mark of inward satisfaction in having performed a good action. I might have scanned the blank wall with equal chance of success. Guileless as a child in most matters, he was helped by his modesty to a matchless show of ignorance.

"Do you believe this tale of Mr. Townley's?" I probed deeper.

"It does not appear likely that an honest man would deceive them in a matter of such importance," he rejoined.

"Now," said I, walking up close to him, "like Annie, I have my surmises, but they point to Mr. Townley only as the instrument of the unknown benefactor—and excuse me for saying that a more worthy tool would not have been hard to find."

My auditor was fidgeting in his chair, casting ominous glances at his hat; but my triumph was not complete.

"And this incomparable friend," I pursued, "is the same, who, with trained seamstresses among his own servants, has extra work sufficient to afford constant employment to the widow and her daughter, whose large plantation, stocked with everything that a provident housekeeper can need, does not produce enough eggs, butter, or honey to obviate the necessity of purchasing each and all of these commodities when old Zack is the vender."

He was on his feet, but I had secured his hat and held it behind me. By this time, my gaiety had made way for feelings more truly heart-felt. I took the hand which would have seized his detained property. I could have bent the knee in reverence before him—this shy, stammering man, who looked more like a culprit than the kingly soul he was.

"If the prayer of the widowed and fatherless can win blessings, you will be wealthy in mercies, Mr. Peyton. You practise what others preach of the brotherhood of humanity."

"It is all I have to live for, Grace—all—all! Let me go now, and keep our secret, little sister."

If I were limning a fictitious character, this friend should, perhaps, be suffered more frequently to occupy the back-ground his humble estimate of himself would persuade him to select; but I have other use for him than merely to prompt him to utter his chance phrase in dialogue and chorus. There is no room upon the list of the world's heroes for those who are great in goodness alone, and my lowly annals are the only pages that the recital of his virtues will ever enrich.

"The only pages," said I? My pen moves more solemnly at the thought of another record, which time can never fade; in whose lines of light no note is made of deeds which men glorify as "Godlike" and "immortal," but where the widower's mite, the Magdalene's box of ointment, the disciple's cup of cold water are encircled by haloes of undying lustre.

His name is there!

CHAPTER VII.

In pity for my loneliness, May wrote frequently. Winter began with a long wet spell, and this had continued for a week when I had a letter from Frederic, written at the lowest ebb of her own spirits, and announcing that his class would meet as usual during the Christmas holidays; therefore, for the first time in his life, he must spend that season away from home. The next mail took to May a *jérémiade* blistered with the drops I had no power to restrain. Forgetful of the hundreds of miles that divided us from one another, I adjured her in the names of friendship and mercy to visit me in my affliction, an appeal that might have softened the heart of a stone, but which, an hour afterwards, I had not the most remote idea would avail ought to remove her body nearer to me.

Judge, then, of the amaze and transport that ensued upon reading the introductory sentence of her reply; "I hope to be with you, Grace, very soon after you get this." An invalid cousin, her intimate associate, had been ordered by her physicians to Savannah to pass the winter and early spring; and although her father was to accompany her, she had entreated May's attendance also. They were to pass Christmas week with friends residing in Richmond, and May intended to brave bad roads and a comfortless conveyance, and spend that time by our country fireside, unless she should be met in the city by a letter from me, discouraging the attempt.

My heart was beating its fastest and warmest thus far; why

should it be checked with a suddenness that caused physical pain, as I read on?

"Herbert Wynne, who is anxious for a glimpse of Virginia Christmas customs, will go with us to Richmond. May I accept his proffered protection to and from Moss-side? If any circumstances unknown to me, would render our coming a source of inconvenience, state the truth without fear, and I will answer that he shall not be offended. Both of us together can but poorly supply your brother's place to you, but I have not read your heart by mine for so long to doubt that you will be more happy to have me with you than if I were away."

I danced into the room where sat my father and aunt, in such a whirlwind of joyousness that both started and exclaimed, "What is the matter?"

"Read and see!" I cried, giving the open letter to my father, and perching myself upon his knee.

He was as much delighted as I could have asked.

"I congratulate you with all my heart," he said. "No news could have been more welcome. I have feared lest your Christmas should be a melancholy one. Aunt Agnes, we must bethink ourselves of all the nice things procurable for the entertainment of our little girl's guests. It is not every year that May visits us in December."

"A pun! positively a pun!" shouted I, clapping my hands. "Father, you rival Mr. Townley!"

He held me upon his knee, his face beaming as by reflected radiance from mine, entering with interest and spirit into all my propositions as to the preparations for, and reception of, the eagerly-expected favorites. Not one stipulation for his personal privileges; not one suggestion of economy or hint of any kind hindered the complete blossoming of my pleasure.

"Very well!" was the conclusion of our consultation. "Consider everything upon the plantation—servants, house, stores, and last and least, my poor services—at your disposal until New Year's day."

As I put up my lips for a kiss he added, "So good a daughter is entitled to some reward. I am only sorry that my wishes for her welfare and enjoyment outrun my ability to advance them."

This was the "top-sparkle" of my cup. How quickly my feet skimmed the floor and staircase that day; how gaily resounded my songs from cellar to roof; how ready were my hands to pull down and set up—too restless to await the sluggish or deliberate movements of the corps of assistants, my father, true to his word, marshalled for my orders. Paint and floors were to be scoured; walls to be swept; windows washed; beds shaken and sunned, and furniture polished. Never before had Moss-side undergone such furious renovation. After portioning out work to the rest, and seeing them fairly at it, I took Martha, my own maid, with me to my room.

The preceding day I had been congratulating myself upon its neat and home-like appearance; but under our vigorous treatment, it was presently as disorderly as the apartments we had left. The carpet was home-made, but new. Its stripes of red and green were bright, yet not glaring, and were well contrasted. I did not quarrel with it, although I remembered that May's chamber was supplied with an ingrain more costly than the best in our house—that upon the parlor floor. I was careful that no other high colors should displease the eye. Counterpane, curtains, ottomans, and chairs were chaste white. White china vases upon the mantel held sprigs of cedar and holly, studded with blue and scarlet berries; and between them—the only place in the room where a picture could be hung—was a drawing Louise had given me as a keepsake at the end of our last session. It was a beautiful female head, with waving hair floating off into shadow; a face, girlish in feature and contour; but in the heavenward look, there was an eloquence of sorrow such tender years should never know, and the mouth seemed shaping a prayer for strength. Even in my happy preoccupation of thought, I stayed the cloth with which I was dusting glass and frame, to wonder at, and admire the beauty that was ever there, however often I might seek for it.

"That's a mighty pretty lady," said Martha, "but, somehow I don't like to look at her. 'Pears to me like her heart was a-breakin', and she was a-prayin' to die. I tries not to see her when I'm a-cleanin' up in here, days. I always want to cry if I do. You're a-sighin' yourself, Miss Grace. Put her back and don't think no more about her and her pitiful eyes."

Frederic's chamber was just across the entry, and was to be prepared for Herbert. Like mine, it had dormer windows front and back; sloping walls, and an open fire-place, its hearth whitened with pipe-clay. My buoyancy received a check from the thought that its inmate must bow his head to pass under the lowly lintel, and that he could stand upright nowhere except in the middle of the apartment. For an instant, all about me was poverty-stricken and mean; but I spurned the unworthy weakness, and fell to work with redoubled ardor. A softer feeling touched my heart as I wiped off and replaced the books on the shelves beneath the slant of one wall.

Again Martha interrupted my meditations.

"It's a mortal pity Mars' Frederic aint comin' home holiday I don' know how you'll stand it, Miss Grace. He is 'quainted wid de lady and gentleman you're 'spectin'—aint he?"

"Yes," I said.

"I reckon he'll be dreadfully put out at missin' 'em."

I "reckoned" so too with a certainty she did not suspect; yet I was equally sure that May would not have answered my prayer so agreeably and unexpectedly, but for my statement that he who would have welcomed her with most rapture, would not be at home to receive her. Free from prudish affectation she was, yet she was at all times governed by the most delicate sense of propriety. She had a deal of character, and resolution to maintain it—this petted plaything of ours. Since it was impossible for my brother to leave his studies, I resolved, with marvellous self-denial, not to tell him of the distinguished honor to be conferred upon the homestead, until it should be too late for him to torture himself with ideas of reaching us in season to get a taste of it for himself. I applied the last screw to this determination on my way down stairs for some article needful in our task.

My father was folding a letter.

"I have sent your love to Frederic," he remarked. "The poor boy has been much in my mind to-day; and although I am aware that it will not compensate to him for the loss of our society and that of your friends, I could not resist the impulse to forward him something with which to purchase a Christmas-box and make merry with his mates."

I wisely forbore to offer opposition, and resigned the useless resolve it had cost me so much to make, without an intimation of its existence to the dear father, who believed that he was promoting his son's happiness in what he did.

One of my choice plants—a double oleander—standing upon the floor, tapped the upper sash of Herbert's southern window with its pink blossoms, and a citronaloes, as tall, made balmy the air of the room to be occupied by May and myself. Every uncarpeted board was brilliant from the application of scrubbing-brush and wax; the yard was raked of dead leaves and grass; a dry covering of gravel rolled into the walks; bed-linen and window-hangings were immaculate, and the last day of waiting, which was that before Christmas, I had not enough to do to beguile one of the dragging hours. My aunt had, in her province, accomplished more than I had in mine, and without one tenth of the bustle. Had a regiment been billeted upon us, we could have fed them bountifully for the week May's letter named as the utmost extent of the sojourn of a gentleman and lady, whose gastronomical abilities were not of the highest order. All was ready here, too, or I would have begged, as a favor, to be allowed to beat eggs and spread icing.

My aunt was an upright fixture in her rocking-chair, which never moved while she filled it. She darned stockings the entire morning with a perseverance wearying to behold. My father had gone to the village—"the Court House"—three miles away, and I had no one else to talk with.

"Aunt!" I ejaculated, as she rolled up the sixth pair of hose. "I wish you would teach me patience."

"I had not learned it when I was of your age," was the response.

The needle recommenced its course, creeping in and out, under, then over a stitch, and the worsted trailed after it. My eye followed it; my thoughts were revolving my aunt's words. I doubt whether this were not the first reference to her early life I had ever heard, for it impressed me as a novel idea.

Youth! and an impatient youth! one like mine! Imagination refused to sketch it as a companion picture to the passionless maturity before me. I could more easily have recognized an extinct volcano in one of the snow-topped granite hills I had seen in the summer.

"Will I ever acquire it?" I asked.

"If it is needful that you should."

"I wonder what teacher will set the lesson?"

"That which instructs all, sooner or later—Experience, I suppose," answered my aunt.

I changed my seat to her footstool, for something in her manner attracted me more than common.

"Aunt Agnes, you will think me very silly; but please explain what you mean by Experience. I have an indefinite notion that it is an unpleasant acquaintance ; yet it is used so vaguely, generally, that it conveys no sense to my mind. Am I to learn to be patient through trial, or will each year quench some of the fire in my blood ? Will it be a short, severe task, or will the work be accomplished gradually and imperceptibly to myself ?"

"I have not the gift of second sight to inform me what means will be employed in your case. They vary essentially in different instances."

I watched the creeping needle awhile longer—in and out, a leap over a gaping hole, then in and out on the other side.

Its motion may have instigated my next speech. "I think I should prefer to have all I must suffer summed up in one lesson ; to grapple with one mighty trouble, and be prepared by it for the battle of life, to meeting with minor difficulties daily, getting under some and over others."

"Most people are obliged to submit to both kinds of discipline," observed my aunt.

"Were you ?" I asked, unthinkingly.

I was frightened at my temerity ere the sound of my voice died away. No increase of coldness resented it.

"Each one of us is apt to fancy his lot peculiar. Mine has, no doubt, a thousand parallels. No mortal suffers more than he deserves, for God is more merciful than man."

"Yet in my short life, I have witnessed what are rightly called 'mysterious Providences,'" I pursued—"afflictions, that would have been cried out against as cruel and unmerited if man had produced them. Were they sent in mercy ?"

"Or in judgment !"

My inquiries were brought to an end. I went back to my chair with a strange sensation of awe upon me. But I had learned something.

This woman, ever calm, ever reserved to hauteur, had not

grown so by the natural process of time; as the oak, whose last century is on the wane, puts forth every spring, fewer leaves, until there comes one March, when the wind that strains and tears its boughs, and the sunbeams that caress them, fail to stir the sap from the roots, where the thin drops dried away in the autumn. The vitality of this heart was destroyed at a stroke. She had said that the work of patient endurance was in some carried on and completed by smaller trials, prior and subsequent to one great calamity; but none of these petty grievances had power over her now. Was she deadened or stoical to their influence? And this was the fate my thoughtless declaration had bespoken for myself! I cast by the book I pretended to read, and roamed from room to room, over yard and garden, followed everywhere by the solemn tone that had sealed my lips—"Or in judgment!"

My father's shout to the hostler recalled me to the house.

"Ha, Puss!" he greeted me. "The morning has been right tedious, has it not? Let me whisper a secret that may lengthen the afternoon and night, in spite of May's presence. I have a present for you and one for her in my pocket, which you are not to see until to-morrow. And now we will try what dinner can do towards relieving us of an hour."

It did this very ungraciously for me. In the hall stood an ancient clock that nearly touched the ceiling. Its broad face was yellow and blotched; the ship and moon, once an accurate calendar of Luna's changes, were fast locked by rust upon their pivot. The pendulum vibrated very dignified seconds at the end of six feet of wire, with a "never-give-up-the-ship" air, and a general expression of irresponsibility for the conduct of any other part of the machinery, while it did its duty in its allotted station; but the striking apparatus wanted its commendable spirit. Five minutes before the hour was to be sounded, a terrifically dismal groan issued from the capacious chest of the chronometer—so doleful, that the hands seemed to dread the stern law that compelled them to order the strokes thus deprecated. At the fatal moment, the grumbling, thumping, and shrieking that jarred the very floor, were appalling and indescribable; then, with a hoarse murmur of exhaustion, the bell was mute for sixty minutes more. The discordant clash was harmony to me to-day, listened for most anxiously, until I felt assured that before it pealed again, realization would have swallowed up expectancy.

Then, like the coward I was, fear and trembling took hold of me. As the safest place, in the panic that possessed me, I went to my father's room. He was four columns deep in his newspaper, and I crept to the rug at his feet. One arm embraced his knee, while I began to examine the cause of this preposterous nightmare.

"Were not those whom I feared to see, dearer to me than any others on earth? that is—correcting myself—next, of course, to my father and brother. Had they not travelled this distance in winter weather to see me, the ingrate, whose knees were smiting together at every sound like the trampling of horses or rattle of wheels? And what is the dread? May will spring to my bosom, and kiss me, as I have pined to have her do, so often since we parted. Herbert's salutation will be more formal, only because custom enjoins the difference. His voice used to be musical—his smile most genial—his conversation more than acceptable; I know he has not altered; where then"—I rated my shaking heart—"where is the use or sense of this disgraceful behavior?"

The whimperer shivered anew, and had no other reply to render.

The premonitory iron groan echoed through the hall, and I started as at the discharge of a gun.

My father raised the paper that he might see me.

"Why, little one! we are growing restless—but courage! we will not have to wait many minutes now."

Which was not the most apropos observation he could have made.

He read on, and I shivered in the same weak, nervous chill, until wheels, hammer, and bell creaked and roared that it was five o'clock.

"There they are!" said my father, rising quickly.

I also saw, through the window, the carriage we had sent that morning to the nearest stage-house. I did not loiter; yet my father was at the gate, shaking hands with Herbert, when I was half-way down the walk. As I came up, he lifted May to the ground, and—whether she made the offer or not, is still a mooted question—he kissed her as he sat her down. Gone was the bugbear that had beset me so pertinaciously, when I caught sight of that sweet face. I had her in my arms, both of us laughing and saying all manner of foolish nothings to keep down the tears.

My aunt was upon the porch. She spoke kindly to May, and rather stiffly to Herbert, although she regarded him with earnest momentary attention. I was blithe as a bird throughout that evening—even when I saw Herbert bow involuntarily as he passed into the parlor, and recollected that this precaution would be necessary on going to his chamber. May and I were in no haste to quit ours after her travelling attire was laid off. She beautified the place, as warm sunshine and freshly-blooming flowers would have done.

Choosing, as was always her caprice, the lowest seat she could get—a mere cushion, around which her dark-blue drapery lay upon the carpet, she lifted her face to me with a sigh and smile of perfect content.

"I am *very* happy, Gracie!"

Had she felt less, she would have enlarged upon her joy at our re-union, her satisfaction with the cottage I had, so shortly before, feared she might despise. I understood all that she meant, and thenceforth, not one sting of false pride threatened my health of mind. Upon most other topics we were fluent, and, to a mere listener, would have been ridiculously diffuse. Yet we rejoined the gentlemen, feeling that the preliminaries of our confabulation had scarcely been entered upon.

My father and Herbert, acting upon the principle of their self-introduction, were talking like old friends; and I was ready to repent the vanity that had hurried us down, in the fear that our absence would be noted and lamented. It was plain that my father had received my darling May rosebud into his affectionate favor. I waited to see him place her in the most comfortable chair in the room, and then gave myself up to be entertained by Mr. Wynne. I had thought him kind and sincere during our former intercourse; but there was now an unreserved display of his real nature: a complete freedom from the bonds of that conventionalism which ruled, in some degree, all in the sphere we then occupied, an earnest truth in look and language, so manifest and so winning, that my esteem and confidence grew to be absolute. But one thing chilled me. In our summer tour, he had learned to call me "Grace," a name I thought very beautiful as pronounced by him. To-night it was "Miss Grace"—occasionally "Miss Leigh." I bore it till tea-time, then entered a protest.

He laughed. "I will tell you a story relative to this matter some day. If upon hearing it, you still wish me to dispense with the 'Miss,' I will be rejoiced to obey."

The evening was not cold, and as a consequence, the parlor-fire was larger and blazed more fiercely than if the thermometer had been stationary at zero. We were driven back by the heat to the centre-table, and there clustered, as hilarious a household as that Christmas Eve saw in all the land. My aunt had least to say, yet several times her features were lighted with pleasurable emotion at a lively sally from May, or the fine play of Herbert's humor. Her stiffness bent before his respectful overtures, and he, as he aferwards told me, was struck with her appearance, exhibiting as it did the remains of beauty of no common cast, and the natural elegance of every sentence she uttered. She inclined to him more and more as their conversation progressed. One precious instant, while May was at the piano, playing with, not upon, the keys, and talking, instead of singing to my father, I took a mental photograph—as distinct to-day as it was then—unsuspected by its original. Fire and candles sent flickers of uncertain brightness over his face; the high brow, heaped with dark hair, the speaking eyes, the mouth small, yet too firm to be feminine—and I thought how benignant was the mood in which Nature had created him. It was an inviting, and certainly an innocent study that engaged me, but my aunt's eye, arrested by my rapt gaze, awoke in me a shame I could neither define nor justify. The glance was rapid and contained no rebuke. There may have been love in it. I could have thought so, had it ever beamed thus on me before. Its significance rendered me more cautious in what direction my regards strayed; taught me the earliest lesson in concealment practised towards one, who had claimed no title from me except that of brother.

At the hour of retiring, indicated by May's languid eyelids, my father, with true patriarchal dignity, collected all his flock; the servants drawn up in a decent row near the entrance, we kneeling about him, while he offered thanksgivings for the priceless, but often unremembered blessings of health, outward and mental tranquillity, and petitions for their continuance, with a richer endowment of spiritual graces.

One grey-headed negro remained after his fellows withdrew.

"Well, Isaac," said my father, "what do you want?"

"You have no objection to us keepin' watch to-night, I hope, sir."

"Who are here?" inquired his master.

"Nobody but our own folks, sir."

"Then you can watch as late as you please. I am not afraid of your getting disorderly."

"Thank you, sir. We won't disappint you, sir;" and he disappeared.

Herbert looked an inquiry.

"This is a custom of which you have not been informed," said my father, smiling. "Shakspeare tells us that chickens sing wakefully all night as Christmas draws near; and our servants add that neither beasts nor birds sleep the night of the twenty-fourth; an example they hold to be worthy of imitation by their master, Man. They—the negroes—collect about eleven o'clock, and pass in prayer and singing the remaining hour of the night proper. This they style, "watching in Christmas"—a vigil often continued into the dawn. I hope they will not disturb your slumbers."

"The novelty of the serenade will prevent any annoyance, I imagine," replied Herbert.

May and I were ready for bed, when a strain of music entered our room. She was instantly wide-awake and curious. The air was very soft, and after I had wrapped her up securely, I yielded to her entreaties to open the window. As I did so, I heard another sash raised in the chamber opposite ours. The cabin of gathering was crowded, as we could see through the door, left ajar on account of the stifling heat within. A hymn was given out, two lines at a time, by Isaac, who stood in the centre of the assembly, and sung with decorous gravity. A prayer succeeded it, by which we were not greatly profited, no intelligible word reaching us. Then came a chorus, ringing energetically through the night, and our pulses leaped to the fantastic, but exciting measure :—

"Swing low the chariot, Lord,
Swing low the chariot, Lord,
Don't leave me behind !"

The singers entered enthusiastically into the spirit of the song, swaying with its swell and fall, rising to their feet, and uplifting hands and eyes, as if to stay the flight of the fiery chariot.

Another prayer, and this time we did not lose a syllable. The speaker was a young man and a Boanerges in enunciation. The fervent, varying tones, that in an educated white, would have been ludicrous in their seeming affectation—as they swelled from his mouth, were music, wild and rude indeed, yet a continued musical theme, expressive as wild, powerful as rude. It detracted nothing from its solemnity, was rather in keeping with its disdain of all shackles of art or custom, that the Deity was addressed as "my Father"—"you" and "your" substituted for the usual "thou" and "they." A written transcript of this extraordinary petition would be tame and most unjust ; would fail to explain its effect upon us, for May was weeping on my shoulder at its close, and my heart overflowed as I listened to the concluding petition :—

"And after you have remembered with abundant blessings, crowded, shaked down and running over, all the saints in the univarsal world ; all mourning souls, seeking for rest and finding none ; all hard-hearted, impenitent, out-daring sinners, who won't come and ask for mercy ; all the sick, the poor, the perishing ; the masters and mistresses of this family, be pleased, O my Father, to look down and remember poor ignorant, sinful John. You are high, my Father, above earth, and stars, and heaven, and I am a creeping worm of the dust upon your footstool ; but you have promised, and you cannot lie, that whoever comes to you shall not be cast out. Be pleased to keep me in the middle of the channel of Faith, keep my heart from evil thoughts, my tongue from evil speaking, and my hands from evil deeds." *

Herbert spoke when he ceased.

"Where did that man learn to intone prayers? for that is the finest intoning I ever heard. We may as well close the windows. There will be nothing better than that."

I awoke once before morning, I knew not why until I put my hand towards May. She was sitting upright.

"Hist!" she whispered, "what is that!"

There were sounds of footsteps about the house; a word or two spoken in an undertone; then the nocturnal trampers passed in the direction of the quarters. My father's door was shut quietly, and I at once divined that the watch being over, he had arisen to advise some stragglers to seek their beds—a not unfrequent occurrence. May was chill and trembling, although she laughed at her alarm, and admitted my solution to be most reasonable; so I gathered her more closely to me, and again she slept upon my bosom.

* A verbatim report.

CHAPTER VIII.

We were aroused by a shock and report that shook the earth and made the windows rattle. It was broad daylight, and beside the blazing hearth stood Martha, in her gala attire, highly amused at our fright.

"Law! Miss Grace! *you* ain't afraid of a Christmas gun, what you've been heerd every year since you was born!"

"It was a cannon, then?" said May.

"No, my dear lady citizen; we have another species of ordnance in the backwoods. A hollow log is charged with powder, or a hole is bored in a tree, and filled with the same combustible, and a slow match applied, with what effect you have heard."

Minor explosions interrupted our toilette, and the cheers from the juvenile corps, who chiefly patronized these demonstrations, gave us some idea of the state of feeling out of doors, before we descended to become eye witnesses of the revelry. A swarm of young Ethiopians, from the tottler upon his trial feet, to urchins of twelve or fourteen years old, paraded with shining faces and clean clothes before the back porch. At sight of me, they were pushed and hustled into line by Joe, a half-grown boy. "Mind your manners, sir!" "Hats off!" "Bow to the ladies, all of you!" were the words of command. Martha brought forward a large basket, from which I drew some trifle for each one; sugar-plums and cakes for the lesser fry, toys, mostly of domestic manufacture, for the elder. Their mothers received from my aunt more useful articles. Children do not value presents according to their intrinsic worth. There was not a girl of them, who would not have chosen a rag-doll in preference to a fine apron; nor a boy, who would not have proved himself as anti-utilitarian, had a whistling-top and a jacket been offered to him.

"You have made twenty hearts happy—a good morning's work!" said Herbert, behind me.

I was on my knees beside the hamper, from which I was removing the sole remaining article, a flashy waistcoat for Joe, who was supposed, in virtue of his semi-manhood, to be above playthings.

"Master Frederic sent it to you," I observed, handing him the garment of many colors.

The lad stared open-mouthed, and did not offer to take it.

"Whar? when, Miss Grace? 'Thought Mars' Frederic was fur 'nough from here—sixty mile and better."

So he is!" I answered, annoyed at this uncivil behavior in one generally so well-mannered. "He sent it to me for you a week ago. I am sorry to have to tell him that it does not please you, Joe."

He came to his senses. "Please me! bless your soul, Miss Grace! the President of Ameriky aint a prouder man dan I is! When you write to Mars' Frederic, put in one corner of your dokkeyment that I'se mightily—I may say 'ternally bleeged, and how I means to drink his health dis happy day in de best 'simmon beer, and how we missed him, and"——

Here the oration blew up in an explosive laugh; and forgetful of respect and etiquette, he jumped up, struck his heels together twice, and went down the steps at a bound.

"Joe's got Christmas in *his* bones—certain!" said Martha, who was his sister, and much mortified at this violation of ceremony. "I reckon he's done taste dat beer a'ready dis mornin'."

May and Herbert enjoyed the scene in all its details, and

relished none more than the part that so surprised me. Joe brought an armful of wood into the parlor while we were awaiting the summons to breakfast, and once more outraged rules by dropping part of it pell-mell upon the andirons, and rushing from the room, again to vent his exuberance of spirits in a guffaw in the hall.

"That boy is bewitched!" said I, vexed, yet amused. "What you now see is not a correct sample of our every day government."

"Which cannot be arbitrary at any time," replied Herbert. "The recollection of tyranny is not so readily lost."

"Breakfast is ready," announced Joe, white apron on and waiter in hand, bolting out the message and backing precipitately. His smothered giggle preceded us to the dining-room, and, although he pulled on a long face when my father commenced the grace, I detected him in the very act of gulping down a laugh at the "Amen."

Under each plate was a small packet which was immediately opened. I had just glanced at mine, a medallion, enclosing my father's and Frederic's hair, and seen that May held its twin, containing a lock of mine, when a sort of buzz went around the table; my head was drawn back, and a kiss pressed upon my lips. Joe treated us to one "haw! haw!" to which its predecessors were modest titters, and dashed through the nearest door for the yard.

It was Frederic himself! his face joy-lit and sparkling, handsomer than ever, as he exchanged greetings with all except his father. After a deal of confusion, all talking together and nobody listening, we were prevailed upon to resume our seats, and Frederic was allowed to clear up the mystery of his apparition at so auspicious a juncture.

"I thought you were to have no vacation," said I.

"We took one," he responded. "We held an indignation

meeting over this curtailment of our privileges as free-born, independent Virginians ; waited upon Dr. Macon in a committee of the whole, and apprised him of our resolution to frolic for a week. He is a good-hearted old gentleman, take him all in all, and agreed to overlook our insubordination. I set out yesterday morning upon a borrowed horse, and arrived here late at night."

"It must have been your coming that awoke us," I interrupted.

May crimsoned and said nothing.

"I suppose so, if said awaking was about one o'clock. Joe, who is a regular night-bird, was prowling around, and to him I intrusted my steed, threatening to cut his ears off if he betrayed me to any of you before breakfast. Father, who does not sleep much more than Joe, put his head out of the window, and as I answered his challenge, he unlocked the door. No one has been in his room to-day except our Eboe confederate, and thus ends the tale of the Midnight Alarm and the Morning Surprise."

"We lack but two of our travelling-party," remarked Herbert to me, as we four were left together in the sitting-room.

Frederic was turning over an Herbarium of his own collecting for May's amusement, and we could converse apart. I had, hitherto, contented myself with casual inquiries about Louise's well-being, but my look showed now that I wished to hear more.

Herbert answered it.

"The world says they live comfortably with one another, and Louise's mother can see nothing amiss ; lauds her as a model of matrimonial propriety. It may be presumptuous in me to pretend to be more sharp-sighted than these competent judges. Wilson escorts his wife everywhere, and it is known publicly that she will not accept indiscriminate attentions from gentlemen. This is unquestionably as it should be—is very well so far as it goes."

His face was darkening, and I spoke.

"I hope she may yet regard him as his excellent qualities of disposition and heroic conduct deserve. There have been instances of love after marriage when circumstances were much less propitious than in this union."

"Do not believe it. Toleration is the best that can be expected. This Louise may practise while in her husband's presence. When absent from him, she has more congenial studies. A woman with a full, satisfied heart has no unhealthy thirst for pleasure, no haunting thoughts to flee. Home and its dear ones concentre her aspirations. Nor is her intellect necessarily cramped because she has, in hackneyed parlance, 'no higher ambition.' For the sake of those she loves she will raise herself to the loftiest standard of womanhood. In the daughter, filial affection will prompt this effort; and the true woman, when rightly mated, will cultivate every faculty, moral and mental, that she may be her husband's pride and soul-companion, as well as his love; that, in the eyes of their Maker, they may form the united Whole He designed man to be in his state of earthly perfection. Am I wearisome?" he checked himself. "I hope not, for I am just coming to the pith of the matter."

"Go on," I said. "I am not quite tired out."

"When, therefore, I meet at ball, rout and soirée, opera, concert, and theatre, night after night, a butterfly, who cannot live in private, mad for this kind of excitement as the opium-eater is for his drug, I write her down in my tablets as one who has an empty or a disappointed heart. There is another class, to whom pleasure's draught would be stale, insipid—women with more head than these, and oftentimes greater capacity of feeling. Over their crucified affections they erect splendid temples to Intellect. They too, drink to intoxication, but in libations to Fame. To you alone can I ever speak my real sentiments with regard to my unhappy sister."

His mouth quivered as I had noticed it when he broached the subject, but he mastered the weakness.

"She has a study-boudoir, the interior of which her husband hardly ever sees. Sometimes, she receives me there, and occasionally I encounter a German professor or a Spanish master. I am more apt to find ladies of an uncertain age, with near-sighted spectacles and very glib tongues. One or two of these bear names not unknown to the public; each of the others is 'distinguished' for something, or she would not be thus closeted. The bookcases are stocked with French, Latin and German classics; Göthe, Kant and Fichte are oftenest upon the table in juxtaposition with English books, as mystical to the plain sense of ordinary readers."

"I see no heinous sin in this," I said. "Louise was a fine linguist, an indefatigable and enthusiastic student of many abstruse branches when at school. Few women have the taste and intellect to follow these pursuits as eagerly and successfully. It is very natural that she should resort to this source of happiness, situated as she is."

"Most natural! Your remark conveys, by implication, the substance of what I said awhile ago. I had rather she selected this species of dissipation than the other, but the extreme of either is incompatible with the discharge of more sacred duties. It is of no importance to me, at present, to recall the circumstances that combined to make Louise the wife of David Wilson; it weighs nothing in the argument that he is her inferior intellectually. Obligations voluntarily assumed, vows in the name of Heaven, are not to be put aside by these considerations. As she would be bound to study with and for him, if his request or need demanded it, she ought, likewise, now and then, to take from Messrs. Kant, Fichte, and Co., one hour of the many they absorb, and contribute something to the happiness of the husband, whose worship is faithful and hopeless of reward. Do not try to persuade me that mine is a heterodox creed to you. I know better. So much," he continued in a lighter tone, "for grave dissertations and unpleasant subjects. Forgive me for intruding them upon you to-day. This is lovely weather—balmy as June—I am restless in-doors. Will you walk?"

Frederic and May were ripe for the proposal, and we spent much of the forenoon in the outer air. It was more than moderately warm, and in the fields, the scent of the withered grass; in the woods, the waving pine-boughs, and the hickory and oak bark, were as grateful perfume as the breath of early spring. On one sunny hill-side we sat a long while. A huge log, stripped of its covering, and bleached by months of exposure, lay just upon the outskirts of the forest. An arable field sloped down from this to a creek, and beyond arose another hill. To our right were visible the roof and chimney of Mrs. Bell's cottage; to the left, a mile distant, we could discern upon higher ground, the village of cabins and out-houses surrounding the more pretentious mansion of Mr. Townley. The blue smoke curled directly skyward, from horizon to zenith, not a cloud shut out one of the sunbeams the earth took in with hushed rapture. There were green mosses beneath our feet, and other patches of livelier emerald upon the banks of the stream, whose dreamy song was musically audible in the stillness. Our voices fell to the same undertone, for we were too joyous to refrain speech. We talked in quartette at first, then, as of old, we paired off; Frederic and May strolling down to the edge of the brook, where we watched them stop to gather pebbles and lichens or listen to the murmur of the water, and after a time, cross the foot-bridge and wave their hands to us from the opposite hill. Herbert and I exchanged smiles full of pleasant meaning; but neither spoke aloud the affectionate hope that bound these two, so worthy of each other, in a life-long tie.

The sun was below the meridian when they rejoined us, yet they seemed to have been gone a very few minutes.

"I regret that I am the bearer of unwelcome news," said Frederic. "Did you not hear the dinner horn ?"

"We did not," Herbert answered.

"It has sounded, nevertheless, and travelled over you to get to us," and about Frederic's mouth there were symptoms of an expression akin to that with which his friend had regarded his progress across the brook. "It was the warning signal, however," he added, "which is blown half an hour before meals are ready. We shall not be too late if we return at once."

A bridle path led through the woods to the house, and midway in our walk we found Uncle Zack, seated upon a stump, a gun laid on his knees, and several hares, his morning trophies, upon the ground at his side, watched by the Newfoundland, Sultan. The old man had removed his hat, overcome by the heat of the day and his exercise. His pepper-and-salt wool was combed into a peak above the organ of reverence, heightening the same into an outrageous contradiction of the spirit expressed by every line of his visage as we neared him. Contemptuous displeasure and dignified disgust were depicted there, and his voice bespoke as much. The exciting cause of his righteous wrath was a personage of his own color and about his age, who bestrode a ragged pony. The rider was comfortably and decently apparelled, yet his aspect was not so thoroughly respectable as that of our old friend. So vehement and engrossing was the altercation between them that neither saw us until Frederic interrupted them.

"How now, Jerry ? what are you quarrelling with Uncle Zack about ?"

Jerry's salute was sulky and devoid of the respectful alacrity with which his opponent jumped up from the stump, and tugged at the grey mountain aforesaid.

"I was remindin' him of a small pint of law, Mr. Leigh; 'sposin' he hadn't never heerd on it," replied the individual addressed.

"And *I* telled *him*, beggin' your pardon, Mars' Frederic, dat I been live in dis world and dis neighborhood mighty nigh as long as he is, and aint never been accuse' of anything onlawful 'till dis blessed day," said Uncle Zack, with rekindled indignation; "dat my mistis is a born lady, one of the fus' and wealthy families, and is 'sponsible for my 'havior and con*duct.* I does nothin' unbeknown to her, and does it stan' to reason dat she would 'low or permit me to act oppose' to a court of justice?" argued the old fellow, growing pedantic to display his knowledge of law and equity.

"What is the 'small point' over which he has been tripping?" inquired my brother of the accuser.

"That statue, sir," answered Jerry, not to be outdone in erudition, "which forbids negro slaves to carry fire-arms."

"I'se no 'slave,'" cried Uncle Zack, irefully. "I'se a respectable servant, and dat's ten million times better dan to be a trifling, no-account free nigger!"

"Fie! fie! I am astonished at you, Uncle Zack," said Frederic. "Don't you see the ladies?"

"Ax thar pardon and yourn, too, sir," apologized Uncle Zack, humbly. "But 'tis aggravatin', Mars' F'ederic, to hear trash like *dat* call me, a 'dustrious, regular colored pusson, 'slave' and 'nigger!' I leave it to you now, sir, if 'taint!"

"It is right hard to bear, I know, Uncle Zack. As for you, Jerry Williams," continued Frederic, "please remember in future that this man is under my father's protection, that he upholds him in all that he does."

"Now you're a-gittin' it!" chuckled Uncle Zack, aside. "Aint he, Sultan, old boy?"

The dog wagged his tail, his quick eye rivetted upon the free negro, with no amicable intent.

"Besides," said Frederic, "nobody wants you to lay down the law upon this or any other 'point,' unless your property is injured. These woods are my father's; Mr. Peyton gave Mrs. Bell that gun expressly for Zack's use. They are as strong law-lovers as yourself."

Jerry jerked up his pony's nose from the ground, where it hunted among the leaves for some bits of herbage that might eke out his scanty breakfast.

"It's none of my business, to be sure, Mr. Leigh"——

"I telled him so at de fust—didn't we, Sultan?" again crowed Uncle Zack.

"But Mr. Townley, sir, is a lawyer, and he spoke with me 'pon dis identickle subject not a week ago."

"There! enough!" Frederic waved his hand. "Pay Mr. Townley to get you of your own scrapes, and don't meddle, either of you, with honest people."

The pony moved off at a shambling gait, and Uncle Zack returned his thanks to his champion.

"It don't look well—'taint right, in fac', for a church member to fight, or he an' I would a' had a tussle 'fore we got through, I'm afeer'd, sir. Poor white folks and free negroes is monstrously alike, to my thinkin', Mars' F'ederic."

"How happens it that you are out gunning to-day?" asked my brother; "I expected you were keeping Christmas in gentlemanly style."

"So I did, sir—for two solid hours dis mornin'—but bless you, Mars' F'ederic, don' you know old Zack warnt born for to play? Too hard work for dis nigger—play is! So, Molly, she took to ironin' 'pon de sly, for fear mistris or Miss Annie'd stop her; and I sot out to lay in a stock of skins. Dis weather's mighty desateful. We'se got to pay for it, and pay well too, if you mind my racket."

"What do you make of these furs?" questioned Herbert.

"Gloves, my marster, and obershoes and tipples—or whatever

de ladies calls dem things what dey wraps up dey throats wid in winter."

"But you do not do all this yourself? You are a genius, Uncle Zack."

"Yaw! yaw! young marster, you've come right nigh de truth, if you mean a Jack at all trades and marster of none—dat's me! aint it, Sultan? My ole woman, she helps me 'bout de nice sewin', 'specially de ladies' shoes."

"I should like to have a pair of your manufacture," said May. "How much time do you need to finish them?"

"I ken make a par in two days, if I aint too much else to do. Bein' as 'tis holiday, I ken let you have yourn done by Saturday arternoon."

"That will do. Will you come to Mr. Leigh's for my measure? I am staying there."

Instead of replying verbally, Uncle Zack fumbled in his pocket for a slip of paper and a clasp-knife.

"Jest set your foot down upon dat, if you please, ma'am. Bein' as how dey's obershoes, I must measure your shoe outside, you onderstand. Whew!" he whistled, involuntarily, as he held up the short strip. "Dat's de leetlest—*jest* a leetle of de leetlest foot I ever see yet. You warn't 'tended to walk, my young mistis. You ought to a' had wings."

Laughing at this compliment, we said "good-bye."

"It is very singular that your servants should conceive so rooted a dislike to their free brethren," said Herbert to Frederic. "Is it universal?"

"I believe it is. They cordially despise them as a class, rank them as an inferior caste, with whom intimacy is disreputable, and intermarriage but one remove from disgrace. The free blacks are, as a whole, the most worthless part of our population; the very refuse of the lower orders. There are some shining exceptions, however, I am happy to say."

"What is the character of this Jerry Williams?" interrogated Herbert. "His demeanor does not indicate any sense of his inferiority."

"No, indeed! yet he is morally not much better than the generality of them. He is a wily fellow, and manages to preserve a sort of respectable standing. He is a rare instance of industry and frugality among his set, and owns property sufficient for his support. From a meagre beginning he has worked and saved until he has accumulated funds to purchase a house, several acres of ground, and a couple of servants to aid him in cultivating it.

"You do not mean that he holds them as slaves!" exclaimed Herbert.

"Why not?" said his friend, mischievously. "Do not delude yourself with the idea that the oppressed race you hear prayed for every Sabbath and harangued about in your political meetings, would not, if they had the chance, wield the oppressor's rod over their brethren in blood and name more fiercely than the veriest brute of a white overseer dares to do now. Take Jerry as an example. No other hands in the country are worked so cruelly, no other owner domineers with like needless severity, for he delights to show his power; likes the office and title of master. So egregiously vain is he of the latter, that he will actually hide himself in the bushes when he sees his servants coming, in search of him, upon which, whether they know his place of concealment or not, they are instructed to shout for 'Master,' until his ears cease to be titillated with the term."

"You are jesting upon my credulity," laughed Herbert.

"I appeal to Grace to verify my statement," returned Frederic, "and for confirmation of another anecdote of the same person. Jerry's cunning does not always parry the consequences of his officious impertinence. A white man—by the way, one of the kind classified with free negroes by Uncle Zack—who resides upon the farm adjoining Jerry's, had a quarrel with him, in which the negro had undeniably the right side. He would have been supported by the community but for his swaggering and uncalled-for publication of the case. Saunders—the neighbor, heard of this behavior, and being as great a bully himself, vowed to thrash him within an inch of his life. Taking two of his friends along to witness the doughty deed, he went over to Jerry's, and finding him in the field, introduced his errand in the hearing of his companions. Jerry was frightened out of his wits, as a matter of course, very penitent, very mean-spirited—and when he had begged himself out of breath to no purpose, whined that 'if Mr. Saunders would just respect his feelins' so far as to take him out of sight to whip him,' he would submit without further ado. The bully rampant was magnanimous; collared the bully couchant, and led him into a wooded hollow where hickories grew plentifully. He cut a stout one, trimmed it for use—when, presto! the actors changed characters. Jerry is athletic and his moment had come. Throwing Saunders down, he set his foot upon him, and proceeded coolly to administer a rousing castigation, yelling at each blow, in the most piteous accents—'Mercy, Mr. Saunders!' 'Oh, pray, sir!' etc., that the unseen and unseeing friends of the prostrate man might not be defrauded of their promised treat. Saunders' groans, if he uttered any, were thus drowned; to call for assistance would be too humiliating; so he bore it then, and kept his secret afterwards to his cost, for Jerry brought an action for assault and battery. Our neighbor, Mr. Townley, was his confidential adviser. He proved by Saunders' two associates all that was needed. Suspicions, if they suspected the truth, were not admissible evidence. They testified to the intent to attack, and the corroborating fact of the withdrawal of the parties into the thicket, finally the cries that came from it, and the verdict was instantly rendered. Saunders was both whipped and non-suited, nor did he escape the 'world's dread laugh' he endured so much to avoid. Mr. Townley told the story. It ran like wild-fire, and Jerry was triumphant." *

"Just as it should be!" cried my father coming out to meet us. "Rosy cheeks and bright eyes, and I trust keen appetites, for dinner is smoking on the table. This weather is superb! Did I not prophecy to you, Miss Grace, that we should have May in December? And here is a frolic on hand for to-night. Mr. Townley called while you were out, with invitations for all of you—Miss Seaton and Mr. Wynne especially mentioned—to an extempore party at his house."

We were ready to embrace any plan that promised fun, and resolved unanimously to attend. The only obstacle to overcome was a scruple of May's. She felt some hesitation at going among utter strangers.

"I wish one of the ladies had called with her brother," she said.

"All three would have been here to breakfast if they had suspected the existence of the point of etiquette that troubles you," said Frederic. "Unless you wish to give grievous offence to our plain country neighbors, you must not insist upon a principle they cannot appreciate."

This settled the question.

Mr. Peyton had, ever since the death of his wife, partaken of our Christmas dinner, and his arrival had preceded ours. It was a never-ceasing surprise to me that he made his way so soon into the good graces of new acquaintances. He was not a fluent talker; was often abstracted and abrupt, and in general conversation, bore an indifferent part. Yet Herbert, who sat between him and myself, fell under the spell of his unspoken goodness and unostentatious intelligence; was respectful, then attentive, and at length, conversed with him almost exclusively.

* Fact.

"Tell me something about your friend," he said, after dinner. "He has a history—has he not?"

My brief sketch did not disappoint him.

"Have you remarked," said he, "or has not your experience of Life been sufficient to teach you that the perfecting touch to human character, the purest type of disinterestedness is accomplished by fire?"

"Oh! do not say so!" I exclaimed, the coincidence of this with my aunt's prediction concerning me flashing upon my mind. "I dread suffering. I have never known it, and I am cowardly. I am happy in my ignorance of evil, Mr. Wynne, and a superstitious alarm seizes me when I listen to these prognostications."

"I prognosticate nothing for you; see no reason why Life should not continue as fair as this day for you through years to come. I hope the noon of happiness has not yet brightened upon you. You court sorrow by indulging forebodings."

I was not so easily quieted. The causeless fear; formless black presence, shadowed my soul with its wings, and ever, as it swooped nearer, I heard the stern tones—"In Judgment!"

In compliance with my father's wishes, May and I sought our room for a siesta to prepare ourselves for the fatigue of the evening. She—happy child! weary with the day's pleasures, slept so soon as she nestled among the pillows; but I was wakeful under the indefinable oppression of what I dared not call presentiment. I was lonely by and by; and to escape from myself, I arose, adjusted my dress and ran down stairs, intending to stroll in the garden while the twilight lasted. A tall figure darkened one window of the parlor. It moved as I was passing the open door.

"Come in!" it said, and I obeyed.

"Did the intensity of my wish bring you down, I wonder?" said Herbert. "You felt no powerful mesmeric attraction pulling you to this quarter, I suppose?"

"None; unless it visited me in the form of a fit of the vapors."

"I thought you lived above the reach of such maladies. It is a fashionable complaint whose contagion I hoped you had escaped."

He spoke dissatisfiedly, and I was ashamed of the slang I had used.

"I have, perhaps, mistaken my symptoms," I said. "Have you never felt a sudden downfall of spirits, unaccountable, impossible to avert, almost as difficult to relieve; a something Mrs. Hemans describes as

> ——— 'the strange, inborn sense of coming ill
> That ofttimes whispers to the haunted breast?'"

"Yes, occasionally, but I refer it to physical causes, or to the natural reaction of the mind after a season of excitement. If this is all that afflicts you, charm it away with cheerful thought. The demon is not a frequent visitor at Moss-side—is he?"

"By no means. My personal acquaintance with him is very slight. If you will not laugh, I will confess to some apprehensions that Mrs. Hemans was right."

"That it was a presentiment? I do not believe in such things, although we hear and read marvellous tales of their verification. On the contrary, all that I have felt and observed leads me to the opinion that the most destructive bolts of affliction fall from a clear sky; that the sun of joy is more frequently struck at one shock from the heavens than quenched in a gradual decline. I have been musing about you here in the twilight."

"About me!" drawing in my breath more quickly.

"About you and your home. This lovely nook meets my ideal of rural seclusion. It is the Arcadia I have hitherto seen but in dreams."

"It is a dear home to me," I said.

"You have no care here; you told me to-day that you knew nothing of trouble," he pursued. "Whoever transplants you to another soil will incur a heavy responsibility. Would it be a selfish act?"

My father's entrance spared me the necessity of a reply, which would have been hard to frame. We were pacing the floor, my hand upon Herbert's arm, and in the wasting light, I perceived my father's start of surprise and inclination to retreat. Herbert did not speak immediately, but when he did, it was without agitation or the earnestness with which he had said his last words to me.

"Our friend, Mr. Peyton, has gone, sir," he remarked. "Frederic and I would have detained him to supper, but he must needs offer his services to gallant a lady neighbor of yours to the party this evening."

"Annie Bell, I presume," replied my father.

"That is the name. She is a protégé or something of the sort of his, Frederic tells me."

I had slipped my hand from its resting place, and, leaving my father in the midst of Annie's story, I effected a noiseless retreat. I would not dwell a second upon the tumultuous thoughts that spurred my brain into a fever; stayed not to inquire the cause of the glow that burned in my cheeks; but ordering May's supper with mine to our room, dived forthwith into the momentous business of our toilettes. The carriage was ready as soon as we were. The moon was near its full, and our ride, as May complained, "only too short."

Mr. Townley's ancestral abode was a two-story brick building, set rather high up on the hill, and environed by what it pleased Miss Malvina to designate as "a pastoral grove." The host opened the carriage-door, and in his creamy tones, bade us welcome, and wished us a "Merry Christmas."

"My friend, Mr. Wynne, Mr. Townley," introduced Frederic —and as May was handed out—"Miss Seaton."

"We are honored by their presence," acknowledged Mr. Townley, at an angle of forty-five degrees.

Deftly, like the natty dandy he was, he tripped up the steps with May, presenting her at the top to "my sister, Miss Townley."

Miss Judy had been wheedled or coerced into wearing a head-dress, a gay, tinsel thing, altered from Miss Malvina's last winter's finery. Her black silk dress had more longitude and amplitude of skirt, and less of body, than her everyday costume. She gave us a loud, sincere greeting, and showed us into her room to remove our mufflings.

"I am very glad you came, Grace," said she, "and you too, Miss Seaton. I am really afraid Malvina would have gone crazy if you had stayed away. Directly she heard this morning that your friends were with you, Grace, nothing would do but we must have some description of a "fuss," and James must ride over and invite you all."

Now, considering Miss Malvina had known three days before from my own tongue that May and Herbert were confidently expected on Christmas Eve, I was tempted to attribute this impromptu "fuss" to another arrival, telegraphed by the sable couriers from one plantation to the other. More company drew off the attention of the elder sister, and we rejoined our escorts in the entry. Miss Malvina, with complexion like a cabbage-rose; her flaxen hair dressed in three tiers of curls, had strained maidenly bashfulness to the extent of meeting Frederic upon the threshold of the parlor door, and as he made no motion to enter, she remained there. He broke her toils with scant show of courtesy when May appeared. She was very lovely that night. Frederic's eyes might have enlightened her as to this fact, had the buzz that ran through the apartment at her entrance failed to do so ; but she was gracefully unconscious that any look or tone of admiration had reference to her. A majority of the younger gentlemen solicited introductions, and all she received with frank ease and impartial cordiality. Frederic maintained the post nearest to her without obtruding his attentions. He was undisguisedly proud of the homage rendered her, manifesting this feeling so plainly that I could not forbear whispering a caution. For this act of sisterly discretion, I got a saucy smile for myself, and a snap of the fingers for the crowd.

There was a crowd, notwithstanding the shortness of the notice served upon the guests. Miss Judy had her clique of matronly housewives and settled elderly gentlemen ; Miss Malvina had asked mostly "girls about my own age," she loved to say—which might, by this data, have been estimated at anything from sixteen to twenty-five. Miss Susan, least social of the three, yet protected in one corner a select few of her chosen associates, most of them as starched as herself. Mr. Townley had not overlooked a neighbor in his rounds, for well as he knew the value of popularity to him now, his ambitious eye pierced the future to the strife of a not distant hustings, when each one of his male acquaintances who was a free man of twenty-one would be worth his vote. I have slandered our neighborhood, if our present hosts are, to my readers, "specimen articles." The Townleys were an old and respectable family, and in general society, upon a level with many, immeasurably their superiors in breeding and education. There were here collected gentlemen who would have trodden the royal drawing-room with as finished elegance as the most thorough courtier there ; men, who had reaped academic and political honors in no mean measure, and women, whose intelligence and refinement fitted them to be their companions.

"I had not anticipated so pleasant a gathering," said Herbert to me. "I am in love with country life. If the lady who has stolen the past half hour from me is a rustic, I award the palm to rusticity over city polish. What a charming, modest, sensible little creature she is! I did not catch her name as Mr. Peyton presented me to her. I suppose you know her?"

"You cannot say too much in her praise," I said. "It is Annie Bell."

"I remember"—he began.

Miss Malvina had overheard the name and interrupted him. "You see, Grace, we could not get over inviting her. She lives so near, and is, besides, a favorite with sister Judy. You must think our society sadly mixed, Mr. Wynne."

"It is a most agreeable compound, Miss Townley—better than any one simple element."

"Does he guess how very simple is that he is now dealing with?" I said to myself.

Miss Malvina fluttered her fan and cast down her pink eyelids.

"You are very polite to say so, I am sure. But we were talking of this Miss Bell. I am ashamed to tell you, Mr. Wynne—we are shockingly democratic here—she is nothing but a seamstress."

"That is all you can say against her—thank Heaven!" said Mr. Peyton, over her shoulder.

She gave her customary scream. "Mercy! cousin Robert! I did not dream you were within a hundred miles of us. I have said no harm, however. Annie is a nice girl—I love her dearly—and Mrs. Bell is a sweet old lady."

"Cousin Robert" was not to be conciliated, for he moved on with a grave bow. Nor had I patience to listen longer. Provoked at her exposure of her own silliness, and the ill-nature I knew to be second-hand from Miss Susan, I made some excuse to change my place, but she caught me by the arm.

"One word!" she said aside, with a forced giggle. "Is your brother addressing this Miss Seaton?"

"Miss Malvina!"

"Now, don't be angry, please! I—that is, we have been troubled to know whether it was so or not. *I* was positive from the beginning that there was nothing in it. Brother says I am a goose; that he is sure they are lovers; and when sister Susan said she must be terribly anxious, to come all this way to see him, brother told her that circumstances altered cases, and repeated some old thing about Mahomet and the mountain."

"A precious pair the everlasting sister and brother are!" I almost said. I had the self-control to substitute a more temperate retort. "Mr. Townley and Miss Susan, and you, Miss Malvina, may cease your speculations. I must have told you before, that Frederic's vacation was a surprise to us all. Miss Seaton was positively informed that he would not be at home this Christmas."

"You are not offended—are you?" still clutching my sleeve.

"Not with you!" releasing myself.

Herbert eyed me quizzically, as I walked off.

"I would not seem impertinent; but I venture to affirm that you have been running a tilt for a friend—not defending yourself. May, Frederic, Annie Bell, or Mr. Peyton has a spirited champion. You *are* spirited—do you know it?"

My ruffled plumes settled under his playful raillery.

"I know that my temperament is rather sanguine than phlegmatic," I rejoined. "I beg you will not suppose that the rise of heat just now was caused by the lady with whom I was conversing."

"I have seen enough of her to convince me that she is incapable of exciting resentment except as the mouth-piece of others more designing."

Ten minutes' talk with him never failed to tranquillize me, and irritating as were the spiteful innuendoes against my pure-hearted

May, as indelicately retailed to me, I cast off the recollection at his command. In my soul, I experienced a secret pleasure at this gentle tyranny, that said even to thought, "No further!" and turned its course at his will. It never trammeled belief; opinion was as free as the wind; its utterance encouraged; but taste he directed, and controlled mood with the power of an autocrat. I have never seen similar strength combined with similar kindness in any man besides. True, I had witnessed the exemplification of this in trifles alone; but they were straws that floated continually on the surface of the tide that could have borne mighty trees along as easily. Still, recognizing this influence as I did, yielding to it without a show of resistance, I would not seek out the root of his authority and my dependence. No analysis of emotions, no weighing of probabilities, no prudent misgivings were concealed under the gaiety with which I mingled in the dance that kept feet and blood in rapid motion. I laughed in real amusement as Mr. Townley slyly observed to my partner of one set:

"It is reported among our friends that a certain gentleman is likely to *Wynne Grace* at Moss-side."

As unembarrassed was my rejoinder to the same partner's comment—"Mr. Wynne is a fine-looking man."

"And as remarkable in character as feature," I said.

The revel broke up at two o'clock; adieux were exchanged, and we drove off. May was delighted with the novelty of the festival; the easy footing upon which everything had placed itself, and yet the unbroken good breeding that pervaded the whole company. The peculiarities of the sisters had amused and interested her—in short, she had seldom, if ever, enjoyed a merry-making more.

"Mr. Townley is a lawyer—is he not?" questioned Herbert.

"Call him an attorney! said Frederic. "The words may

be exactly synonymous, according to our manner of using them, but to my ear the latter suits him better. Why do you inquire? Was he professional in his management of you?"

"I have never occupied a witness-box, but I have a vivid conception of the feelings incident to the position," replied Herbert. "He cross-examines so dexterously, shapes his queries so ingeniously, that it is a positive pleasure to be pumped by him. Nor, judging from my brief experience, is he prone to let slip opportunities of amassing information, although there may be nine hundred and ninety-nine cases out of a thousand that it will never profit him. He reminds me of a class of economists who are forever buying bargains, things for which they have nc present use, simply because they are cheap, and may serve them some good purpose twenty years hence."

"Why, how could you learn this?" I inquired. "He surely was not guilty of prying into the personal history of a stranger and his guest! I am at a loss to understand you."

"'Prying' is too coarse a term for the adroitness, with which, in a chat of half an hour, he made himself *au fait* to the leading events of my manhood, youth and infancy; climbed the branches of the genealogical tree up to the names and residence of my great-grand-parents, which was as far as I could go. There we exchanged places, he instructing me as to my probable pedigree back to the Norman conquest. He is ready this moment, I will warrant, to make out an armorial ensign for me, not a quartering omitted or slurred over."

"In the name of all that is impertinent and ridiculous, what did the fellow mean?" exclaimed Frederic.

"Not to rust for want of practice, I imagine," returned his friend, his good-humor invincible. "I was a bargain, and he bought me up cheap—as I have intimated, for I was amused, not worried, and let out the line as fast as he was disposed to pull it. He would sift even a chancery suit to the bottom, or prove it to be what many wickedly declare it—a bottomless den of iniquity. If my cousins-Norman, as he decided any connections I may have over the water to be, should ever leave me legatee to a fortune of fabulous amount, I would write forthwith to him to supply whatever my memory had dropped. Commend me to a man who understands his business!"

CHAPTER IX.

Three more days of beauty and of joy ; of witching weather and unalloyed delight in the same ; the third a Sabbath, that restrained our sporting, without marring our happiness ;—and there arose a Monday's sun, as glorious as its immediate predecessors. We were making the most of the swift hours now, for but one day besides this remained for our intercourse. Our separation was an interdicted topic, and at the breakfast-table we spoke not even of the morrow.

Mr. Peyton had furnished Frederic with the means of gratifying an ardent wish, hitherto frustrated by the lameness of my horse ; viz. a ride with May. Herbert and myself, according to this plan, had no choice but to be mutually agreeable and while away the time of their absence as we could. My father received early that morning, a line from Mr. Townley, notifying him of an examining court of magistrates, to be held in the village at noon, to investigate a case of petty larceny—a call which he, as a justice of the peace, could not disregard. The lawyer came by our house in time to help May mount Black Bess, Mr. Peyton's special pride. Frederic placed himself at her side ; my father added a warning both were too gleeful to remember—and they were off, May's green habit and white plumes streaming back in the air, parted by their flight.

"A fairy-like vision !" said Mr. Townley, with his ever-ready smile. "Steed and rider are well matched."

Herbert followed my glance to the sleek sorrel, Mr. Townley's riding-horse, and answered by a look of arch intelligence

We had a laugh at our ease, when he and my father jogged down the lane ; the very gait of the animal, an ambling pace, his head nodding complacent wisdom right and left, being an imitation of his master too faithful for a burlesque.

"Now," said Herbert, "what have you to do between this and dinner ?"

"Nothing, except amuse or vex you."

"One—I do not say which of these—you can effect by equipping yourself for a walk. The house is chill and damp after this dry, warm air. We will go, if you please, to the hill we visited the first day we spent here."

"And whither we have been every day since," I said ; "but we could not show better taste."

The shadows of the leafless trees, fringing the hill-top, lay upon the earth in arabesques as motionless as if cast by carvings of stone ; the wind-spirits had rocked themselves to sleep in the highest boughs, and the wondrously-beautiful sunlight that had lent a wierd-like charm to our festal week, still bathed the winter landscape, like the smile of heavenly love on the cheek of age.

And there, beneath the blue sky, in the breathless, enchanted silence of Nature, Herbert Wynne told me of his love. How the revelation was made, I cannot tell. A thousand vain efforts have showed me that I cannot recall one of the words which conveyed to me the most precious gift of my life. I know that my tongue was spell-bound ; that to the wild current of emotions that flooded my being, when his meaning burst upon me, succeeded a sense of awakening from a ravishing dream to a reality a million-fold more blissful—that when he implored me to speak, I could only falter—"Let me think !" and bow my head upon my lap. I did not shut out the brightness in closing my eyes. I had never seen the full glory of Life until now. My relishful summer pleasures, my autumn reveries, intangible, dissolving views as they were ; the overflowing joyousness of the past few days—what were they all but faint premonitions of this ? Every girlish ideal of earthly happiness, every yearning for affection were here met and more than realized. What wonder that my answering movement to his entreaties was to lift my streaming eyes towards Heaven, and murmur in passionate gratitude, " O, God ! I thank thee ! "

Herbert's instant impulse was to uncover his head, and our united heart-song of praise, voiceless to human hearing as the slumbering air, went upward through the sunshine.

When we could talk, I heard of the birth and growth of his attachment ; learned that his intentions were matured ere he decided to accompany May ; that Moss-side would have had him as a visitant had she never thought of coming South.

I raised my eyes, but let them fall again.

"You have no right to do that," he said. "I love my authority, and your thoughts are now mine. I demand them."

"I wanted to ask you why you love me."

This was uttered in true humility. When he would make me his equal, I comprehended my inferiority, and trembled lest he should be blind to it until it was too late to retrieve his mistake.

"The question I have been listening for !" he said. "You have never been told that you are attractive in person and manner ; have no suspicion of your popularity in your circle of acquaintances ; wonder that Louise should have clung to you later and more firmly than to any other friend ; that May should love you as a sister ?—which, permit me to remark parenthetically, I hope she will be some day. These things are all news to you, Grace ?"

"Now you are jesting," I said, "and I was in serious, almost sad earnest. I do not rate myself among the repulsive or utterly unattractive. I am young and lively, therefore not destitute of charms, but you know as well as I do, Mr. Wynne"——

"That gentleman has departed this life to you," interposed my auditor, with becoming gravity. "If you have aught to say to *Herbert*, pray proceed."

Rather disconcerted, I continued—"I was about to say, that while I may be on a par with the average of young ladies, I am much below the standard you must have formed. I have neither Louise's genius nor May's loveliness of face and disposition. I am a country girl, untried by care, new to the world, unformed in manner and character"——

"Excuse me, but you are monopolizing the conversation"—I was again interrupted. "I am not speaking lightly now, dear Grace, so listen! That you are a child in world-knowledge, I rejoice to think. It enhances the purity of the gem I have won; and I trust the unperverted instinct of your woman's nature, your quick penetration of character, more than all, your moral principle to keep you still unspotted, true to yourself and to me. So far as your mind is concerned, I am better informed than you are, and I might say the like of certain traits that time and occasion will develop. You have not sounded the depth of your own heart; dream little of its powers of endurance; its rocks of resolution and hidden fires of passion. Passive as this hand now rests in mine, you have latent strength, that if aroused, would change it to unbending steel, and deny it to my touch, if the heart above which you sternly folded it were beating its last. You would not bear sorrow patiently, Grace—I feel this. You would return buffet for buffet; wrestle with the storm that would bear you to the dust. But that you are 'untried by care' is not the dissuasive you suppose, any more than is the conviction that it will find you rebellious, when it does visit you—for oh, my darling! we will meet Fortune's shocks—all Life's woes together. You can, you will bear anything for my sake, and a strong arm and brave heart, nerved by the thought of your love, will break the violence of every blow aimed at you, or be crushed in the attempt."

"Must we look for clouds to-day?" I said. "Who told me only last week that we courted sorrow by forebodings?"

"We will no more of them!" he responded. "And one must have keen sight indeed to espy blemishes in our heaven. We will accept the gracious omen of our betrothal-day!"

As the flush of excitement burned more steadily, we accustomed ourselves to think of matter-of-fact minutiæ. I shrank slightly at the beginning, but he demolished the barrier by reminding me of the brief space intervening before our separation, an allusion that drew me at once more nearly to him.

"Your father!" he said, at length, "I shall speak to him of this before I leave. Frederic, the dear fellow! shall not sleep to-night until he hears it all. Is it your wish that any other of your friends be apprised of it at present?"

"By no means. I should be painfully embarrassed were any formal communication made. If it were proper, I could desire"—I stopped.

"To break the intelligence to your father yourself, you would say."

"How did you discover that?" I asked.

"No matter. That was your meaning, and you shall do as you like in this. But, Grace, it will carry a pang to his bosom. You are his chief treasure; will he resign you to the care of the acquaintance of weeks? I could not blame him if he refused to sanction my suit—and what then?"

"He will not! You wrong him—indeed you do!" I replied warmly. "He never denied my most trivial petition."

"This is not a trifle," he said.

"And therefore he will weigh the consequences of a negative more carefully," I urged. "Is this the most formidable difficulty you apprehend? To my way of thinking, there is much more danger that your mother will frown upon a mésalliance with one who has no prétensions to fortune, style, or"——

His fingers were upon my lips.

"I am a man and independent!" he said. "I select a wife for myself, not for society!"

His scorn was to me the echo of Louise's maledictions upon the false system that had laid her heart in ruins.

"Moreover, Grace, you forget that Mrs. Wynne is not my mother. From you, hereafter, I can have no concealments. I owe her respectful duty, for she did not drive from her husband's board and roof the orphan boy bequeathed to him by a dying wife—his early and best-beloved. I fed, slept, played and studied with her children. My uncle would have it so, and he enforced his will by measures so extraordinary as to tame his politic lady into a show of acquiescence. I love—I revere him, if only for what he has been to me; and I have faith to believe that, incrusted as his affections seem to be with business cares and selfish interests, there is yet a place in them for the legacy that no longer needs his guardianship. Since Louise's marriage I stand alone in the world. I have never had a home. Grace, will you make me one?"

What appeal finds more ready entrance to a woman's heart? When we bent our reluctant steps towards Moss-side, I had promised to share this home whenever he required it; to bear its ark of treasure over land and flood, if his footsteps led the way.

My father had not returned, and we dined without him. Then May and I betook ourselves to the cozy upper chamber, according to our afternoon custom, while Herbert and Frederic smoked their cigars in the porch or yard. May seated herself in my lap, took my face between her hands and studied it; her eyes beaming with mischievous enjoyment. I could not deny her a returning smile, and finally both laughed aloud like madcaps, neither of us could say at what. I could have cried as heartily afterwards, in default of something better to do, had she not grown serious too.

"You need not tell me anything, Gracie, if you will but let

me take for granted what I choose. I was advised of Herbert's movements up to this morning, and I judged from his face at dinner-time that he was not heart-broken. My own friend! what a prize you have gained in his love! I am so happy for you!" and she kissed me over and over again with other, and yet more fond ejaculations.

In what warm colors she drew my—our future, in the talk that ensued! and I was well satisfied to hear the praises she lavished upon my betrothed. Through the window we could see two tall forms walking up and down the path leading to the summer-house, engaged, my beating heart said, in converse similar to ours. Thus went by the hours until the increasing darkness veiled her face from my sight. Frederic met me at the foot of the stairs, and held me back to put his arm around me and touch my forehead with his lips.

"My sweet sister!" was all his whisper, but it relieved me of embarrassment at his presence.

He had an accurate ear and admirable taste in music, although comparatively ignorant of the rules of the art, and he obeyed May readily when she sent him to the piano. The outline of her figure, the head drooped in thoughtful attention, was dimly visible to us against the western window; the rich chords that vibrated upon the twilight air were struck by an unseen musician; and at the far side of the apartment, Herbert sat beside me, as was now his right, the fast blood throbbing in the palms laid against each other, reporting faithfully each heart-beat, for our tongues had no language for this hour. I could laugh to scorn presentiments and goblin fears; and my soul, with the presumptuous confidence of youth, shook its wings exultantly at the expansion of its horizon; its new anticipations already looking beyond the bliss of the present, and saying, "To-morrow shall be as this day, and even more abundant!"

Joe brought in lights, an unwelcome piece of official politeness.

"Carry them out!" ordered Frederic. "Nobody wants them."

"Supper is 'most ready, sir; and, Miss Grace, marster done, come home. He look mighty sick!"

I ran to his room without delay. He lay on a lounge, his hat, gloves, and riding-whip upon the floor, as if he had thrown them down immediately upon his entrance. His ashy paleness and contracted brow betokened great pain; and kneeling beside him, I inquired the cause and symptoms of his illness.

"My head aches violently, my daughter," he said, without unclosing his eyes.

He was subject to intense suffering from this disorder, and his answer rather soothed than disquieted me. I rang for a cup of strong coffee, and a hot foot-bath; bathed his temples, and loosened the heavy over-coat he had not laid aside. He groaned from time to time, and this unwonted expression of anguish startled me. Each moan I answered by a word of love and sympathy, which, more unusual still, elicited no reply. I could not bear the sight of the closed eyelids and compressed mouth.

"Dearest father!" I pleaded, "can you not speak to me—to your little Grace? Tell me how I can help you. May I send for the doctor? Is there nothing in the house—nothing that I can do to ease this terrible pain?"

He looked up at me. His eyes were sunken, and appealed to me with an agony that forced tears from mine.

"You cannot relieve me, my dear. I must bear it. Do not let your aunt come in. Bolt the door! I can see no one except yourself."

He was just in time, for my aunt and Frederic met upon the threshold that minute. I stepped out to them; represented this as one of his most severe neuralgic headaches, and advised them to leave him to me who was always his nurse in these attacks. I heard cautious steps go past the door to the supper-room ; then their return, and I could not stir from my watch. Half an hour later, I ventured to speak again.

"Are you no better, father ?"

The dry lips motioned, not said, "No better."

"You would be more comfortable in bed if you could endure the pain of moving. May I call Frederic to assist you ? The poor fellow is very uneasy, and wishes to see you—to help me take care of you."

He paused a moment before he replied, "Call him, then."

Herbert came into the dining-room while I was drinking my tea.

"Is your father very much indisposed ?" he asked with solicitude. "Can I do anything for him or for you ?"

"Thank you—I believe not. I hope he will fall asleep soon. He is about to retire now."

"Joe," to the young butler, "Miss Seaton will be obliged to you for a glass of water. She is in the parlor. You are pale and dejected, dearest," as the boy departed on the improvised errand. "For my sake, do not give way to fear. The frequency of these attacks is a proof that they are constitutional and not dangerous. One thing more—you must not sit up alone to-night. If there should be any necessity for such a watch, Frederic and I will divide it. I am jealous of any exaction upon your health and spirits. Have you time to look at the stars one instant ? to inhale one breath of fresh air ?"

We encountered Joe in the hall, bringing back the scarcely-tasted water ; and with the precocity of his race, he bestowed on me a knowing grimace, appreciative and confidential, and unseen by my attendant. We tarried out-of-doors but an instant, as Herbert had promised, only made one turn to the gate and back ; yet I re-entered the sick-chamber refreshed in body and in mind, stronger in hope and desire to alleviate the pains of the beloved invalid. Frederic stood by his pillow, trying to persuade him to take the coffee I had prescribed.

"No! no!" I heard him answer. "It will do no good."

"It has never failed to help you before, father dear," I said, playfully. "It is not like you to discard a friend who has given you no offence. Pass over the cup to me, Fred. He cannot refuse me."

Again that imploring look—longer and more fixed upon me.

I offered the cup to his lips, "To please your daughter, father! Drink it because you love her."

He swallowed it unresistingly. As I stooped to kiss my thanks, he enfolded me in an embrace, sudden and fond—impassioned even in its fervor.

"I *do* love you, darling!" he said. "Do you believe me?"

"Believe you, dearest father!" I replied, striving to preserve my cheerful tone; "I should be very miserable if I doubted it!"

"Will you believe it, forever?" he persisted, holding my hand locked in his, and gazing wistfully into my eyes.

"Forever—so long as I live! Can you sleep now that you have heard me declare this? I mean to turn Fred out and stay with you myself, until you obey this part of my prescription also. He must look after May and Mr. Wynne."

My voice may have changed slightly at the latter name, for he started; then his brows were knitted in a sharper pang, and he turned restlessly to the wall.

"You had better go," I said aside to Frederic. "Talking disturbs him."

"I had rather be quite alone," interposed my father—"quite alone!" repeating the words incoherently. "I must think—sleep, I would say! You are good children. You have done all that you can for me; but if the room were perfectly still, and the candle put out, it would be better for me—and for you."

I touched his hand. It was cold, not feverish. He noticed the movement.

"I am not delirious or dreaming. I wish— Kiss me once more, Grace! God bless you!" and we were obliged to go.

I listened without the door several times in the course of the evening, and found all quiet. At bed-time, he was apparently in a profound slumber, and my dreams were all of the forenoon.

"The last day!" said May, with her awakening thought; "let us make it a happy one, Grace. To-morrow grief will be inevitable."

My patient was better, and smiled feebly upon me as he said that the pain in his head was gone. I enjoined him not to rise until late, and was surprised at his submission to a request disregarded upon many previous occasions. At eleven o'clock, he quitted his bed for the lounge, complaining of debility and drowsiness. This unforeseen confinement added to my anxiety on his account, perplexity on my own. I had tried vainly to muster the courage I had thought, the preceding day, would come of itself to enable me to introduce the subject uppermost in head and heart; and had arrived at the determinate conclusion that Herbert must assume the whole conduct of the delicate business.

He was not superior to the natural inclination to triumph over me, when, after a world of hesitation and falterings, I managed to communicate to him my changed purpose; could not withstand the temptation to boast a little of the sagacity that had foreseen this sequel.

"And lest you should be cast down at the discovery of your faintheartedness," he said, "let me tell you that I love you the more for the timidity which I understand, although you do not. I intended, at the last, to be my spokesman and yours; but thought it no harm to amuse myself with your shy approaches to the awful *dênoûment*."

"And do you feel no trepidation?" I inquired; "no trembling—no impeded articulation?"

"I!" drawing up his stately figure in the conscious strength of manliness. "I glory in the task! and were my nerves less firm; if I knew what it was to dread the face of mortal man, the recollection of what depends upon my action would brace me for the undertaking. My main—my sole regret is that this trial—for it will be a trial to him, Grace—must, of necessity, fall when your father stands in need of rest. This, and this alone, would tempt me to postpone it for a day or two; but since we are compelled to go to-morrow, I must speak this afternoon—*now!* What frightens you, Gracie?"

I was trembling all over. "I don't know," I could hardly say.

"Shall I guess? You dread my return to you with a lugubrious visage and general sheepish expression, to whine over the lecture—richly merited, I admit—administered by your justly-incensed parent for my audacity in thus creeping into his fold, and coaxing off the fairest of his flock. And what right have I to do this?" he went on, musingly. "Come to me, darling!"

He stroked back the curls from my face, and scrutinized every lineament.

"His youngest—the only daughter left to gladden his home; the pride of his eyes; the stay and comfort of his age. Oh, Grace, what atonement can I ever make to him for robbing him of you? Can the devotion of my life recompense you for the loss of such a father? Weeping, my dearest? Are these tears for him or for yourself, or because you repent your promise to me, and grieve over my disappointment?"

I clung to him in reply, and hid my face in his bosom; all coy scruples forgotten at the mere imagination of losing him.

"I love the touch of these clinging fingers," he said, fondly. "They are as frail to the sight, as strong in their grasp, as ivy-tendrils. Will they always be satisfied with their present support, I wonder?"

"Your wonderment is arrant hypocrisy," I said, rallying. "I could ask a more pertinent question—will the oak never be ashamed of its parasite?"

"'Parasite!' out upon the vile name!" as if it had stung him. "A clever botanist you are! You are no stunted moss—an eye-sore upon the trunk; nor mistletoe, never seen until the boughs are stripped of leaves. The ivy has its root in the earth that imparted life to the forest giant; and grow with, and twine into the oak as it will, it retains its individuality. I would not have your character and personal identity merged into mine, Grace. I have learned to love the ivy—ivy let it be to the last! My time is up, dear one! I must leave you."

"Your time! leave me!" I repeated. "What do you mean?"

"Simply, that, anticipating that your courage would desert you after the manner of Bob Acre's, I sent a message by Frederic to your father, asking permission to wait upon him at as early an hour as should suit his convenience. I received for reply that he would see me at four o'clock. Your centenarian in the hall there, croaked out the five minutes' signal awhile ago. I would not fail in punctuality on this of all occasions. We shall not be closeted very long, I fancy, if what you and your brother have flattered me into believing, be true. You are going up to May—are you not? Leave your door ajar, and when you hear the first line of 'Sweet Home' whistled in the lower entry, come down. There goes the crazy old sentinel!"

A hasty caress; one beam of love, joy, encouragement thrown back to me from the door—and his fleet step resounded through the passage leading to my father's room.

May's packing was not entirely finished, and I busied myself in helping her. She was aware of the negotiation transpiring below; and while she, like myself, was in no suspense as to its termination, she appreciated my tremor and joined in my earnest "Oh! that it were over!"

"Another thing, Grace," said the sympathetic angel. "We are forgetting that your father does not expect to have you with him all your life. Every parent looks forward to the marriages of his children as probable events, and becomes familiarized to the idea. Yours will feel your departure as a personal bereavement; but, at the same time, a load will be lifted from his mind by the reflection that your comfort and happiness are sure; that you are removed beyond the chances of dependence or loneliness. I may be a selfish reasoner, for my interests are with my affections, on Herbert's side. I long to have you settled near me. I suppose my second trip southward will be to countenance the final step by my presence and aid—our next journey in company be another bridal tour. Poor Louise! how different from—how much happier than hers!"

Thus she prattled, in her cooing notes, attuned by Nature to Love's own music; sometimes working with me; pausing frequently to lay her cheek to mine, to play with my hair, or perform some other act of soothing tenderness that might allay my impatience; never, while maligning herself by speaking of her selfishness—a principle unknown to her save by the hearing of the ear—never, I say, referring, however distantly, to the pain of the nearing partings to herself. Yet did I not know that, untold as was their love, she and Frederic would suffer well-nigh as keenly as the two who were openly betrothed; that their absence from each other would have much less to assuage its bitterness, since their correspondence, if direct, must be confined by certain limits laid down by worldly-wise formalists; that, whatever of sickness or distress might befall one, the other must support the tortures of absence and suspense—that they must suffer apart.

"You may revisit Virginia on a bridal tour, and earlier than you now pretend to think," I said, and halted purposely to mark the influence of the speech.

The slender neck was straightened in queenly hauteur, but only for a second; the following thought-flash revealing the absurdity of her suspicion of my meaning.

I continued, without appearing to observe the transient touch of offended dignity: "Mr. Townley is evidently captivated. He told me yesterday that he had seldom beheld a more enchanting *May*-den. I trust my emphasis pointed the pun as well as his does."

"Most of his witticisms should borrow an edge," said she. "Happily for his puzzled auditors, he is not averse to playing chorus himself to his compositions."

As directed, I had left the door unclosed, and I here heard footsteps down stairs, I could have been sure were Herbert's. They came, too, from the quarter towards which I was listening for signs of his return, but there was no summons, and I was provoked at the trick of my excited nerves.

"This conference is tedious!" I sighed.

"That shows how little you know about debates upon such questions," rejoined May. "The marvel is to me that they are settled under two or three weeks. Your father would demand time for consideration of an offer for his plantation. There would be an infinity of chaffering and counting of costs on both sides"——

"Do you insinuate an analogy in this to my case?" I retorted. "Am I a chattel to be bargained for—to be sold or withheld without reference to my will or pleasure?"

The jest was cut short by a low whistle, much more indistinct than I was expecting to hear. It stopped short at the end of two or three bars, and I colored high at the vision of the smile which had hindered him from executing the signal as agreed upon. To gain composure, I brushed my hair and smoothed my collar. He should be repaid for his saucy glee.

"Don't make him wait!" remonstrated May. "Have done admiring yourself in the glass! You are in excellent trim; and if you were not, he would not perceive it. See that you bring me an explicit account of the sayings and doings in the late Council of Two, and don't show yourself up here again before night!"

She pushed me from the room. A glance showed me who was standing upon the lower stair; and I studiously averted my eyes as I descended, although I could not conceal the roguish expression that contended with the pout I assumed for the occasion.

He led me into the parlor; shut the door behind us; tightened the arm that encircled my waist until I exclaimed with the pressure; then released me abruptly and walked to the mantel-piece, upon which he rested his forehead and groaned, "O Heavens!"

I sprang to his side, and pulled away the arm that shadowed his countenance, my tongue palsied with the intensity of my alarm. He sank into a seat, and drew me again to him; his every feature indicative of overmastering distress.

"Darling! my darling! how shall I give you up?" escaped him. "And this will draw down misery upon you, too, my poor child! I hoped that my love would be a blessing, not a curse to you. Oh! that I had died before I had seen this hour! Do not despise my weakness, Grace! I was so hopeful! This blow is too sudden!"

Still I could not stir, or articulate a syllable; could just wring my hands and gaze into his pale face—my own as bloodless.

The working lips were pressed together by one resolute effort; the face grew calmer, yet more deadly white, and he spoke slowly, commanding himself to the enunciation of each word:—

"Grace! your father positively forbids our marriage!"

I gasped for breath. "Why?" I inquired.

"He assigned no reason. He has one, he says, which is all-sufficient to bear him out in this denial, but it cannot be communicated to you or to me."

"You must be mistaken," I said, incredulously. "This is so unlike him!"

"He neither spoke nor acted like himself," responded Herbert. "He became stern at the last, as if angry at my importunity, and declared that while you remained under age he should never yield his consent to our union, and, if you chose subsequently to defy his authority, you should know and bear for yourself the consequences of your disobedience."

"Herbert! you are dreaming! My father, my kind, gentle, indulgent father could not say such cruel, harsh things to you, whom he likes and respects—he has said that he did both—and of me, the child who loves him so dearly—his only daughter!" and I wept aloud.

Herbert was silent, only holding me closer.

"Let me go to him, please!" I prayed. "He cannot be unkind to me. There is some misapprehension—some false impression that I can clear away. Let me go!"

"No!" restraining my struggles to rise. "I have his final answer, and he has my promise that all solicitation shall be suspended until you have attained your majority. You could produce no arguments that I have not used. I expressed my candid belief that your happiness depended upon the success of my application; represented that ours was not the love of a day, a hasty, thoughtless whim; I even dared, in my desperation, to allude to Frederic's friendship for me and his avowed approbation of our engagement; and going further, I asked if he himself had not suspected the object of my visit, and why he had not sooner discouraged attentions which had betrayed my sentiments to every one who had seen us together."

"And what answer did he make?"

"I had rather not repeat it," his brow reddening.

"I will hear it!" I said, resolutely.

"He reminded me that he was not responsible to me for his actions; a remark he modified when I was about leaving him. Then he offered me his hand. 'Mr. Wynne,' he said, apparently moved by thoughts of my situation, 'this unfortunate affair has cost me as much pain as it has you. That there exists an impassable obstacle to the fulfillment of your request implies no want of moral or social worth in yourself. I esteem your character, and shall always remain your sincere well-wisher. I should grieve were your intimacy with my son broken up. As my daughter's *friend* you will never be unwelcome at Moss-side. Once more, however, lest you should misconstrue my frank expressions of good-will, I must repeat that the alliance you desire is impossible.'"

"What can be the meaning of this mystery?" said I. "Did he drop no hint that could serve as a clue?"

"None; or if there were any, I am unfit to trace one of them—do not remember it."

He hid his face in his hands, and I sat watching him as before.

"Grace!" he said. "You are stunned, but with surprise. You do not understand—do not begin to realize that we cannot remain as we now are—that we must part!"

With a bitter cry, I flung myself upon his breast, and supplicated him not to forsake me. What else I said in my frenzy of grief I was not conscious of then, but I raved wildly. I had wept until now in ignorant sympathy with his wounded feelings, without the power, in my bewilderment, to comprehend the weight of the blow; still less to look forward to the unavoidable issue. Nor could I listen yet, so violent was the storm of passion. I caught, in the intervals of its bursts, loving words, beseeching me to be comforted ; felt kisses upon my hands and wet cheeks, knew that more than one drop bedewed them from other eyes than mine ; yet it was not until I lay upon his arm, sobbing with exhaustion, that he could prevail upon me to hear what it was necessary should be said then. He hushed me first as a mother would her infant ; wiping away the tears, and murmuring terms of endearment, and forcing smiles that must have made his heart bleed afresh.

"You will not leave me, then ?" I begged like the child I was.

"My darling ! you are too weak to talk of that now. Remember only that I love you—that nothing can change that love."

I remembered far more ; my brain would work, rebellious even to him in its torture. The heart, lately dissolving in sorrow, was chilled into stone as the truth was unfolded. This, my earliest-born, my only love, must be sacrificed by the iron hand of duty. Soon I sat upright, my fingers firmly interlocked, my sight bent upon vacancy—thinking, thinking ! condemned to decide and pronounce the death-warrant of the victim. Five minutes, or an hour may have elapsed before the trance was over. To me, it was years—and years that changed the girl into the woman.

The sentence of fate was uttered in the composure of despair.

"I must submit to my father's will !"

"And I to yours !" was the low reply.

Then I arose to go, I knew not whither, but it was meet that the interview should end then and there. I had reached the door when he recalled me.

"Grace !"

I turned. He was standing where I had left him, his hands outstretched.

"Have you no farewell for me ?" he entreated.

Not the burning kiss upon my forehead or the suppressed agony in the "Heaven bless you forever, my precious lost darling!" stirred the congealed current.

I said "Farewell" in a measured voice that did not sound like mine, again passed the doorway, lost the last ray of his presence, and my soul gave one fearful shudder—but one—as the Arctic blackness received it.

CHAPTER X.

Christmas and its guests had departed ; and with them the false show of summer skies ; the deceitful breath of summer zephyrs. Lights twinkled no more from every window as night draped the white walls of Moss-side ; quick-moving forms glanced no more over stairway and hall ; rambles by hill and field were unthought-of, and in the garden-walks, the snow lay untrampled, unbroken, except by the blasts that ploughed and packed it into drifts. From morning until noon, from noon until dark of the stormy Sabbath, I sat alone in my chamber, watching the tempest. Its fury had forbidden much sleep during the night, for dry leaves and twigs rattled against the casements like hail, and ever and anon, stout boughs snapped in the driving gale and went hurtling through the air, while the building itself rocked and creaked at the rude blows dealt upon its seasoned timbers. With daylight, its wrath began to subside into sullenness ; to the finely powdered snow, wheeling and scudding at the caprice of the wind, finding its way into every crevice, even to the inside of our dwelling, succeeded large, slow-falling flakes, descending ashes of desolation upon the shrouded earth. The air was still, save when a "whuddering" breath swept by, and moaned away its life among the hills. No moving thing was abroad ; up to the doors of the kitchen and cabins, the surface of the yard was smooth as unwritten paper. The ear ached with the sepulchral silence that reigned throughout the house ; silence that was shocked, not awakened, by the challenge growled by the grim warder in the hall to the hours, as they passed in their funereal march.

The scene was fraught with mournful suggestions. My mood would have suggested none other; nor could imagination depict aught else so gloomy as the real Present, arrayed in contrast to a Past but one week old; Nature's most radiant smile and fiercest frown; the light-hearted child, affluent in love, and the sorrow-bowed woman, who, in her desolation, was without comforter.

Frederic had exceeded his furlough by a day, to condole with me, and try the efficacy of expostulation with our father; but was discouraged in both attempts; I meeting his affectionate consolations and hopes for coming days with apathy, resembling indifference, and my father, by an unwonted exercise of authority, silencing question and remonstrance by the declaration that he had discharged his duty, and looked for submission from his children. Frederic said that he was nevertheless greatly moved while issuing the mandate; acting as one upon the rack of necessity, and charging him with a message to me—the sole communication, direct or indirect, that had passed between us on the subject.

"Say to your sister, that for nineteen years I have never deceived her confidence; never thwarted a wish whose gratification could conduce to her happiness. Let her ask herself if it is probable or possible that I could condemn her to what she is now undergoing without a cause sufficient to warrant me in the adoption of extreme measures. Her sufferings may equal—they cannot surpass mine. If I believed that it would mitigate hers, I would, although I have no right to do so, acquaint her with the nature of the objection which I consider—which I *know* cannot be set aside. She has been a loving child heretofore. If I forfeit her affection, I can go down to my grave in sorrow—I cannot alter my resolution."

I had no response for Frederic's indignant amazement; did not second his imprudent motions for overt rebellion.

"It can do no good," was my unfailing reply.

But did this demeanor afford contradiction of Herbert's assertion that I would not bend wisely before the storm? No maniac, dashing his manacled hands in the face of the keeper who would chastise him, ever resisted more determinedly than did I. I had nothing to win by complaisance, nothing to lose in following the dictates of the smarting heart, whose first cry, after the paralysis of the blow went off, was of foul, undeserved wrong, of injury unprovoked and irreparable. I scorned to weep when others were by; but neither would I wear a lying smile. A parade of woe was only less obnoxious than a hollow mockery of mirth. When household laws required me to join my father and aunt, I occupied my place at the table and fireside, and performed the light duties that fell to my lot with mechanical fidelity. I had no means of ascertaining whether my aunt had been definitely informed as to recent events, if I had been curious to ascertain this. If I thought about it at all, it was to take for granted that she was in my father's confidence. I fancied that I detected compassion in her treatment of me, and she relaxed her taciturnity in some degree when my father was present, it seemed, to cover over the void made by mine.

His kindness sustained no abatement from my cold reserve. He addressed me with the affection of former days, and more secretly, but as constantly, studied my convenience and wishes. Pensive he was to melancholy, but not morose or petulant. Attributing this, as I did, to our estrangement, which was, I argued, his work, my heart hardened at the recollection. I totally discredited the theory adopted by Herbert and Frederic of an inscrutable mystery that rendered him irresponsible for his decision. I believed that our hopes had been sacrificed, if not to arbitrary caprice, to some prejudice, unjust as deeply rooted. Louise's sneer recurred to me with such subtle force as the Tempter understood how to impart.—"Although your happiness now seems to be his chief aim in life, when an issue of this nature is raised, he will not scruple to overthrow your air-castles; to teach you that this is a world of realities, unsuited to the growth of Romance."

"She was better versed in human nature—in man's nature—than was I—silly dupe!" I said aloud on this lonely afternoon. "The Love that elevated me into a region of divine and peaceful bliss, was Romance to him. When its very memory is lost, and I can creep in the dust as resignedly as the other worms I once despised, I shall enjoy the more solid satisfaction of feeding upon realities. I had rather that the snow were weaving my winding sheet!"

The ashes, grey against the clouds, whiter nearer the ground, fell unceasingly, and more mournfully as the pale daylight sickened to its death.

"What have I to live for?" I asked myself. "Were Time to blunt this sorrow, can any art restore the bloom to life? And this that rives my soul, which has covered the earth with sackcloth, is what one hears carelessly styled 'a disappointment!' an affliction transcended by the failure of the least important scheme of business; not to be mentioned in the same breath with the decease of an agreeable acquaintance; nor in the same day with a bankruptcy! I am weak-minded, for it crushes me; miserably destitute, for I have been deprived of my all. I cannot stupefy my heart, or hush its wailings. Yet such grief is never fatal; is so slight in its direst extremity that one must smother it in her chamber—forget it when abroad. And why? If he had been in outward form, by man's appointment, my husband, and parted from me for months, even for weeks, I might seclude myself and weep over his absence, with more than the indulgence,—with the sympathy of my friends. But, again I would know what remains for me when the wound is staunched, if I live until then? When I am twenty-five—thirty—forty—how will Life appear? Upon what is my heart to subsist through those tedious years? What will supply its springs with refreshment? Will it stagnate into a noxious pool, offensive to all about me, or dry up?"

A brief gust whirled the snow-flakes, howled in the chimney, and screamed around the gables. The storm within arose with it.

"There are pious people doubtless, who would consider this a capital opportunity to sermonize upon the vanity of earthly hopes, the danger of creature-love, the wisdom and mercy of an unintelligible Providence. In my blind folly, I would once have esteemed these appropriate teachings, judiciously adapted to quell the murmurings of a bruised spirit. I give them to the winds now. Rejecting all human ministrations, I stand boldly before Him, who, they would persuade me, has dealt the blow, and inquire its cause and purpose. Am I stricken because I opened my hand to receive His mercies, the gifts I had coveted, yet so sinlessly that I did not repine while they were withheld? Did I, in truth, forget the Giver in the very earliest transports of my joy? The most fervent prayer that has ever winged from my soul was the thanksgiving that consecrated the moment of our plighting. Though unclothed in suitable words, the offspring though it was of a spirit often undevout, it was sincere and pure as mortal thoughts can be. They may prate to me of the sinfulness of undue affection for vessels of clay. I loathe the hypocritical cant! I recognize as distinct a law of my being compelling me to love the man, as that which impels to adoration of the Creator. If this be regarded as my shame, I glory in the reproach! if it is branded as idolatry, I proudly profess that I am an idolater!"

A shriek—not loud—but which thrilled me through and through, stirred the solemn darkness gathering in passage and hall. To me it was deadened by distance and closed doors, but I followed in the direction from which I thought it had come, to my father's room. No attention was paid to my knock and I lifted the latch unbidden. My father knelt in the middle of the chamber, chafing the hands and bathing the brow of my aunt, whose corpse-like appearance possessed me with an awful fear. Hurrying forward, I assisted in the application of the remedies. My father was unmanned the instant my entrance relieved him from these necessary duties.

"I have killed her!" he whispered to me. "I might have known that she could not bear it, but she insisted upon the explanation. I am a curse to everything I love!"

"Hush! hush!" I said, almost as much agitated. "She breathes again! Had you not better stand back out of her sight?"

Her reviving was slow and painful, and when she opened her eyes they were dully vacant.

"Aunt!" I called, terrified. "Do you know me?"

No answer, but the same meaningless stare.

Her brother addressed her with no more effect. Two of the servants were called in to help carry her to her apartment. She was borne in their grasp, a dead weight; one arm hanging powerless from the shoulder. While disrobing her, this helplessness struck me, and I hastened in quest of my father, to impart my suspicion of a paralytic stroke. Medical aid could not be obtained on such a night. John, the young class-leader, of whose gifts in prayer I have spoken, offered his services on this errand of mercy.

"I dare not let you go, my good fellow," said his master. "Neither you nor the horse could live to reach Dr. Hamner's."

"You aint sure of dat, Marster. No 'fence, I hope, sir; but

'taint for you nor me to say whether the Lord wouldn't spar' me, and, for the matter of dat, de horse too, if we was bound 'pon His work. Miss Agnes is wuth heap more dan me, and 'pears like twarn't much better dan murder to let her lie dere, all night, a-dyin' maybe, and I warm and well in my bed."

His master changed color ; and, as if shaken in his resolution, walked to the door to take another observation of the weather It would have been pitchy dark, had not the reflection from the snow shed a ghastly glare over objects near it ; and the hall was instantly filled with the driving flakes. The porch-steps were completely buried, and a bank, several feet in depth, lay against the house.

" God help us," said my father, shutting out the storm. " We can get no assistance from man while this lasts !"

The sturdy negro turned away disappointed.

" John," said his master, gratefully ; " you are a faithful boy, too faithful to be risked in such a chance as this ride would be. In the morning, if possible, you shall make an early start for the doctor's. Until then, keep yourself comfortable. I hope Miss Agnes is not so ill as we think. At any rate, we can do nothing except nurse her as well as we know how "——

" And *pray*, sir," subjoined John, with respectful emphasis. " The Lord works Himself, when He's tied our hands. Least-ways, Marster, it's our business to call 'pon Him in times of trouble, and if dese aint sech, I never see none."

The homely phrase was often in my mind during the vigil that appeared endless. My father walked the adjoining room hour after hour, his muffled footfalls my only relief in the loneliness of the night. Once, the rising wind was blent with music, an unearthly, dirge-like melody, but it breathed of cheer to my spirit ; for, with a glimmering of John's simple faith, I remembered that " prayer moves the arm that moves the world," and I blessed the pious souls that had collected, undaunted by cold and tempest, to supplicate for the unconscious being whose life might then be near its extinction. I would have hailed with pleasure any token of pain. Groans, convulsive struggles, would have been more endurable than this stupor. She breathed heavily, her eyes sometimes open, but blank as ever in expression. There was nothing to do except to keep her warmly covered and swathe in hot flannels the limbs on her right side, which natural heat had deserted.

Most of the time, I sat by the fire, where I had a fair view of her, and while Milly, her colored attendant, dozed upon the rug, I quailed before the reflections that rolled in upon me. The evening of the last Sabbath, we four young people had watched a red sunset from the arbor in the garden ; and, led by our own care-free hearts, to thoughts of the other extreme, some one related the fable of the Egyptian courtier, whose compliments to the prosperous fortunes and undisturbed happiness of his host, were interrupted by the latter, who conducted him to a veiled niche, and drew aside the drapery which concealed a skeleton

At the moral—" a skeleton in every heart and home,"—Frederic cavilled.

" It is certainly not of universal application," he said. " I detest this doleful philosophy which magnifies every mote in the sunshine into a cloud. The clear days are the rule—showers and storms the exceptions. Where is the skeleton in any of our hearts ? Has one lurked in a secret closet of dear old Moss-side, lo ! these many years, and I, never, by accident, rattled its dry bones ?"

" It has !" I said to myself, now. " Through our merry childhood, our happy youth, we have frolicked in its shadow, and not suspected its existence. This is its unveiling !" and I shook with fright as real as though its fleshless jaws were gaping before my eyes. " Hide it away as we may, it can never be forgotten. If that insensible woman could speak, and would part, for one moment, with the reserve that has so fenced her in for years, I feel that she could show a mysterious connection between her sorrow and mine. What has revealed this to me, I cannot say, but I am not more certain of her illness and of my grief. Reason disputes this ; puts it down with a flat contradiction. 'As well,' she says, impatiently, 'arraign the hoary-haired man who has slept with his fathers a score of winters as the murderer of the infant, whose grave is not yet sodded.' I have not learned to reason yet, and if I had, I should appeal to higher authority in the intuition that has whispered this belief to me. If I had not loved, and mourned a thwarted love, *she* would still be erect in her stately bearing, invulnerable to fear and anguish. How those proud features bid defiance to disease ; seem to hold Death himself at bay ! At my age, as she told me, she knew nothing of patience. At her's, I shall be like her. The idea does not terrify me as it did a fortnight since. I would have cried then—'Let me die first !' Now, the thought of hardening and freezing into the monumental stone of Love and Hope—the youth of the soul—is received as the decree of Fate, with which I want ability and will to contend."

The morning light showed me, in the mirror, a visage so wan, yet so settled in all its lines, that I stopped to examine it ; to trace in it the resemblance to the statue upon the bed. My manner, as I moved about the house, directing the servants, produced a visible change in their free, affectionate deportment towards me, the youngest pet of the whole family—white and black.

"Poor Miss Grace is stunned-like," I overheard the cook remark to Milly. "She looks like her own ghost !"

It was too cold to snow, and there were signs of breaking among the clouds whose offensive alliance had been so disastrous to us. John, at my father's command, waited to see these indications terminate in a flying rout, and as the sun darted a glance of greeting at the earth, he was in the saddle. Dr. Hamner lived but four miles from us : yet, urged as he and the messenger were by the emergency, it was past noon when they reached Moss-side. My aunt had moved and spoken in the interim, but the palsied side was still pulseless clay, and her tongue vainly attempted to enunciate an intelligible word. The doctor remained with us overnight, and while he confirmed our opinion that it was a case of partial paralysis, delivered us from apprehension of her imminent danger. The remarkable constitution of the patient might, he affirmed, effect almost a miracle in favor of a recovery, which, if not entire, would yet restore, in some measure, the use of her limbs.

"This must, however, be the work of time and care," he said. "She may be the cripple you see her now for weeks—perhaps for months."

This was the beginning of my assumption of the responsibilities of nurse and housekeeper ; duties that, of themselves, would have tamed youthful levity, and clothed the countenance with premature gravity.

Mr. Peyton broke through the drifts between his house and ours so soon as the report of our affliction spread to the Linden plantation ; and the next day, Miss Judy rode over, unattended, upon a stout cart-horse ; a blanket pinned about her knees and feet, and in other respects so bundled up that the twinkle of her black eyes was all that identified her as our strong-minded neighbor.

My aunt's face brightened at sight of her. With the courtesy which had become her second nature, she glanced significantly at her disabled right hand, as she feebly extended the left.

"No apology, Miss Agnes !" replied Miss Judy, giving it a hearty squeeze. "I am too glad to have a chance to shake hands with you at last to mind which one I get. James tried his utmost to prevent my coming. He would have it that you would think me a meddlesome intruder ; but, said I, 'Here I have lived close by Mr. Leigh's for twenty years, and been on the best of terms with him and his all the time ; and now that they are in trouble, and about Miss Agnes, as fine a woman as ever breathed '—begging your pardon for saying so here, madam —'I'd never respect myself, and never look them in the face again, if I did not try to help them in some way. If I am unwelcome,' says I to James, 'I'll find it out the minute I set foot in the house, and I can but come back as I went.' "

My aunt's lips moved.

" She says that she is much obliged to you for your kindness, and happy to see you," my father interpreted. " For my part, Miss Judy, I do not know how to thank you "——

She cut him short. "Don't bother yourself to do it, then. All I ask is something to do while I am here. James wanted to scare me, who am older by seventeen years than he is, with some bug-a-boo story about catching cold, or getting stuck fast in the snow. I laughed at him, and had Billy, the strongest animal on the place, saddled, and as I expected, I got over safe and sound."

Her loud voice was curiously subdued, and she was evidently rattling in this style to sustain our spirits with hers. Dissimilar as she and my aunt were, there was much mutual esteem, and, as Miss Judy had said, uninterrupted kind feeling between them. As the worthy spinster tiptoed her thick-soled boots to the least possible squeak ; re-making the bed for the night, in which, pushing aside Milly, she deposited the patient when it was ready, her plain physiognomy was goodly to behold. It enlivened her charge, as did her somewhat boisterous cheerfulness our usually silent evening meal. She remained in the dining-room when it was over, to prepare some beef-tea, and benevolently exerted herself to amuse me. My conscience smites me now for the indifferent success that rewarded her ; but she did not choose to remark my ungrateful listlessness.

"Now, Miss Agnes," she said, re-claiming her station as chief nurse, "I am going to send Grace to bed, willy-nilly."

"Thank you!" was imperfectly articulated, but the intonation was one of gratitude.

"Exactly!" rejoined Miss Judy. "We understand—you and I—that young people need more sleep than those of my age. Don't be fretted with me, Grace, honey! Your aunt can't get on so well with me perhaps, but we can manage somehow for this one night. You are a first-rate nurse and the best girl I know. There aint many who could or would have scuffled with sickness and housework as you have done. It has worsted you a little, and a night's rest will set you up again. Tell your aunt 'good night,' for you must pack off right away. And Grace! don't worry about getting up early in the morning. If the servants want the keys, I'll give them to them."

As I went out, I heard the ready reply that met the invalid's efforts to speak, before the labored sentence was half through

"Exactly, ma'am! a treasure she is, worth the picking up, as I tell all the young men."

I smiled bitterly, and wearily dragged myself up to my room.

Martha, whose anxiety to contribute to my welfare increased with my gloom, had bestowed extra care upon the chamber, in the prospect of my occupying it for an entire night, a luxury in which I had not indulged myself since the day of my aunt's stroke. Lamp and fire were nicely trimmed, suffusing the walls with a pink tint; the coverlet of the bed, folded down neatly, disclosed clean, lavender-scented sheets, and the plump pillows, their ruffled cases yet glossy from the smoothing iron, wooed me to rest. A low lounge was wheeled in front of the hearth, and I threw myself along it, tired out in body, but too wakeful in mind to think of adopting the regimen Miss Judy had strictly enjoined. The pencilled head above the mantel was well brought out by the light; and while I gazed into its unfathomable eyes, brimming with grief, I remembered the pity that used to move me at its study ; the wondering conjectures as to the nature of the woe that could so steep her being. In my morbid depression now, I found fault with the artist that she had not painted passion in its might ; so serene were the uplifted regards in comparison with the rayless darkness in which I was walking. " Is any sorrow like unto my sorrow ?" was the language of my heart. Then I smiled again in withering scorn at Miss Judy's straight-forward essays at match-making.

" She is happy," I said, " because she has a soul that finds suprem econtent—all the food it craves—in her crops of grain and vegetables. Did she ever thirst for affection, ever gain it, and find it more precious than her life-blood, only to see it poured out to waste as forbidden poison, while she was maddening with torture ? Pshaw ! she would laugh, until the rafters rang at the question. Women are not all constituted alike ! Oh ! if my nature were mercurial or sluggish !"

The hall-clock trembled in every joint under the protracted agony of twelve strokes. I had not undressed, only moved twice to replenish the fire; still lay upon the lounge, so immersed in my musings that I did not hear the door open. I started very slightly at the apparition which confronted me, for I was far from suspecting its proximity. It was attired in a blue calico dressing-gown, whose perpendicular folds were uninterrupted by any cincture at the waist, and its tight sleeves declined familiar acquaintance with the bony wrists. A voluminous night-cap, three parts frill, one, plain linen, contained the grey hair and projected over the astonished brows that went up with the hands at my reckless imprudence.

" Is Aunt Agnes worse ?" I asked. " Am wanted ?"

" No. I stole up to make sure that you were comfortable and were sleeping soundly, for I could not get your altered looks out of my head ; and when Miss Agnes dropped off into a nap,

I says to myself, 'maybe I'll be less uneasy if I look in upon the child;' and here you are, wide-awake, and looking worse than ever!"

The good soul swallowed a sob.

I got up in very shame, and began to undress, when she set me down again and unhooked and untied with great energy, never pausing to speak until my wrapper replaced the day-dress, and she pronounced me ready for bed.

"Where I mean to see you, before I budge a step!" she said, decidedly.

I tried to smile as she tucked the blankets around me. "You are very kind, Miss Judy. I am sorry I have annoyed you."

"No annoyance, honey! *You* couldn't vex me. I set as much store by you, Grace, as if you were my child, that is I think I do. I've trotted you on my knee and rocked you to sleep on my bosom a hundred times, when you were a puny, sickly baby, and if I had not come to love you then, you would have showed me how since. I have had trials myself, lost father and mother and brothers, had a deal to do and suffer in this world, but the thought of all my ups and downs don't trouble me near so much as the way you are breaking under your burdens."

She was patting my hand with her hard palm; a motion, that was somehow both affectionate and deprecatory.

"Don't think that I mean to scold you, Grace; but you must not look too much on the dark side. The Lord has some meaning in our afflictions: in one way or another, every one of them is for our benefit. Many's the time I would have given right up, if it hadn't been that I was certain of that. It is natural that you should feel lonesome and anxious, but, honey, try to shake it off, and remember how many blessings are spared to you. Worrying, even if you don't speak it out, does no manner of good to anybody and hurts you. Your aunt notices it, I see. Her eyes follow you around the room, just as your mother's would, if she had lived to see you in this trial. Too many people care for you for you to be down-hearted."

I thanked her as well as I could for the swelling in my throat, and she was gone. I cried myself to sleep, an abundant flow of tears that tended to restore the health of body and mind. This simple lecture, diffuse and wandering as it was, touched me more than the tenderest sympathy of either May or Frederic. But the demon of despairing misanthropy awaited my awakening in the morning, and my pillow was not more free from traces of the salt deluge that had flowed over it the night before, than was my heart from the melting influence of our neighbor's friendly counsel.

CHAPTER XI.

Another winter, and yet another, had come and gone, and Spring was fast yielding to the fervid caresses of Summer.

One warm afternoon I established myself and my work-basket in the summer-house at the foot of the garden, to have, as he expressed it, "a comfortable confab" with my brother, Dr. Frederic Leigh, by this time a practitioner in a thriving town in another State. He had been guided in his choice of a settlement by the circumstance that this place was the residence of our elder brother, besides ourselves, the only surviving child of our parents. Edmund, Frederic's senior by eight years, had removed to C——, upon arriving at his majority; had been successful in business, and married a lovely girl, who, in the two visits she had paid us, had won our unqualified approbation of his selection. To this spot another flower was shortly to be transplanted, for this flying peep at Moss-side was Fred's bachelor farewell.

"And you will not go with me, Grace?" he said, regretfully.

"I cannot!" I replied. "My duties here bind me down. There is no option in the matter."

"I do not see this," he persisted. "Aunt Agnes requires very little attention, and grows less infirm every day. She is competent to exercise a general supervision of domestic arrangements, and your trained servants may be safely entrusted with the rest."

"I should have no pleasure in my absence," said I. "There are many things that ought not to be committed to others. Aunt would miss me constantly. I cannot go, Frederic."

"May will be grieved—inconsolable!" he returned with his

old, boyish pout. "I doubt whether she will consider the ceremony valid if you are not bridesmaid."

"I have written to her that it is not in my power to be present, and believe that she will be satisfied with my reasons. I wish you could bring your bride to see us on your return journey."

"Not this summer, sis. She has been somewhat delicate lately, and our proposed trip to the sea-shore is the best means of strengthening her. We are to live with Edmund and his wife for the first year, you know?"

"Yes, I heard you say so. It is a good arrangement."

"And then," he went on, animatedly, "we will have our own snug dove-nest of a cottage, where a certain beloved sister of mine will always find a room prepared especially for her. Grace, how can I ever be thankful enough for the mercies that overrun my cup? I have the best sister, and am soon to be blest with the sweetest wife in the universe; am prosperous in my profession, robust in health; what more can any reasonable, or unreasonable man desire?"

"You have been signally favored," was my answer.

"Sister," he resumed, in a more quiet tone, "there are some subjects on which I wish to speak with you"—and he hesitated.

I waited to hear more, but he appeared reluctant or doubtful how to proceed.

"There is one," he said, at length, "which you once forbade me to mention. Will you remove that prohibition for five minutes?"

I felt the color slowly leaving my cheeks, but I answered calmly, "If you ask it, certainly!"

"You were twenty-one in March," he continued. "Did you not receive a letter from Herbert Wynne?"

"I did."

"Did you answer it, and how?"

"I gave it to my father, who replied to it."

"Grace! Forgive me, sister; but was that kind, was it just to one whose constancy has entitled him to your most gentle and respectful treatment?"

"He had both from father, whose letter I read and approved. A milder refusal would not have been worthy of the name."

"What reason did he state for continuing to deny his consent?"

"He reiterated his former reply that an insuperable objection existed, whose character he was not at liberty to divulge."

"What can that be?" He arose and walked to and fro upon the grass-plot. "Have you ever pushed him with inquiries about it?"

"Never."

"Have you no suspicions?"

"I used to have, but I dismissed them, long ago, as worse than useless."

"How composedly you speak! as if you had no care or feeling in the affair."

"I *am* composed," I said. "I do not pretend indifference."

He came and sat down at my side.

"Would you know, dearest Grace, what is the one shade upon my happiness? The thought that you are wearing away under a hidden sorrow! You would tell me that you are not ill in body, but grief does not always sap the foundations of physical health. You are not the Grace of two years ago."

"I am older, and have more to employ my mind and hands," I interrupted, dreading further examination.

"You evade my question! will not confide in the brother, from whom, in times past, you could not conceal a thought! Still I must speak while you permit it. Far be it from me to incite you to disobedience to the will of the father, who has, except in this most inexplicable instance, been a model of indulgent kindness. This exception, while it has tried my faith in, and affection for him, has shaken neither. It has only proved him fallible, whereas we believed him faultless. A more upright soul, a truer heart were never bestowed upon man. Yet, Grace, he is unjust in exacting your blind submission to his law. In any other parent I would call this downright tyranny. No pledge of silence, if we may imagine the possibility of his being bound by such, should prevent him from allowing you a clue to his couduct, that you might decide concerning it for yourself. I am disposed to regard his impenetrable secresy as an overstrained point of honor, for what cause imposed, or by whom, I cannot divine; or, else, as morbid delicacy, yet more incomprehensible. What I would have you ask yourself is this: 'How far is it lawful and right for me to yield to what may be a whim; what is not, so far as I can ascertain, the result of just, unbiassed judgment? Is the child forever to remain a slave to the parent's will, when her own mature discretion descries neither reason nor expediency in his commands? May there not be duties to myself and to another that are paramount to his claims?'"

"These arguments are trite to me!" I said, wearily. "I have reviewed them so often! My work and place are here, where I was born—where I shall, most probably, die."

My heart added, sighingly, "Would that the time were near!"

"Am I, then, to understand that you do not look beyond the limits of Moss-side? that you are quite contented here?"

I could not supply a direct answer to this, so I said, "Is there not a proverb—'With expectation, desire shall fail?'"

"Enough!" he rejoined, with feeling; and there was a protracted pause. I sewed, and he pulled a sprig of honeysuckle to pieces.

Brushing the fragments from his palm, he recommenced—

"You are a noble creature, Grace! I reverence your heroism. Do not interrupt me! This is no preface to further efforts to tempt you from the path of action your conscience has chalked out. I want to inquire into the motive that keeps you in it."

"Duty!" I said laconically.

"Duty—to whom?"

"Can you ask? To those to whom alone I owe it—my father and aunt."

"So I supposed. Few natures are capable of self-denial and joyless labor like yours. The bravest faints sometimes upon the battle field. What bears you up?"

"Will and necessity."

His countenance fell. "That was not what I hoped to hear. I have too recently begun to lean upon a higher Power myself to instruct you; but dear sister, there is a strength that revives while it supports; not only lifts the drooping head, but gladdens the sick heart. My hopeful prayer is that you may seek this."

He said no more, for I did not encourage this topic, and there ended all that was confidential in our interview. Little did I dream of the inexpressible consolation, I would, in after times, find wrapped up in that short sentence!

He left us by sunrise the next morning, freighted with love and good wishes. As was my custom, I stood at the gate until he reached the bend in the road that was to rob us of his form, and shook my handkerchief to the wave of his hat, thrice-repeated; then, as though his heart-shout was—"Now for Love and May!" he dashed the rowels into his horse's sides, and was out of sight.

I went into my aunt's room to aid her in her toilette, which being completed, she leaned upon my shoulder and tottered into the breakfast-room, where the servants met with us for morning worship. As she was prevented by her lameness, from kneeling a stand with a cushion upon it, was set before her easy-chair, upon which she bowed during the prayer. The head of the table had, of necessity, been relinquished to me, whôse part it was, likewise, to carve her food into morsels of the proper size to be taken up with her fork. Her helplessness in no wise detracted from the dignity of her demeanor, and her malady had altered nothing in the expression of her regular features. If a ruin, she was one that impressed the beholder with veneration, not pity. Her chamber was my sitting-room, and thither I repaired when the overseeing and planning for the day were through. Habited in her conventual robe of black, her cap as severely plain in its fashion, her hands laid together upon her lap, she sat for hours without change of posture, sometimes without speaking. Her eyes were weakened by sickness, and I read to her from one to two hours of every forenoon. Her books were of a strictly religious cast, comprising theological treatises that are not generally supposed to possess attractions for women. She had her favorites, and they accorded with the austere stamp of her piety.

In my fresh-hearted girlhood, I would have yawned over these works as tiresome homilies upon subjects as foreign to my taste as enigmatical to my understanding ; now, their gloomy paintings of the corrupt earth and the sinfulness of its human inhabitants, their exhortations to mortification of the flesh as the primal move towards the purity of the soul, the pre-eminence given to irksome duty over selfish pleasure, begot in me a species of interest ; and—without my being aware that I was influenced in the slightest measure by their teachings—shaped both thought and deed. I had no right conception of the new heart they insisted upon as the indispensable preparation for the new life I flattered myself that I was leading. Explaining the numerous allusions to it as technical terms for a reform of purpose, an intention to live no longer for the world and the vanities thereof, I accounted myself to be diligently working out my salvation; earning acceptance from the righteous Judge, who had arrested me in my idol-worship, and who was to be propitiated by the sacrifice, not merely of the first fruits of labor and life, but of all carnal delights. Life was not desirable; I could meditate upon Death without terror; and my longing for rest must, I convinced myself, be the cravings of the immortal principle for heavenly joys. I did not call myself a Christian; and I was perhaps never less likely to become one, although upon this latter proposition I had then a different opinion.

Had I read fewer books; had introspection been less of a study with me; had I looked more into the hearts and lives of others; sued for information from those whose experience was superior to mine, the duration of my delusion would have been shortened. Mr. Peyton's boundless charity of motive and act; Annie Bell's cheerful toil and filial piety; even Miss Judy's homespun virtues might have led me to suspect that "Religion undefiled" had no inherent affinity with asceticism. If my intercourse with my father had retained the affectionate confidence with which I used to impart to him every sentiment, I would have required no other safeguard against the errors that beset me. But—owing to an obstinacy that might have enlightened me concerning the weightier matters of the law, if I had not been too much engaged in summing up, to the last mite, the tithes of anise and cummin, my share in our tacit reconciliation was incomplete. That this inflicted much and poignant suffering, I could not doubt. Perhaps a candid examination of intentions and feelings would have dragged to the light a reptile from which I would have fled in horror—a lurking serpent of revenge, feeding upon the reflection that as I had received, it was now in my power to give. No word of tenderness from me repaid his; in the even current of our common existence, no skill was necessary to steer clear of the unsafe points and shoals. There were additional furrows in his forehead and cheeks, and more snow fell nightly upon his head ; yet the genial smile and pleasant remark failed not to greet whoever expected them. His sister's devotion to him was perceptible in look and gesture, rather than in any audible token of regard.

Our morning lessons over—for studies they were, and arduously pondered—my father joined us and talked, or read, in his turn, something of his own selection, while my never-ending needlework went forward. Dinner was served at one o'clock, and my aunt's afternoon siesta liberated me from confinement ; freedom which I improved by rapid walks in unfrequented ways, sometimes stretching two or three miles from home. This habit I had acquired when the fever of blood and brain drove me abroad, and there were still seasons when I sought in swift motion and subsequent exhaustion the most effectual quietus of which I had any knowledge.

One spot I sedulously avoided. I had seen it once since the hour that had hallowed it to me forever. In the early spring of the year before the last, I was threading the woods in its vicinity, and emerged unexpectedly from the cover of the trees upon the cleared hill-top, within a dozen steps of the storm-bleached log. It was a bleak day ; clouds, blue-black and grey, rolling over their sullen masses before the March wind ; the fields on both sides of the brook were ploughed up, and the damp clods lay rough and stiff as they had been heaved by the share. My dream of fairy beauty was destroyed ; I cared not to look again upon the wreck.

The above, then, is a programme of one day's occupations and recreation at Moss-side, concluded by an early supper, evening prayers, and retirement to our several apartments at ten o'clock in summer, nine in winter ; and this twenty-four hours was the pattern for its successors for months together. The news of Frederic's marriage was duly transmitted, discussed with some show of interest, a record made in the Family Bible, and the circle disappeared from the stream whose progress might have seemed rest, so unvarying were the barren shores it washed.

I visited more frequently at Mrs. Bell's cottage than anywhere else; yet sincere as was my regard for mother and daughter, few of these calls were prompted by friendship alone. They must have observed and felt wounded that necessary business with one or the other was introduced during my stay, were it brief or long; but no signs of offended pride or feeling resented this change from the familiar friendliness in which Annie and I had been trained. Frederic had called his blushing May "wife" for five weeks before I bethought myself, in the course of a ramble that way, that Annie would like to hear the particulars of an event so interesting to her old playfellow.

The air was sultry, and I languidly crossed the little yard to the porch where both ladies were sewing. Annie drew a rocking-chair to the door, untied my bonnet and laid it aside, and Mrs. Bell furnished me with a mammoth fan of turkey-feathers. I was not chided for my long absence, or interrogated as to its cause. Mrs. Bell was motherly, Annie as cordial as if its period had been measured by days, not weeks. The latter commenced the conversation by inquiries about Frederic's movements, upon which theme I forced myself to speak cheerfully. There was no echo in my heart for such music as bridal chimes, and so palpable to me was the want of these vibrations, that I marvelled every one did not perceive the loss. With Annie, the answering note rang clear as a silver bell. I listened and gazed at her with envious admiration.

"What would I not give for her freshness of soul, her ignorance of the woes that make men selfish!"

Old Zack stopped at the threshold to salute me.

"You're a mighty stranger dese days, Miss Grace," he said, less scrupulous than his superiors. "Miss Annie and I been wondering what had 'come of you. *She* gits right down 'bout it sometimes."

"Miss Grace has very little time for visiting, Zack," replied his mistress for me; "and neither you nor Miss Annie have a right to think hard of her for not leaving her sick aunt."

"Dat's a fac', mistis, jest what I says to Miss Annie. Miss Grace, is you seen de fashionable bee-hive I been put up in Miss Annie's flower-guarden?"

I had not, and went with him and his young mistress to examine it. He added some skill in carpentry to his other accomplishments, and this really ingenious little edifice was constructed after the style of "one he had seen at Mars' Robert Peyton's." A clumsy but efficient apparatus for conducting water from the well to the garden was "like one Mars' Robert had told him about," and he had sent over one of his men to help lay the hollow logs that served as pipes. The old man's sense of his own importance, which he by no means underrated, did not blind him to the exemplary character of his useful coadjutor. Where "Miss Annie's" interests were concerned, the two seemed to have labored together most harmoniously. The most valuable plants in her flower-beds were raised from slips and seeds supplied by the choice collection at Linden; a flock of fan-tail pigeons, that pecked food from her lips when she would suffer it, owed their parentage to a pair presented by him, and the splendid Newfoundland, Sultan, her devoted serf and fearless protector, had been sought for far and near before the donor was suited in the gift he designed for his protégé.

"Mars' Robert!" said Zack, throwing himself into an oratorical attitude, "he is one of de salt of de earth, Miss Grace. Neber you mind 'bout han'some faces and slick tongues! He aint got neither; he's as bashful-like and modest as a lady—but, I tell you, dere's de beauty in his heart, and he keep de hinges of dat smooth wid oil!"

"It is hot here," remarked Annie. "Shall we go in?"

"Uncle Zack has been eulogizing Mr. Peyton," I said to Mrs. Bell. "He is very much attached to him."

"He well may be," she rejoined, "since he, with the rest of us, owes more to him than to any other person living;" and she proceeded with a second edition, refined and enlarged, of Uncle Zack's encomiums.

This was all stale to me, nor did Annie manifest any of her mother's enthusiasm. She colored slightly at some passages in the old lady's discourse, as if she dreaded this zealous partiality might appear over-strained, and looked relieved when "Mars' Robert" was dismissed. I arose to go, and she accompanied me part of the way, chatting about matters she fancied might divert me, with a disinterestedness I failed not to notice. Even my dulled heart—dulled to everything except my individual griefs, was moved.

"Come and see me often, Annie," I said, at our parting. "Ours is a changed household, and presents no allurements to a young person, but you may do us some good."

An eager, trembling flush mantled her face. "If I could only make you happier, Grace!"

She kissed me hastily, as if afraid to trust herself to say more, and ran back towards home.

I stood still a minute, looking after her. Why should she desire my happiness? why continue to love me? My neglect and indifference to her society were evidences how lightly I valued her friendship, and there was nothing about me calculated to please a lively girl. I was too proud to ask her pity in my private sorrow, and had I uncovered the least portion of my heart, this must have been the emotion aroused.

"Besides," I said, walking on, "it would be unnecessary cruelty to tell her of trials she has never experienced, which she may never meet. Up to this moment, I am the sole sufferer, and alone, I will bear it all!"

"The sole sufferer!" I sighed, as the thought struck home. "I should die if that were indeed so. Am I prepared for that day? for its coming may not be distant."

In peevish anguish I cried aloud: "Shall I never be resigned?"

"'She *whispered* as she went for want of thought,'" said a voice beside me, that, mellifluous as it was, affrighted me as the roar of a cannon would have done. "Or do you speak from the abundance of the heart, in excess of thought?"

"I was not conscious that any one was near me, Mr. Townley," I replied, with a touch of anger at his cat-like approach.

He chuckled. "It was an attack in am-*bush*. I saw you coming, apparently in a meditative mood, and quitted the path for that thicket."

"An ill-timed piece of impertinence!" was my thought, nor did I try to conceal its expression in my face.

He was blind to the demonstration. "I am fortunate in this meeting," he pursued, picking his way over the dusty grass, never soiling the tips of his boots. "I am on my way to your house."

"Ah!" I said, absently, for I was preparing myself for an unpleasant walk. Our suave neighbor had never ranked highest in my list of associates, and latterly, his civilities had been more marked than agreeable. I had an instinctive persuasion that none but interested motives actuated him even in the ordinary forms of politeness, and, without the most remote idea in what service he intended to employ me, was on the watch for some demand. The shape it assumed astounded me, nevertheless—an explicit offer of marriage, less elaborate than I had believed him capable of composing, in consideration, perhaps, of the humble taste of the lady thus honored. When my wits and breath returned in sufficient quantities, I answered him in the commonplace suitable to, and customary on, like occasions.

"What you have said has surprised me greatly, Mr. Townley."

"Pardon me, but I do not understand why it should, Miss Grace. One less sagacious than yourself might have anticipated this consequence of my intimate acquaintance with your virtues and charms. The matter for wonder is that this declaration should have been so tardy. I could have made it with as much truth more than two years since, was upon the eve of it indeed, when a circumstance, adverse to all present hopes on my part, compelled me to defer it to a more propitious season."

A meaning look called up the blood to my temples, but a second's pause decided me not to speak upon a provocation that might, after all, be unintentional. He could have no certain knowledge of the event to which I imagined he had reference, whatever his serpent eyes might have gathered from outward signs.

"Let by-gones be by-gones," he resumed, with a kind of light condescension. "We all have that in our memories which we would fain consign to oblivion. The clouds of yesterday need not, perforce, overcast the sun of to-day."

"Your apophthegms are riddles, sir," I returned coldly. "Not being an adept in solving such, I must request of you the favor to speak plainly."

It was his time to be surprised, and the counterfeit was ably managed.

"To what could I refer, unless to the dangerous illness of your aunt, which unfitted a lady of your beautifully sensitive feeling for the entertainment of any proposition relating merely to yourself, important as such proposition might seem, if presented in an undisturbed moment? Engrossed as you were with amiable cares on her account, cares continued to the present time, I may be excused for delaying the presentation of my suit."

The advantage he had gained by this adroit reply was as ap

parent to me as it was to him, and pique afforded me strength to say, "Since my answer is the same that you would have received then, I cannot but deplore a delay that may have caused you inconvenience and some degree of anxiety."

Curbing my satiric inclination with the recollection that the form of respect he maintained should be repaid in kind, I added, "I am sure that you prefer frank dealing to any play of fair words. I cannot reciprocate the attachment you have professed, and have no disposition to tamper with the feelings of a friend. Therefore, we will, if you please, drop this subject now and forever."

His thin skin revealed the flush that dyed the roots of his sandy hair, and the blue light I had once before seen, gleamed in his eyes; then his face was composed into a proper and decent regret.

"I honor your candor; but I am not altogether ready for the demolition of the most cherished hope of my life. In your compassionate fear of inflicting further pain by heightening my expectations, should you deliberate upon my proposal, you overlook the possibility—not an unheard-of thing in a lady, by the way—that you may change your mind. I will wait whatever time you may set, and exculpate you from any design to trifle with my affections, should your final resolve be the same you have just expressed."

"It is needless," I rejoined. "My decision is unalterable. I beg you to accept it as such at once, Mr. Townley."

"This is indeed remarkable," he said, thoughtfully. "An unprecedented case!"

"In your experience, perhaps," I returned, growing fretful at his tone and unmanly persistence in a suit that displeased me "There is no coquetry in my conduct, however much you may have met with in others."

"I am not the beau-general you intimate, Miss Grace; nor

can I submit to the imputation from you, just at present, with the equanimity I usually study to preserve in the presence of a lady."

This warrantable hit at my ungenerous taunt again gave me the worse side of the contest, for contest I began to understand it to be. I tried to close it by one effort.

"Mr. Townley," I said, "this is downright trifling on the part of both. You claim, and it may be justly, an intimate acquaintance with my disposition and traits. You cannot accuse me of vacillation in the past, and never has my mind been more firmly made up than it is in this affair. I offer no encouragement. I should deceive you grossly were I to hold out the supposition that any amount of time or thought could make me waver a hair's breadth from the answer you have received. Importunity may disgust, it cannot move me."

"The reply in substance which your father made to Mr. Wynne!" was the sneering response.

A deadly faintness seized my heart; and the momentary check of the blood in vein and artery was followed by a tumultuous rush, a beating like ten thousand pulses through my body; my head swam, and I caught at a tree to save myself from falling.

"You seem overpowered!" were the words that restored my failing consciousness. "Accept my arm. Permit me to find a seat for you."

I recoiled from his touch, and as fast as my limbs would carry me, I hurried along the path to Moss-side, now in sight, praying inwardly for power to support me to its gate. Mr. Townley kept pace with me, and I could not shut my ears.

"You were under the impression that the history of that love-passage was confined to your household? There are unerring signs that betray blighted affection, though all tongues be discreet. No gossip, male or female, who has seen you since your lover's departure, has read these amiss in your countenance and deportment. I have tendered to you an opportunity of confounding their wise saws and knowing predictions, and you have treated it with disdain. Your father has never entrusted you with the reason of his opposition to your union with the man whose 'professed attachment' you *could* 'reciprocate,' I believe?"

I did not speak, but continued my irregular race, my hand against my heart, that its palpitations might not entirely deprive me of breath.

"In this instance, I construe silence into *dis*sent. Mr. Leigh has more prudence than I gave him credit for. A dangerous secret should be guarded carefully; and if one would have it remain a secret, he had better blazon it in the newspapers than admit a woman into his confidence. This was no business of mine, except as everything relating to you affected me more or less; and the principle of self-preservation cautioned me not to stand by tamely and let the prize be born off by another; when, thanks, in part, to his obliging communicativeness, I was in possession of a story that would stop all proceedings, even nullify a contract matrimonial, supposing the preliminaries had been entered upon. I have suspected that your filial devotion has sustained some damage from your father's seeming perverseness, but this should not be. If I did not esteem Mr. Leigh my confidential client, I could show you, in a word, the propriety of his course. Had his courage failed, Mr. Wynne, knowing half as much as I do, would have discarded the thought of the alliance."

"Mr. Townley!" I said, facing him. "What object you can have in this brutality, beyond the gratification of an unmanly spite, it is hard to say. I have endured your insults because I am a woman and unprotected. You imagine yourself secure in the certainty that I will not report your language to my father, whose age would not permit him to become your antagonist; but there is still one whose right it is to defend me. Every word of this conversation goes, by the next mail, to my brother, whom nothing can detain from my side if I require his aid."

"Do it!" he cried, with unruffled coolness. "The spirit goes with the blood, I see! I have enough regard left for you to warn you of the consequences of this rash action of yours, should your brother's conduct justify your expectations."

He leaned towards me, and, his eyes glittering like blue steel, exchanged his tone for one of menace. "His aim may be true, his blade keen, yet my shot is surer to pierce a vital part, my weapon will destroy not life, but what you may prize more dearly—the honor of your family. If you are unbelieving, ask your father the value of the stake for which the game you propose would be played. Hearken to my advice, Miss Grace, and do not wantonly alienate a friend, who, as an enemy, could overwhelm your house with infamy."

"Infamy!" I repeated.

"I have said it!" he replied, sententiously.

We were at the yard-gate, the goal that had seemed to elude my uncertain feet, so long had they been in gaining it. My father was pruning away the dead branches of a rose tree. His head was uncovered, and the evening sun slanting athwart his silvered hair reminded me of the "crown of glory" upon the hoary head, "found in the way of righteousness." Giddy and sick as I was, his open brow and benignant smile were decisive proofs to me that the abominable insinuation of guilt of his that could entail ruin upon all of his name was a vile fabrication.

The gate was inhospitably fast to Mr. Townley, and my father had to lend him some assistance.

"You are pale, my daughter," he observed. "Have you walked far?"

"To Mrs. Bell's," I answered. "The weather is oppressive."

Mr. Townley relieved me in his easy way. "And our fair pedestrian, thoroughly trained as she is, is not quite adequate to a three mile *heat*."

"You had better lie down, my dear," said my father. "Mr. Townley will remain to tea."

"I thank you, sir, but my sisters will be expecting me home. I called by to deliver a letter I brought from the office, thinking that it might be from Frederic, and you would like to have it immediately"—I was obliged to hear as I trod dizzily up the walk and steps.

A fit of hysterical weeping was the vent of outraged feeling—so protracted and violent, that it was dark when I ventured to present myself in my aunt's chamber. Her chair was by the window, and the candles were yet unlighted. I apologized, while repairing this negligence, for the lateness of my appearance, pleading extreme lassitude produced by my warm walk.

"I hoped you were enjoying yourself abroad," she said, kindly, "and I have needed nothing. You should not abridge or hurry your excursions on my account. You are too much confined. I have thought of it much this afternoon—and all for me!

She sighed heavily. These exhibitions of feeling were extremely rare, and I never knew how to receive them.

"I am better satisfied here than anywhere else," I replied "You must not vex yourself about what I do not think a hardship."

She was in the humor for talking. "I have been thinking of Frederic, too, and his pretty wife. I wish he had brought her home directly they were married. Their happiness would have inspirited us all. They must be a handsome couple. Is he less near to you since his wedding?"

"No, ma'am. During his engagement I became accustomed to the idea of resigning him. As he cannot live with us, we should be glad that he has some one to make a desirable home of the residence he has selected."

Her solicitude reverted to me. "When they are settled, you must leave the old people to look after each other for a while, and pay them a visit. There must be happier days in store for you."

Her grave features, as she said this, wore some resemblance to her brother. Had she appeared thus to the child or girl, my responsive burst of affection might have broken the ice-wall between us, and I tasted something of the sweetness of a mother's ove. I experienced no such inclination now.

I rolled her chair out of the draught, if any there was stirring in the murky atmosphere ; laid everything in readiness for her early retiring, and led her into the supper-room. The seat at the foot of the board was vacant. Joe had seen his master "go out towards the quarters about half an hour before," and reckoned it was to see "Uncle Reuben," one of the negroes who had been ailing for a day or two. Our rule in such cases was to proceed with the meal without sending for him. It was soon over, and I had seen my aunt in bed and stolen out to seek calm from the repose of the night, when my father's step grated on the gravel-walk.

"How is Reuben, sir ?" I inquired.

"I have not seen him, my daughter."

"You're very tired," I continued. "Will you have your supper ? It is waiting for you."

"I wish none to-night—thank you."

He kissed me a "good-night," and went slowly on to his room. His melancholy turns were seldom attributable to any direct and recent agency, and departed as they had come. My own mind was too much oppressed to conjecture concerning his sadness

The recollection was revived by Martha, who entered my chamber, as I was undressing, to deliver a letter her master had sent.

I had the presence of mind to order her out so soon as I recognized the superscription—then I stood for many minutes, unable to unfold the sheet or to re-read the address, which was my father's, in Herbert Wynne's handwriting.

CHAPTER XII.

"My dear Sir:

"If the painful duty Friendship imposes upon me could be performed by any other hand, mine should never write what will shroud your home in gloom"——

Thus far I read. My terrified mind grasped the rest, it seemed without the help of the organs of vision. My brother—my brave, fond, beautiful brother! the bridegroom of one month—was no more! He was bathing with a party of gentlemen in the surf; ventured too far; was overtaken by the undertow, and carried out to sea; the next mountain wave dashed his body upon the beach—untenanted clay! Brief history of the quenching of the one remaining light of our hearts!

In the midst of his grief, the father remembered the young creature who had so lately murmured, "'till death do us part," with no presage of this speedy and fearful release from the obligations she assumed. It was her wish, Herbert stated, to have the remains interred in a cemetery near the home to which she would now return; and, dearly as he coveted the mournful privilege of laying his boy to rest beside his mother, my father wrote instantly to Mr. Wynne, ordering that all should be done as May requested; to herself, a letter of the most affectionate sympathy. My aunt was ill for days after the intelligence was communicated, and there could not be—I said impiously—angrily—a drop remaining in the vial of wrath which had been poured upon our devoted family. The seditious horde of blasphemies that rushed up from my soul, at the stroke of this calamity, put my self-righteous imaginings to flight. Dust thickened upon the covers, and canker blackened the clasps of my Bible. From a Pharisee, I became an infidel, practically—to myself, a confessed rebel, stubborn as hopeless.

The reader cannot desire more ardently than I to pass rapidly over this, the dark age of my life. My heart revolts at its details; my hand would fain seal the tear and blood-stained pages forever. Is mine too sorrowful a tale? Oh! if the sun and dew of God's visible mercy still abide upon your home; if lover and friend have not been put far from you—yet believe that thousands of aching spirits upon the earth that is all smiles to you, will testify to the truthfulness of the picture you condemn as too gloomily shaded. No artist has ever dared to give the thunder-cloud upon his canvas the inky hue of that which sweeps across the heavens we love to think of as eternally serene; and even those to whom Sorrow has been, at some time, a familiar companion—when the footprints of the destroying angel are effaced, forget how dense was the darkness of his presence. Men are most skeptical as to the gregarious nature of trouble, taught though it is, in aphorisms which condense the wisdom of generations past—illustrated in their sight daily. Truly sings the greatest of living poets—the magician, whose harp is the vast heart of humanity:

——"Disasters come not singly;
But as if they watched and waited,
Scanning one another's motions,
When the first descends, the others
Follow, follow, gathering flock-wise
'Round their victim, sick and wounded,
First a shadow, then a sorrow,
'Till the air is dark with anguish."

The mother could tell of the fast procession of little coffins across her threshold after Death had once halted there; the husband may relate how among the cluster of short mounds in the family burial-place, arises one longer and higher, where, worn with watching and grief, *she*, last of all, lay down with the lambs she could not save from disease and decay. Many a doubting Elijah is appalled by the wind, the earthquake, the fire, before the still, small voice whispers of peace and love to his bewildered soul.

With the December snow came another black-sealed letter to drain the tears unwept for previous calamities. My brother Edmund had lost his wife, the lovely girl whom, ten years before, he had introduced to us as his bride. We could show no outward tokens of respect to her memory, for there were none but sable garments and sad faces at Moss-side, but while the affliction was to us slight when compared with the bereavement we had recently sustained, we mourned for the widowed husband, the motherless child.

"I have just heard again from Edmund," said my father to me, one evening; "and must consult you before I reply. He is perplexed what to do with his little girl. 'She has been most carefully raised by the best of mothers;' he writes, 'and I should be wanting in duty to her and to the departed, were I to expose her now to the subtle temptations and glaring evils of a boarding-school; or undertake to have her instructed under my own roof, when my personal superintendence must necessarily be irregularly exercised; my best attempts fall far below the watchful guardianship of the parent she has lost. A girl should be educated by a woman. I cannot do mine the injustice to deny her this need of her nature. A man of business is, of all others, the least competent to a task so difficult and delicate. Now for my petition, which is so bold that nothing but this exigency could force me to present it. Will our Grace accept this onerous charge for a while, at least until I can settle upon a second-best plan? Lilias is a child of warm feelings and some quickness of intellect;

is easily controlled by those she loves, and she will soon become attached to my lovable sister. Your experience, my dear father has proved how nearly an aunt can supply a mother's place. Tell Grace that I do not press this imposition by arguments or persuasions. She knows what an inestimable benefit she will confer upon me and Lilias by granting my wish. If she decline the responsibility, I cannot blame her, and shall love her none the less.'"

This proposal acted like the charge of a galvanic battery, arousing me, for the time, from my lethargic state. I was, I told my father, reluctant to enter into any engagement to teach a child, whose preliminary tuition had been received from the accomplished woman I knew my sister-in-law to have been.

"Her father could not have made a more unfortunate selection," I said. "I am unversed in the habits, even in the plays of children; and as to nursing, any girl eleven years old, who has younger brothers and sisters, could manage better than I."

"These are things that come naturally to your sex," answered my father; "Lilias is a healthy child of nine, not a babe in arms, you must recollect; and in the science of games, she probably needs no instruction. She will, as Edmund says, contribute to your cares, now too laborious for your age and strength."

"I am quite well, sir, and have not enough to do," I interrupted in my ordinary tone of indifference. "Nothing else agrees with me so well as constant occupation."

He sighed, and I read in his look the yearning to hold me to his bosom and weep with me over the mutual sorrow that had left us so little joy, upon which our minds could dwell; but my aspect was uninviting. These endearments belonged to an age now dead.

"I wish we could fall upon some other mode of providing for Lilly," he said, seriously. "I have all confidence in your ability to do what your brother desires, so far as moral and mental training goes. I am unwilling, however, to subject your health to the danger of increased confinement and the anxiety you will experience while your distrust of yourself continues."

"I will take her," I said, quietly.

He paused in surprise. "Have you counted the cost—do you think?" he asked.

"I have, sir. Since you are surety for my most doubtful qualifications, I do not hesitate to pledge myself to the performance of minor duties. Please say as much to brother from me. Will he bring her to Moss-side himself?"

"So he proposes, and if your conclusion is favorable, he would like to have the journey over before the weather renders the roads impassable. She will be a pretty Christmas gift for you, if they can reach us in season."

It was rather singular, and to me ominous of a conspiracy between him and Edmund, that they arrived on the eve of the very day he had named—an anniversary with me, one of the many against which I had erected a black cross, marking the grave of murdered hopes. The evening was cold and wet. A drizzling rain had been falling since noon, at which time we expected the travellers. Dinner, delayed two hours, was at length served up, and went away untasted. My aunt soon resigned the hope of seeing her nephew that day; and should the mist thicken into a storm, they would, she thought, be detained for the remainder of the week in whatever quarters they had found shelter. My father's more hopeful disposition argued differently.

"Unless one of them was sick, they started from —— this morning while it was fair," he represented, "and it is not like Edmund to heed weather. They have a comfortable conveyance, and are perhaps hindered by the miserable state of the roads. I shall not give them up before dark."

My faith in his son's perseverance or my desire to see him and his companion was less strong than his, and deeming it useless and imprudent to join his lookout at the front door, after one glance at the chilling fog-folds that dimmed the nearest trees, I went up to my sanctum, now as perfect a "Growlery" as Mr. Jarndyce would have had people believe his. Upon my lounge, then, I established myself with the selfish congratulation—"One more quiet night!"

"What influenced me to send for this child?" I questioned myself for the hundredth time. "Was it not that I courted still heavier burdens than those under which I am bending; a casting down of the gauntlet to the Destiny they may call Fate, Providence—what they will—that appears intent upon overcoming me? A most Christian-like motive! this is sisterly affection! but I do not affect to be guided by Christian principles; I ceased to be a sister when Frederic died. This brother I scarcely know: I pity his child with an unloving pity; yet I remember her as an engaging little creature five years ago. I will be kind to her, for I am not inhuman—win upon my affections she never can. There is nothing there to lay hold upon. "My lovable sister!" Edmund wrote in unconscious irony. How could he guess that I have grown to be the antipodes of the girl he last saw me? He may object to leaving his daughter with me when he sees the change. This will disappoint my father, for I foresee that she will usurp my old place with him. To me it will be neither mortifying nor distressing; I have done my duty in consenting to her parent's request, and shall not object to his removing her from a baneful neighborhood."

I said this out mentally, without a tear or a shudder. I honestly considered myself impervious to further suffering, incapable of forming other attachments. This hardening of heart and conscience is the legitimate effect of an egotism of sorrow, and this luxury I had feasted upon to the utmost. I was firm in the belief that I hated myself, while by a perverse contradiction, my dismal delight was in the contemplation of the woes linked in, identified with my being. I had been upon my feet the greater part of the day, and was more than tired of waiting ; so, rolling myself up comfortably in my deliciously sombre fantasies, I dozed gradually into a confirmed slumber.

I was aroused by a noise at my door, as of some one opening it with care.

"Is supper ready, Martha ?" I inquired, not raising my head; for she, of all the household, moved so noiselessly.

A rustling passed around the head of my couch; and between me and the fire stood a diminutive figure with short, fair ringlets, blue eyes and skin dazzlingly white above her black dress. This hue alone precluded the idea of a supernatural visitation, and my brain, cloudy with sleep, did not at first, wholly scout the possibility of such an appearance.

"Who are you ?" I said, confusedly, half rising.

"I am Lilly Leigh. Grandpapa told me I should find Aunt Grace in here."

She stood quite still, her hands behind her back, and gazed steadfastly at me, neither abashed nor forward.

"I am your Aunt Grace," I said. "Will you come and kiss me ?"

She advanced promptly, pursed up her mouth ; demurely performed the salute, and retreated to her former stand-point.

"When did you get here ?" was my next question.

"A short while ago."

"Is your father down stairs ?"

"Yes, ma'am."

I could not help smiling at the prim gravity of her childish face ; and she stepped nearer to me, encouraged by the gleam.

"Shall we go down and see him ?" said I.

"If you please, ma'am."

I took her hand. She clung to me as we entered the passage.

"Are you afraid?" I asked her.

"Not exactly," in a whisper; "but I do not like the dark very well."

In the lower entry, she stopped, shook out her apron, and tried ineffectually to smooth her curls.

"I have been riding all day, you know," she apologized. "I am afraid papa will shake his head at me."

"I will attend to that," I assured her, whereat she was comforted to follow me to my aunt's room.

My brother said nothing at meeting me; only put his arm over my shoulder, as Frederic used to do, and embraced me tenderly. When he trusted his voice to ask after my health, mine was low and tremulous. The brothers had seldom been thought alike during the lifetime of the younger, but the resemblance of feature and tone touched me now, as I had boasted, an hour before, nothing could ever do again.

My father came to my help. Lilly, by his directions, had paid her respects to her great-aunt pretty much after the precise fashion of her introduction to me, and now occupied his knee.

"Did our tiny witch here surprise you?" he inquired.

"I was asleep, sir, when she came up, and mistook her for a real witch," I replied.

Her teeth shone through the parting lips for a second, and her eyes sparkled with amusement; then the lids dropped modestly.

"It was a stroke of dramatic effect for which I am disposed to applaud myself," my father went on to say. "I judged that the slight bustle of arrival was unheard in your room, and, when I at last discovered a living Lilly in the bundle of cloaks, shawls and hoods, I carried her up to your door, unfastened it and slipped her in."

The small lady's behavior at supper, and while her seniors discoursed afterwards, justified her father's account of her training.

A child's chair, a remnant of my nursery furniture, had been provided for her, and planting it under her grandfather's elbow, she sat mute as a mouse; looking much of the time straight into the fire, wide awake with the novelty of her situation, and the need she felt of comporting herself with the utmost decorum. I marvelled what busied her infantile brain, for there was intelligence in the large eyes. She was an object of curiosity to me, some almost forgotten reminiscences of my own childhood being all the key I had in the unfamiliar study presented to me. I hoped devoutly that she was not one of the pattern children (I had nearly written patent!) so extolled by parents and friends. Would she ever wear high-necked aprons, hunt hens' nests and climb cherry trees, in which exciting pastimes my father abetted me, to the horror of my staid aunt? Could she laugh aloud and stretch those white-stockinged, trim ankles in races upon the lawn with the frolicsome pup her thoughtful grandfather had purchased for her? Would she always know her lessons; never drop books and abridge the hours for practising scales and exercises, to chase butterflies and string jessamine necklace? I would not have said it, even to myself, but I did not dissent from my father's remark, "Lilly will break in acceptably upon our monotony, Edmund. Old things and the spirit of past days have held sway here a tedious time. She will act like an infusion of fresh blood upon our domestic system."

Rapid, scarlet blood it was that dyed her cheeks at this mention of herself, which I had not supposed she would understand. The same happy smile that had lighted her face before, flitted over it, and she inclined her head towards the caressing hand that met its flaxen profusion. Once only, she quitted her seat before the summons to bed. My father had opened the Bible for prayers, and I arose to place my aunt's stand before her. In doing this, I accidentally struck against her footstool. Lilly flashed across the rug—no other word can express the motion—

and replaced it before I could stoop to repair my carelessness, and was as speedily back in her corner, grave and still, as befitted the approaching service. My father looked surprised and gratified, Edmund gratified merely ; but he did not commend her for this or anything else, by word. A glance of approval and a frown from "Papa" were her highest meed of praise, her severest punishment.

I fancied that she would have avoided Martha, when she offered to undress her, and making some excuse for dispensing with her services, I myself unfastened and drew off the clothes that seemed ridiculously small to my unpractised fingers, as they passed lingeringly, with a pleasurable thrill, along the dimpled shoulders, the rounded limbs.

"Shall I lift you into bed?" I asked, when the night-dress was tied and the ringlets combed out.

"Not just yet, if you please, Aunt Grace," and the clear treble faltered in greater embarrassment than she had before displayed.

"Is there anything you would like to have?" I said, as gently as I could.

"May I—will you let me read one chapter in my Bible?" her eyes more pleading than her timid voice.

"Certainly," I said, but I was none too well pleased with the request. This had been one of my childish customs also ; a duty rigidly adhered to by my aunt in her own practice, and as rigidly exacted of me. I retained a vivid impression of the smarting eyes which would not be rubbed open ; the drowsy wanderings that interpolated the sacred text ; the downright slumbers that sometimes concluded the exercise, while my guardian pored with undisturbed attention over the prosy commentary I hated so heartily.

"I am afraid she *is* a pattern miss!" I said peevishly to myself. "I had rather she were a downright miscreant who would give such puritanical farces the go-by whenever she could"

She did not nod as she read—I wished she had. I would have liked her better for the lapse into baby-nature. Nor did she peep furtively at me to see if I were observing her precocious piety. The psalm was brief, I noticed from my chair, where I pretended to be equally engaged with a novel; but she was in no haste to run it through. When it was done, she returned to the pages a bookmark, embroidered with the initials of her mother's name; and, without hesitation, having perhaps selected the spot beforehand, she entered the narrow space between the bed and the wall, and knelt down. I reached forward and secured the book she had left upon the table. It was bound handsomely, without any tinsel filigree-work, and upon the fly-leaf was written—"*Lilias Leigh—From her Mother.*" "*Remember now thy Creator in the days of thy youth.*" "*When thy father and thy mother forsake thee, then the Lord will take thee up.*"—*Nov.* "15*th*, 18—."

The recent date, the tremulous chirography told the affecting story, I subsequently learned from the daughter. It was a mother's latest gift; the inscription was penned upon a death-bed. Cut to the soul for my uncharitable strictures upon what I had chosen to construe into an ostentation of goodness, I put the volume back, as she issued from her hiding-place. Her eyelashes were moist and her countenance very pensive.

"I am ready now, aunt," she said, "but I am too heavy for you to lift. If you will show me where I am to sleep, I can get into bed by myself."

I replied by taking her light weight in my arms and depositing it in the feathered nest she hardly indented.

"I will be with you presently," said I. "You do not fear to lie alone for a minute or two, do you?"

"No, ma'am. I am very much obliged to you," and she turned her cheek to the pillow, I supposed to sleep.

There was no movement from her when I lay down. It occurred to me that she was unnaturally quiet, and I abated my breathing to listen for hers. It was muffled and not regular, as in healthy slumber, and the strange suppression troubled me. Not to lose a sound, I imitated her stillness, and she, more readily deceived, no doubt, believed my unconsciousness real. A choking sob escaped her ; then a plaintive cry, imperfectly smothered—and the flood-gate was raised. She wept bitterly, though not loudly ; her frame heaving with woman-like agony, indescribably painful in the mere infant she seemed. Before the warm, sweeping tide, the snow and ice I had labored to pile around my heart, dissolved. If one atom of humanity still survived within me, this child-woe must have developed it into growth.

And in the haste of my anxiety to alleviate her distress, I called her by a name I had sternly vowed should never be uttered again by my lips; the sweetest of Love's appellations ; the title *he* had given me in the bliss of our soul-union—in the throes of our soul-parting—a word as holy to me as the memory of his love.

"Darling !" I said, drawing her towards me. "What is the matter ? Tell aunt Grace !"

She nestled in my arms, like a lost, frightened bird. "Mamma ! mamma ! I want my dear mamma !"

I covered the hot little face with tears and kisses, my bosom swelling against hers.

"My poor babe !" was all I could say.

"I can't help crying sometimes, Aunt Grace !" she sobbed, mistaking the cause of my silence. "I miss her so much at night !" and repeating the beloved name, she wept afresh.

"There ! Lilly dear !" I soothed. "She is happy now in Heaven."

"Then I wish I was there too !" she exclaimed, impetuously.

"Hush! hush! that is wrong, Lilly!"

"Why, Aunt Grace? I know she wants me as bad as I do her."

I was nonplussed for an answer to this, and evaded it.

"Would you leave your papa? Think how lonely he would be."

"I cannot live with him, he says," she replied.

My ill-judged consolation must be amended. "Not now, perhaps, dear, but one of these days he will come back for you, and until he is ready to take you to his home, you will stay here with us"—and, some inspiration dictating to me—"I will be your mother."

The violent sobbing ceased. "Will you?" said she, with breathless eagerness—"and will you love me and call me your 'little Lilly?' You did not look to-night as if you ever would."

"You shall see," I replied, confidently. "Can my little Lilly sleep now?"

"If you will kiss me, I will try."

With her hands folded in mine upon my breast, her pure breath flowing over my cheek, I watched out the hours until the hoarse clangor of the clock rang in the day of—"Peace on earth, good-will to men!" The stilly midnight, that had so often waned for me in sleepless wretchedness, witnessed the birth of an unknown feeling, the feeble upstarting of the germ implanted most deeply—latest uprooted in woman—the yearning, tireless, immortal principle of maternal affection.

My Christmas gift was astir betimes on the morrow. She was wonderfully metamorphosed—the others said by the night's rest. Some tincture of shy propriety showed itself at intervals, but the air of strangeness to things and people was modified into the ease of a guest, who, although not altogether at home, feels that he is welcome to his friend's house. The volatile mercury of youth had risen superior to its late depression, but she had not forgotten the scene, or the compact that closed it. Me, she accepted as her protector and guide in the weighty, as in the minute affairs of the day, but without quoting her authority for the adoption. Aunt Grace was now "Auntie," and in process of time, "Auntie dear"—sweetly-toned syllables, to which my heart would have pulsated in the moment of dissolution.

Excepting hers, there could be no "Merry Christmas" among the white family at Moss-side ; but the servants considered downcast visages positive sacrilege upon their grand carnival. Their presents had been prepared, in obedience to their master's unselfish will, but I had designed to appoint my maid almoner in my stead. Lilly's lively interest in the juvenile Ethiopians, to her as unwonted a spectacle as would have been a crowd of young monkeys, chattering English, suggested another substitute. The morning was unfavorable for out-door parades, and the distribution took place in the dining-room. Joe, in all the splendor of a tall shirt-collar and a buckram stock, deigned to officiate in his capacity of Chief Marshal ; directing his main energies to the initiation of his troop in the use of the scraper and door-mat. My aunt occupied her chair by the fireside ; my father and brother surveyed the array from the background.

Lilly's was the centre figure. Her feet twinkled, rather than stepped, from end to end of the huge basket, and her eyes danced yet more merrily ; from her wind-blown curls to the tips of her restless toes, every nerve was alive with enjoyment. I called the destined owner of each article, as she exhibited it, and if I were occasionally backward in my duty, it was that I might have the secret delight of hearing her silvery—"Auntie dear!" a reminder spoken anxiously, if I appeared abstracted, but never impatiently. There was a native grace in her manner of presenting the gifts that awoke audible murmurs of applause from the older servants, who were lookers on in the doors and hall, and elicited her father's proudest smile. Catching every name as I pronounced it, she addressed the one who answered, as she transferred whatever she held to his possession, and subjoined some observation she deemed appropriate.

"Julius," she would remark, "this is a fine humming-top! I dare say you can make it go nicely."

"Mary, see what a beauty of a doll! almost as large as you are—and the best of it is, she will not break if you let her fall."

"Why, Jimmy!" to a wee fellow who was led up by his larger sister; "here is a great horse—all of gingerbread! enough to last you a week."

"This, Auntie dear?" picking up from the bottom of the hamper a dandyish cane, varnished black, with a gay cord and tassel at the head.

"That is for Joe," I said.

The colored exquisite bowed up the room, and almost prostrated himself as he received this finishing touch to his Sunday suit.

"It is very becoming, Joe," said Lilly, archly—a naïve satire that provoked us all to laughter. Joe's good-nature and conceit forbade him to see aught but a compliment in this speech, and he replied with a volley of thanks and praises.

"The flatteries of the season to you, Miss Lilias," was the peroration—"to your most worthiest pa; my reserved master; my respectful Miss Agnes, and admiring Miss Grace. Long may you live and reign in this tabernacle, whar we have the pleasure of beholding you now, and when you leave it for a more happier home of your own, may I, Joe the butler, be honored by waitin' 'pon your flourishing table!"

The iris of Lilly's blue orbs was amply relieved by a white ring around them, when he was through. She was self-possessed enough to say, "Thank you, Joe!" seeing that he waited for an answer, and somewhat sobered, walked back to her father, whose amusement banished the melancholy from his brow, as he set her upon his knee.

"Auntie," she whispered, touching my arm, and motioning me to bend my ear, that the query might not wound "the butler," who was bustling about us—"Did he mean that he wants to wait on my table when I go to Heaven?"

CHAPTER XIII.

Mr. Peyton brought with him to dinner a visitor and a namesake of his own—Peyton Elliott—a fine lad of fourteen. He was the son of an intimate friend of his host, who, in consideration of the loneliness of Linden, often lent the boy to his godfather for days or weeks, as the case might be.

I had dressed Lilly in a black silk frock, edged upon the shoulders and sleeves with lawn frills, and its sombreness further mitigated by worked pantalettes, very full, which granted but a tantalizing glimpse of the pretty feet they shaded. I do not like to see children wear mourning any more than I like to see the morning sun overtaken by storm-clouds ; but she was passing fair in her sad-colored robes. She stood by me, as Mr. Peyton and his charge entered, and the regards of both were instantly riveted.

" She is strikingly like her mother," said the former aside to me, as he held, in his kind way, the hand she gave him. " Where is her father ?"

" He will be in directly. You will find him much changed, Mr. Peyton."

" I look for that, Grace—I look for that ! No man knows better what he has gone through than I do—no man !"

He was fluttering the leaves of a book, taken up at random, from the table. Well acquainted with his mood, I let him alone.

" Do you remember "—he resumed as ramblingly. " No ! you

were very young—not larger than that little niece of yours, there—but you may have some recollection of when Edmund was married."

"I recollect it perfectly," I said.

"There was great feasting here then. A lovely woman she was—a lovely woman! I was at the dinner party, the first given him—the last Mary ever attended—the very last! It runs constantly in my mind to-day—constantly!"

He never named his wife except in conversation with those upon whose friendship and sympathy he was certain he could rely, for he was not a man to unlock to the world the depository of his most sacred feelings.

"I studied the question of coming over to-day for a whole hour," he said.

"Why, Mr. Peyton? Could you doubt what reception you would find, however circumstanced we might be?"

"That was not it, Grace. I thought Edmund might suffer more for seeing me—that was all! You don't need to be told what it would cost me to stay away from your table on Christmas-day."

My brother interrupted us. With unfinished salutations falling from their tongues, they wrung each other's hands until the nails were white with the pressure, then sat down in adjoining chairs, and tried to chat with the freedom of "lang syne."

"Lang syne!" The words sighed through my soul in pathetic minor cadences, such as the wind breathes in autumn nights among the tall grass of grave yards. By the gravitation of habit, my mind sank into the slough whose quaking depths it had come to make its home. Wantonly I recalled each souvenir of another Christmas-day; mustered every joy that blent in the glorious halo which begirt its memory; not to win forgetfulness of the darkness that followed, but to compare the picture with the present; to change Eden at a stroke into a ruined garden, half-ripe fruit hanging blighted upon the dry boughs—for music, the plaining of mateless birds over empty nests.

A touch upon my knee disturbed my reverie.

"Auntie," said Lilly, seeing that she had aroused me. "That little boy looks lonesome. What can I get to amuse him? It is too wet to play out-of-doors."

Her patronizing air was laughable when I surveyed the young gentleman whose forlorn condition she commiserated. A manly fellow, older than herself by five years, and nearly twice her height, for her stature had not kept pace with her intellect—the "little boy" would have been diverted or chagrined by the implication of her seniority. She was in very sober earnest, and in reply to my advice that she should go and talk with him, objected in the same cautious undertone: "But I can't think of anything to say. I don't know anybody that he does, or where he lives. I wish I did, for I do feel very sorry for him."

"Where is the book of engravings grandpapa gave you this morning?" I inquired. "Maybe he is fond of pictures."

Her eyes lighted up. "He won't think me bold if I begin to talk to him, will he?"

"By no means. It is your duty to entertain him in your own house."

She departed, satisfied, in quest of the stepping-stone to the acquaintance. The book was a folio volume, but she returned, carrying it dexterously, so as not to appear to require assist ance.

Peyton got up to take it from her.

"No, thank you!" said she. "I can hold it. Aunt Grace thought you would like to see some pictures, and these are new and pretty ones."

She graciously awarded him permission to spread it open upon the centre-table and draw up seats. He was gallant without pretension, and entered upon the inspection of the prints with a flattering show of interest. I forgot my dreaming in watching them, and I saw, one by one, the others present glance at them with significant smiles. Lilly's voice was never shrill or loud, but her utterance became quicker, the inflections more varied and expressive as they went deeper into the book. Engaged herself, heart and soul in her employment, she had no perception for the stolen gaze her companion, ever and anon, bestowed upon her kindling face ; no suspicion that he coaxed her to more detailed explanations to hear her talk, not to gain the information she artlessly supplied. Unperceived by her, I sauntered to the back of her perch. The plate under examination was the overthrow of Pharaoh's host in the Red Sea.

"What is it ?" asked Peyton in pretended ignorance. "A freshet ?"

Lilly was too polite to laugh, or speak her surprise at his deficiency of Biblical lore.

"O, no ! that is—not a freshet in a river. You remember the story of how the Israelites got out of the land of Egypt—the ten plagues and all that."

"Not very well, I believe," rejoined the embryo diplomatist. "Tell me more."

"God sent plagues upon the Egyptians until Pharaoh was willing to let the children of Israel go," pursued she, still shunning any appearance of superior knowledge. "They came off in the night—'six hundred thousand men, besides women and children.' "

"They must have had hard work marching in the dark," interposed Peyton. "Didn't some of them get lost ?"

"No ; they couldn't, you know, for the pillar of fire went straight before them the whole night and showed them the way. They travelled pretty well until morning, and then was the trying time ! The wicked king was sorry he had let them go out of his country, and started after them with a great army, horsemen and chariots—the best soldiers he had. He came in sight of them just as they reached the Red Sea, and you see there was a mountain on this side, and one on that"—pointing to the picture—"the Egyptians were behind them and the deep water before them"——

"Decidedly a ticklish situation!" commented the listener.

"Yes; and the poor Israelites thought so too. They began to quarrel with Moses, the good man who had done so much for them, for bringing them away from their homes to be killed or drowned; and he prayed to God to help them. And the Lord told him not to stop to call even upon Him, but to tell the people to go forward."

"How could they?" said Peyton. "Were they to step right into the water?"

"Ah! but it was not their business to ask Him any questions! He said, Go forward!' and He would not have ordered them to do it, if He had not meant to help them through their trouble. Don't you recollect about Abraham, when he thought he would be obliged to kill his son? and Jacob, whose brother met him so kindly because God had put it into his heart to do so? Well, the next thing that happened was that the pillar of fire moved backwards and settled down right between the Israelites and their enemies.

"Why, I should think they would have gone back too," said Peyton; "they were to follow it every way—were they not?"

"Not when they had been told to 'go forward!'" replied the monitress, with emphasis. "Then the Egyptians could not see through the cloud, for it *was* a cloud to them; and Moses stretched out his rod over the water, and it divided and stood up in two high walls, with a great, wide, dry road in the middle."

"A *dry* road!" exclaimed the dissembler; "when the water was there one minute before?"

"Yes ! a dry road !" retorted Lilly, firmly ; "just as dry as this carpet, for the wee bits of children went over 'dry-shod.' God can do anything. He could have dried up the sea entirely if He had pleased. It was not like man's work. His people got safely to the other side, and the Egyptians started in too, still chasing them. They were, maybe, half way across, when, all at once the waters rolled together over them, and swallowed them up. That must be Pharaoh himself in that fine chariot, with the crown on his head. I can't help wishing he had not gone in—poor fellow !"

"You called him a wicked king awhile ago. Didn't he deserve to die ?"

"I suppose so, or God would have held him back ; but I think Moses and all the rest of the Israelites must have felt badly to see the whole host, every one of them, destroyed."

I would not check her prattle by being detected in the act of eaves-dropping, so sought my seat.

"'Except ye become as little children—'" I said to myself, as their tones played upon my ear. "That child, with her unquestioning faith, hears and obeys the 'Go forward !' of revelation and of Providence, while I, in my wilderness, can only stand and murmur !" and wresting the infantine teacher's words from their original application, I repeated, "the Egyptians could not see through the cloud, for it *was* a cloud to them !"

Peyton and she waxed merrier and more familiar, and the engravings being disposed of, she tripped over to me with a second petition.

"May we play 'Graces' in the hall, Auntie ? We will be very careful not to strike the clock or windows."

Their laughing voices, and the clattering of the hoops and sticks were distinctly heard in the parlor, and cheered the saddened countenances there.

"She is my consolation," said Edmund to his friend.

"I can well believe it," was the reply. "My house is doubly gloomy and desolate after one of Peyton's visits. I am anxious to adopt him, but cannot quite gain his parent's consent. What can be more inspiriting and home-like than the patter of children's feet, the sound of children's mirth?"

"As enthusiastic a baby-lover as ever!" observed Edmund. "I must make interest with you for my pet—constitute you sponsor extraordinary, when I go away. Not that I doubt her happiness here; still less do I fear that she will not be affectionately nurtured, but she cannot have too many friends."

"I have one daughter here now," said Mr. Peyton. "I raised Grace, and am very proud of the job," tapping me on the head.

"You have slight cause for this vanity," I returned.

"Well, well! that is your say. Keep your opinion and I will keep mine. The best wish I can make this blossom of yours, Edmund, is that she may grow up to be like her aunt."

"Heaven forbid!" was my thought, as I reflected upon the misery, the rank poison-growth he innocently invoked for her. And more like a prayer than anything I had breathed for months, arose the wish that this unpolluted lily might be saved from the mildew and worm that had ravaged my heart, and a determination that so far as in me lay, she should be spared even the knowledge of evil.

A swift taunt opposed this glimmering of desire. "How can that be when melancholy faces meet her at every turn? when her caresses are responded to in solemn taciturnity, or are unnoticed in the absorbing care of the hour? when the bosom, which is her nightly resting-place, is ever convulsed with sighs or cold in despair? Is this house, peopled with the shades of the departed, where, from hour to hour, human steps never resound, a fitting habitation for this gay young creature?"

"It shall be!" I said. "If it be a cross to sacrifice my

habits and inclinations to secure this end, I accept it. I have defied hardship before in mere perversity of spirit. I invite it now, for the sake of another."

In the might of this resolution I worked through the day, worked hard, and so far as others were concerned, successfully. But evening, the gathering time of memories, approached, and my tired strength began to waver. It was raining fast, and our guests were to remain with us through the night. The gloaming anticipated the usual season of its dusky coming, by more than an hour. My aunt had retired to her chamber; in the sitting-room, my father, Edmund, and Mr. Peyton smoked chibouques, and talked in a hum no louder than the dropping rain. Lilly and Peyton were kneeling on the seat, under the window, their foreheads against the glass, counting the pools in the yard and the trickling streams from the eaves.

Whither should I repair, and in what society, except to the Growlery, and alone—with myself—Grace Leigh, and her oft-told grievances? The humble sofa I had made a Procrustean bed, the rack whereon I tossed through my most bitter hours, was in readiness; likewise the fire, its licking flames and red-hot caverns furnishing new images of unrest when fancy became jaded; likewise the pale portrait over the mantel, its features untouched by years, its woe changeless; likewise the swarm of stinging, black-winged thoughts, awaiting my lying down to settle upon their voluntary prey. There were enough real sorrows to bow me earthward, without loading myself with imaginary horrors to grind me into the dust. Weak and wicked, I suffered them all. A drowned form, with sea-weed matted in his hair, hands clenched in the death agony, was borne into my view; and the sough of the night wind was the wave requiem. Then knelt in speechless desolation the bride-widow, her nuptial robe torn off to make way for sable shroudings, her girlish beauty destroyed by weeping; weak, trembling, helpless—she whom Heaven had just seemed to bless with the best of earth's treasures. Near by, his face averted that he might not behold the wreck he could not repair, the woe no mortal balm could assuage, was another figure, like a young pine, swayed by this resistless storm; the friend, who had snatched my brother's body from the exulting billows, who had poured his own breath into the lungs that were never, alas ! to heave again ; whose hands had composed his limbs for the grave and helped to lay him there ; whose tears had flowed for him and for us ; the more than brother to her—the utterly bereaved—her advocate and helper ; to me the honorable and fervent lover of my girlhood ; the constantly mourned of every hour in my unhoping Now ; who, stainless in truth, abiding in affection, irreproachable in thought and deed, was, nevertheless, to be neither brother, lover, nor friend to me now, nor evermore. The beating rain was the tramping of a train of weeping ghosts, winding round and round the house, bearing the ashes of Life's most precious things in mocking honor of this—my Christmas festival !

"Auntie, dear," was spoken at the door. "May I come in ?"

"Yes, Lilly."

She rustled past the head of the lounge as upon the evening before, but instead of standing aloof, as then, she crouched down upon the floor, leaned her elbow upon the side of my cushions, and touched my brow with her lips.

"Were you asleep ? do I disturb you ?" she queried, apprehensively.

"No, my love. I like to have you here."

She played with the rings upon my fingers, slipping them off and on.

"I was lonesome, Auntie, and came to look for you."

My heart bounded. Lonely for *me !* Could this be so ?

"Where is Peyton," I asked.

"I left him in the parlor. I am tired of playing, although he is very kind and funny. Somehow, I do not feel like laughing and talking after it gets dark ; and so, as I said, I was lonesome, and wanted you. I love you, Auntie !" pressing her soft face against mine.

Was she a spirit of mercy ? Did a secret magnetic current pass from her love-full soul to mine, worn and withered ?

"And I love you, darling !" I cried, catching her to my breast with a vehemence that almost alarmed her.

"Auntie," she commenced, as I released her, "may I talk to you about my dear mamma ?"

"If it will not make you too sorrowful, Lilly," for the big drops in her eyes were sparkling with the firelight.

"No, ma'am—at least I will try not to cry, for she asked me to remember her and speak of her sometimes, and not to fret papa or myself by thinking that she was dead, but to believe that she was very near me when I was good and loved God"——

"What, dear !" I interrupted.

"She hoped, she said, that He would let her watch over me when I was a poor, motherless child ; that she would beg Him to make her my 'ministering angel.' Do you think He did, Auntie ?"

"What do *you* think, Lilly ?"

"I hope that she can see me and be with me. Sometimes, I feel sure she is not far off."

Her rapt face shone like that of the angel she appeared to welcome. Whatever was my belief in the beautiful theory taught by the mother, and received by the trusting child, I beheld in it a blessed consolation to the latter ; a harmless delusion, if they were mistaken in their translation of spirit-longings ; one rich in peace and comfort to the survivors, as to the parting soul.

"She cannot forget you, Lilly," I said, "and it is sweet to think of her as present with us."

"Then she knows how good you are to me," she responded, again, fondling my face, "and that I am already quite satisfied to live here at Moss-side, with you and grandpapa, and that I have two mothers now—one here, and another in heaven!"

"Yes—yes!" I assented, unwilling to shake her happy faith.

She did not move or speak for some time.

"Auntie," she whispered, finally, "you have some friends that you love in heaven, too, haven't you?"

"Yes, dear Lilly," my manner a mournful contrast to hers.

"Your mother is there—isn't she?"

"Yes; she died when I was very small—several years younger than you are now."

"And Uncle Frederic," she proceeded, "he is with her, I know, for mamma said he was a Christian. Oh! how we all cried when we heard that he was"——

"There, love! no more!" I entreated. "O, my brother! my brother!" giving way to a paroxysm of grief, the first tears other eyes had seen me shed since I wept in Herbert's arms.

"Dear, dear Auntie!" murmured the sweet voice, broken by sobs, "please forgive me! I did not mean to distress you—indeed—indeed, I did not! I thought you would love to talk" —and breaking down completely, she cried with me.

I was refreshed, not exhausted, by this salutary indulgence, and regained my self-command sooner than did she. Taking her upon my lap, and kissing away her tears, with many assurances that I was neither wounded nor offended, I bade her tell me all about the uncle whose playfellow she had been.

Very dear were these gleanings of the later months of his life. In the beginning the sensitive narrator proceeded warily, scanning my features for any return of the late tempest of uncontrollable emotion, but as I continued calm, she cast off fear, and related just such incidents and particulars as I wished to hear; sketched domestic scenes and social virtues with a loving fidelity that proved the stand he had gained in the hearts of his brother's family and stranger friends. He it was who, by his frequent stories of our childhood and highly colored paintings of his unworthy sister's charms and excellences had prepared Lilly to love me. The rain still beat and the wind moaned, but it was not the dirge to which I had listened through two winters past, for within my soul were angel-voices, and in my sight, an angel's form.

From that night, my dependence upon her began. The germ which had put forth under the rain of her tears, was baptized anew by mine, and day by day, the thread-like roots spread and strengthened ; twining tendrils wound about the slender support that bore them up well and bravely. Our Lilly was not a saint —still less was she a genius. Her father had described her truly as an intelligent, warm-hearted child, in whom whatever was lovable and good had been fostered, and evil propensities restrained. Her ministry to me was as spontaneous as her mirth. Her delicate intuition advised her that there existed the need of a reconciling medium between me and my kind, a need she supplied, without comprehending ; which her unformed mind certainly never attempted to follow back to a primary cause.

Edmund tarried to see her domesticated, and after a touching farewell, wended his way back to his place of business, homeless and solitary. Our household fairy drooped her pinions for a while, but they were too buoyant to succumb entirely to the heaviest pressure. Soon the quaint old homestead was resonant with her carols and her gleesome laughter, and her feet skimmed its floors as gaily as though these were not haunted precincts—a skeleton in every corner. From her they were mercifully veiled —the phantoms that glided past, and walked with me, wherever I moved were, viewless, and therefore undreaded by her. I had not so much leisure now to heed them. Active duties were driving out sickly humors. The moping needlework absorbed less of my attention, for Lilly's lessons were of greater importance. She must have exercise, and my walks were shorter and more diversified ; amusements, and the piano, discordant from disuse, was retuned ; a closet fitted up for a play-house, and stocked by myself. This tiny cog in our machinery accelerated the slow rate of its revolutions, and the web that rolled from it was interspersed with light, graceful designs, and hints of brighter coloring, among the formal patterns, in dead, neutral hues, that had hitherto formed our bundle of life.

CHAPTER XIV.

It was a clear, bracing morning, and my pupil was restless to have done with books.

"This is a beautiful day, Auntie," she said, between a recitation in Geography and one in Arithmetic.

"Very beautiful!" I replied, unsuspectingly. "Now for your rule, Lilly."

It was correctly repeated, the questions in mental practice and the written sums approved, and she ventured further.

"It will be nice walking about twelve o'clock—don't you think so?"

"We will try it," answered I. "Have you any particular jaunt to propose?"

This was what she waited for, and her straight-forward rejoinder showed that she was indisposed to prolong the guileless manœuvering.

"Yes, ma'am. I should like very much to go to the ice-pond."

"And why the ice-pond?"

"Because the men are at work there to-day. Uncle Sam told grandpapa this morning that the ice was thick enough to be cut out, and grandpapa said that the hands were to go down and get it right away. I would so dearly enjoy seeing them pull out the great shining blocks, and load the wagons with them! Joe says they glitter just like silver."

"If Joe's eloquence has been exercised in behalf of the expedition, opposition from me would be thrown away," thought I.

"If we get through our studies early, Lilly, we will talk about joining the workmen."

"Grandpapa has gone too," finished she. "I saw him ride down the back lane, not long ago. Won't he be surprised to see us?"

Dispatch was the soul of her duties until the tasks were accomplished. Well wrapped up in cloak and furs, she danced delightedly around the room, as I attended to some final preparations for my aunt's comfort while we should be away.

"Lilly dear," I said, reprovingly. "You may trouble Aunt Agnes if you jar the room."

The invalid smiled. "No fear of that! She moves too lightly, and I enjoy her flow of spirits. Be very careful of her, Grace. Is she warmly clad? It is piercing cold."

"See!" said Lilly, opening the wadded skirts of her mantle; "and we walk so fast—Auntie and I—that we never know what the weather is."

"Young blood is warmer than mine," remarked my aunt, slowly rubbing her palsied hand. "I am too apt to forget how hard it is to chill it, for I am never warm myself."

Lilly ran to her to say "Good-bye," and held up her face, pure as a snow-drop, for the salute none ever denied as her lawful perquisite.

The wind was, in truth, very cutting, while we travelled the exposed plains and higher grounds, and we were ready to slacken our gait to take breath, when we gained the shelter of the woods. Icicles fringed some of the lower branches to which the sun and wind had imperfect access; the brown leaf-carpet was powdered with hoar-frost, and the twigs we brushed and trod upon snapped spitefully. No child of the forest could have boasted more ruddy cheeks, a more elastic bound than my city-born companion. She sprang over fallen brush-wood, mounted rocks and stumps, flying, every other minute, from the path, in search of these inviting obstacles ; and once a peal of laughter, melodious as a wood-nymph's call to her mates, drew my notice to a headlong race after a startled hare, down a slope, encumbered with undergrowth and logs, to which she paid no more regard than did the four-footed puss. She rejoined me, still on the run, her hood hanging by one ribbon from her finger, a comic mixture of regret and mirthfulness in her countenance.

"Auntie dear," she panted, "I am very sorry—but it caught upon a naughty limb, and, of course, it was impossible for me to stop just then, for I wanted to see where the hare's nest was. I thought I could remember the very spot where I dropped the string, but when I lost the rabbit, which, I am sure, must have run into the ground, all the trees looked exactly alike, and my ribbon was not upon any of them. I did not like to keep you waiting, and ran back to tell you. Was I very careless ?"

"Rather—I must say," I returned, smiling, and restoring the liberated curls to their confinement.

"I believe I could find it if I were to hunt a while longer," she proposed.

"It is hardly worth while to do that. I will pin your bonnet on now, and give you another string when we go home. How flushed you are ! You will injure yourself by such violent exercise, if you get cool too suddenly. We had better walk on together to the end of this piece of woods."

She restrained herself to my pace, only darting aside twice to pick up nuts, until we were out of the forest, and beheld the sheen of the ice through its girdle of shrubbery trees. Clapping her hands, she flew from my side with the speed of a loosened arrow. I remarked, in my more deliberate descent of the hill, the absence of signs of human life, where we had expected a busy scene, and upon the bank was met by Lilly's disappointed, "Why, there is nobody here !"

"Perhaps you did not understand grandpapa's orders," I suggested.

"Indeed, Auntie, he said just what I told you! Joe heard him too, and wished he had not so much house-work to do, and could come down here with the rest."

"Grandpapa changed his mind then, I suppose," I said.

"Are you certain this is the pond, Auntie?"

"Yes, dear. Come, let us look at it."

To console her, I led the way to the edge, and pointed out the beauty of its dazzling surface. It was a narrow, oblong lake, fenced about with hills except at the northern extremity, whence poured the blast that had given to "Leigh's pond" the reputation of producing the thickest ice in the county, and that coated it across when other waters were uncongealed.

"After all," was soon the juvenile philosopher's conclusion, "it would not be half so pretty if it were all cut up, and we can come here another day, when they do begin to clear it out."

"If we had skates now, we could have fine sport," said I. "I have skated here many a day when I was a girl."

Nothing would do but I must relate the excursions Frederic, Annie Bell, and I used to make for this pastime; how Annie and myself were fearful and awkward, and incurred numberless falls in punishment for our want of courage, and the exhilarating enjoyment of the rushing sweep from end to end of the lake, after we had conquered all difficulties. I pointed out the smoke of Mrs. Bell's chimney over one of the hills, and made her fairly shout with the tale of a disaster that befell me, one freezing day, when I tempted the ice upon the running brook that fed the pond, and atoned for my rash trust by a plunge in mud and water three feet deep.

"I scrambled out, dripping, and shaking with cold," I said; "there was no fire nearer than Mrs. Bell's, and although I ran every step of the way, my frock and stockings were stiff frozen when I got to her house."

"This looks strong!" said she, stamping upon the slippery sheet.

"Oh, yes! it would bear twenty men, or grandpapa would not think it ready to be packed away. I can walk on it without falling. Shall I lead you to the other side?"

She consented with great glee, although she breathed hard and short for the first few steps. The taste of excitement made her importunate for more.

"I can teach you to slide," I said; "that is something like skating, but much easier to learn."

I retained my hold of her while her footing was uncertain, but when she once stood firmly on her feet her poise was so just and elegant, and such the pliability of her body and limbs, that, to gratify her and myself also, I omitted this precaution, and stopped my own course to watch hers. I had removed her fur cape, that she might not want for additional clothing when the heat of motion was over, and the wind buoyed her cloak into streaming sails as she floated, rapid as the wind itself, hither and thither, wherever her ecstatic fancy willed. The pin I had put in her hood was an inadequate substitute for the lost ribbon, and a sudden turn in her zigzag career left her head bare. This was unsafe exposure, and I called to her to cover it. She snatched up the bonnet and swung it around, shook her curls over her eyes in pretty willfulness, and running and sliding, started up the pond, looking back at me, roguishly defiant.

"Too fast, Lilly!" I called again—when she disappeared beneath the ice.

Superhuman speed and skill bore me to the fatal air-hole—masked by a crust, which had broken like glass at a touch. She arose where she had sunk; the bright ringlets came up within reach of my grasp, and a terror-stricken face looked into mine.

I seized her, felt her drowning clutch upon my sleeve, shrieked some words of encouragement, dragged her from the chasm, and in the effort to throw her far upon the solid ice, lost my balance.

"She is safe!" I uttered, mechanically, before I realized my own peril. Indeed, I knew nothing of it beyond a simultaneous sense of extreme coldness, and a stunning blow—then I must have gone down without a struggle.

I slept a long time; for a thousand fragmentary visions that visited my brain, while I lay insensible to external things, recur to me even now. Some were nightmares, with which I grappled when I could not flee the horrid spectres; but most were beautiful dreams of summer scenes and sunny hearts—a lapsing of mind into a channel blocked up and forbidden when reason's sway was potent; revelled in, during her dethronement.

My waking thought was that the morning was at hand, for a reddish light shed a faint illumination through the chamber. With this indistinct impression, I shut my eyes, steeped in the delicious languor that pervades the enchanted land on the borders of sleep's realm. Unlovely shapes presently invaded this domain; witch-hags, with weazen features and claw-like fingers, gibbered and grimaced at me; perched, moping and mowing upon bed-posts and pillows. Their whispers buzzed, at length, into intelligible sentences.

"She can't stand it long," said the ugliest gnome of the crew. "Her pulse is very low, and her complexion ghastly. I notice to-night that there are purple circles around her eyes and mouth—a sign that does not fail once in a hundred times. I should not wonder if she were to die to-morrow."

"The doctor has hopes of her still," answered more human tones. The beldame troop of elves vanished, and in their room were the shadowy outlines of two figures, life-size and life-like. By the hearth sat Mrs. Bell and Miss Susan Townley. Miss

Susan's were the lineaments of my impish tormentor ; and at her wiry whisper, my flesh crept as at the grating of rough steel.

"He may say so, and not believe it himself, and he may believe it and not be right. I don't pin my faith to his sleeve. Besides, nobody can ever tell what he does think—he goes on at such a rate ! I know something about sickness. I've nursed some in my life, and can judge of some things as well as other people that are thought wiser. If this girl's life is not going out as fast and certainly as that candle is burning down, I will never undertake to speak my mind upon another case."

I hearkened without alarm. I knew the doomed girl ; but what was my personal interest in her, I could not understand. I appeared to have a double existence, and neither of the two was more than a half developed being. Yet what concerned either of my selves, it behooved me to hear, and my senses served me truly in gathering every word.

"I will hope on to the last," said Mrs. Bell. "She is almost as dear to me as my Annie. I trust in God's goodness not to lay heavier burdens upon His children than they can carry, and her loss would kill her father and aunt. She is their all, now."

"There does seem to be a fatality hanging over that family," pursued Miss Susan, complacently regaling her nostrils with a pinch of snuff. "It's been one misfortune after another, ever since they moved into the neighborhood, and nobody knows how long before. The old man lost his wife, a son and a daughter in three years, and a good deal of property, I've heard. Things went on smoothly then, until here come his sister's sickness, Frederic's death, and most likely, the death of this one too—all in a lump, as it were. Queer—is it not? that the two youngest should both die by violence—as we may call it—anyhow by accident. It seems to me like a peculiar Providence."

Mrs. Bell's manner savored of displeasure. "I do not know what you mean by a 'peculiar Providence.' If you would say that this is a mysterious dispensation, I agree with you that we cannot see why the righteous should be so afflicted, and that Providence alone can perceive any need of the discipline."

This was not Miss Susan's meaning, she said, true as it might be, and as she hoped it was.

"We are blind, erring creatures, the best of us, Mrs. Bell, and require chastisement—some more than others dream of. Hidden transgressions are often visited by punishment that astonishes and puzzles a man's nearest friends, who can't believe that he deserves it. There is some significance in every blow. That is what I alluded to when I wondered if both these children being drowned"——

"Grace was not drowned," Mrs. Bell corrected, testily.

"But she would have been if they had not pulled her out directly," was the rejoinder. "As I was saying, Mr. Leigh, good as he is, may be aware of some secret reason for this form of affliction. If I were in his place, I should lay it to heart."

"As, no doubt, poor Mrs. Allison over there, did the deaths of her four babes in one week, from scarlet fever," retorted Mrs. Bell; "as Mr. Peyton did the loss of his wife, when he had neither kith nor kin besides upon earth; as you, Miss Susan, may in the Lord's time, be called upon to mourn for your own relations. Ah!" sighed the matron, shaking her head, "it is not for us to judge of the dealings of the Almighty, to apply the lessons He sends! For anything we know, Mr. Leigh—a patient Christian he is! may be set up as an example for our imitation, and we could not have a worthier, Miss Susan, to show us how a mortal like ourselves may 'glorify God in the fire.' By their works ye shall know them. The widow and the fatherless can relate more of his than those who are raised above want;" and moved by grateful recollection, or her own eloquence, she applied her handkerchief to her eyes.

Miss Susan's sour lips took on a superfluous curl; but, baffled in one quarter by blunt sincerity, she tried another avenue of aspersion.

"His daughter does not favor him much in certain respects. She was passable in looks and manners when she was growing up. Now-a-days, I can make nothing of her. Annie is intimate with her; have you ever heard of her having been engaged in a love-scrape or having had any other cross? I strongly suspect something of the kind. I told her so once, and she turned as red as a beet."

"Annie does love her, as do I, with all my heart," returned the hostess; "for a better girl does not live hereabouts. I never heard a whisper of any love-affair; and as to her blushing when you charged her with one, it would have been strange if she had not been confused. Young ladies are apt to color up at such accusations, as they used to do in your day and mine, now gone by, Miss Susan."

This home-thrust sent Miss Susan's hand again to her pocket for the snuff-box.

Mrs. Bell went on. "Grace has enough to wear her down, anxiety, and nursing, and her brother's death. They were perfectly devoted to one another."

"Humph! so I've been told. She had unbounded influence over him, I know. Of that we had proof in his marriage. She made the match, out and out."

"No disparagement to her if she did!" contended Mrs. Bell. "Some who had less right to interfere, would have rejoiced to assist him in the choice of a wife, and not suited him at that."

Two stabs from the charitable old lady in the same number of minutes! The high bridge of Miss Susan's nose trembled with the powerful sniff that drew in the aromatic dust from her thumb and forefinger. Sne rapped the painted lid, to be ready for the next emergency.

"Well! well! you see what has come of this affair. She hasn't much room for bragging of her work. Her brother is dead and her friend a widow!"

"Miss Susan! Miss Susan!" her hands upraised devoutly. "If you hope to obtain mercy for yourself, be merciful! One would suppose that you triumph in the troubles of your neighbors. Not that I believe it, but you do shock me, imputing blame to those whose misfortunes call for pity; whose sorrows are directly from the hand of the Lord. Just picture to yourself that lone lamb a widow, in the very month that first saw her a wife! It's enough to make a heart of stone ache!"

"She was a flighty, flirting butterfly," replied Miss Susan, flintily. "It is to be hoped that this affliction will sober her, and be sanctified to her good."

Here something sounded through my head like a breaking string. I gasped and fainted.

Dr. Hamner held my wrist and Mrs. Bell bathed my face, when I could see again. Annie leaned upon the post where the fiendish hag had squatted.

"Where is she?" I said, staring around me.

"Who, dear Grace?" questioned Mrs. Bell and Annie together.

"She—the one that said Grace Leigh was dying! I saw her and heard those very words."

Mother and daughter exchanged glances.

"You are dreaming, my love," answered the latter.

The doctor's bushy eyebrows met in his frown. "What stuff has been talked in her hearing?" he snarled. "You are a goose, Grace Leigh, and your *she* whoever she is, is a greater. 'Dying,' forsooth! I dare you to die without my leave! If I live as many years as you have got in advance of you, I shall bury my great-grandchildren. People don't die in this degenerate age for less than two doctors. Six would not kill you. Pah ! pooh ! confound meddlers, I say !"

This gruff vaporing was a sedative to me, and decided my doubts as to whether I were really in the flesh.

I smiled, and he nodded.

"That is sensible ! If you speak before I am through my story, I will cut your tongue out, and then, as a spunky woman, you will *not* live, out of spite. Where are you ? At Mrs. Bell's, with Annie to cry over and nurse you. How did you get here ? You were trundled in a wheel-barrow by old Zack, who found you in the road, and strained his back in hoisting you into his vehicle. What were you doing on the ground ? You are too hard for me. The most plausible theory is that you tripped your toe, or twisted your foot, or swooned, or performed some other feat as characteristic of your sex, and in falling, cut your head with a pointed stone that lay, as we Irishmen say, 'convaynient.' Now, you have all the information you could ask for, if you were to gabble half a day, and as talking is thus proved to be irrational, be a rational animal, and eat your breakfast instead—a light luncheon, which old Molly will be offended if you refuse."

"One question, doctor !" I said, feebly.

"Out with it then ! and mind that you know how to count, for I won't hear more. I am sent for in a plagued hurry to see a man who has the croup, chicken-pox and consumption, and was dying of each when the messenger left him. What is it ?"

"When did I hurt myself ?"

He rammed his fists into the huge pockets of his great-coat. "That is more Mrs. Bell's business than mine. You have trespassed upon her for bed and board and messes uncountable, since yesterday afternoon."

"Then I cannot be very ill," I was about to say, but he threatened me with an imaginary gash in his own tongue, and

I held mine. With the weakness, I had the docility of a child.

Dawn superseded candle-light. The doctor, warning us with assurances of his speedy and overwhelming vengeance, if we dared to speak a monosyllable, beckoned to Mrs. Bell, and Annie was my only attendant. I would have addressed her, had she not put her finger to her lips, in token that she was an accomplice of the facetious physician in whatever the scheme was he had on foot—some jest, I was foolish enough to imagine. I poorly merited his epithet of "rational animal," for my mind was torpid, while the physical portion of me lazily enjoyed the sensuous ease of the slumbering nerves and relaxed muscles, the *dolce far niente* of the earliest stages of convalescence. My bed was soft, the chamber summer in temperature, and my once ever-active imagination could conjure up no Elysium equal to a perpetuation of my present state, no horror exceeding the pang of moving. The window-curtain was pushed aside by a chair, undesignedly set against it, and through the aperture not an inch wide, a sunbeam found entrance. The motes, rising to starry lustre in the golden stream, sinking to annihilation below it, were my playfellows, until the ray narrowed to a pencil, the pencil to a line, the line to a hair-stroke, and the sun had passed. Then I slept and awoke that I might gain a relish for another nap. The doctor's burly figure was beside me several times—why, I had no idea. Conjecture upon this or any other subject was too troublesome for the Sybarite body, and it might have drugged its nobler mate with Lethean waters, so abject was its submission. During all the day I heard not a footstep or a voice. My waiters were bodiless mutes for all the noise they made. It was kind in them, I thought, and the exertion of this trifling amount of gratitude was an opiate that lasted me two hours.

I dreamed that I had other visitors, benign in presence and loving in deed, for they sprinkled my couch and anointed my forehead and hands with fragrant essences. I stirred at waking, and there was a flutter of unfurling wings, while on my hand, resting upon the counterpane gleamed a tear-pearl, not yet cold. A vase, in dimension suited for a doll's centre-table, had been placed on a stand by the bed, and from it sprang a pale-green stem, bearing six white hyacinth-bells. I counted them carefully, after divers unsuccessful attempts, and perceived their odor, so delicate, it seemed but the lingerings of my dream. The spring floweret recompensed me for the absence of the sun-ray, for it was always there to greet my eyes. In the darkest hour of night, the taper afforded me light to discern the snowy petals bowing meek in rest or humility. Fragile as they were, a knowledge of my real condition would have led to a doubt whether they might not, in fading, be strewed upon my coffin, or still blooming, still fragrant, be pressed by my dead hands over a motionless heart.

But the morrow broke, brightened and wasted, and evening found me yet alive and conscious to all pleasant influences, oblivious of the existence of pain and woe, just breathing enough to show that I lived; just sensible enough to prove myself a "rational animal."

CHAPTER XV.

The faces of Mrs. Bell and Annie were more cheerful, that of Dr. Hamner graver upon the third day, and one skilled in the knowledge of the character of each, would, from these signs, have augured well for the patient. The eccentric knight of gallipots and powders was happiest in situations that would have distracted an ordinary man, and dismal, when others saw every reason for rejoicing. It was a common saying that he cracked jokes with dying men and swore at those who recovered. It is certain that his jests to me at this morning call, were fewer and more forced than upon prior occasions, when he had arrogated as his prerogative, the whole of the conversation carried on in the sick-room. The fourth, he was reserved and moody ; the fifth, cross.

"I am better, thank you !" I replied to his salutation.

"I am glad you have the grace to thank me for it," he growled. "You will be as short of memory as the rest of them by the time you can stand upon your feet. Put out your tongue ! That's the way the world goes ! How can I feel your pulse when your hand is bobbing this way and that ? It is 'dear doctor,' and tears and blessings, when Death is knocking at the door, and when I have, by fisticuffs, and kicks and wrestling, day and night, driven off the bugbear, the tune is changed. 'What an old bear !' 'A shockingly rough, vulgar creature, whom we would not patronize, you know, if he were not the only experienced physician in this part of the county, you know, and one must submit in illness to a great many disagreeable things, you know, my dear,'" mimicking the languishing lisp of a fine lady. "It is downright laziness that fools you into keeping your bed; yet I should lose your custom, and thereby, a thick slice of my bread and butter, if I did not humor you—treat you according to your folly."

"I think I am rather weak, doctor," I said, in timid expostulation, persuaded, notwithstanding, that I was in some degree culpable, so emphatic was his declaration of the cheat I was playing.

"And so would Samson have been 'rather weak,' if he had steamed between the blankets for eight days, and been coddled with toast and panado. Mrs. Bell, have you obeyed orders with regard to that old maid—I beg your pardon—and hers! that youthful friend of the very undecided age, who is addicted to snuff and evil-speaking?"

He withdrew to the fire-place as he spoke, and Mrs. Bell's reply was undistinguishable. Not so his.

"My respects to her if she shows her peaked phiz within your doors again upon a similar errand, and say that, ignorant quack as she thinks me, I can kill those who are green enough to employ me, without her valuable assistance; and that when I am so bereft of brains as to go into partnership with a woman, she won't stand more than a fifth-rate chance of the appointment."

"Doctor, when may I go home?" I inquired.

"To-morrow!" said he, tersely.

"Are they well at Moss-side?"

"Yes; and I have pocketed a bribe to imprison you here so long as I can manufacture pretexts for doing so—they get on so grandly without you."

I laughed.

"It is the truest word you have heard me speak to-day, Miss, believe it or not, as you choose! But you may go home to spite them whenever you are ready. Get up! stir around! never mind if your head is giddy! that is not a fault, but nature in female brains. Go down stairs to dinner, walk out with Annie this afternoon, and by the morning you will be as strong as an elephant. If you prefer to travel in style, Zack's wheelbarrow is at your service. A bottle of opodeldoc will be an acceptable reward for any further demands of that sort."

"Nonsense!" said I. "I cannot walk down stairs and up again."

"Then, lie still!"

"Why have not my father and Lilly been to see me?" I asked, revealing my wounded feeling.

"Where was the use? You did nothing but sleep, sleep, sleep like a beggar in the sunshine. They were here yesterday, the day before, and the day before that—saw you breathe and heard you snore. You must not look for them again in a week. They cannot wade through snow a foot deep."

I cast my eyes unbelievingly to the window.

"Don't credit that either, hey? Jump up and see for yourself! Oho! you can't? Until you can, trust the report of veracious people!"

"Annie," I said, when he had gone, "has there been a snow-storm?"

"Not such an one as the doctor described," she returned, "but the ground is covered."

"Then Lilly ought not to venture out," I soliloquized.

My hands were in their usual position on the outside of the bed, and as I lifted one, the light was visible through the wasted fingers, as through mother-of-pearl, a phenomenon that filled me with amazement.

Annie marked the motion and my expression.

"You did not know how thin you had grown—did you? You must reflect that you have taken a very small quantity of nourishment and no exercise since Dr. Hamner has been your jailer."

"In eight days!" I said. "I had not supposed that one could fall away as I have done in that time."

"You have the evidence of your own sight," Annie replied. "Do not be discouraged. Take heart and recruit with like rapidity. You are decidedly better to-day, the doctor says. He recommends, however, that you talk very little. What an antipathy he professes to our sex! He has a kind heart, though, and has been unwearied in his cares to you. It is a sore temptatation to be with you when I must be dumb, but I will try to resist it for your sake. I am impatient to have you up and well. Now! silence is the order of the day."

This is, perhaps, the most appropriate place for me to recount the incidents of my rescue from a watery grave and my transportation to the abode of the benevolent widow. Old Zack was, on the forenoon of my adventure, foraging in the woods adjacent to the pond, for game in the shape of hares and partridges, and light-wood for torches and kindlings, attended by Sultan. Drawn towards the lake by the sound of Lilly's laughter, he was in sight of us at the moment of the catastrophe, had I looked for other succor than what I could extend. Hale and sound in wind, he reached us as speedily as a young man could have done. His shout was unheard in my frantic haste. Lilly was cast almost to his feet, and the waves had not closed after me when the Newfoundland dashed in among the fractured ice. Lilly was unhurt, and thoughtless of her freezing apparel in her concern for me. Zack dispatched her, piloted by the sagacious Sultan, to his mistress's house, bidding her "run fast to keep life in herself and me;" enfolded me in his shaggy dreadnought coat; disposed me ingeniously in his hand-cart, and trundled, as if fifty lives, more precious than mine, hung upon his celerity.

The reason of the solitude where Lilly had promised me we should see all the working force of the plantation, was, that my father, upon a personal survey of the premises, differed from the man whose report Lilly had heard, and declaring the ice too thin for his purpose, postponed getting it out until the following day. The hands dispersed to other avocations, and he, by a singular coincidence, rode by Mrs. Bell's to inquire how she fared in the inclement weather. He had arisen to go home, when the door was burst inwards by Lilly, beside herself with fright and distress. Annie carried her off to bed, and the others hastened in quest of me. In falling—and this was anohter crumb of truth in the doctor's fiction, founded upon fact—I had received a wound in the temple, not from a "convenient" stone, but a more formidable projection, jagging the side of the air-hole. The cut was dangerous, the blow severe. The night of Miss Susan's neighborly watch was the eighth of my delirium, instead of the second, as they would have had me believe. The imperious Irishman prohibited the utterance of anything that could recall the memory of my accident, justly fearing its agitating effects. Upon his accommodating conscience, he imposed the inventions that slipped like oil from his tongue, when, for the success of his art, he considered it necessary to do evil that good might come.

These details were doled out to me as my insatiate inquiries demanded some satisfaction. The whole story was not gained until I could sit up in my room, and Aunt Molly's arms were the palanquin, wherein I rode down to the lower story every day to dinner. The old woman and her husband regarded me as their foster-child, in right of my deliverance by the last-named. They were privileged dependents, never feeling their servitude, and more prone to speaking their whole minds than was their nominal mistress. Their propriety in me they asserted jealously. Zack paid his respects in my chamber the same day that my father was admitted to a waking interview ; and every luxury the country afforded at that season was, through his instrumentality, provided for me. Sultan, too, he trained to march up stairs at his heels, and bear a part in the ceremonial of the audience vouchsafed to him. Thus they presented themselves, the morning of the day fixed for my going home. Zack stood near the door; my canine preserver walked up and touched my hand with his nose. I patted him—license, as he understood it, to rest his black muzzle upon my knee, and while I talked to Zack, his intelligent eyes never quitted my face.

"I wish I could tell you how much obliged I am for what you have done, old fellow," said I to him. "He looks as if he might know what I am saying, Uncle Zack."

"He does, Miss Grace. Dat cretur is 'nough sight smarter dan most folks. When you fell into dat ar hole he never waited for no orders, but before you could say 'Jack Robinson,' he duv straight down arter you."

"I owe him a great deal, Uncle Zack, but much more to you. I shall never forget your goodness in saving my life and waiting on me while I was sick."

"'Taint nothin' to speak of, Miss Grace. Anybody might 'a done all dat and not 'served 'thank ye' for it. I'se mighty glad I happened along jest in de nick of time. Sultan, dar! he was de feller what worked—warn't you, Sultan?"

"Ah, Uncle Zack! I have heard the story from beginning to end; how you rolled your wheelbarrow up the steepest side of the hill, because it was a shorter way than by the path; and I was a heavier load then than now."

"You was dat!" showing his teeth. "You warnt a bag of feathers, I can tell you, yet I never knowed but what you was, 'till I see yer pa and mistis running up to me. *Den* my arms did ache, I 'low. But for all dat I never strained my back, if Dr. Hamner did say so."

My father had deposited with me a sum of money, that I might tender him and his wife a substantial token of my grateful remembrance, and I here begged him to accept his share of it. He hung back, in an awkward dilemma betwixt his dislike to receive what appeared to be remuneration of his services, and his dread of wounding me.

"We don't want no pay, Miss Grace," he stammered, twirling his sorry wool hat and shuffling from foot to foot. "Me and Sultan would 'a done jest de same for any drownin' dumb beast, let alone one we sot so much store by—one of our chillen, as it might be. You and Miss Annie stans pretty nigh together in we-all's hearts—don't dey, Sultan?"

Sultan gave his affirmative wag, and looked back to my face.

"And de ole woman—she feels jest zactly as we do—don't you, Molly? So, Miss Grace, if you'll 'member us as friends, and drop over to see us whenever you can spar' time, we won't say no more 'bout money."

"I don't mean to *pay* you, Uncle Zack. I am not rich enough to do that. This is for you to buy a keepsake with, something to remember me by, when I leave you."

By dint of reasoning and a feint of hurt feeling, I finally carried my point.

"Aunt Molly," said I, as she shut him out. "I hope you listened to what I told Uncle Zack, for I have not strength to go over it again to you. Will you please take this from me?"

"If it will pleasure you, Miss Grace. You can't help knowing dat I don't like to do it."

"I do know it, Aunt Molly, but I must make you do as I say, this once," dropping the purse into her hand. "You have been like a mother to me. God bless you for it!"

"I pray night and mornin' dat He will, Miss Grace!" was the unexpected reply. "I will never be satisfied, I tell Him, widout He answers my prayer. I says to Him, 'You been snatch her from de water whar she would 'a found her death; now save her from de second death! Dis is de blessin' I asks.' You've thanked Zack and Sultan and me for de little He lef us to do. We didn't deserve it, but He does. His mercy calls for everlastin' praises out of your mouth."

She was not so garrulous as her stronger half, and now courtesied respectfully and left the room. Pious negroes rarely omit an opportunity to cast in "a word in season." Every occasion of universal joy or calamity, a marriage, a death, illness and recovery, are to them seed-times. Molly had not withheld her hand, and the Lord of the harvest would count her guiltless, although she sowed upon a rocky wayside.

At noon arrived the carriage, with my father, to take me away. Annie was to accompany us and remain at Moss-side a day or two. Mrs. Bell wept over me, in saying "good-bye," and I was too weak to refuse an answering tear. Dr. Hamner rode up, in his sulkiest temper, as we were starting, and was careful that we should not be flattered by what he represented as "a chance encounter, he having forgotten that he had given me leave to decamp." He felicitated Mrs. Bell upon this riddance, and claimed her thanks as his due for having contrived it; counselled my father to the purchase, or loan, if he could not be bought, of Sultan, to guard me in my peregrinations; scowled at me, and gallopped off in his accustomed "plagued hurry."

We had another, and a less agreeable meeting on the route. At the fork of the road, Mr. Townley ambled by on his glossy sorrel. He raised his hat to the carriage, and sent in a search-warrant glance through the window. Annie supported me upon the back seat. I was looking towards him and met his gaze. He changed countenance, perhaps in surprise, perhaps in remorse for past cruelty to the ghost-like being whose life seemed trembling upon a breath; perhaps with far dissimilar emotions called forth by seeing me in that locality.

"He startled you, did he not?" inquired Annie.

I murmured something in response, and put my hand upon the

scarred temple which throbbed at the least excitement. My father's scrutiny was not foiled by this pretence of physical ailment. He became serious despite his efforts to wear an unruffled front to me. What he discovered, it was impossible for me to conceive, but I had a presentiment that he was not far from guessing the truth.

Dear old Moss-side! It's familiar loveliness caused a vibration of a rusted chord in my bosom—bare as was its grove, sere its verdure. Lilly came flying down to the gate, and close after her was Martha, sobbing hysterically behind her clean apron. My aunt met me with a fervent but silent greeting, and she, likewise, drew out her handkerchief the next minute. I did not wonder at this invariable manifestation of pity, when I saw myself in the mirror in my room. At Mrs. Bell's I was an invalid, and examined the reflection of my figure daily for signs of improvement; elated when Annie's observations, joined to mine, detected a tinge of healthier coloring, or we imagined that an angle was plumping into a curve. Here the image I had seen equipped for our ill-starred walk, was as plainly before me as if it were painted upon the glass, and within the same frame, were features, scared by their own shadow; the forehead bloodless as bone; the hair dropped short on one side, scanty and ragged on the other; lack-lustre eyes; cheeks pallid and shrunken, and lips streaked with the black lines of fever. Fascinated by the contrast which should have occasioned a recoil, I looked long and fixedly; then turning away I avoided the sight for weeks afterward. A morbid, selfish distaste for society had made me a recluse before my sickness; necessity, backed by pride, secluded me now. Yet with the accessories of debility and mortified vanity, discontent was not so absolute in its dominion as when health and good looks were unimpaired.

The white hyacinth, her offering beside my sick-bed, was an apt emblem of Lilly herself. As through eventless hours, when although I knew it not, I was balanced between Life and Death, I had feasted my dim eyes upon its chaste beauty, inhaled its subtle perfume as a breath of healing, so, in my days of languishing and tedious recovery, I drank in vitality from her companionship and affection. Spring advanced punctually; garden and field and forest lured her abroad, but no extravagance of temptation had power over her, when she fancied that I needed her. While away from me her every act evinced a thought for my solace. A very Flora, she would appear in my presence, garlanded with leaves and flowers, and bringing for me blossoms of her choosing, she would suffer no one else to cull; wild violets, forget-me-nots, tender-eyed innocents, and anemones, you felt it would be cruel to handle roughly. These decorated my apartment and conversed with me of her in her absence. "May she not be to me the harbinger of a new spring?" Hope sometimes whispered; but my familiar demon, the cockatrice-egg which had hatched a viper, put to death the friendly intruder. "The human heart has but one spring"—it hissed. "You have had yours; gathered its flowers, eaten its fruits."

One Sabbath forenoon, I was alone at home, the others, including my aunt, having gone to church. I was nearly well, and wearying of confinement, I strolled over the garden until my faltering limbs and labored respiration impelled me to rest in the summer-house, so frequently mentioned in former chapters. The grass was warm, as I laid out my feet in the sunshine; the bees were humming over the strawberry beds and in the apple trees; and the birds, unsinning Sabbath-breakers, were discussing and working upon the architecture of their nests.

Who has not recognized in the resemblance of one day to some other anniversary of soul or affections, an influence more moving than is exerted by a fac-simile likeness of face to face? It may be the light of a mellow autumn sun, the scent of ripening orchards, or the spectacle of fields of billowing grain, that acts upon the tide of feeling. "How like!" you say. It is all the tongue can do, but memory is busy. What matter that the bearded grass tinkles its seeds in paths you trod that September noon; that brambles bind the clods above the form then walking or sitting beside you; that the orchard is now a thoroughfare, barren and dusty, and the fertile field a naked common? Ten, twenty, fifty years are but a second to the leaping mind—and you have everything as it was then. But were you to stand bodily, at such a time, upon the self-same spot, and with the same air and sky and sun, find your other surroundings unchanged, save that you are there *alone*—this is a concurrence of associations, a blending of cherished objects to create a blank, that racks the stoutest spirit—yet a pain, the heart would not exchange, intense as it is, for actual present pleasure.

Such bitter-sweet meditations were mine. This was the counterpart, in atmosphere and scenery, of Frederic's last day at the homestead. I recapitulated its incidents; sat with him on the brown bench; hearkened to his pleading, and deputed Duty to reply. His concluding sentence arrested me. "I have too recently began to lean upon a higher power myself to instruct you, but, dear sister, there is a strength that revives, while it supports; not only lifts the drooping head, but gladdens the sick heart. My hopeful prayer is that you may seek this."

In instant connection followed Molly's, "Save her from the second death! This is the blessing I ask. I will never be satisfied without He answers that prayer."

"One entreated consolation for me, the other safety," I mused. "Was their object one? if so, what is it? Why do I say to-day that these prayers are not yet answered?"

To this inquiry I was unable to reply. I, the offspring of Christian parents, dedicated to the Lord in my cradle;

instructed in the faith, learned in theological disquisitions, was as dumb as the most benighted heathen, when this direct question was propounded. My knowledge of my misery, it is unnecessary to repeat, was perfect as any lesson was likely to be which had been so diligently and incessantly conned. The assurance that comfort was in store, if I would seek it, was soothing—but why safety? Why am I endangered? by what?"

"By sin," replied my orthodox memory.

"Sin—sin"—I said, reflectively. "As an idea, an abstraction, I comprehend it; but what are my offences against the moral law? what transgressions have made me amenable to its offended majesty?"

Then I recollected the remark of a beggar-woman, whose necessities I once relieved. Soaked with rain, and soiled with mud, she knocked at our door, and spread before us her pitiful case—a dying husband and starving babes. "Miss," she said to me, when needful succor had been extended; "I am a sinful creature, I know, but it does appear to me that all my punishment must be in this world."

And under this impression, I gathered the mangled remains of the hopes, the blackening corses of the joys that had walked, hand in hand with me, in life's morning, and heaped them in the sight of Heaven, a propitiation for my iniquities. In return, I demanded peace and exemption from further chastisement, here and hereafter. I had beforetime tried the efficacy of meritorious works—self-denial, penance of the flesh—and the structure, irreproachable in my estimation, had been filled to its sandy foundation by an unlooked-for flood.

"All Thy waves and Thy billows have gone over me!" I prayed. "Will not they suffice to cleanse whatever pollution adheres to my soul?" I sued not as a beggar, but as one who had a right to the privileges of the children of the Kingdom. The filling lungs, the healthful bound of the blood, the re-strung muscles had acted sympathetically upon the mental system. I was tired of a monotony of grief, and graciously willing to accept what degree of happiness I had capacity to enjoy, ready for a change, and since an external one was improbable, this introversion of vision was most natural. The consideration of insurance against danger—"the second death" of Molly's prayer—was secondary to that of temporal tranquillity. Nor do I believe that signal deliverance from peril predisposes the heart to repentance, makes it a better absorbent of Divine truth, after the peril is over. If while I had stood at the entrance of the dark valley, my position had been described to me, I would have quailed in mortal fear; but now, that every step carried me further from the frowning gates, the remembrance that I had well-nigh passed them begot hardihood, not gratitude. It is this rarely-absent peculiarity of human nature that causes its students to sigh in doubt, scarcely removed from hopelessness, over what are called "death-bed repentances;" and the histories of a large proportion of those who have recovered after such an experience, add powerful testimony to the truth of this opinion. Unswayed, then, by fear, unmoved by a review of the mercy which my sable instructress had told me, "deserved everlasting praises from my mouth," I asked a renewal of heart and conduct—regeneration—while I secretly ignored its necessity; reformation, while I held my daily walk and conversation to be worthy of a sanctified believer.

The sun shone; the birds sang; the bees hummed—and "through Nature" I strove to "look up to Nature's God." Gentle, faithful teachers are her voices to him whose ears have been first opened to the accents of heavenly wisdom; who traces everywhere the signet of his Father; hears in every breeze whispered messages of that Father's love. To the carnal and unspiritual, this book of revelation is in a dead language. My prayers ascended no higher than my head ; the aspirations I labored to make devout, were disjointed lip-service, interrupted by wandering thoughts and fits of forgetfulness, leading me off and away from the golden ladder, I tried to vision from earth to the foot of the throne.

"I do not progress an inch," I said, at last, in fretful discouragement. "My mind grows more misty ; my heart more cold. Yet there must be some meaning in the theme that engages so many lofty intellects and melts the hardest hearts—the reconcilement of man to God."

The rattle of carriage wheels disturbed my solitude, and tones, clearer, more sweet than the bird-music were heard. "Auntie dear ! where are you ?"

"I will ask Lilly," I resolved, as I obeyed the call.

CHAPTER XVI.

It was Lilly's practice to resort to my chamber when dinner was dispatched on Sabbath afternoons, and, when after a detention of half an hour in my aunt's room, I went to my own, I expected confidently to see the demure little figure in her rocking-chair in the chimney corner, intent upon a volume of Scripture stories, or something else from her "Sunday library," as she had named the uppermost of her book shelves.

The chair was vacant; the books untouched. I seated myself to wait, doubting not that a few minutes would bring her to her post. Fifteen loitered by, and full of my scheme, I was impatient of the unreasonable delay. I sauntered to the window overlooking the kitchen-yard and its background of cabins. In the largest of these, which was tenanted by John's mother, I saw, through the door, a circle of dusky forms surrounding my missing fairy. Her head was bending towards the book from which she read—a book, I knew at that distance, for her Bible—and on the still air an occasional reverent cadence arose to my window. I compared this scene with the formal readings my aunt used to hold on the evening of the hallowed day; the upright, uneasy postures of the victims ranged around the dining-room; nay, with my unsuccessful endeavors to secure punctual attendance when, to fill up every hour with tasks, I appointed meetings for a like purpose. The seriously-inclined, the church-members, mostly the middle-aged and the old, were always in their places; but the ear of the younger ones, the belles and beaux, and the children I could never gain. A group of these last sat upon their heels on the ground in front of Lilly; Martha and Milly, the smartest coquettes on the plantation, stood at the back of her chair, decorous and unsmiling, although more than one gallant visitor was in the audience; and the harum-scarum Joe, arrayed for a courting expedition, permitted his pet cane to be stolen, as it dangled from his finger, and converted into a hobby-horse by a sly rogue, not out of his petticoats, while the colored Brummel leaned within the door, one foot upon the step, his hand supporting his chin in an attitude of charmed attention.

"'A little child shall lead them,'" I found myself repeating. "O for their impressible natures and her undoubting faith!"

When her step sounded on the stair, I was reclining, with my habitual air of lassitude, upon the lounge, a book closed upon my finger, as if I had been studying.

"Where have you been, Lilly?" I inquired, carelessly.

"To Aunt Amy's cabin," she said, a slight glow coloring her brow.

"She must have been very entertaining to keep you so long," I said, but without rebuke.

She paused, then answered firmly, as if to overcome the rising shyness, "I have been reading, Auntie—reading from the Bible. They cannot learn much in it for themselves—that is, most of them cannot."

"You are very right, dear. You could not have been better employed. Is this the only time you have done this?"

"No, ma'am. Grandpapa said he had no objection; that he quite approved of the plan, so I go out whenever they send for me, and then you see, Auntie dear, there is no danger of my putting myself in their way."

"How happened you to think of this first?" asked I.

"While you were at Mrs. Bell's I read a good deal to Aunt

Agnes, and as one of the servants stayed constantly in the room, several of them heard me, and one Sunday, Milly brought me word from her mother that they would like to hear a chapter or two from the Bible, and I went."

Her somewhat anxious vindication of herself from the suspicion of officiousness, and her lowly hearers from any personal partiality in their choice of a reader, was at once interesting and amusing.

"I, too, have a favor to ask," said I. "Are you too tired to read to me, just as you have been doing to the servants?"

"No, indeed, ma'am, if you wish to hear me."

She spoke diffidently, and I accounted for the request by saying, "My head feels badly, and the sound of your voice will relieve it."

"That is so like mamma!" exclaimed she. "She often set me to read for her when she was sick, too restless to lie quiet or to sleep, and then she would have no book except the Bible. If she were easier, and strong enough to hold the book herself, the one that she liked next best was 'Rutherford's Letters;' but I could not understand that so well. She said the Bible soothed her better than medicine."

I felt like a convicted hypocrite as this artless parallel was drawn. Lilly was turning the leaves of her precious volume.

"She marked ever so many chapters that we studied together. Have you any choice, Auntie, or shall I read you one of her favorites?"

"I shall like it, I am sure," I said. "Begin where you please."

Her selection was the portion containing the parables of the ten virgins and the talents delivered to the three servants, and my personal application of the moral of each was, on the whole, satisfactory to my self-love. I was not drowsy or slothful. If my lamp were not trimmed and burning, it was not because I had spared any pains to procure oil—and was I not searching for light even now? My talents, by which I understood, not only the mental endowments generally so called, but all opportunities for doing good—I had exerted to the utmost in my limited sphere. Had it not passed into a proverb that my labors of disinterested benevolence were undermining youth and health? The Pharisee spirit advanced a step nearer the Holy of Holies, and spiced its petition, or, more properly speaking, its demand, with a boastful show of good works.

Lilly was reading more slowly when my thoughts fixed themselves again:

"'He is despised and rejected of men; a man of sorrows and acquainted with grief; and we hid, as it were, our faces from him; he was despised and we esteemed him not.

"'Surely'—and there was a feeling, although involuntary stress laid upon the word—"'*Surely* he hath borne our griefs and carried our sorrows; yet we did esteem him stricken, smitten of God and afflicted.

"'But he was wounded for our transgressions; he was bruised for our iniquities; the chastisement of our peace was laid upon him, and with his stripes we are healed.

"'All we, like sheep, have gone astray; we have turned every one to his own way, and the Lord hath laid on him the iniquity of us all.'"

Her voice sank almost to a whisper as she proceeded with the sublimely mournful prophecy, and when it was finished, she did not offer to follow it with another chapter. Her stool was by the head of my resting-place, she leaned back out of the range of sight, and laid her forehead against the cushions.

I took the book from her, and read for myself the page that had pierced my soul.

"He was wounded for *our* transgressions; he was bruised for *our* iniquities."'

"For mine?" I inly questioned. "What was my share in this intolerable chastisement?"

"*We have turned every one to his own way.*" A lambent flame seemed to leap along each letter.

My "own way?" I *had* chosen it; turned to it; persisted in it; been torn by its thorns; suffocated in its quagmires; lashed by its furies—had clung to my muck-rake, which only heaped up miserable garbage—odious poisons—while, from the strait way beyond, beckoned this loving One, borne down by my griefs, carrying my sorrows, yet loving still—entreating still—and when, at the Father's chastisement, I plunged on in my mad course, even more reckless of danger or His pitying call—lamenting, with more than a mother's yearning over her wandering child—"You will not come unto me that you may have life!"

"Lilly," I said, breaking the troubled silence, "did your mamma ever explain this chapter to you?"

"Yes, ma'am—often."

Less ignorantly, but as earnestly as inquired the Ethiopian prince concerning the same passages, I asked—"Of whom did she say that the prophet is here speaking?"

She did not mistrust my design, but was not so simple as to be imposed upon by my affected want of knowledge. Thinking that I intended to examine her upon this one of her early lessons, she replied promptly, "Of Our Saviour."

I should have said, "Of Christ," and in the very common form of expression she employed, I felt the power of a new beauty, a richer depth of meaning.

Availing myself of her willingness to be catechised, I continued—"When were these prophecies fulfilled?"

This was too general a question. She asked me for her book before she could reply, and the perplexity did not leave her countenance after she had re-perused the portion under inquiry.

"It is hard to answer you, Auntie, without going over it all, a verse at a time, and that would tire you."

"Take as much time as you like, and tell me in your own way, dear."

"Mamma showed me that part of this was fulfilled while Our Saviour was upon earth—in His works and sufferings, and his being despised and rejected by the Jews, His own people, who did not believe that He was wounded for their transgressions and bruised for their iniquities, when He died upon the cross to save them. They thought that He was smitten by God for his own sins; that He was as wicked as the two thieves they crucified with Him!"

"You said that this partly fulfilled the prediction—how and when did the rest come to pass?" maintaining my character of catechist.

"She told me that sinners in every quarter of the world were now rejecting Him; not only the poor heathen, and Jews, and Mahometans, but in Christian countries, those that will not take Him for their Saviour, who do not love Him and pray to Him, and trust Him to show them the way to heaven."

"But if they believe that He is the son of God, and everything else that the Bible teaches, and break none of His commandments, yet are not Christians—what then?"

"They cannot keep the commandments unless they are His children and He helps them," she replied, confidently. "I don't mean that they will lie, and steal, and kill—but you know, Auntie dear, a Christian must do a great deal besides."

"Must he? what?"

"Why, Auntie! you talk as seriously as if you were not a million times better and wiser than I am."

I winced, but kept my ground. "I want to hear your ideas, Lilly. You must not forget something else you once told me of your mamma's teachings."

"I remember! I remember! She said I must learn to express my thoughts, and be able to tell what I know, so that others can understand me. I have a notion about your question—one of my own. Will you hear that?"

"I had rather have it than any borrowed one," rejoined I. She was speaking from the heart, not reciting now.

"You saved my life last February, Auntie, dear—almost died to do it. What would you or anybody else say if I were never to thank you for it; if I did not love you better than I ever did before, and loved twenty other people just in the same way; if I were to run off every morning because I did not like to stay with you, and spend all the day in the woods with naughty children who hated you, and whom you had forbidden me to play with; if I were not to think of you oftener than I could help; and when I came home at night, should eat the supper you had fixed and go to sleep in your bed without speaking to, or kissing you? Why I would be worse than Sancho, for you can't coax him from me; he follows me everywhere, and says 'thank you' as plainly as a dog can."

"Very well!" I said. "Go on!"

"The Saviour has done more for us than you could ever do for me. He died to save us from everlasting punishment; He gives us our lives, and homes, and friends, and when we are wicked and sin against God, He begs Him to forgive us. Mamma said that was the meaning of His making intercession for the transgressors. Oh!" she added, holy fervor outspeaking in eye and voice—"He is *so* good! 'the chief among ten thousand, and altogether lovely!' and I do love Him with all my soul—don't you, Auntie?"

"I am afraid not, Lilly."

The child gazed at me in utter amazement—incredulity, wonder, grief, chasing each other over her truth-telling face; and when I sustained the look with a gravity that forbade the sup position that I was jesting, or wished to try her faith, she burst into tears, and threw herself down beside me.

"Auntie! dearest Auntie! you were not in earnest! Please take it back!"

"I cannot, Lilly. I would not have said it, if I had dreamed that it would have affected you so, but I spoke the truth. Forgive me, love."

She kissed me, and sobbed, instead of speaking.

"You will hate me now you know how wicked I am," I said, even in that moment, thinking more of the loss of her love than of the cause of her grief.

"No! no!" winding her arm around my neck; "but I am so sorry! I thought, I thought"——

"That Auntie was a Christian," I supplied what she could not articulate.

"Do not cry so bitterly, darling! Perhaps you can help to make her one."

She started up. "If I could! but I cannot do anything—nobody on earth can! Won't you pray to our Saviour to teach you to love Him? Don't you want to be one of His people?"

"Indeed I do, Lilly!" and I uttered it in deep sincerity.

Her beloved Bible was again her resource. A drop from her wet lashes fell among its leaves, as she hurriedly sought the texts she wanted.

"'Come now and let us reason together, saith the Lord. Though your sins be as scarlet, they shall be white as snow; though they be red like crimson, they shall be as wool.

"'Ask, and ye shall receive; seek, and ye shall find; knock, and it shall be opened unto you.

"'Him that cometh unto me, I will in no wise cast out.'

"He loves *you*, dear Auntie!" was her comment, in tender reproach, as she rested her head upon my shoulder.

"I will try to be what you wish, dear one!" I murmured, humbled to a sense of the nature of the state which had produced such pain for this innocent, right-hearted child. This agitation, flowing from a cause apparently so unlikely to create it in one of her age, would have struck me as unnatural had I seen it in any other person. Nor, with my thorough knowledge of her religious training, her conscientious observance of sacred duties, her extreme tenderness of feeling, had I anticipated the shock my declaration would give her. I had no doubt of her piety, whether she had been sanctified in her earliest infancy, or her plastic nature been gradually moulded by the Spirit of Grace, under the teachings of the mother, whose last months had been devoted to her. My error was in overlooking the fact that she had never been instigated to seek examples of the class of so-called "Christian" unbelievers, she had portrayed. "Mamma" had informed her that there were such, and it was entered as a clause of her creed. Her own experience had furnished her with an imaginary illustration of how this anomaly might exist; but in her abounding charity, she attributed a partnership in her Faith to every one she knew and liked. The discovery that she, to whom she had transferred the affection and duties she had paid her mother during her life-time, was a stranger to the love she esteemed essential to earthly happiness and future bliss, confounded her.

She dried her eyes, and, with admirable tact, endeavored to reassure me of her love, without adverting to what had occasioned pain on both sides. She even clung to me with increased devotion, a sort of tender anxiety, as if she would contribute her utmost to fill the void in my heart. All the evening, she was quiet and grave, replying readily and sweetly to whatever was spoken to her, following me with a wistful, loving gaze. Nor did the shadow pass as it had fallen—in a moment. Morning and night as she knelt to present petitions inaudible to mortal hearing, I knew that the sigh and tear mingled with that prayer were for me, and redoubled my self-accusations at the reflection of my unworthiness of such an intercessor. It was a baby-hand that grasped my skirts, but no afflictive judgment had so hindered my downward course.

Imperceptibly, slowly, her mission was accomplished. It was not a child-seer, a creation seraphic and sinless, that turned my feet, but a creature of earthly birth ; inheritor of our human frailties ; sportsome in her childish mirth as her pet lamb ; yet one whom the Saviour of babes and men had taken in His arms and blessed. Led by her, I came, broken in spirit, though not by temporal woes ; a suitor for pardon, not for present ease ; and cast myself where she delighted to bow—at the bleeding feet of the Crucified, to experience the fullness of the promises to those who "shall receive the Kingdom of God as a little child."

CHAPTER XVII.

The burning heats of the dog-days were diversified by heavy rains ; vegetation was rank, premature in growth and in decay. When the sun was not cloaked by clouds, he extracted from marsh, and water-course, and sodden meadows, steaming vapors, reeking with pestilence. In what form the Destroyer would appear amongst us could not be foretold, but we looked forward with certainty to a sickly season. Sanitary rules were in force upon every plantation ; a strict watchfulness was exercised over the improvident menials whom no danger, prospective or present, can incite to care for themselves.

The storm broke alarmingly near to us. Lilly and myself went over, in the cool of the early forenoon, to stay until evening with Annie Bell. I had not heard from her for several days, and doubted not that everything was going on well at the cottage.

"Why, Auntie !" exclaimed Lilly, as we came in sight of it ; "there is Dr. Hamner's horse tied to the rack !"

She was correct. There was no mistaking the gaunt, hard-ridden public-accommodation, or the sheepskin strapped upon the saddle.

His owner stopped us at the gate on his way out.

"Good morrow, young ladies !" in his briskest style. "Upon my soul, Grace, you begin to play the Rose to this Lilly."

"Is any one sick here, doctor ?" I questioned.

"It is going to be a hot day—broiling ! and I have to take whatever comes, if it cooks my brains. Never marry a doctor, Miss Lilly, unless you think a widow's cap becoming to your order of beauty. Human life is uncertain, and death is certain to overtake the doctors before it reaches any other class of men. This has kept me from marrying—a sentiment of refined philanthropy that does honor to the species—if I do say it."

He stood in our path, and unable to obtain the intelligence by my own observation, I pushed him again with the anxious query, "Who is sick here, sir?"

"Ah, yes! I beg your pardon for obliging you to repeat the inquiry. I am growing forgetful in my old age. It is the old woman, and a bad time she is having of it!"

"Not Mrs. Bell!" I ejaculated.

"Och! botheration! Did you ever see me so forgetful of the forms of decency, whatever might be the exigency, as to denominate a respectable, middle-aged matron, with a pretty daughter, too—an 'old woman?' I allude to the wife of the Lord Paramount of these premises."

"Aunt Molly? Is she very ill?"

"Much nearer her end than I thought you were to yours, last winter, when I perjured myself by swearing that I believed you would outlive me. You may yet, in spite of that prophecy; but if she is alive to-night, I shall be surprised. Here!" for I was undoing the gate with impetuous haste; "you need not rush in to deliver my verdict. Not two minutes since I comforted old Zack by the adage we physicians are obliged to wear into flimsy tatters—'While there is life there is hope!' Hold on, I say!" himself holding the latch down with a grip like a vice. "After this, do you and that lily-of-the-valley of yours keep your weak little bodies housed in the heat of the day, or I shall have more practice than I want. Live lightly—not starvingly, understand! but prudently; laugh as often, and mope as seldom as your sentimentalism will allow. My respects to your negroes, one and all, and tell them I will poison—'trick,' as they would say—every one that makes himself sick. Take no medicine, and above all, avoid the sunshine. We are going to have rare works here this summer. Do you hear me, or are you so wrapped up in your concern for dear old Aunt Molly, as to be unmindful of your own danger?"

"I hear you, sir, and thank you;" but I was trembling in every limb, and knew that Lilly's white, shocked face was a reflection of mine.

"That is well! Stay here until evening. There is nothing contagious in this disease. Don't be scared into ever believing that there is. Annie wants you badly, too. As for old Molly, if we were all as fit to die as she is, it would be better to take the same conveyance, without regard to terms. Heaven preserve you both! You have kept me here listening to you too long already. Bless these women's tongues, I say!"

The house was empty, but Annie met me in the back porch, her eyes inflamed with weeping.

"You know, then?" she said, as the fervency of my embrace testified my sympathy.

"Yes; I have seen the doctor."

"What did he say?"

"That 'while there is life there is hope,'" employing, before I thought of it, the very phrase which had sounded like such miserable comfort from him.

"Just as I feared!" she said, sadly. "It is all he can say; you will not leave us to-day, will you, Grace? I was wishing this morning that I had some means of sending for you. I could not ask Uncle Zack to go."

I regretted that Lilly was with me, for Aunt Molly was sinking fast, and I was loth that she should be a spectator of the pangs of dissolution, hear the lament of the bereaved. She divined my trouble, the instant I returned to the room where I had left her, and spoke of my visit to the sick woman.

"You are afraid I will be in the way, are you not, Auntie?" she inquired.

"Not just that, dear Lilly. I fear lest you should be lonely, having to stay in-doors, or be terrified at the idea of Aunt Molly's sufferings."

"You must not feel so—must not think one minute about me. If I can wait on you, help you the least bit, you will call me, and until you do, I can sit here and work—for I brought my sewing—or read; and if I get very tired, I can go to sleep. I will not trouble you."

"You can never trouble any one, darling," I responded.

I found books and pictures, and whistled to Sultan, who lay at the door of Zack's cabin. He arose and obeyed; his hanging head and slow walk indicative of dejection; nor could any arts inveigle him into the house. He licked our hands, wagged his tail in sorrowful recognition of our caresses, sighed, and went back to his post.

"Let him stay, please!" pleaded Lilly, pityingly. "He is too much grieved to play. How strange that he should know!"

Mrs. Bell had been a constant watcher by the bedside since the beginning of her servant's illness, four days before, and was now overpersuaded by us to lie down for an hour. Zack sat on a chest in the darkest corner of the room, his forehead supported by his clasped hands—only echoing, by a suppressed groan, the moan pain forced, now and then, from his patient wife.

In the scorching noon-tide, a shadow fell upon the threshold. Annie did not move or look around, yet the intruder passed directly to her side and took her hand before he noticed me. Molly opened her eyes.

"Mars' Robert! it is good in you to come over so often! I am worse to-day. I am goin' fast!"

"No—no, Molly! I hope not!"—he could just say in a choked voice, "We cannot spare you yet—we can't spare you!"

"It does look as if he"—directing her glance to Zack's crouching figure—"and mistis couldn't spar' me, sure 'nough, Mars' Robert. I donno how they'll git along, but the Almighty

Master does ; He's fixed a way, or he wouldn't have called me so sudden-like. It's *His* time, Mars' Robert ! His will be done" —and less audibly, she added—"in earth as it is in heaven."

She was silent for a minute, then joining her hands, repeated as if she loved each word—

"There's nothing here deserves my joys,
There's nothing here like my God !"

Mrs. Bell was too uneasy to remain away more than the exact length of time she had set, and when she resumed her stand, she observed a change for the worse. Little refreshment was partaken of by any of us—even Lilly refusing to eat.

"Is Aunt Molly dying ?" she interrogated me privately.

"I am afraid she is, my love."

"Is she happy ?"

"Very. She is a Christian, and death is not dreadful."

"It was not to mamma !" her eyes darker and darker. "Auntie !"

"What, dear ?"

"I should like to send a message by Aunt Milly to mamma."

"My darling !" for the request was startling.

"Why not ?" asked she. "Aunt Molly is going directly to heaven—the same heaven where my dear mamma is. She will see her, and I want her to tell her that she left me a very short time ago."

"But you believe that your mamma is with you very frequently—that she watches over you herself."

"Yes, Auntie ; but I can't *know* it so well as that Aunt Molly will meet her. This seems *so* sure !"

"Come, then !" I yielded.

She trod on tiptoe through the yard and across the floor of the cabin. Molly's cheeks and eyes were hollowed, but the latter were bright, and she spoke clearly. A smile greeted Lilly, who put her fingers into the swart hands, clammy with the damps of death.

"Don't be afraid to see Aunt Molly die," said the old woman. "It isn't nigh so hard a thing to go through as folks think, when the blessed Jesus stands 'pon the other side of the river. Love Him, honey! He will never leave you nor forsake you."

Lilly looked inquiringly at me, and I nodded assent.

"Aunt Molly," she began, tremulously, "I want you to do something for me. My own mamma went to heaven eight months ago. You will meet her when you get there. Will you talk to her about me; how much I think of her, and love her; how happy I am in my good home, and that I am trying to live so that I may go to her when I die?"

The faith of the dying Christian was as simple and as strong as that of the child.

"I will, dear! I'll look for her, and find her, for there 'the rich and poor meet together,' and all sing one song—'Worthy the Lamb'—what is the rest, Miss Annie?"

Annie bent over to wipe the wrinkled brow and murmured in her ear—"'For Thou wast slain, and hast redeemed us to God by Thy blood out of every kindred and tongue and people and nation.'"

"Hallelujah!" repeated Molly. "I shan't need to be told what it is when I've heard one sound of the golden harps."

Zack sank on his knees, and buried his face in the coverlet. She strove to raise her arm, and her mistress guided her hand to his head.

"We've been lived many a year together, old man," she said, affectionately. "A kind and a faithful, and a hard workin' husband you've been to me; and if anybody but the Master had ordered me to leave you, I'd have hung to you at the risk of my life. We won't be separated long, for you aint young and hardy—you've 'most counted your three-score and ten. Keep up your heart and listen for the chariot wheels. They'll be along presently. Watch and pray, for in such an hour as you think not, the Son of man cometh."

She had addressed her mistress and Annie before my entrance, and now fixed her wasting sight on me. The words were distinct, but the breath was failing.

"Do you mind what I said to you last spring, when you was gettin' well, Miss Grace? I've prayed it ever sence. Sometimes, Satan would cast me down with sayin' that it was no manner of use—you'd never come out on the Lord's side; but says I—'The Lord meant her to do something for His glory, else He'd have left her to perish in the ice. Anyhow, He's told me to 'pray and pray again,' and I'll 'bey Him. I could die shoutin', if I knowed you was in the right path."

"I trust that I am, Aunt Molly," I said, softly.

"Do you love the Saviour?" she asked with reviving energy.

"I do!"

She put her cold palms together and gazed upward. "Lord! now lettest Thou Thy servant depart in peace, for mine eyes have seen"——

The chariot caught the rejoicing spirit ere the thanksgiving was ended.

I sent Lilly home by Mr. Peyton, and remained at the cottage until the funeral, which took place the next afternoon. Only the negroes from the nearest plantations, my father and two or three other gentlemen, whom Mr. Peyton had left nothing to do, attended the burial. The grave was in a clump of trees back of the garden, on a hillside overlooking the spring. As I stood upon the brink of her narrow home, I could see a bench set in the root of a giant oak, where I had often beheld her on washing days, singing at her toil. Near it were an empty tub and the charred remains of the fire she was tending, when stricken with mortal sickness. Zack was stationed at the head of the grave. The poor old man was not noisy in lamentation, but the salt rain trickled over his furrowed cheeks, as, oblivious of what custom styles the "decencies of grief," he neglected the handkerchief some officiously kind friend had thrust into his hand, and only dashed away the water as it threatened to blind him entirely to the coffin, the last visible link that united him to her he had loved so well. Next him were Mrs. Bell and Annie, weeping as for a sister and a mother.

One of Mr. Peyton's servants had brought a Bible, and when the body was lowered into its place, his voice arose above the sighing of the mourners, the rustling of the leafy branches overhead:

"But I would not have you ignorant, brethren, concerning them which are asleep, that ye sorrow not even as others which have no hope."

He read only the few verses that, after this, remained to the end of the chapter; but no monarch ever had a grander funeral service. Then John's trumpet lungs called forth the echoes from the nearest hills. Like a song of victory after battle ascended his prayer; praise—all praise for the translation of one who had received from her Master the "Enter thou into the joy of thy Lord;" an earnest plea for consolation for the afflicted, and that the minds of the living might be moved to solemn meditation by this event. The rattle of the clods upon the boards was drowned by a hymn raised by another colored man, for the gentlemen committed the conduct of the exercises wholly to the friends and companions of the deceased.

"Why do we mourn departing friends?"

was sung with the combined power of forty voices to the immortal melody of old "China"—music so married to these words that it were a crime ever to divorce them.

We left her there; the dying glories of the sunset lighting up the low heap of red earth, where lay one who should claim a part in the first resurrection; on earth an indigent slave-woman; in Heaven, the "King's daughter all glorious" without as "within."

My father had, early in the day, sent over one of his women, as a temporary substitute for Mrs. Bell's mainstay, and Mr. Peyton instructed his confidential body-servant to discharge Uncle Zack's duties and minister to his wants during the night. The freshness of the evening air tempted us to walk home by the rising moon, but prudence prevailed. We were learning to distrust Nature's blandest moods, and none were more deceptive than these cool, moist nights, so welcome after the sultriness of the day. Shut up in a close carriage, my father, Mr. Peyton, and myself conversed of the death-bed, and the late interesting scene; of the virtues of the departed, and the gap made by her loss.

"Mrs. Bell cannot keep house without her," said my father. "If she were able to procure other help, no three women can supply her place."

Mr. Peyton returned no relevant answer.

He followed me into the hall, when I would have gone to my aunt.

"Grace!"

"What is it?" I asked, halting.

"I must go back to Mrs. Bell's after supper. It will not do for them to be alone to-night. Can you give me five minutes' chat with you presently?"

The merest intimation of my wish would have sufficed for my father. I preferred the straightest course. I called him from the parlor when I was ready to go in; told him frankly that Mr. Peyton had something to say to me in private, and commissioned him to delay supper until I should signal the conclusion of our business.

"I can trust you both," he replied, playfully. "I have no fear of your flirtations with your great-uncle."

Neither had I, and the embarrassment of my life-time friend, which would have been alarming in most men, did not stagger my confidence in his god-fatherly and fraternal attachment.

"You think me very foolish, I dare say," he brought out at last. "I am acting more like a shame-faced boy than a man who has numbered forty-two years. It is no boy's age, Grace—no! nor yet a youth's. I have ceased to be young, that cannot be disputed—can't be disputed!"

"You are in your prime yet," I responded, "and the heart is not old. Many lads of eighteen are more *blasé* in feeling. You will always be young, Mr. Peyton."

"Do you think so? Let that be as it may, can you justify me, with my almost half a century, for wishing to wed a girl twenty years my junior?"

This was coming to the point, assuredly; and my father, although intrenched against suspicion behind his belief in our relation of adopted uncle and niece, would have been startled from his fancied security by this abrupt approach to a personal application of the case under consideration. My woman's wit interfered to save me from a mistake so mortifying.

"If she loves you, Mr. Peyton, she will not consider this disparity otherwise than as a reason why she should trust you the more; will be thankful that your experience can cover her want of it."

He looked at me approvingly. "What judges you women are of each other! Why, that is just what she says!"

"And in virtue of our coincidence of views, may I not know who 'she' is?"

"Cannot you guess?" with heightened complexion.

"Annie Bell," said I. "She is the nearest, so I begin with her."

"You need go no further," was his reply, his diffidence vanishing instantly. "I love her, Grace, and she has engaged to marry me."

"From my very soul I congratulate you!" I said. "She is admirably adapted to you. You cannot fail to be happy together."

"Thank you. I know your mutual affection."

He was grave, but happy withal. "I shall be a different married man now from the lover-husband of fifteen years ago; less impulsive, less sanguine, less demonstrative of my fondness, but not less fond. Twelve lonely winters have I lived at Linden; lived in the memory of my first love; nor is her image to-day dimmed by the hopes that are chasing the gloom from my heart. Annie would not esteem me, were this so—I know she would not! I do not apologize for marrying again. I should scorn to excuse myself for loving and marrying her. The world may call me foolish and her mercenary"——

"She is not that!" I interposed.

"I agree with you. We who have known her from her cradle, may dismiss misgivings on that score. That she has come to love me I am bound to credit, for she has confessed it, and her truthful tongue could not utter a falsehood. Why she has done this, is a mystery I never expect to solve."

"It is comprehensible to me," I smiled. "I would enlighten you, were it not that you would quit the house before I was half through."

Aunt Molly's death would, he thought, serve him as an argument for hastening the nuptials. The day, and indeed the month were not yet fixed, for their engagement was but three weeks old. There was only an indefinite understanding that, by winter, the cottage should be closed and its establishment transferred to Linden. Our five minutes was spun out to sixty, and after tea our conference was resumed.

"By the way, Grace," he came back to say, when his horse was brought up at his order; "you may give your father a hint of the position of affairs. You and he are our best friends."

Without this pretext, it had been my purpose to visit my father's chamber before retiring. His affectionate "Come in, my dear," answered my knock at the door. He was reading by his study table, but shut the book with an expression of pleasure.

"How is my daughter to-night?" he inquired, taking my hand as I stood by him. "You have had much to weary you since yesterday morning."

"I am not wearied, however," I replied.

My conduct to him had sensibly altered with my changed feelings; yet something, a nameless but stubborn bar, had, up to this time, prevented a complete restoration of our old freedom. The wall crumbled more and more now, and had it been adamant, I would have brought every art affection and religion could suggest, to bear against it.

"Well?" he said, throwing back his head that he might see my countenance, and smiling in his genial way. "Has Mr. Peyton gone? Has he proposed and been accepted? and when is the bridal to be consummated?"

"Too many questions at once!" I made an effort and seated myself upon his knee. "Mr. Peyton has gone; he has proposed and been accepted, and he will be married directly to—Annie Bell!"

"Is it possible!" The perplexity that had followed the beginning of my announcements, slowly spoken on purpose to mislead him—fled before delighted astonishment. "She will have a model husband and a comfortable home. I wish them joy most heartily!"

I told him all that I knew of their plans, and enjoyed the zest with which he received each item.

"It is getting late," I remarked, at length; "and I have something to say about myself."

"Say on. I will listen all night, if your story lasts so long."

It was not so short nor so merry as that which I had just related; yet his interest was more absorbing, his emotions more powerful. As I finished with the account of my open profession of a faith I had dreaded should prove unfounded, until the question of the dying saint had probed my heart, he wept outright. Then, I felt that other prayers had joined Lilly's on their heavenward progress; fathomed his love; appreciated his long suffering, and father and child were reconciled.

The hall-clock tolled one, as I kissed him and listened to his benediction. I raised my window for a moment, but the unwholesome fog that rushed in caused me to drop it. The moon was yellow and sickly through the baneful veil, and the earth had a cadaverous hue like that of a shrouded corpse. Dr. Hamner's prediction returned to my mind; but it was not the sentence of doom. That the danger was very near us; that no arm of flesh could avert it, did not terrify me. Trustfully, I said over a verse of a hymn Lilly had recited the previous Sabbath:—

> "God is the refuge of His saints,
> When storms of sharp distress invade;
> Ere they can offer their complaints,
> Behold Him present with His aid."

I had looked upon Death bereft of his sting; upon a grave to which victory was denied; and while I besought safety for the bodies, as peace for the souls of those I loved, there was delicious repose in casting all my care upon the Omnipotent; in leaving them in trust with the All-merciful. Of Annie and her dawning happiness I thought; of the sterling heart she had won; of its morning of joy after the night of years; of the parent weeping with rapture over the new birth of his returning prodigal; of the darling babe, out of "whose mouth" was "perfected praise;" and putting resolutely behind me the irrevocable Past, I blessed God, in singleness of heart, that the "lines had fallen to me in pleasant places."

CHAPTER XVIII.

Dr. Hamner was a wise soothsayer. Our section of the State was renowned for its healthfulness. Its inhabitants had hitherto enjoyed an immunity from summer epidemics and autumn fevers, and jealous for the credit of their neighborhood, many combated the theory that the plague which fell upon them so suddenly, was generated in their own rivulets and fertile low-grounds. It had been imported, they averred ; the question was from whence, and by whom ? From these idle fallacies sprang the report of contagion, resulting in embargoes and quarantine regulations. In spite of the non-intercourse acts, the work of destruction went on. The physicians slept and ate in the saddle ; rode from dawn to sunset, from sunset to dawn, and were the principal means of communication between the nearest neighbors. Moss-side was visited by the scourge—but lightly. None of the white family sickened, and although there were, at one time, seven servants down, some of them dangerously ill, all recovered except two very young children. This exemption might have been ascribed to our situation upon an airy ridge, a mile from any of the larger flooded creeks ; and to my father's foresight in enjoining dietetic discipline, when less judicious masters scoffed at his over-carefulness ; but it was more in consonance with our feelings and the truth to return thanks to a Mightier Friend for the mercy.

Mr. Peyton, undismayed by warnings and croakings of personal infection, continued his visits to us, and, as a matter of course, to the Bells. Early one morning, while Lilly was saying her lessons to me at the breakfast-room window, Black Bess cantered up the lane. My father was busy with his shrubs in the yard, a favorite recreation with him. I distinguished Mr. Peyton's rejoinder to the inquiry after the health of his household—"About the same; no new cases"—and proceeded with our books, peeping, once in a while, through the jessamine sprays, in expectancy of his coming to seek me. They walked and talked, up and down the main alley, until I forgot to watch them. My seat was very comfortable at that hour, and I retained it when Lilly gathered up the school furniture, and ran off to her play. My mind was tranquil; my fingers were busy upon a garment for my "little daughter," a term she especially affected. For some reason, the two pedestrians diverged into the path that ran around the house, and by the same fatality, stopped beneath my window. I leaned forward to say a playful "good morning" to our friend, but it remained unuttered.

"Why depend upon living down this calumny, when by noticing it publicly, you can kill it forthwith!"

"Time heals all wounds, even those in the reputation," returned my father.

"It has torn this one wider," said Mr. Peyton, excitedly. "The rumor has been spreading under the crust, as it were, for nobody knows how many months. Mrs. Bell heard it last winter, from divers quarters, and being wiser than her neighbors, kept it to herself. I can recollect numerous references to it which I treated as beneath my notice. Yesterday, as I have said, it was bruited about on the court-green, and discussed at the tavern dinner-table. I contradicted it then, upon my own responsibility, and now beg you at least to authorize me to ferret out the origin of the slander. Mr. Leigh, you have been a father, an invaluable friend to me—an invaluable friend! I am not apt to quarrel, as you are well aware; but were this my affair, I would adopt the course I recommend. I would, indeed, sir! It is the plain duty of self-defence."

My father's profile was presented to me. The mouth was rigid, the brows contracted.

"And what will you advise," he said, huskily, "if I admit the accusation?"

"Miss Grace," requested Joe, politely, besom in hand, "I am ready to sweep out this department, but I dislike to remove you. Perhaps you won't not object to dust. I never raises a 'strordinary quantity."

Without answering, I escaped from the room, and ran upstairs. Lilly was in my chamber, and I took refuge in the one opposite, locking and bolting the door, to keep out, I could not say what pursuing evil. I fell upon the bed and stopped my ears. "Calumny," "wounds to reputation," were phrases of dire import. The skeleton had never appeared more ghastly than now. Figures danced before my eyes; bells rang and water roared in my ears, and in the scarred, still tender temple was a fast beating, like the striking of an alarm clock. By and by, I became sufficiently collected to think over what I had unwittingly heard, and define my terrors. What was this rumor which was moving every tongue? What had this man of spotless life, of blameless piety, to apprehend from the babble of ingrates whose love of scandal outweighed the respect they owed him as their host, their neighbor, some, as their benefactor? On what vulnerable side had this slander attacked him, that he should cower under the whip, and feebly decline Mr. Peyton's generous offer of vindication?

I had raised myself to a sitting posture, and my regards were attracted by an end of faded ribbon hanging from a drawer. In the idle curiosity that sometimes seizes us in humors and at seasons seemingly the least propitious to its production, I sauntered to the bureau, and opened it. The streamer was attached to a defaced portfolio, crowded into a scrap-drawer. I remembered Miss Malvina's nondescript design, the farewell gift to

Frederic, the session he spent with Dr. Macon. I did not smile or weep, although its associations might well have betrayed me into either emotion. It was as if the skeleton had lifted its bony finger and designated the spot where I could find a clue to the author of the mischief, whose brewing had so affected us. I saw not the odd devices painted upon the tattered card-board ; nor were my meditations of the enamored artiste. Mr. Townley's insolent charges against the head of the family he desired to enter, notwithstanding the infamy he boasted he could pull down upon them at his will ; his base threats and browbeating of a defenceless woman—galling as they were, were swept into nothingness by the avalanche of sorrow that burst upon us the same day. Whenever they had occurred to me since, they were despised as the impotent ravings of a rejected man, burning to avenge an injury to his overweening vanity ; for of nobler passion I believed him to be totally incapable. Like the venom of the enraged toad, his might blister slightly, but could not empoison the blood.

Then the conversation between Mrs. Bell and Miss Susan, when they thought me delirious, was sifted for evidence bearing upon this point. "Mrs. Bell heard it last winter," Mr. Peyton had said, and it was not unlikely that the innuendoes of the acid spinster were the prelude to bolder assertions. Another picture was lifted into the light by obedient Memory ; the dinner, the day after our return from the North ; my father's illness and the snaky gleam of the lawyer's cold, shallow eyes ;—these were scattered links of one chain ; but I had not the skill to fit them together.

"If he would confide in me !" I said, burning drops welling forth at the idea that this had been declared to be an impossibility. "Explanation cannot restore the love and troth this mystery lost to me ; but surely, I could comfort him. Can he bear this augmentation of his burden alone, unsupported ?"

He *did* endure it silently—without complaint; with the heroism of a Spartan, the cheerfulness of a Christian. The silver hairs multiplied more rapidly; the lines of grave thought were ploughed still deeper; but the man, the master, the parent, was the same. Once I entered his room unexpectedly, to consult him about administering some medicine to one of the sick, and discovered him wrapped in reverie or devotion, his grey locks spread over the pages of his Bible, which lay upon the table. It was too late to retreat, for he was conscious of my interruption, and I made known my business. The requisite drug was in the medicine-closet, and I unthinkingly glanced at the book he left open when he arose to procure it. There was a tear-blot in the middle of one leaf, and without approaching nearer, I read in the large type, the verses thus marked:

"Wilt Thou break a leaf driven to and fro? and wilt Thou pursue the dry stubble?

"For Thou writest bitter things against me, and makest me to possess the iniquities of my youth."

And I, emulating this example of patient affliction, refrained from saying or doing anything that evinced any acquaintance with the concealed wound, or the dart that now festered there. His outer life was for others, and such I strove to make mine also.

We were at dinner one day, when Dr. Hamner paid a professional visit to the plantation wards. His tough constitution withstood the draughts imposed by his duties at this critical period, and his joviality ran higher as the epidemic waxed more virulent. He came in, rubbing his hands and proclaiming that he was "hungry as a wolf!"

"What of the sickness, doctor?" I asked.

His ravenous gaze was not to be diverted from the chicken my father was carving with all possible speed.

"Add the wing, if you please, sir—a bit of the breast, not

omitting the dressing—now gravy it, Mr. Leigh, and I am your obliged servant. The sickness, did you say, Miss Grace? I will trouble you for the tomatoes, Joe. Are those cucumbers in that dish? Excuse me—I see my mistake. There is no vegetable more refreshing after a hot ride. I have swallowed a peck of dust this morning. Some of the roads are getting horribly dry."

"I regret your disappointment in the matter of the cucumbers," said my father, "but your prohibition was too strict to be slighted. The hogs are the only epicures in that line on the place."

"All right! perfectly proper! but"—shrugging his shoulders in his Hibernian fashion—"those rules do not reach me. I snap my fingers at such humbugs. My breakfast, sir, was ham, and eggs as hard as boiled brickbats; three cups of coffee, half sugar, six biscuits, a plate of buckwheat cakes and another of blackheart cherries, topped by a glass of iced buttermilk, sir. 'Do as I say, not as I do,' is my motto to you. Your health is my concern; mine is nobody's, thank goodness!"

"You are very busy still, I suppose," I edged in.

"Busy! my dear young lady, it is enough to kill an elephant; and as I do not happen to be an elephant, I survive. I am direct from Peyton's. I hear he is going to espouse little Annie, down in the hollow over there."

"So it is reported," said my father.

"Then one more blamed fine fellow will be spoiled into a married man. Heigho! so the world wags—'marrying and giving in marriage,' as saith the good Book. Annie is a nice girl, and if there are such marvels as tolerable wives manufactured now-a-days, she will turn out to be one."

"How are the servants at Linden?" I questioned.

"Oh! so-so! Peyton ruins them with kindness. I am dragged from pillar to post whenever I go there. Old Winny has a "misery" in her side, brought on by the apparition of the spinning-wheel; Josh faints when ordered to his grubbing-hoe; Dick gets dead drunk off "a thimble-full of drops," he has been told are a capital preventive, and one and all are enrolled upon my list. The lazy vagabonds! as if the market were not overstocked with specimens of their sort!"

"Are there any very ill amongst them?" My father superseded me as inquisitor.

"Humph! two or three will have to swim for their lives. But not one of them is so badly off as James Townley."

"Mr. Townley!" I exclaimed, while my father turned as pale as ashes.

"I did not know that he was sick."

"Another potatoe, Joe!" said the imperturbable doctor, "and the pickles, if you please. Sick! I don't call him sick—he's past that. Nine chances out of ten that he makes a die of it."

My father pushed back his chair and left the room. I must maintain some guise of self-command.

"This is shocking news, doctor. When was he taken ill?"

"The fact is that he deserves all he is enduring for his obstinacy. He was ailing somewhat last Friday, when I chanced to meet him in the road. The day was scorching, or rather stewing, and I ordered him to 'right-about-face,' and go home—but no! a couple of executions must be levied, ten miles off. 'Duty before pleasure,' he said. 'To-morrow I will begin to nurse myself.' 'You will need medicine and nurses both before to-morrow morning, you avaricious nose-grinder of the poor!' I hallooed after him. He chuckled that sly, knowing laugh of his, and rode on. By sunrise next day, I was sent for by Miss Judy, the only sensible, well-behaved one in the family. If she were twenty years younger, six inches shorter, and a hundred times handsomer, I'd marry her to get her out of the set.

James may stand it. I have seen worse cases get well, but I won't stake my reputation upon any guess that he will live four days more."

I had to let him run on, for I was too perturbed to speak. He threw his saddle-bags over his arm the instant he had dispatched his repast; strode out; mounted his Rosinante, more gaunt and disconsolate-looking than ever, and went forth gaily upon his endless round.

The door of my father's chamber was bolted on the inside, and remained thus, most of the afternoon. Towards evening, he emerged from his retirement, and called to a servant to saddle his horse.

"You are going to ride then, sir," I observed, waylaying him in the entry. My suspense would not allow me to let him depart without seeing and speaking with him. I wished, yet dreaded to ascertain for myself the effect of Dr. Hamner's intelligence. He looked jaded, but perfectly calm.

"Yes, my love," and without any change of manner, he added, "I am going to see Mr. Townley—to assist in nursing him, if need be. If they desire it, or it appears to be expedient, I shall stay there to-night. There is probably no other gentleman in the house, and if his condition be what the doctor describes, it is not right that his sisters should be left alone at this crisis."

"Dear father! the risk to yourself!"

"Is trifling, my daughter. With my health, I can support greater fatigue than that of a single night's watching."

I sat up late, awaiting his return, in the vain hope that his services would be unnecessary; that this painful act of charity would not be exacted from him. It was long after Lilly's bed-time when I reluctantly locked up the lower part of the house, and went up to her, but she was awake.

"I am glad you have come, Auntie," she chirped gratifiedly.

"Have you been lonely?" I asked.

"No ma'am. I am thoughtful, I believe, and my thoughts will not let me sleep."

"And what weighty matters engage them?" I said, stroking her cheek, amused at her unchildish gravity.

"I am thinking about Mr. Townley. Will he die, Auntie?"

"I hope not, dear. I know no more than you do."

"Is he a very dear friend of grandpapa's, that he has gone to take care of him?"

"No, Lilly," I was compelled to reply. "To do good to our *friends* is not the Scripture command."

"He is not an enemy, though, is he?"

"Has grandpapa any enemies, do you imagine?" I answered.

She laughed. "What a foolish question for me to ask! What put it into my head that you and he did not like Mr. Townley? and I know there must be something wrong in him if you do not."

"My little Lilly jumped at two conclusions. I hope you have never heard either of us find any fault whatever with Mr. Townley; and if we had, every day, it would not be a certain sign that he was not quite the man he should be."

"It would be to me!" rejoined the perverse lady, whereupon I feigned to box her ears and bade her go to sleep.

There is no beam of light more true than the ray from a child's eye; no test of character more surely to be depended upon than the unwarped instinct of a woman-child.

In my prayers that night, I earnestly remembered the sick man, and him whom he had malignantly aspersed. For one, I supplicated health of body and a softened heart; for the other, the tried disciple of the meek and lowly Redeemer, I implored relief from the trouble that tracked him relentlessly, murderously, I feared lest it should prove in the end; for mental anguish was telling upon his once vigorous frame with a weight more cruel than that of years. He was in his place at breakfast. My tongue clove to the roof of my mouth, when I would have asked the state of the patient, and his worn, sad look was no index to the truth.

"I left Mr. Townley no worse, Grace," he said, reading my solicitous glance. "He is very ill, however, and I have promised to be with him to-night also."

"Will you be able?" I expostulated. "The weather is excessively hot. Does not regard for your health warn you against this second watch?"

"If there were any one to supply my place, I might be indolent enough to conjure up objections," he replied. "You have no conception of the difficulty of obtaining assistance in tending the sick. Five of Mr. Townley's negroes are prostrated by the disease; Miss Malvina is a novice, unfit to be in her brother's chamber; Miss Susan is hardly convalescent after her attack, and Miss Judy, strong and courageous as she is, burst into tears when she saw me. No help can be hoped for from the surrounding plantations. Most of the well members of the different families have to perform hospital duty for the rest, and those who could be spared, are so imbued with this notion of infection that neither humanity nor friendship can prevail upon them to brave the chances of taking the malady."

"Did Mr. Townley recognize you?" I inquired.

"Yes. He is conscious, although his weakness is pitiable. Several times I thought him dying, so low was his pulse. He says little, and only to signify his wants. Heaven grant he may outlive this spell!"

There was no hypocrisy in this ejaculation. From the bottom of his heart it arose, and the recording angel wrote it down with a smile. I read him to sleep that forenoon, and during the dreamless slumber of hours, I did not quit him. His placid features were a study and a lesson to my undisciplined spirit. Whatever was the dark sorrow overhanging him with mysterious gloom, it wrought in him no revenge towards man, no rebellion against God. He drank the wormwood humbly, without repining. Remorseful thoughts of my estranged affection, my hard judgment and repellant bearing, mingled repentance with the veneration I felt for him now. In trusting my Heavenly Father, I had parted with doubts of my earthly protector. I manifested no desire to learn what motive besides Christian benevolence carried him day by day to Mr. Townley's; nor did he intimate that any other swayed him, except by a brief sentence, uttered in a transport of gratitude, when his charge was affirmed to be out of danger.

"Grace! God forgive me! but there was one second in which I wished for his death instead!"

"We are your debtors forever!" sobbed Miss Judy, who came over to Moss-side with the tidings, the same day, not knowing that Dr. Hamner had already imparted them. "The good Samaritan was not so kind as you have been to us, Mr. Leigh. Said James, just before I started from home—'Tell Mr. Leigh I have no words to thank him with, but if I do get over this, my deeds shall speak for me.' And *I* say that none of us can ever do anything towards repaying you—yet it will be made up to you—I know it will!"

CHAPTER XIX.

Five years rolled tranquilly away, signalized by no melancholy changes in our home and neighborhood. My aunt's health had amended perceptibly; my father was not, in appearance, one day older than at the close of the summer of the pestilence; Lilly had attained a stature below the medium height of womanhood, indeed, but one which was likely to remain her maximum, and her curls were darkened to the rarest golden chestnut. Her father had married again, three years after the death of his first wife; an event that excited much commotion and trying suspense at Moss-side; a commotion quelled and a suspense ended by the bridal visit. My sister-in-law was in nothing undeserving of the succession to Lilly's mother. Her self-sacrificing spirit, displayed at the outset of her married life in resolving to spare our treasure still to our craving hearts; her generosity in waiving her right to the daughter she received into full affection, from the instant of their meeting, laid us under a weight of grateful obligation, and called down upon her head a shower of loving blessings. Lilly had been to see them since the birth of a baby-brother, named for our father, "Archie," and in whose face the fond parent fancied he could trace a likeness to our lost Frederic.

Another nephew, and a niece, not the less beloved because they were such in heart alone, and not in blood, were claimants upon my thoughts and time. The whilom solitary halls of Linden reverberated to the shouts of infantile voices; the music of childish prattle made glad the heart of its master. For him happiness seemed to have reversed the wheels of Time ; with the gift of these young lives to his care, had also been bestowed the renewal of his youth.

The Townley establishment had undergone material alterations. Miss Malvina had transferred her susceptible heart and substantial corporeal frame to the keeping of an elderly farmer, resident in another county, who had already buried three wives. To the languishing step-mother, nine children looked for parental instruction and control, and were doomed, I fear, to disappointment and anarchy, except at the seasons of Miss Judy's visitations, when her sterling sense and indefatigable industry righted some of the disorders in the turbulent household. The brother, too, had submitted his supple neck to the noose hymeneal ; had tested the capacity of his heart to support a weight of bliss, by taking to himself a buxom lass, weighing twelve stone, and "worth," in match-maker's phrase—"a cool thirty thousand in her own right ;" which right, of course, became the enraptured bridegroom's. How far he had redeemed his pledge of service made to my father in the transient thankfulness for his recovery, I could not determine. I deemed it most likely that if he were the author of the reports which had raised Mr. Peyton's friendly ire, he had, without bestirring himself to contradict them, compromised with conscience upon mature reflection, when the danger from illness was fairly over, and preserving a circumspect silence, trusted to the natural demise of an unjust report to reinstate his slandered neighbor in the favor of the community. That this did occur was owing to the probity of the victim and the erasive operation of Time ; not to the repentance of the calumniator. I could judge of the estimation in which my father was held, only from outward tokens of respect showed by his associates, and these were manifold at the period to which this necessary retrospect brings me.

Two winters had been blessed by the society of our widowed

May; still the unclouded pearl, brighter, purer for the sombre setting. At her last visit, and ever since by her letters, she had extolled the merits of a celebrated physician in her native city, who had proved himself remarkably successful in the treatment of such diseases as my aunt's, and tried to inspire us with faith sufficient to make trial of his skill. The idea gained plausibility to my father's mind at every presentation; nor could I discredit the accounts of wonderful cures for whose authenticity she vouched. Edmund was consulted, and he strenuously advocated May's views. Dr. Hamner shrugged his shoulders until they saluted his ears, and advised us to "pack off by the next stage."

"I have heard of more miraculous recoveries in the Mother Country," he said, assuming the brogue he never practised unless when he designed to ridicule. "Faith! they raise a man from the dead there by the howly help of a corner of St. Peter's pocket-handkerchief; though its meself that doesn't believe that he ever had one. A paring of St. Matthew's thumb-nail, or a button from the flap of St. Luke's overcoat might answer your purpose. Although an apostate from Mother Church, I may have influence enough at head-quarters to procure you whichever you prefer."

"But seriously, doctor," said my father, "do you discourage this plan as an absurd venture? Is there, in your opinion, the slightest hope that it will be productive of good to my sister? As a friend and a physician whom I trust, I beg you will be candid with me."

"I will, sir! My counsel is, try this fellow, if you are assured that he is not an unlearned or knavish charlatan in his profession, and by all means, take the journey. You wish to see your daughter-in-law, and should Miss Agnes derive no benefit from the practice of Dr. What-you-may-call-him, your time and trouble will not be thrown away, or hers either, for change of air and scene will undoubtedly improve her general health. Thus much as a friend. As a physician, I will frankly avow that I have hitherto considered your sister's complaint almost incurable by medicine. Nature occasionally takes the patient in hand, and puts to shame our drugs and panaceas, but the dame is chary of these favors, through an amiable fear, perhaps, that men will get entirely out of conceit with an art that, once in a thousand times, helps her in a job. Yet I am more cautious than I was once ; am acquiring humility with crowsfeet and grey hairs. My father never saw a steamboat or a railroad car—I have travelled in both. My grandfather died of the small-pox—now, thanks to Jenner ! I have enough of the ounce of precaution in my pocket-book to render an hundred men invulnerable to the loathsome destroyer. Wisdom won't die with me. Set that down as a spick-and-span idea, and hope, as I do, that this all-curing brother M.D. may be what Mrs. Leigh describes him."

"Thank you !" said my father, warmly. "Will it be trespassing too much upon your time and kindness if I ask you to join your persuasions to mine to reconcile my sister to this movement ? She is desponding, and you, in whom she has unbounded confidence, are best qualified to deal with her."

My aunt had been uniformly disinclined to a proposition in which she certainly was most nearly interested. The doctor, who was faithful to the trust reposed in him, found it difficult to rebut her reasonings, and reply to her interrogatories, without committing himself to the opposite side of the question.

"I had rather James Townley should cross-examine me upon the witness-stand, than pass through another such ordeal," he remarked confidentially to me, at the conclusion of the debate. "But we've carried our point, and next month—June—you are to begin your pilgrimage to this King-cure-all."

For the evening reading, my aunt selected the history of the paralytic, whom his bearers lowered from the house-top into the court where Jesus was. As I read, she sat, as was her custom, rubbing the deadened member, slowly and constantly.

"You see!" she said, when I was through, "that Power alone, which could forgive sins, could heal the palsied man."

"And why may He not be moved in your behalf?" I asked.

"The day of miracles is over," replied she. "Yet I am willing to go—useless as I feel it to be—for your sakes."

My attendance was indispensable, and I urged no objection. The decision was made, and I would not, if I could, have revoked it, however forlorn might be the hope of a favorable result of the experiment. I had my hands full of work, morning, noon, and night; but my heart did not wait for leisure to complain. How I fought the Past; wrestled and prayed in private, and in the haunted midnight, no one suspected; and I blessed the Giver of strength that this was so; that my smile deceived even the father whose watchful gaze followed me everywhere; who, with his knowledge of my former life, must be prepared for some sign of awakened memories; of the conflict which was, in reality, going on.

Trunks were packed; arrangements made to leave the house in care of the servants, for Lilly was to stay at Linden while we were gone; and, as there yet remained an idle afternoon of the last day at home, I proposed a farewell call to the Peytons, instead of awaiting the one they would be sure to make to us. My father had letters to write, but would, if these were finished in season, come for Lilly and myself. It was not very warm, and we preferred walking the short mile of plantation-road, lying, for the most part, through spicy pine woods, or the less dense shade of oaks.

"How much Linden is improved since Mr. Peyton's marriage!" observed Lilly.

We were ascending the hill upon which it stood, and as I recalled the deserted air that used to hang about its dingy walls and wide, empty porches, unpainted during the widowerhood of its owner, the scene before me was one of striking beauty. Painters and carpenters had been at work throughout the building, not re-modelling, but repairing; and heavy as was the style of the old structure, it was no more gloomy and tasteless. The lawn, close-shaven, and green as emerald, was enclosed by a white paling, with great gates opening upon the graceful sweep of carriage-way. In the centre of the circle thus formed was a magnificent elm. The rest of the shade-trees were of the species which had given name to the place. This was the home of Annie Bell—"the seamstress," as Miss Malvina designated her. An unavoidable comparison of the present situations of the two came up in my mind.

"There is a buggy—Mr. Townley's, I believe," Lilly's quick eyesight next discovered; "and Mr. Peyton is playing with the children on the lawn."

Baby Mary, the youngest, called, by Annie's particular request, after Mr. Peyton's former partner—was mounted upon Sultan's back, sustained in her seat by her father, while upon the other side trotted Master Robert, an urchin of four summers; a bold miniature of his mother, and on this score, somewhat spoiled by Mr. Peyton and Mrs. Bell. He was a generous, warm-hearted boy, however, and showed unfeigned delight at his sister's rise in the world. She had another, and a higher, shortly, for Mr. Peyton, catching a glimpse of us, swung her up to his shoulder, and, pursued by Robert and Sultan, ran down to the gate to meet us. Thus escorted we proceeded to the house, and were ushered into the great parlor, where Mrs. Bell and Annie entertained Mr. and Mrs. Townley. Mrs. Peyton was more matronly in dress and staid in carriage than in her girlhood, but the happy smile, the natural sweetness of speech and manner were all hers yet. She felt the alteration in mere externals less than did her acquaintances. Mr. Townley, for example, universally affable though he was, understood, and expressed in his deportment, the difference between the daughter of the brown cottage under the hill, and the mistress of one of the best estates in the district; between the sewing-girl who fitted his sister's dresses and stitched his wristbands and collars, and the wife of Robert Peyton, Esq., whose popularity would ensure his election to any office in the gift of his fellow-countymen—Mr. Townley's acme of public favoritism.

The small lawyer was very diminutive, as he appeared from the penumbra cast far across the floor by his wife, and paid his respects. He still wore shining boots and unimpeachable broad-cloth; linen, speckless and wrinkleless, and parted his hair down the middle; was inquisitive as a woman, and sly as a fox, and still perpetrated puns upon every possible, and what would have seemed to plain, sensible people, impossible opportunity. He handled the reins of conversation with his accustomed airy sprightliness; while his wife, laced up at the peril of stays and blood-vessels, in a broad-plaided silk with four flounces, fanned herself in the most capacious chair in the room, and mourned over the hot day. This sylphid bore the name of Eva! A host of lovely images; the beautiful creations of poetry and romance arise to deprecate the profanation, but truth is stern and fact is immutable. I repeat it—she was christened by, and answered to, the title of Eva. Her husband had confided the circumstance of his engagement to Mr. Peyton by means of a riddle in this shape, "I have now a prospect of obtaining *Eva*-ry blessing I can desire,"—which happy device, if not immediately intelligible, was, at any rate, characteristic.

Our projected journey was the chief theme of chat. The leopard's heart was not transformed. More than one scratch reminded me of what I had learned long ago—that although policy might dictate the concealment of his claws, they were sharpened for use. One might have supposed that his grudge against me would be overlooked—more than forgiven, inasmuch as its cause had indirectly enabled him to pluck this richer and larger prize from the scales of Fortune. But in the eye of Law and Equity, a result which I had no intent to produce was not an atonement for actual and personal offence. With the pertinacity of a little soul, he let pass no chance of such petty retaliation as I only would perceive and feel.

"It has been a number of years since you visited New York, Miss Grace," he said, smoothly.

"Yes, sir." I turned to reply to something said by Mrs. Bell.

"Let me see," he calculated, "I was there the same summer —six—*can* it be seven years ago? I was a grown man and a beau of Miss Grace's even then, Eva; but gallantry and truth compel me to say that she was *very* youthful—a mere school girl, in fact; too young to vex her brain about broken hearts and vows as brittle. Miss Lilly, we are listening every day for tales of your conquests. I trust you will display more leniency to your subjugated admirers than your aunt has done."

"I shall aim to copy her in that, as in other respects," said Lilly. "She has never led me astray as yet, and I am willing to tread in her footsteps to the end of the path."

"You could not select a safer or more flowery road," assented Mr. Townley. "The sorrows that befall you there will be such as Providence appoints; none of them the fruits of misdirected affections or rash contracts. You will never lose a friend or create an enemy by your own act."

Annie, in her simplicity, smiled at me lovingly, yet in amusement at what she regarded as high-flown compliment. Lilly gathered a different meaning from my countenance, and bowing slightly in acknowledgment of Mr. Townley's gratuitous remarks, she coaxed the infant from Mr. Peyton, and began tossing it and discoursing in baby-patois, more barbarous than Greek or

Hebrew to our ears, but perfectly intelligible to herself and Mary, who crowed and jumped in prodigious enjoyment.

"It is not your purpose to travel about much, I understand," continued my persecutor.

"No, sir. Our trip is one of business, not pleasure."

"Business, which it is my earnest wish may be happily accomplished," he responded. "You have acquaintances in the city, however, who will not leave you in seclusion. They will enliven your dutiful retirement with their society. Besides your estimable sister-in-law (to whom please present my remembrances and kindest regards), you have another intimate friend there—have you not? I refer to the lady at whose marriage you assisted in 18—."

"I shall see her, doubtless," I answered as negligently as I could; "but our sojourn will be short, and my time fully occupied with my aunt."

"Is the agreeable young gentleman who honored one of our Christmas gatherings with his company—the brother of the very lady in question, I believe—now a resident of New York?"

"I do not know, sir," I said, truly.

"Nor whether he is still unmarried, I presume?" growing more impertinent under the mask of playful raillery.

Instead of avoiding his mocking smile, I looked him steadily in the face. "I know nothing about his present locality or condition."

"Really, Mr. Townley," interrupted his wife; "you shall not tease Miss Grace any more. She takes it so beautifully that I don't see where you find the fun in pestering her with questions. Where is the sense of worrying yourself about her beaux? You are, for all the world, just like the dog in the manger."

The most skillfully-aimed shaft of repartee could not have entered where did this blunt, random shaft. Mr. Townley was disconcerted; so rare an occurrence was it, and the general effect upon the listeners so ludicrous, that a laugh was raised at his expense. His wife chimed in with the round, unctuous "ha! ha!" one always expects from obese good-nature, and fanned herself more vigorously to evaporate the perspiration the exercise had driven out upon her forehead. Her liege-lord tarried a decent time, that his withdrawal might not have the appearance of a retreat, and signed to her to prepare for the leave-taking.

He gave me as a Parthian arrow, a revised edition of an ancient pun.

"I have a presentiment that this contemplated visit is to deprive our neighborhood of one of its most valuable ornaments. You have lost none of your *Wynne*-ing qualities since your earlier expedition to this same hunting-ground, and some of us are tolerably posted up as to your exploits in those days. May similar success crown your efforts in this case—or chase, I might better say perhaps."

This clause was for my private ear.

"Don't believe a syllable of the soft talk he is dosing you with there, Miss Grace!" called out Mrs. Townley. "I know him! and I tell you he is the grandest hypocrite alive."

"'There's many a true word spoken in jest,'" said Mr. Peyton, rejoining us, after having helped the lady into the carriage. "That's a man in whom I have no confidence—none whatever!"

"Do not say that, Mr. Peyton," returned Annie. "He has his faults, but he must have his virtues too."

"You will go far and search keenly before you discover many," was her husband's reply. "You don't know him as I do, Annie—you don't know him as I do! But let him pass. So, Grace, you set out to-morrow? and when am I to come for Lilly?"

"Early in the morning, if you please, sir. I hope you will not find her a troublesome charge."

"Troublesome!" exclaimed he and Annie in concert.

"You deserve that we should keep her from you always, in punishment for that slur," added the latter. "We will do our best to save you from home-sickness, Lilly; and with the aid of the children, I think we may succeed in a measure. It is to be lamented that Linden offers no facilities for swelling the list of conquests of which Mr. Townley speaks."

"Lilly's conquests!" I said to myself, on our return walk. "Is this already the cry? and she nothing but a babe and our toy! How preposterous!"

I looked then, with stranger-eyes, at the form tripping by my side. Girlish it was, but not childish; slender, without fragility; well-strung and free of motion as was that of her greyhound. Her bonnet swung upon her arm, the slight moisture induced by walking imparted additional gloss and a closer curl to her hair; the carmine and snow were, at once, blent and contrasted in her complexion; to me, she was exceedingly beautiful.

"Auntie," she ended the silence, ignorant of my gaze. "May I ask a very silly question?"

"As many as you choose, darling."

"I must preface it by a truthful remark, which you may class with Mr. Townley's flatteries," she continued. "Auntie, dear, you are intelligent, pretty and good, and these things are as apparent to others, as to me. Martha and Aunt Amy have a never empty budget of stories of your admirers and the repulses they received. Mr. Townley hinted as much this afternoon. There must be some foundation for these traditions. Were you so very cruel in your bellehood? It is unlike you, it seems to me."

"I was neither a belle, nor cruel, my love. The servants exaggerated to maintain the honor of the family, whose escutcheon they consider would be stained by the admitted fact that one of the ladies of the house lived and died an old maid from necessity."

Lilly laughed. "You cannot deceive me with any such prevarication as that. My belief in the nursery and kitchen gossip is firm. I thought," more gravely—"I have often wondered whether a sense of duty or your own pleasure kept you single, whether you would not have been happier married to one you loved, than even in your sweet home with us. Then again, it appeared probable that your heart was so well satisfied with the love of those nearest to you now, that you never knew the need of other affection."

If the chimera of her perpetual babyhood had not been abandoned ten minutes before, this language would have dissipated it. Untrained in the conventionalism which instructs young ladies to deny that they have ever had an idea upon a subject that often excludes every other from meditation, locked-up diaries and dreams—she avowed to me that she had had speculations of her own; that she was cognizant of the existence of one sentiment sufficient in itself to supply the heart with food, and that there must be a reason for every exception to its universal dominion.

I could not jest. This budding of the woman's nature was too holy, too solemn a revelation to be sported with. I had lost my play-thing, but in its stead was a treasure to be guarded with more jealous vigilance. With the knowledge of Love, how soon would come its experience—how soon its woe? I thought of my Christmas vow, when her laughter had a novel tone to me.

"O, Father!" I prayed now, "help me still to ward off sorrow, everything that can blight this spirit!"

"Lilly," I said bravely—not without cheerfulness—"time was when I *did* feel the want of another love; when it was mine, to have and to hold, I imagined, forever. God saw fit to deprive me of it. I live without it ; live contentedly, happily, in the home, with the dear ones He has spared. I desire nothing to replace what once absorbed my being ; I shall die as I live, unmarried. If Love be a spirit-need, darling, believe me, wedlock without it is the spirit's bane. Do not torture your imagination to conceive me as spinning out a life of wretched loneliness, for this would be untrue. There is one Fountain that quenches every thirst, and with this, I have so many other blessings that I must devote the largest place in my prayers to thanksgiving."

The rosy mouth was in a quiver, and the brown eyelashes lowered.

"But, Auntie, you must have suffered in the beginning—before you saw the wisdom of the disappointment."

"Shall I tell you who lifted me into the light ?" I asked.

"Yes, ma'am—a very dear friend he must be to you now."

"She is ! A dearer earth cannot supply—for she is my Lilly—my little daughter—my reconciling angel—my everything lovely and beloved !"

Her eyes ran over ; but her countenance was illumined by a smile more joyous than the summer daylight.

We had reached a curve in the road, and hearing, in advance of us, the rapid strokes of hoofs, stepped to one side, barely in time to clear the way for the rider of a fleet, mettled animal, dusty and wet with fast or long travel, yet galloping as upon a morning hunt. The cavalier uttered an exclamation and reined up, seeing us so near him. He was handsome and young, the incipient darkening of the upper lip proclaiming the promise, rather than the presence of manhood. There was no lack of grace in his apologetic salutation—"or assurance either !" I decided, as a half-smile flitted over his face, and a scrutinizing glance succeeded his start of surprise. Doffing his hat, and bowing again, until his black hair almost mingled with his horse's mane, he swept on at the same gait.

"Who can he be?" wondered Lilly. "They said nothing at Linden about expecting a guest, and this road leads nowhere else."

My father met us a few rods further on. The horseman had passed him, and had bowed, but he had no recollection of his person, only that he was a bold rider and seemed to be a traveller. Our curiosity was temporary. It expired before we arrived at home, and was quite forgotten, with its object, by the morning.

CHAPTER XX.

Mrs. Seaton, May's mother, was a widow, whose household, once numerous, was now reduced, by marriages and removals, to herself, her daughter, and one son, the youngest child. Unwilling as my father was to impose upon her hospitality, he could not, without wounding her and May also, decline her pressing request that we would make her house our home while we were in the city. For the invalid and myself, he accepted the invitation, alleging the convenient location of his hotel to the principal business mart as a reason why he selected it for his abode.

It was night, and May and I, wrapped in our dressing-gowns, were in the depths of a six hours' dialogue. As a particular favor to herself, she had asked me to share her chamber. Over against her chair and workstand, where she must behold it whenever she raised her eyes, hung Frederic's portrait, so like his living self that my heart heaved achingly at every inspection of it. Who could have judged that the mouth, about which lurked the arch humor I had seen there a thousand times, the dilating nostril, the eye alive with soul, were copied from the inanimate clay? Yet so it was. Among the visitors at the seashore, that fatal summer, was an eminent artist, who formed an acquaintance with my brother, matured by the unceremonious customs of a watering-place into friendship. All through the night that followed the catastrophe, this man, at his own desire, watched alone by the corpse. By daybreak, his pencil had sketched the outlines of this picture, and from the image imprinted upon his retentive memory, he supplied the rest. A month later, the widow received it, marked by no name, accompanied by no message, save what was written upon a slip of paper attached to the frame—"From *his* friend and yours." The matchless workmanship would have betrayed the author, had no other evidence been forthcoming, but the eccentric donor refused thanks, and never confessed the benefaction.

This story was an old one to me, and not mentioned in our conversation.

"You have not named Louise Wilson," I said, in course of time.

"Because we have so many more pleasant things to talk about," was May's rejoinder. "Her life is all public; that of her husband, all private. She is ostentatiously happy in her fame, he undeniably miserable in his home."

"Bravo for our gentle May!" cried I. "That is an antithetical sentence worthy of an accomplished satirist."

She blushed. "If I expressed myself with sharpness, it was in an unguarded moment. Personally, I have no ground for fault-finding with Louise. She is kind to me when our paths intersect, which is more frequently than one would think who knows the contrariety of our views and pursuits. We exchange calls with some regularity; and she never sees me that she does not inquire after you. The bond of our school intimacy has outlasted natural affection, it would appear, for her neglect of her parents is notorious."

"Have they quarrelled!"

"It is said they have not. Mrs. Wynne professes to feel great pride in her daughter, but Louise informed me, the last time she was here, that she had not been to her father's for nearly a year. She has one child, a boy, for whose mental progress she is extremely solicitous."

"He must be a comfort to his father," I said.

"The sole comfort he has, setting aside his business, to which he is devoted. But the little Howard is haughty, as beseems his name, and begins to rule and hector the parent whom no one in the house affects to respect."

"So true is it," I mused, "that when a wife despises her husband, the world imitates, although it may scorn her meanwhile."

"Have you read any of Louise's writings?" questioned May.

"Some fugitive pieces," I replied.

"Which she does not publish now. Her most elaborate work is just out. I finished it yesterday, and laid it aside for your perusal."

"Do you like it?"

"It is powerfully written; as to the rest you must form your ideas for yourself. It is no ordinary tale of fiction. There is purpose as well as power in it. Reviewers are divided pretty equally with regard to its beauties and defects."

The sounding waves of the mighty, invisible ocean to which I had hearkened in awe seven years before, broke around my couch this night with more articulate roar. I required no interpreter but the review of my life since then, and the histories intermingled with mine. The moonlight poured in through an unshuttered window and showed me the portrait on the wall—the head that reposed on my bosom. Somewhere upon this moaning, never-quiet sea, was another lonely skiff that would have sailed beside me through all the voyage of Life. Was it tempest-tossed, or peacefully moored in untroubled waters? Although so near to one another, our prows were not to touch in kindly greeting; our courses must ever be diverse.

The morrow dawned upon me, sleepless, feverish, heartsick. My aunt was fatigued by journeying, and did not leave her chamber during the day; and there I lounged, a semi-invalid, and read Louise's book. Had May surmised my unhealthy state of feeling, she would as soon have given me a deadly poison.

The Press disseminates scores of such works in this day; this was the first I had seen. Woman the oppressed and Man the oppressor; Woman the slave; Society, Civilization and Religion as preached by Man, the enslavers; these were the texts insinuated rather than boldly propounded by the initial chapter, and when the attention was enchained and sympathy enlisted, the reader had glimpses which broadened into views—views that expanded beyond the horizon of present vision, of Woman's innermost soul in its ample development; superhuman in intelligence, scarcely inferior to Divinity in unblemished, incorruptible goodness—of her Mission, the regeneration of her race, and the undisputed possession of her appropriate sphere. In this, she should be enthroned, no lower than the angels, while he who had ruled her, purified, by her influence, from the gross amalgam of his original nature, should be well-pleased to occupy a subordinate place, and adore as queen and priestess the radiant Immaculate. With inimitable address, the author worked out the problem of Life to this demonstration. She craved the admission of one postulate, viz., that a reform was needed, and this no one withheld after her artful introduction, where not a false or one-sided representation was discernible to the most critical research, and what had been left out was never missed. To feminine tact, she added the fearlessness of the Reformer, the zeal of the Radical. The vices of one sex, the temptations of the other, the applause that hailed triumphant villany, the ban that cursed the error of the weak and trusting—were exposed so independently as to convey an impression of moral sublimity in her who wielded the pen. In her Utopian Paradise, the least poetical of the senses was refined into a medium of spiritual gratification; birds and blossoms taught celestial truths more clearly than the Bible; in a lily was material better worth study than the lives of prophets and apostles—and to the clarified visual organs were vouchsafed seraphic apparitions, the "myriads" who, in Milton's time, "walked the earth *unseen*."

This, and much more, I drank in, never staying to question the source or the elements of the sparkling draught. Pearls of fancy, diamonds of wit, the blood-red ruby of passion gemmed the bowl, and dazzled my wavering perceptions of good and evil. I read swiftly; by dark the volume was finished. I was miserable to wretchedness as I closed it. I had not the dauntless spirit of the defender of "Woman's Rights;" was too cowardly to buckle on armor for the crusade to which she exhorted. One of the many million serfs she portrayed—shackled, hand and foot, by despotism—what hope had I but in death? Her Millenium would come too late for me.

"Are you here, Grace?" said soft accents.

"Yes—come in, May."

She groped her way through the obscurity, sat down upon the sofa, and took my head in her lap, fondling it as if it had been an infant, and crooning in undertones an old ballad. Presently I recovered heart to pull her lips down to mine.

"You are good as ever, my dearest sister!"

"Are you unhappy this evening?" she queried. "Your voice sounds sad. Or is it weariness?"

"I am depressed, and I must be weak, or I could master my spirits better," I replied.

"Louise's story is answerable for some part of the melancholy, I fear," said she. "Am I right?"

"I do not deny it. The reflections it has engendered are not the most advantageous to self-ease."

"It is a *bad* book, Grace! pernicious to morality, ruinous to the healthy contentment of the mind. I read it with the infatuated interest you have exhibited to-day, and its work upon my feelings was, I doubt not, identical with what you now experience. You have heard of the Irishman, who, having instituted a suit against a fraudulent debtor, was observed to weep profusely while his counsel was speaking. A bystander had the curiosity to inquire the cause of this extraordinary demonstration.

'Och ! and shure I niver had an idee of how badly I was thrated 'till the gintleman explained it so gintalely !' he blubbered. So I was in blissful ignorance of 'Woman's wrongs'—in blissful apathy to the glorious cause of 'Woman's rights,' until yon harmless-looking volume told me the story. I cannot meet argument with argument, for Louise's intellect is logical as brilliant, and mine is neither. I cannot gainsay her report of unjust legislation, and the arbitrary oral by-laws of popular sentiment against our sex. Every permanent reform is gradually wrought, and the time for amending these abuses will come as quickly and as surely without our declaring ourselves in insurrection. It is degrading, Grace ! I am not a slave, nor are you, and no sophistry should mislead us into making such a concession. Against what are we to take up arms ?"

"We are woefully dependent, May."

"Not more than Man is upon us. In the symbols of royalty, the external trappings that belong to power, he is the sovereign, as he is physically our superior. There are men who employ brute force to maltreat children and women ; but what is their proportion to the multitude of tender fathers and kind husbands ? I love—I reverence a good, wise man as the masterpiece of his Creator. Rulers there must be, and since I perceive in myself no vocation for the office, I had rather submit to his jurisdiction than to a female autocracy."

May had pondered these subjects better than I, but I objected to this remark—"May there not be a medium, a division of labor and of power ? Why lodge all authority in the hands of one ?"

"Would you have then a government like the feet and toes of Nebuchadnezzar's dream-image—a mixture of iron and of clay ? And this reminds me of what struck me most unfavorably in this work. You and I, Grace dear, believe in a God, a heaven, and a Bible—in this last as entirely as in the other two. Is it not a significant token of the fallacy of many of these modern 'isms' that they wrest the plainest passages of Holy writ ; erase some as spurious, and if hard-pressed to establish their systems of doctrine, cast discredit upon the whole. 'If Woman,' say Louise and her disciples, 'is declared by Scripture to be weaker than he who has basely usurped the title of lord and governor,—is enjoined to be subject to his will, to serve him in humility and meekness, we discard the Bible that teaches such monstrous tyranny.'"

"Oh ! now you *are* too severe !" I exclaimed.

"Am I ?" her voice gaining earnestness. "It is the fault of my understanding, not of my heart, if my judgment is harsh. I have spoken out the best meaning I can put upon Louise's fine-spun dissertations, her grand theories concerning 'natural religion ,' and the 'higher law of instinct,' the 'newer and divine revelation of intuitions,' and 'spirit communications.' What do these expressions signify if not what I have said ? Are not these teachings inculcated in every page, in every line ? 'Spontaneous affinities ;' the 'infinitude of the finite ;' the 'Iris-chain of beautiful truth that conducts the receptive soul to deeper, sublimer spirit mysteries'—are terms which I am not ashamed to say I do not understand. They belong to the cant of the sect, for sneer as they will at 'sectarian dogmas,' they are a sect, and cant after their fashion, more than did Cromwell's Roundheads."

"Poor Louise !" I sighed, after an interval of painful thought. "If she had been a happy wife, this book would never have been written."

"There," said May, "you have the key to every incident of her public career, every doctrine she advocates."

I could see that she looked at the cherished portrait.

"Only the other day," she continued, "I was reading the 'Records of Woman,' and dwelt tearfully upon this definition of her wants and 'mission,' penned by one who poured forth the plaint of her own grieving heart in the lines."

There were tears in her voice now, as she recited them.

"'Thou shalt have Fame!' Oh, mockery! give the reed
From storms a shelter, give the drooping vine
Something round which its tendrils may entwine;
Give the parched flower a rain-drop, and the meed
Of Love's kind words to woman. * * * * * *
If I could weep
Once, only once, beloved one! on thy breast—
Pouring my heart forth ere I sink to rest!
But that were happiness—and unto me
Earth's gift is *Fame!*'"

Our family group was collected in the parlor for a social evening, when "Mr. and Mrs. Wilson," were announced. Their entrance reversed the order of the footman's words, for Louise sailed in upon us ere I could rise to receive her. Her figure was fuller, and, I thought taller, than when she was first married, so majestic was her mien. She kissed me with a sentence of greeting, beautifully turned and delivered, and continued the round of the little company, while I was transfixed in a sort of stupid wonder; lost in the endeavor to connect recollection and observation.

"Sappho! Corinne!" I said, over and over again. "Is this Juno, the pitied sacrifice of a mother's ambition, the unhappy, unloving consort of a man she held in utter contempt?"

This directed me to him. I was pained by the alteration in his appearance. The hair was thin upon the crown of his head, and tipped with iron-grey; his face and form were spare to leanness; he stooped in the shoulders, and had a slouching gait at variance with his former brisk step. The hand he gave me was unbending as a piece of jointless wood, and his bow was effected by machinery as stiff. He crept into a chair, and would, I believe, have been a speechless fixture the whole time he stayed, but for Alfred Seaton's good-nature. He seated himself near the hermit-corner, and talked "business."

Louise was gay and chatty.

"It has been seven ages since we met," she said to me, "or are not twelve months reckoned an age in your rural retreat? I should suppose not, or, at least, that the greybeard of the scythe and hourglass has forgotten to mark the passage even of days upon you. As I look at you, it seems but yesterday that we parted."

I might have rejoined that the stranger who was yesterday presented to me, would have acted as much like the friend of by-gone hours as she did. It was not affected indifference, but the nonchalance of one used to the world, who smiled at early loves and hopes as sickly dreams. She was in party costume, and the robe, in texture and hue, was in keeping with her position as a wife and mother. But the corsage retreated from the bosom and shoulders with a freedom that caused my cheeks to burn with unsophisticated blushes, and the arms were surmounted by an ornamental band—a capital to the rounded shaft, and which was called by courtesy, a sleeve.

"I am engaged out this evening," she excused her brief visit. "I only dropped in here to welcome you to our midst. When shall I have the pleasure of seeing you in my own house? I do not receive morning calls except upon my 'at home' days, and I do not wish you to present yourself in that mêlée. Cannot you and your sister favor me with your company to dinner on Thursday?"

I left the reply to May, who was disengaged, and I consented to go, with the proviso that should my aunt be worse or require my presence, I must be excused. The next day was the medical examination, and Dr. ——'s judgment reanimated our courage and infused something of our hopefulness into the patient's heart. A letter from Lilly completed the cure of my melancholy.

"Has our encounter in the pine-wood with the 'Wild Huntsman' escaped your mind?" she wrote. "If not, know you, Auntie dear, that this phantom was very substantial flesh—being no less a personage than the 'little boy,' Peyton Elliott, whom, he says, I patronized with infinite condescension, the Christmas of my installation at Moss-side. He has been at college for four years, and is now improving his emancipation by what he is pleased to term 'loafing' at Linden, and for which perfect idleness I can devise no more expressive epithet. He is kind and sociable with the children and myself, and Mr. Peyton is much attached to him."

To Louise's, therefore, we went on Thursday, at an hour, when, as I told May, dinner-guests at Moss-side were thinking of going home. The establishment was handsome; in nothing resembling the picture one is apt to sketch of a literary lady's abode. Louise was the polite hostess, the life of the party, which numbered some half-dozen beside ourselves—all talkers but Mr. Wilson. He sat at the foot of the table and performed the duties of carver and decanter-master with a spiritless air that was really pathetic.

My vis-à-vis was a bald gentleman with spectacles; next him was a lady capped and spectacled; then May, and then a young man of flaxen complexion, moustaches and hair to match, and a double eye-glass pendant from the upper button of his vest. Although I knew this house to be the resort of a certain clique of literati, I had not expected that any, even of the lesser lights, would be invited to waste their effulgence upon a couple of Louise's schoolmates, who were unknown except to a small private circle, and anything but "progressive" in taste and aspirations. The conversation at table was on a par with such dinner-talk as I had participated in many times before, and when called upon, I bore my share in it without diffidence.

There was more company in the parlors when we repaired thither.

My eyes ran eagerly through the rooms in a quest, unavailing as unwarrantable.

"Did I hope to see him here?" I asked myself. "Should I not have shrunk from the meeting instead? It is best thus. Shame on the heart, that bravery should desert it at this late day!"

But I was repeating in my old way—"Nevermore!" when May addressed me.

"Do you know, sis, into what goodly company we have fallen? Here is a varied assortment of one dramatist, two editors, three poets, four poetesses, and five prose authors—I did not say 'prosy,' by a slip of the tongue—did I? In short, our host and ourselves are the only undistinguished persons in the room."

"Indeed!" said I, looking around me, and somehow expecting to descry the labels affixed to the celebrities she had named. "Where are they all?"

"The play-writer leans against the wall in that corner. He was my neighbor at dinner—he of the sandy love-locks and quizzing-glass. He is talking to a poetess and an authoress."

"They look very much like other people," I remarked, naïvely.

"And talk like them, too," she responded. "There is one person here whom you will not object to meeting. Do you note that young man standing at this end of the piano; neither talking nor yet dreaming, but bearing himself like a sensible gentleman, ready to do the one if occasion offers, and who never gives way to the other in society?"

"I see him. Who is he?"

"The author of the exquisite poem for the sake of which you forwarded the —— Magazine to Lilly."

"May! you are not in earnest?"

"Why am I not, my dear?"

"He is so youthful," I said. "He is neither pale, tall, nor lachrymose."

"Cogent reasons—all of them, why he should never attempt poetry," she replied. "Add to them that he eschews spectacles and trims his hair, and any jury would acquit him of such a deed. Or, if a touch of doubt remained, I could clear it away by representing that I am personally acquainted with him; that he often converses with me, a nobody, when there are somebodies by—and that I comprehend and admire everything that he writes."

He smiled and bowed now, and came over to speak to her. A figure rather short and square-built; a good-humored, healthy-colored face; a sparkling eye—these were the results of my hasty scanning of the personage whom she introduced to me. As she had said, he spoke as he looked, the simple gentleman. The stored imaginings, rich and glowing as the treasures of oriental mine and forest, were not with him baubles to be sported with by the frothy surface-waves. Yet, as we became better acquainted, he permitted us to see a stray flash; the ripple was sometimes a cleft, through which shone the bright and precious things of the depths. To me, he was kindly attentive, obscure stranger as I was, uninteresting as I appeared at the first. I rejoice that this was the outward stamp of the only confessed poet I have ever known, and that my conceptions of the class are formed from it. The Aurora of Fame was then just touching his brow with faint prophetic gleam. It is now broad day. Where then one tongue, one heart uttered his praise, a thousand shout it now. May thousands more yet echo it!

Mr. Wilson, all this while, was secluded in his nook, between a pier-table and a voluminous window-curtain. I think he had an instinct for discovering out-of-the-way places, and he immured himself in them whenever he could. He noticed nobody, and nobody noticed him. His eyes were generally engaged in the perusal of a patch of the carpet, about a foot square; his hands were crossed at the wrists upon his lap. A broken-spirited and a miserable man I knew him to be, and I pitied him from my soul, as I traced the seams of care and toil in his visage—toil, that she whom he had wooed lovingly, won exultingly, might maintain the state her imperious pride demanded ; care, ah ! what of care and anguish had not tried his heart ?

I summoned hardihood, when I thought myself least observed, to approach him. He made way for me to pass, and was confounded when I took an ottoman near him instead. His lips parted twice before a sound came forth.

"I hope you are well this evening, Miss Leigh."

"Quite well, thank you. Mr. Wilson, I have a favor to crave from you."

He bowed.

"I want to see your boy. I watched for him when the dessert was brought, and then hoped that he would be in the parlor. He is not sick, I hope."

"No ;" and he seemed really gratified. "Children are noisy, and his mother does not often send for him to the drawing-room. He takes his meals in the nursery. His mother thinks rich food is injurious to him."

"He is asleep now, I suppose."

"He may be ; but he is frequently awake later than this. His mother prefers that he should not go to bed too soon. She thinks too much sleep will make him heavy."

"Master Howard, too, is a monopoly enjoyed exclusively by his mother, it appears," thought I. "Is the nursery forbidden to visitors ?" I inquired.

"No ; that is—I believe not. His mother invites her friends up occasionally. I do not know whether she is willing that any one should see him in the evening."

"She will not refuse me, I think," answered I, intercepting Louise on her way by us.

"What is it?" she asked.

"I am desirous to make the acquaintance of your Duke Howard," I said, "and am begging Mr. Wilson to grant me admittance to his domain at this unseasonable hour."

"You can go, certainly," was her reply. "Mr. Wilson will, with pleasure, show you the way."

With a reverence to her and to me, he offered his arm. Words were superfluous—had not she spoken?

The nursery was a commodious and elegant apartment, but, as it seemed to me, rather fanciful in some of its appointments. The pictures, with which the walls were lined, were principally allegorical, altogether beyond the comprehension of a child. There were busts and statuettes, and directly opposite the muslin-veiled crib was suspended a large, beautifully carved alabaster cross, with a wreathing serpent—a mystic symbol, whose meaning I could not appreciate. Vases of flowers were set about on brackets, above the reaching baby-fingers—teachers of Nature's beauties, which the pupil would have been too happy to exchange for a handful of dandelions and wild grasses, if he might litter the floor with them. Books there were, in plenty and variety; of toys, there were none, except a philosophical apparatus, which, at the moment of our entrance, the heir of the house was insisting should be broken in pieces to aid in the construction of a store he was building of books.

"I will! I say I will!" he screamed vociferously. "Give it to me, or I will complain to mamma, you old thing!"

The opposing force was a Swiss-French woman, an amphibious creature—nursery-maid and governess, whose rising wrath sank when she beheld us.

"Master Howart is indispose', I tink," she said, courtesying. "He is a lamb most times, madame."

"Papa," roared the enraged lamb, "make Félice reach down that for me!"

"My son! will not something else answer the purpose? What do you want me to get for you instead?" Mr. Wilson faltered, eyeing in fear the angry countenance, babyish though it was.

"I will have that, and nothing else!" persisted the boy, obstinately; and there was in look and voice a painful resemblance to Louise, as I had seen her at the beginning of her wedded estate, before her heart-petrifaction was thorough.

"But what will your mother say, my son?"

"*I'll* see to that!" with an air of superiority.

"Well," submitted Mr. Wilson, "let him have it, Félice. If he breaks it, I can buy another to-morrow."

The amphibious lady did not remove her black lace mitts and the hands they adorned from the pockets of her apron. Inclining her head yet further towards her left shoulder, she objected positively to the concession.

"Pardon, monsieur, but madame have ordered expressément Master Howart nevair to play wid dat when she not here to give it him. *I* obey order."

By implication, the stress laid upon the personal pronoun in this clause said, "Whether *you* do or not!"

"What shall I do, Miss Leigh?" prayed Mr. Wilson, in distress. Between awe of the unmanageable boy, and his mother, who controlled everything about her, his dilemma was undesirable.

"Howard," I said, but hopelessly, "what will you do with that clumsy toy? I do not think it pretty."

"I do! and I want it to build my store with," he returned, crustily.

"I should not call it a very good thing for that."

"That's because you don't know, you see. Those posts"—pointing to the cylinders supporting the crucible or boiler—"are exactly like some I saw to-day to a store down town, and I *will* have them!"

"Where is your house? Let me look at it," I suggested.

Diverted by this turn of the subject, he forgot the coveted article for a minute, but that was long enough for Mademoiselle Félice to whip the queer machine that had begotten the ferment, under the ruffled, be-bowed scrap of silk, which was the foundation of her pockets, carry it into the dressing-room, and be back to her position by the bedstead, lace mitts ensconced as before, and an innocent smirk upon her hard lips. Then Howard, who had been explaining his building plans to me with alacrity and intelligence, returned to the original charge, and detected the trick.

"The lisping of infancy is the dialect of angelic communities," said his mother's book. This stout six-year-old had lost the recollection of its very elements, for in no vocabulary seraphic, in use among the élite of the "lower spheres" even, could have been found the epithets he launched at the entire party, individually and collectively. In Billingsgate and a French Billingsgate, one might have sought with better chance of success. The amphibious lady was unmoved in smirk and attitude. Mr. Wilson, goaded to action, placed his hand in pacification upon the head of his hopeful scion. He struck it off, and an oath, sounding and furious, burst from his mouth.

"Had not we better go down, Miss Leigh?" said the insulted parent, his leaden complexion crimsoning with mortification and suppressed feeling.

"Go along!" shouted Howard, taking this movement as an acknowledgment of defeat; "and never come in here again! I'll tell mamma of you all. She'll show you who is master."

Mademoiselle Félice sidled to the door; courtesyed anew, an obeisance compounded of maid and governess, and was "vair sorry madame should have seen Master Howart in one such misfortune."

"When you come again, he will be dispose' in body, and in vair good temper—parfaitement aimable, madame!"

Silently, we wended our way down the spacious staircases, so carpeted that no step creaked in the descent.

"This is splendid misery!" I thought, "and this abject sufferer is its owner!"

Disrespectful as the idea was to her as my hostess, it obtruded itself: "Is this Louise's tyrant? and this her manner of prosecuting reform? Must the wife's emancipation necessarily involve the husband's slavery?"

It was a crude notion, and is here set down as it entered my cranium at the bottom of the second flight; but it was to me what Louise's sect would style a "spirit manifestation," and I am inclined now to regard it as less nonsensical, attendant circumstances considered, than many of the Socratically-put arguments that upon the pages of "My Mission? What?" had seemed unanswerable.

CHAPTER XXI.

There had been further additions to the company while we were out. This I observed casually, as I obeyed Louise's beckoning finger. The magnet of a select circle, she was in high bloom and spirits. She swept aside her flowing robes to make space for me upon her divan.

"My friend, Miss Leigh, Dr. Harney."

A grey-haired gentleman, with an eagle eye and a benevolently smiling mouth, arose and bowed.

"Pray go on!" said Louise to him, "or stay! let Miss Leigh be informed as to the subject of the controversy. You have missed much by not hearing it," to me. "Such opponents do not often engage one another."

I gave a thought to the less refined warfare I had witnessed in the meantime; but signified my curiosity to be instructed in the merits of this one.

"Briefly then," continued Louise, "inasmuch as any description of mine will be a witless affair to those who have listened to the debate, and we are impatient to have it proceed, Mrs. Rowland laments the poverty of real life in the matters of romance and poetry, and Dr. Harney asserts that all of both, contained in written story, is meagre in quantity and quality, when compared with the dramas and tragedies acted out before us and by us every day we live."

She spoke lightly, yet not scornfully, and the disputants were satisfied with her statement.

Mrs. Rowland had seen, perhaps, fifty years of the barren

existence she protested was "insupportable to a craving intellect and sensitive heart." A sharp, quick utterance ; a pair of sharp, quick eyes lent a shrewish character to her discourse, while Dr. Harney's courtesy was unvarying. Her aim was to show how the contact of man with his fellows, under the present constitution of society, blunted his nicer feelings ; "rendered gross his spiritual faculties ;" "materialized his ethereal essence."

The doctor's mouth twitched as she brought out this expression. If aught so intangible could be handled, he did it politely but with ability. I was getting mystified by more transcendental jargon, when he introduced a little story, narrated with no straining after effect, in unvarnished English, made eloquent by his feeling manner and its truth.

"In the summer of 18—, the city of —— was decimated by the worst plague that has ever cursed our Western country. All who could quit the place fled from it ; but there were thousands left upon whom Death might feed. Hospitals were crowded; graveyards overflowed ; and neither nurses nor sextons could be hired in sufficient numbers to supply the increasing need. Business was suspended ; loss and gain were disregarded when the question "to die or to live ?" was forced upon every man's consideration. In my rounds through the principal hospital, I was thrown much into the company of a young physician, who had emigrated from this State to try his fortune in a less thronged field. He was a grand-looking fellow ; straight as an Indian, and the picture of healthful, vigorous manhood. His strength of nerve was marvellous. He bore sights that whitened the faces of veterans in the service, with an equanimity and a presence of mind I have never seen in any other person of acute sensibilities. While there was a glimmer of hope, while the breath of a patient lasted, he ceased not to exert himself for his recovery. No spectacle of disease and woe was so revolting as to daunt him, yet I have known him to weep in womanly softness over the remains of the poor wretches, who had no claim upon him except that of humanity. He was the favorite of all in the wards—the sick, their nurses and his brother doctors. Day after day he walked beside me with a fleet tread fatigue could not make languid ; the restorative of his voice and smile doing me as much good as it did the sufferers, who watched and prayed for his coming.

"I loved him as a younger brother, and as the pestilence began to subside, I set my wits to work upon the surest method of aiding him in his professional course without hurt to his delicacy. My own practice was extensive, and short as had been our intercourse, I resolved to invite him forthwith to become my assistant ; in time, my partner. Upon this business, and nothing else, I, one day, called at his room. He was sick, he said—how oddly it sounded from him ! and was just thinking of sending for me. I attributed his fever and debility to overwork, and commanded him to keep his bed for the remainder of the day. Within the hour of my departure, he was summoned imperatively to visit some one who was dangerously ill. Feeling better at the thought of action, he arose, dressed and went out upon what was his last errand of mercy. That night, a messenger, in hot haste, aroused me from sleep to attend my friend. He was already in a critical condition. He told me this before I could apprise him of it.

"'While I am sensible, doctor,' he said, 'I would intrust you with one or two final commissions.'

"No hero of romance or poetry, Mrs. Rowland, could have manifested more fortitude, no martyr more resignation.

"'Don't think of final commissions, my dear boy,' I answered, with a choking in my throat. 'Your iron frame will show brave fight, and as like as not, come off victorious.'

"'I hope so, doctor ; but I do not agree with you that this is the most likely termination of the struggle. I stand almost alone in the world, for I am an orphan, with no near relatives; but life is precious, and there are other loves than those of childhood's home.'

"He drew from his bosom a locket, hung by a ribbon about his neck. 'Look at that, sir!'

"It was the miniature of a very beautiful woman.

"'She is my betrothed,' he resumed; 'the spring of every effort becoming a man that I make; my star and prize, set steadfastly before my face in whatever direction my Fate conducts me. My death will break her heart. Is it a wonder that I wish to live?'

"'And live you shall—for her—if there be efficacy in mortal skill!' I returned.

"'Thank you!' squeezing my hand. 'But should this fail, you will take charge of my effects, and write to her—gently, tenderly, doctor! for the shock will be great. She loves me!'

"The pathos of these three words I cannot describe to you. A volume of written poetry could not convey so much of devotion and agony. He gave me her address; added instructions touching some unsettled pecuniary concerns, and resigned himself to my care. The best medical aid the city could supply was obtained; consultations were held hourly; no means or pains were spared. For two days he battled for the life which was *hers*; on the third, he sank. The miniature, a tress of her hair and her letters moulder with him in his untimely grave.

"This was love until death. It is an everyday story, Mrs. Rowland, but the secret of two lives is infolded in it."

"And the lady?" questioned a gentleman.

"I wrote to her, as I had promised, and never received a reply. I hardly expected one, although it would have comforted me in my affliction, and could not have augmented hers."

"What became of her? or did you lose all trace of her with the end of this correspondence?"

I could scarcely believe my own ears, when Louise's unaltered voice fell upon them. Her eyes were clear and dry, while mine were filling fast.

"I do not even remember her name," said Dr. Harney; "having destroyed the address when I dispatched the letter, nor is it of consequence. Other things have covered over, in my mind, this episode in an eventful career. It was recalled by the conversation here to-night. By to-morrow, I shall have packed it away again in its hiding-place. A novel-writer would have intensified more; would have put the tale into a better form. I have told it in my way, to serve my purpose. If I have been prolix, as well as inartistic, I crave your indulgence."

There was a disclaiming buzz, eager and complimentary, as he said this. I did not join in it. I had fewer words, more thoughts than any of the rest.

A sultry July twilight; the great, unseen river booming without; a darkening room, bestrewed with bridal array; a crouching figure, crushed by memories; mournful, fitful tones, that repeated the very story to which we had just now listened; its finale—"Deep in my heart there is a grave—sealed fast! for I trampled down the earth myself—beat it hard! No grass grows there; no tear ever wets it; no sunbeam ever strays through the darkness to light it; My former self is buried there with *his* memory."—This was the picture, these the sounds that visited me. Where was now that grave? Forgotten, with the thought of that in which lay the mortal remains of her early love—the martyr-hero!

"Can it be?" I said, wonderingly.

"If our written romances could win our readers to interest as genuine and flattering as Miss Leigh has showed in your narrative, we should ask no higher meed of praise," was Louise's remark. "Truth, nature and heart—these are better than all the studied graces of stage-effect, doctor."

She left us with this, to shine upon others who claimed hospitable notice ; still radiant, self-poised, inimitable ; the cynosure of envious and admiring regards.

Mine sought out May as a relief from this excess of brilliancy. She yet wore her mourning-dress, and the pensive cast of her features did not date back to the period of our early intimacy ; but upon the forehead and lips was enstamped a serenity sorrow could not disturb, nor time take away.

"Peace and stoicism ; Religion and Philosophy—which best befit the woman?" said my invisible monitor ; and again I wondered whether I had not been favored, twice in the same evening, with an "inward illumination ;" whether my spiritual intuitions were not undergoing the "purification which should eventuate in their infallibility."

Louise was importuned for a song—I guessed from the gestures and countenances of several who pressed about her.

"Why does she refuse?" queried the dramatist of Mrs. Rowland.

"To enhance the value of the consent which will come in due season," she replied, cynically. "Men rush most anxiously after denied blessings."

"Mrs. Wilson seldom sings at her own parties," said May's gentle, firm tones. "I hope she will break through this rule to-night, however ; you have not heard her"—to me—"for several years—have you?"

"No ;" I said ; then inwardly, "I do not care to, now ! I suppose her style of music too has undergone a reformation, and I am weary of alterations for the worse."

I had two disappointments ; one, at seeing her approach the piano, leaning upon the arm of the young poet ; the other was delighted astonishment, when like a breath of summer wind, the song stirred the air, and silenced every other voice. I could have imagined her the Louise I once knew and loved, so like were the notes to those she used to carol frequently and freely as do birds in Spring-time. I arched my hand over my eyes, and listened to the round, liquid tones that brought me the love-song :—

" There is a fountain in the dell,
And it singeth evermore,
As the laughing waters leap to light,
And tinkling crystals pour.
All day, to catch the sun's warm kiss,
The eager wavelets swell;
And a wild and joyous thing of life
Is the fountain in the dell.

But when its god has looked his last,
And woods grow chill and dark;
And stars upon its glassy breast,
Dart but a fleeting spark,
There comes a ceaseless, wailing sob
From out the heaving well;
And song and dance are hushed till morn,
In the fountain in the dell.

My heart is like that gladsome fount,
When thou, beloved, art nigh;
To meet thy loving eye and smile
The billow riseth high.
The circling ripples bound in glee
Beneath the genial ray—
And cheerily! O, cheerily!
Singeth the dashing spray.

And like it too, it sadly sinks
When its day of joy is o'er;
And from its secret depths, a sigh
Struggles for evermore.
All through the long, long weary night,
It maketh plaintive moan;—
For life and beauty leave the wave,
When Thou and Hope have gone."

" One of her own lyrics !" sneered Mrs. Rowland, incautiously as before, for May was now out of hearing, and I was too stupid or too insignificant to be regarded. "Is that in good taste, do you think, Mr. Armour?"

The play-writer screwed his mouth to one side, and perked his eye-brows, without speaking.

"My dear Mrs. Wilson!" Mrs. Rowland called, as the songstress neared us; "I cannot thank you enough for the soul-treat, the spirit-banquet you have deigned to grant us. I did not know until you sang it that the exquisite poem I have so enjoyed was ever wedded to music."

"Carsini is the composer," replied Louise. "The verses were a juvenile production, whose resurrection was accomplished by an accident. They found their way into print without any connivance of mine, for I am too conscious of their demerits. I should not have sung them, had I not been urged to it by my friends here, and"—glancing over her shoulder to ascertain that the individual spoken of was at a safe distance, and bending towards Mrs. Rowland—"Carsini himself is present."

"I believe you!" I wanted to retort. "I am only ashamed of myself for fancying that you could write and sing thus now from choice."

A gentleman entered unannounced, and without bustle, when I was eying May interrogatively for the signal of going. Louise advanced some paces and saluted him with more show of cordiality than she had evidenced at the appearance of the mass of her visitors. A singular fascination drew my attention continually towards them as they stood in the middle of the floor; she, speaking volubly, and with much animation of expression and action; he, slightly bent to listen, dignified and calm, responding where verbal response was needed; but she consulted his eyes most frequently when she paused for an answer. His height exceeded that of any other person present, and this, with his proud bearing, aroused a pain at my heart. The face certainly did not bring up kindred associations; yet I was troubled by a familiar look that taxed my memory to refer it to its former possessor. Those deeply-set eyes had once read mine as they were now reading Louise's; those teeth had parted, in the same dazzlingly-white line, the moustache from the crisp beard below. Their voices were drowned in the prevailing hum, but I knew that his was subdued in pitch, and skillfully managed; melodious in persuasive argument; in its every cadence a sneer, when the subject admitted of sarcasm. An antique seal-ring upon his left hand, unique in form, I recognized as readily as if I had handled it a hundred times; and when he twisted it reflectively, in the most stirring part of Louise's address, the action was just what I was waiting to see. Where had I known him? especially where in company with her? They had talked and I watched them before this—if nowhere else, in my dreams.

The conference was over for the present. Louise accepted his arm, and they moved through the apartments, dispensing words and smiles at their convenience, to the various groups scattered here and there. I stared on, I doubt not, like an untutored rustic, until Louise detected me in the act. A momentary and irrepressible gleam of amusement flitted over her countenance. Heartily vexed with myself and with her, I steadied the offending orbs, after Mr. Wilson's manner, upon a figure of the carpet, and pored over its convolutions with a closeness of application surpassing his.

"Miss Leigh," said the commanding tones of the mistress of the house, "allow me to revive your recollection of a travelling companion—Professor Dumont."

The stranger of the White Hills it was, who, resigned in my favor by his hostess, expressed, in gentlemanly terms, his pleasure at our reunion.

"I have ever retained a most agreeable remembrance of our accidental acquaintanceship," he said. "To meet again, under the roof of one of them, all the ladies of that harmonious travelling party, is a surprise, delightful as complete."

"There have been many changes since then," I replied, without thought, or I would not have seemed to solicit his sympathy in what was melancholy in these events.

He bowed his head in respect to the dead and the sorrowful living—a motion of marked grace.

"I have learned, to my regret, how deplorable some of them are. I have, once or twice before this evening, had the privilege of paying my respects to your sister, Mrs. Leigh. As Mrs. Wilson happily remarked awhile ago, you are also sisters in a conspiracy to cheat Time of his tribute-tax."

"We have paid it, I believe, sir—if not in shrivelled skins and silvered locks, in some other currency equally as acceptable."

"The world is no wiser for your integrity," he was pleased to say. "But where is Mr. Wynne? I do not see him here."

"He has not been in at all, I think," said I, unfalteringly.

"Ah! yet that is nothing uncommon. He does not make one of our number upon these 'literary evenings' so regularly as his sister's wishes and ours could dictate. While deprecating his taste in this respect"—there spoke the old polite scorn!—"I am constrained to award him, in everything else, my hearty, unequivocal esteem. His abilities are more than respectable, and, if directed to worthier objects than trade, would win for him reputation of a higher order than the pittance of fame that deludes mediocrity into the belief of its own stupendous genius."

His glance, sweeping and comprehensive, was not flattering to the bevy of literati within its scope.

"Mr. Wynne is successful in the line of life he has chosen, I hope," I dared to say, led on to the risk of exposing the inner chamber of my soul, by my desire to gather some tidings of one who was never absent from thought, who had not been named in my hearing for years.

"I hear nothing that contradicts this impression which I have derived from the never-ending 'disappointments on account of business' that frustrate so many of our social plans; the clamor and hurry of his establishment, and his interest in operations, sufficient in number and intricacy to throw a man into a brain fever. Yet this money-making would not be so odious in Americans, were it not pursued without intermission from the cradle to the grave ; from the introductory marble 'swap' to the sexagenarian's investment of the half-million in stocks. Your people know how to amass. They do it cleverly, and spend—excuse me for saying it—awkwardly. The science of Leisure is the only one of which they have not, at least, a smattering. When they do pretend to recreate, it is play with one hand, work with the other ; spending here and scraping in there ; the right eye softened with enjoyment of the beautiful in Nature or Art ; the left wide-awake for a keen bargain, a lucky speculation."

"This description does not correspond with my idea of Mr. Wynne's character," observed I.

"Nor was it intended as a personal portraiture," he answered. "As such, it should rather stand for Mr. Wynne the elder than for the son, who has trodden the dusty highway but a little while. Mr. Wilson, our host, is, in jockey-phrase, thoroughly broken in harness. In the natural course of events, his more spirited brother-in-law will be as tractable—as tame."

I was uncomfortable, hot and uneasy, yet not daring to defend the absent from the charge of this woeful depreciation.

The next question did not cool my flushing cheeks.

"You have seen Mr. Wynne since your arrival in the city—have you not?"

He was turning his ring, and not looking at me ; why then my awkwardness in forming and articulating the reply?

"No sir—he has not—I have not had that pleasure."

"Business again, doubtless! A finer form does not walk Broadway. He is a Herculean Apollo. Mammas cry, 'Ah! what a catch!' and daughters echo 'Ah!' from their very hearts ; and he, unhappy youth ! is voted 'heartless,'—a 'magnificent statue,' because it pleases him to remain fancy-free. He is waiting for an angel and a fortune ?"

I could hear no more of this.

" Have you been a resident of New York long, Mr. Dumont ?" I inquired, changing the topic, disposed as he was, for some reason, to expatiate upon it.

" I am a cosmopolite," rejoined he. " 'Every land is my home.' My sojourn in this place will not extend over this month. I have been here since the middle of April. Having no local attachments, when one set of faces grows to my sight like a twice-told tale, I migrate. Other whims move me sometimes. This year, I am following the footprints of Spring, the vernal breezes and the snowdrops. When I lose the coy nymph in an Arctic iceberg, I shall set forth upon some different chase. One soon comes to the stale dregs of the flask unless he makes variety his motto in the choice of vintage."

I was more alert than civil to him in my obedience to May's sign of departure. I hurried her until we were in the carriage and the illuminated windows behind us ; then leaned back in the darkness and wept unheard.

Herbert had always been my superior. I could not have loved him else ; but it was not with a superiority to elicit encomiums from this callous worldling, in whose estimation feeling was a weakness, Religion a nursery fable. Sorely did I lament the impulse that had betrayed me into the indiscretion of speaking with him of one, never mentioned in my most confidential talks with May, my soul-sister. I was punished as I deserved to be—more severely, perhaps. I was accustomed to regard the separating chasm between us as impassable ; never to be bridged ; but, until this, it had been the work of my own hands ; it was I who repelled, not he who receded. To some the distinction may seem strained ; no woman, however disinterested in her desire for a lover's happiness, will fail to appreciate it. This statuesque Apollo, smiling disdain upon Cupid's manœuvres, was as unlike the image enshrined in my heart, as was the driving man of business, the commercial machine or the wary fortune-hunter. My oft-repeated asseverations of disbelief, the more vehement as my sinking heart declined to receive their comfort—failed to disperse the mists that accumulated about the cherished shrine. Years of absence had spared it, untarnished; a breath from lips I knew to be false in most things, had sullied its glory. Unjust, most unkind I felt this to be, but I could not prevent it.

My eyes were heavy, my motions inelastic as I set about the labor of disarraying myself of my dinner-dress, while May chatted on, unheeding my discouraging replies.

"And Mr. Dumont vouchsafed an entertainment of half an hour in length, to one auditor!" she said. "You must have made an impression. Did you know him before Louise introduced him?"

"No."

"He is the lion of this season—upon exhibition 'for a few days only,'" she continued. "You may recollect my ancient prejudice against him? If he ever divined it, he bears no malice. He is invariably polite and conversational when we meet."

"Louise presented him as Professor Dumont," I forced myself to say. "Of what is he Professor, and where?"

"He has occupied some place in a French University, I understand—I do not know what chair. His stylish appearance, courtly manners and versatile talents have obtained much favor for him in Louise's set."

"I do not like him!" returned I, snapping my slipper-string, as I tried to untie a knot.

"Nor I, if I must be truthful," said May. "There is nothing

real about him, to my eye. As to his age, nobody hazards a definite opinion. He wears a toupée scientifically adjusted, yet an acute observer can detect it; his whiskers are dyed, brown as they are, for they were nearer auburn when we travelled with him, and his teeth may be his own, either by right of purchase or as the lawful gift of Mother Nature."

I smiled sadly. This dislike I traced back to the impressions transferred from Frederic's mind to hers; saw that she had never parted with the aversion he had professed, from the moment of our encounter by the way-side, with the so-called Frenchman.

"He may be thirty, forty, fifty—some guess that he is sixty years old," she went on. "Alfred, who has been in company with him occasionally, protests that he is the Wandering Jew."

A handsome bouquet was handed in at the door the following morning.

"For whom?" asked May, as the servant brought it into the breakfast-room.

"Miss Leigh," was the reply.

"The token of some conquest made last evening!" she cried, clapping her hands. "Look for the card."

There was none, although we searched carefully. The footman did not know the person who gave him the flowers, nor did any surmise as to their donorship meet with acceptance. Alfred Seaton, upon whom my suspicions rested, denied the act or any complicity therein. Other gentlemen were named—May even bringing up Mr. Dumont; but their claims were voted doubtful; and the beautiful offering continued to be the theme of many a jest and conjecture. These were redoubled by the arrival of another the next day, and still a third with a succeeding, until they became, as May said, "a daily institution."

Gradually I became thoughtful at their coming. Who was the friend who thus continually remembered that I was an exile from the bowers of Moss-side? Why did he shun my sight and thanks? Who had a motive for concealment beyond a puerile desire to mystify us; a ridiculous fondness for the anonymous? I studied every flower for an answer to these questions. Refined taste I read in their selection and grouping; liberality in the variety of choice and scarce plants. Were tender thoughts committed to the speaking of their fragrant sighs?

"This is folly," I said, resolutely, one evening, awaking from a reverie over the freshest and most lovely of all. By seeming accident, I had left it in my chamber, instead of upon the parlor-table. In truth, it was for minute inspection, that I might dream over it at will. And what dreams were shaped by its odorous incense! Time, care, duty did not mar delight as intoxicating as I was wont to revel in when Life was new.

My aunt's voice, in conversation with May in the entry, awoke me with a shock.

"You forget," I pursued, hastily rising and pushing away the vase, "that chasing bubbles is children's sport. You caught yours, and found out their nothingness too long ago. You should have learned other lessons by this time. Who was the main figure in your silly musing? Confess it to yourself. Can anything in imagination be more preposterous than the supposition that he has chosen this method of re-establishing a correspondence he promised never to renew—a promise he has kept now for five years—which you have every reason to believe he will never be disposed to violate? I am disappointed in you, Grace Leigh! I hoped you were a strong hearted, right-headed woman. You are proving yourself a sentimental girl. Carry these flowers down to the parlor; put them in a conspicuous stand, where you cannot avoid seeing them all the evening, and let them preach to you of your frail heart—your unstable resolutions."

I did so; setting them where the blaze of the chandelier

revealed the very veins in the leaves, invaded the privacy of every perfumed heart. And having some fancy-work to employ my fingers, I sat at the same table, and stayed my needle, now and then,to pluck a petal or pinch one into fragrance—not caressingly, but as I would have toyed with clover blossoms at home.

Louise surprised us by another call, and in her train, meekly walked her husband. I did not lay aside my sewing. I braved the scornful pity of those haughty eyes; made myself liable to the touch of a lash that never inflicted more than what appeared a touch, but which, like the knout, seldom failed to divide nerve, sinew, and flesh at one smarting cut. I was proof against it to-night. I smiled to myself as I thought how humdrum my tastes, how aimless my existence must seem to her. I accepted her condescension; looked up to her, for all she knew to the contrary, as the glow-worm does to the star—unenvying, unambitious, supremely content with the glimmering spark that shows him only the clod he rests upon. She was a distinguished woman who had a "mission," and was fulfilling it in the sight of men; I an humble country-girl, without beauty or fortune; settling down into the estate of matronly maidenhood; incapable of comprehending the principles of which she was the expositor.

As before, her stay was brief—this time because she "had letters to write."

"I have been made very happy to-day," she said, "by the receipt of several communications which testify that I have not labored quite in vain. Of course, representing, as I do, doctrines, instead of seeking merely to amuse the Public, I have drawn down upon me a storm of abuse from the lordly sex, and must submit resignedly to the fate and title of 'strong-minded woman.' I only hope they will inscribe it upon my tomb-stone. Posterity will call that an honor which was meant as obloquy. But from the oppressed, the lowly slaves, to whom

I have dared to preach freedom; from souls made earnest through suffering, I have had blessing and encouragement which would strengthen me to endure tenfold more opprobrium. I work the more diligently for the abuse; the more heartily when I hear in every throb of my own bosom, the indignant cry of thousands of my sisters against tyranny."

She would have looked grandly upon the rostrum at that moment; her eyes lustrous; the crimson blood centring in her cheeks; her bust swelling with the emotion she described. She had arisen to go, and stood by chance, near the middle of the apartment; "a striking picture," and "an able actress!" said Alfred Seaton's gaze. Youth as he was, the majesty of emancipated womanhood failed to awaken any more exalted sentiment. The other "tyrants" in our number were hardly more moved by this seditious outbreak. My father surveyed her kindly, rather sorrowfully, for he reverenced the old-fashioned type of feminine perfection; but he was not abashed by her contempt or intimidated by her lawless language. Mr. Wilson was picking up his hat and stretching his limbs—weighing anchor, that he might be ready to follow his consort the instant she set sail. There was a dead pause of some seconds when Louise stopped speaking, no one being prepared with a suitable reply, and to prevent embarrassment, May accosted the quiet husband:

"Mr. Wilson! you love and cultivate flowers. Can you tell us the name of this?" singling out an unknown beauty in my bouquet.

He hung back, as if afraid of the vivid circle of light within which she was standing.

"I cannot—I suppose not—I do not think"—he commenced, and a confused muttering finished the answer.

"See it!" May said to Louise.

The prophetess vouchsafed a look. "This should have been gathered from my conservatory," she replied. "It is a new variety of the ——" some unpronounceable name I had never heard before—" which I have not yet seen anywhere else. I am confident it is not to be found in the public gardens. Mine was imported by private hand from the West Indies. Still," she added, laughing, "I do not presume to identify it, since I am ignorant how it came to be here."

May would have told the story, but her teasing glance towards me crossed one from her brother, that admonished her to be discreet.

"I am the present proprietor of the suspected article," I said. "For its antecedents I do not pretend to be responsible. I know no more of them than you do. The nine points of possession are all for which I have any care."

Louise examined the spray slightingly, as if tired of the paltry discussion. "The tenth point can, I imagine, be established by Mr. Wilson."

He was fidgeting by inches towards the door, in perturbation obvious to any one who chanced to look that way. At this direct reference to himself, he let fall both hat and cane, and stooping to reach them, struck his head a sonorous blow against the wall. A very red face, and one grievously discomposed by pain or shame, he presented to us upon the recovery of his perpendicular.

His wife smiled, as did the rest of us, but with less commiseration than was exhibited in our countenances.

"I was saying," she resumed, still carelessly, "that I have seen this plant nowhere except in my greenhouse; and since Miss Leigh is in the dark as to its history before it became her property, I relieved her curiosity by saying that you, probably, were directly or indirectly the donor, especially as I noticed you busily engaged arranging a bouquet this morning."

No answer rendered the discomfited culprit, arraigned and convicted in this sentence.

I pitied him. "I am truly grateful to you for your thoughtful kindness, Mr. Wilson," I hastened to say, "and particularly request that if yours was not the direct agency in bringing me so much pleasure, you will not undeceive me. I prefer thanking you. Your playful *ruse* in sending the flowers as you did, has afforded us considerable amusement."

"It was nicely managed," May followed me. "We are all much obliged to you."

"I should be, certainly," said Louise, "for reminding me of my neglect in not having invited you to explore the conservatory, and gather whatever you wish. My gardener brought the best recommendations, and judging from what I see of his management, was not over-praised. It is enough for me to luxuriate at the banquet of beauty and fragrance that ever awaits me there. I verily believe my floral pets know me, and love my visits. I draw much of solace and joy from them."

"You never handle the watering-pot or the trowel—do you?" inquired Alfred.

"Not I! I would not degrade my thoughts of the holy ministers by associating them with drudgery. To me, they are the spontaneous efflorescence of the soil; emblems of the triumph of the Beautiful over the merely Useful. I leave the tilling, and watering, and pruning to Maclean and Mr. Wilson, who is an amateur in the pursuit."

This classification did not offend the second person included in it. With his customary low-spirited bow all around, he tacked and fell into the wake of the full-rigged frigate sweeping majestically ahead of him, typifying the "victory of the Beautiful over the merely Useful" more distinctly to the optics, physical and mental, of the observers, than her "holy ministers" could ever succeed in doing.

And my dreams about my gift were the thinnest air—not even so substantial as bubbles! Right thankful was I that Dame Reason's lecture had disabused my mind of romantic vagaries before the mystery was unravelled. I said with sincerity that I was glad to know Mr. Wilson as the author of the benefit. I was touched by this mark of his friendship ; saw in it the budding of feelings which, under different auspices, might have flowered into actions worthy of the nature God had bestowed—which the adverse influences of his home had bruised and blighted.

I was in a mood that night to write an appendix to Louise's book, and this would have been its import—"Women ! Sisters ! in piling the blazing beacons that signal your resistance to thralldom old as the earth and time—take heed lest you trample out the fires upon your own hearth-stones ; in the contest for the laurel of Victory, have mercy upon the humble flowers springing up close to your doors ; before you take your lives and reputations in your hands and go forth to battle for the world's regeneration, hear one word of appeal in behalf of 'Domestic Missions!'"

CHAPTER XXII.

I WAS writing to Lilly, and very happy in my intentness upon my task, when May entered our chamber, somewhat out of breath with climbing the stairs.

"Ah! you are busy—agreeably busy!" she said.

"Do you want me?" asked I.

"No; quite the reverse, just now. There is company down stairs. I have a call that may detain me some time, and to beguile your solitude of weariness, I have brought up a book for you to read. You are employed, however—and if Lilly is your correspondent—entirely to your satisfaction. I will leave the volume here for future need."

I thanked her, and assured her of my comfort; but she tarried until I raised my eyes from the paper to see why she had not joined her waiting visitors. She was contemplating me, from the other side of the table, with a peculiar expression of saddened tenderness.

"Why, dear May! what is the matter?" inquired I, apprehensively.

"Matter! nothing! only I *love* you, Grace!" She came around to me and took my head, after her own sweet way, in her arms. "Best, dearest of sisters!" she said; then releasing me, she laughed. "It was one of my spasms of fondness, Gracie. They come over me in sudden waves, when you are unusually lovable. Now, I will go. Shall I find you here when I am at leisure?"

"Yes," I answered, and I was alone.

It was not hard to account for the rise of this "wave." In my happiest humors I was said to be like the portrait above her chair. A flash, a smile upon my features ofttimes brought the moisture to the eyes of Frederic's father and wife. This day I was almost gladsome. The sunny side of Life was displayed to me. My aunt was improving under Dr. ——'s practice; my father's health was robust, and his spirits excellent; our friends were the personification of kindness; my intercourse with May was balm and wine to my soul; and I was communing with my best-loved, my child. A late letter from her, replete with affection, was open upon my desk. And this was a part of my reply:—

"Your love is unspeakably precious to me, darling, far more dear than your modesty has ever allowed you to dream. If I were required now to designate the greatest of the countless temporal blessings which the Father has streamed into my cup, I should unhesitatingly name you, my 'Christmas gift.' That was a pretty conceit of our fathers'—was it not? Yet neither of them set a just valuation upon the treasure they were conferring upon me. Those were my days of shadow, Lilly! shadows, whose depth appalls me in the retrospect. I prayed then, as I grew to love you, that the like might never rest upon you. I thank Heaven that this is impossible, for the inward light—your inalienable right as a child of God—will prevent their closing in about your soul. This safeguard was not mine in those times. I shall never forget what pointed significance there was to me in your innocent explanation of the print, 'Pharaoh's Overthrow;' when unsuspected by either of you, I listened to your prattle with Peyton Elliott,—'And the Egyptians could not see through the cloud, for it *was* a cloud to them.'

"In two weeks, at most, the doctor will liberate Aunt Agnes, with instructions how to continue the blessed work we dare to believe he has begun. Spare yourself the uneasiness you tell me you experience in the fear lest I am more closely confined than I was at home, with you to relieve guard. May contends with me for the honor of playing tire-woman and nurse to the relative, whose patience and virtues endear her to us. I pass much time in the outer air, quite as much as is comfortable at this season. Not a day elapses without some sight-seeing excursion, and I go frequently into company by May's desire. She has a circle of congenial acquaintances, who show us many and acceptable attentions. Your staid Auntie is in danger of becoming dissipated at her advanced age."

Sunlight, lucent amber as that then dancing over the peaked gables of Moss-side, slanted upon the page as I concluded the epistle. I sang snatches of popular lays, while folding and sealing it ; and then, so at-home was I about the premises, I descended to the kitchen to seek a post-boy for the document I was anxious should go by the earliest mail. The obliging footman was "intirely" at my service ; and I bounded up the narrow private staircase, forgetful of May's guests ; without a thought indeed of where I was, or what I did, for I was caroling,

"Be it ever so humble, there's no place like home."

Had not my mind been in advance of the letter, *en route* for that Southern Cottage, I would not have sung that air of all others in the universe. I never did it wittingly—the reader knows why.

From the upper landing, I passed into the entry leading to the snug breakfast-room, where I had never known May to receive her friends. Yet, as I came along the passage, some one stepped back into the door of this apartment, and shut himself in. A gentleman it was, for he did not move so briskly that I could not see his arm and the hand that held a hat. I was streiken dumb, and lost no time in leaving to him the clear course he coveted,—"for my sake, most likely," I reflected, when I was safe in my chamber.

"What a figure I must have made!" I said, laughing, notwithstanding my annoyance; "tramping from the top to the bottom of the house, like a rude school-boy, and practising vocal exercises with all the strength of my never-weak lungs! I will apologize to May when she has dismissed her terrified cavalier."

But she was in a hurry, and I did not detain her to hear my excuses.

"I have to go out on the street for awhile, Gracie," she stated, looking troubled as I fancied. "I do not like to leave you, but mamma will be happy to have you sit with her. I ought"——

"To run away forthwith," I interposed, "and take shame to yourself for insulting me by an apology, as if I were a stranger within your gates, and a stickler for ceremony. No more words! Be off! and a lively jaunt to you!"

"*That* it cannot be!" she rejoined, smiling, while the tears seemed ready to flow. Checking herself, she kissed me twice, and saying anew, "I love you, Gracie!" ran out of the room.

"I hope nothing disagreeable has happened," I thought. "It is some household errand, I suppose."

Composing my ease-loving limbs upon the sofa, I chose the book May had left me, as a substitute for Mrs. Seaton's society. I had passed the paper-cutter but thrice through the leaves, when a card was sent up for "Miss Leigh"—"Mrs. William Wynne."

Shaking fingers added the needful finish to my morning toilette; failing feet carried me into the august presence.

"My dear Grace! I am overjoyed to greet you!"

A fashionable embrace permitted me to touch the silken and lace outworks of her bodice; the blonde trimmings on the inside of her hat kissed my brow as lightly as her lips did mine.

Before I gained a seat, the see-saw, of which I retained a vivid recollection, was in motion. I "was looking charmingly," etc., etc., etc.

"But my dear girl, you have wounded me inexpressibly by not informing me that you were in town. I am actually afraid to ask when you arrived."

As she, nevertheless, took breath, evidently to give me room for a response, I put a period to her affectionate suspense by saying, "We have been here nearly three weeks."

The lavender gloves approached each other, crushing to invisibility, the cobweb mockery of a handkerchief.

"Naughty, cruel creature! how can I forgive you? If I were less attached to you, I would take my leave without another word. Where have you been? what have you been doing, that I have not heard of you?"

I told her of my aunt's sickness; that it had drawn us to the city, and been my principal care during our stay.

"Then, too, Mrs. Wynne, I could not know that you were ignorant of my visit. Having seen Louise repeatedly, it was natural to suppose that she might have communicated the fact, unimportant as it was, to you."

"Poor, dear Louise!" sighed the mother. "Her engagements really overwhelm her. But for her genius and her zeal, she would sink under the burden. You must pardon the oversight, my dear. She has such a number of weighty concerns upon her mind that we ought to be lenient if she is guilty of neglecting what are momentous affairs to other ladies."

At sight, she gauged me by her daughter's measure; made of me a harmless, nothing-in-particular puppet; and the perception of this nettled me more than Louise's condescension. In the Brobdingnagian world of Reform and Progress, I was content to be Lilliputian; to be sheltered by my nothingness; but to my mind, Mrs. Wynne's superiority of years and wealth hardly entitled her to assume this tone.

Ignorant of this mounting independence, she proceeded, "Have you been to her house?"

"Yes, madam—once."

"Is she not delightfully situated?"

"She appears very happy, and lacks for nothing that wealth can procure," I said, guardedly.

"She has secured a most fortunate settlement," was the tune to which she swung me. "I bring her forward as a model to her younger sisters, a shining example of the advantages of a rational union, opposed to the objections that attend mis-called ove-matches. She has the best of husbands—one who never contradicts her; never interferes with her designs. Mr. Wilson is an eminently sensible man. I was conscious of this when I consented to the marriage; but he has surpassed *my* expectations. He is willing to leave to her judgment all that pertains to the household establishment, taking as his share of obligation the work of providing means for the accomplishment of her wishes. He reaps his reward in seeing her surrounded by luxuries, and enjoying herself in her own way. He is a very remarkable person."

"So I think!" I uttered, in sober veracity.

"Depend upon it, my dear Grace, there is more certainty of happiness in these marriages which young ladies are apt to cry out against, because of the disparity of disposition and taste in the parties united. Where there is unison of feeling, perfect congeniality of sentiment, both weary of the sameness. It sounds well to talk of walking the same road, but if you will excuse a homely phrase, a double track is better. Now Louise and Mr. Wilson never quarrel. Not a hard speech has ever been exchanged. They agree most amicably to differ, and avoid the repeated collisions to which loving couples who *will* walk together are constantly liable."

"Yours is an ingenious theory, Mrs. Wynne," said I, amused at her overt worldliness; her refined repudiation of a fallacy sanctioned by ages, held as undeniable truth by many generations. It occurred to me, too, how close was the similarity between her very material views and the etherealized doctrines inculcated by her daughter. Did this conjunction of extremes then form "the faultless circle of Truth, effulgent and eternal," of which the latter had written? a sentence untranslatable otherwise to my literal comprehension.

"Amelia is not at home," Mrs. Wynne was saying, "or she would have called with me this forenoon. It affords me pleasure to announce to you that she is likely to follow her sister's example in the course of the coming Fall. She has contracted an engagement with an excellent gentleman, a particular friend of the family, and perfectly eligible in every respect."

I had heard of this prospective alliance before, but deemed it wisest not to say so, lest her keen-sightedness should read the remainder of the information I had received touching her "eligible," viz. that he was nearer fifty than forty years of age, cramped in intellect, ungainly in person, cross and parsimonious, and reputed a millionaire.

"The match has the unqualified approbation of her father and myself. Having her real good most at heart, we could not refrain from congratulating her and ourselves upon her prospects. I am happily disappointed in the giddy girl's choice, for her volatile spirits and tendency to willfulness have caused me some misgivings as to her destiny. She is acquiring stability of character and sobriety of demeanor now—a marked change which commenced the very hour of her engagement. Dutiful children are the greatest pride and delight of a faithful mother's heart. In my imperfect way, I have endeavored to discharge my duty to mine, and, up to this time, have been amply repaid for my labor and anxiety."

The cobweb performed a journey to her eye upon an unnecessary errand, for the placid orbs were dry as Sahara, still and frozen as an Alpine glacier. Her maternal affection, as I have said elsewhere, was her distinguishing trait. As she advanced in life the hobby had become an idiosyncrasy, paraded as one whose interest must be apparent to everybody, and therefore was never out of season. I was meditating upon this, and calculating the probable amount of nature and of habit combined in her foible, when she scattered addition and subtraction right and left, by an unlooked-for shot.

"You have had a visit from Herbert to-day?"

"Madam!" I ejaculated.

She said it over, unmindful of my dying color and irregular breathing.

"Herbert, my son, has been to see you to-day."

It was an assertion, not a question, yet I denied it.

"No, madam—I should say, not to my knowledge."

How I blessed the window shades and curtains that shut out the prying, tale-telling light!

"I stopped my carriage upon the block adjoining this, to leave a card, and saw him come out of the house, accompanied by Mrs. Leigh," persisted the lady, impaling me with those unmoving eyes.

I rallied to sustain the inspection.

"Ah!" affecting to see through the whole affair as clearly as she did through my deceit; "May came to my room to say that there was some one below, and that she was going to walk. I do not think she mentioned that it was Mr. Wynne, but I was writing and did not pay a great deal of attention to her."

"They maintain their ancient Platonic affection with much constancy," said Mrs. Wynne. "He is more attentive to her than to any other lady. Some comment upon this and hint broadly at the growth of a more romantic reciprocal sentiment; but I try to silence the report. Herbert has not forbidden me to continue this course; indeed, he was actually angry that his brotherly regard should be so misinterpreted. I proposed that the exhibitions of his esteem should be more prudent; but he is a headstrong boy, and I got only a black look and a surly negative for my unfortunate counsel. I perceived I was touching upon delicate ground, and have since repressed my uneasiness in his presence."

I detected the latent spite her utmost tact could not hide. Her motherly feeling was as nominal as his sonship.

"I have wished that I could speak unreservedly with Mrs. Leigh upon this subject, for I fear that she may have formed an erroneous idea of my feelings and actions in this business. May I rely upon you, Grace, you, who used to be so lovely a peacemaker—to free her mind of any notion that I am, or ever was, averse to her union with my son? She was the chosen and familiar associate of my Louise, and in those days, had my affection and confidence. Although our intercourse is more distant now, these feelings remain unaltered. She is still very pretty; is amiable and intelligent; her standing in her circle cannot be questioned—she would acquit herself creditably in any; what motive could I have for objecting to her entering my family, if she were Herbert's choice? That she is not, or that there is, at any rate, no definite betrothal, I have declared to be my belief. My object in reverting to this, and to you—to whom it may be painful to think of her second marriage with any one—is that I may right myself in your sister's eyes, if I have suffered. I am sensitive as regards my place in the hearts where I have gained a footing. The danger—the chance, I mean—of their marrying is lessened, if not removed, by Herbert's departure. As I said to a lady yesterday—a believer in the engagement—he would not leave his native land for three years, if it contained his future wife—he knowing her to be such—particularly as it is optional with him to go or to remain."

Was this frankness an artful stratagem to enlighten me as to the futility of any schemes I might have upon her son, or did she design to insult May, and poison my mind with suspicions of her fidelity to the memory of my brother? These questions shot through my brain while the rockers were in mid career, but the closing remark expelled them.

"Where is he going?" I gasped, the cold sweat breaking through my skin.

"You may well be amazed, my dear. A young man of his prospects, his home ties, his patriotism! It appears impossible—unnatural! but so it is. He sails this afternoon for California, that semi-barbarous country. It is a hare-brained notion, I fear; yet Mr. Wynne will not raise a finger to dissuade him, and other of his friends encourage him to believe that if he can found a branch of his business there, it will prove very lucrative. So he has set his face to the Southwest, and no mortal power can stir him from his purpose. Men rail at our caprices. Between ourselves, it is because we infringe upon theirs when we venture to indulge our whims."

"Mr. Wynne sails this afternoon, you say? In what vessel?" My voice did not tremble now.

"In the Benjamin Franklin. He called here to say 'Farewell,' I presume. His resolution was hasty, that is, his announcement of it to us was; but he is more reserved to us than any of our other children are, or ever will be, I devoutly pray. Now, my love, what is there to prevent you from stepping into my carriage, and riding home with me to partake of a family dinner? You used to be domesticated with us during vacations, and when you paid us that welcome visit at Louise's marriage. Mr. Wynne will be charmed to meet you. You have a great admirer in him. He it was, who hearing from Mr. Wilson that you were so near us, told me where to find you. Come! what say you to my plan for pleasing him?"

"That it is impossible for me to do it to-day. I thank you

for your invitation, and him for his favorable remembrance, but it is out of my power to go with you. I will try to return your call before I leave for the South."

I felt that my manner was restrained and high, and I did not care. "If she would only go!" groaned my heart. "Oh! why does she stay? Am I not tortured sufficiently? Have not those pale-blue eyes looked their fill?"

I could have stamped; wrung my hands and cried aloud with impatience; but I set my teeth tightly and stiffened the jerking muscles, until blonde and lips, a second time, honored my face, and I lost her and the swing at the front door. Slow and hard fell my footsteps upon the stairs; slower and harder was their beat upon the chamber-floor; but passion raged with tornado violence. Sometimes I checked my walk to feel my hands, to look at my reflection in the mirror, in very doubt of my identity. I felt congealed flesh, the blood purpled under the nails; I beheld an ashy visage, with eyes of living fire. I knew myself to be possessed of a legion of demons.

His then was the society from which May succeeded so ingeniously in banishing me; his, her escort in the walk that was to be so brief, and had already lasted, it seemed to me, hours. He came hither frequently—daily perhaps; but with the like clever manœuvres, they continually hoodwinked me. When I tripped through that private entry, but a door divided me from him. I had seen his hand—a step nearer—and one glimpse of his face had been mine—a glimpse for which, in my frenzy, I would now lie down and die. He had heard my voice. Did its tones, did the melody they warbled revive no visions pleasant and mournful to the soul? or were the innuendoes of his wily mother—who insinuated belief while professing to doubt—true, and brother and sister forgotten together in the allurements of a later, more fortunate love? I stopped before the portrait, and the lightful eyes took the anguished stare of mine. I wept while I looked—

hot rain that aggravated the heart-burning. Once I had my hand upon the frame to turn it to the wall; a token which she should see and recognize, the instant she entered; but I drew it away, and left it to smite her with the beauty she once loved.

She was coming! The step approaching, languid with fatigue or heaviness of spirit, was still hers. I dressed my face in a hypocritical smile, the just return for what I expected to receive. But hers was beamless, and her voice, gentle and affectionate, wanted the ringing music that belonged to it.

"Have you been very lonely, Grace, dear?" she said, tossing her bonnet and mantle upon the bureau. "I am sorry I remained away so long a time."

"I have not suffered from solitude," I returned. "You enjoyed your walk, I hope."

"Not very much, and I have come back with a headache."

"Lie down!" I advised. "If you rest in this shaded room for an hour or so, you may get over it."

She complied, and feeling very much as if I were heaping coals of fire upon it instead, I bound her brow with my hands.

"Dear Grace!" she said, faintly.

A drop oozed from beneath her eyelid, and trickled down her cheek. A sense of self-reproach arose in my bosom. I remained silent, holding her head and looking into the countenance which had never yet deceived me.

"I have had a trial this morning, Grace, a sore trial," she continued, "yet it was not so much the personal grief to myself, as sympathy with another. I cannot tell you its nature now."

"Do not!" I uttered impulsively. "I trust you, May."

Her eyes opened in surprise upon me at this singular exclamation; but I did not explain my meaning. I placed pillows for her aching head, and kissing her before I commended her to the healing influence of sleep, I called her "sister."

"You are my own blessed sister, May! I shall never address you by any other title."

"Never!" was her response. "It is the dearest and proudest to me that you can use."

I left her, with the pictured face beaming down upon her from the wall, smiling its blessing upon her sinless slumbers, and I bore myself and my misery to another part of the house. Miserable I was, after the transport of unjust doubt and vindictiveness had subsided. Assurance that I had wronged her faithful heart did not mitigate my suffering. What "trial" was hers if not that she had been forced to reject the offer of a love more hopeless, less constant to its original object, although that object still lived, than was hers, dedicated to the dead? This was a hypothesis, obvious in its probability, but it wounded me less cruelly than the thought of the thousands of miles, the months and years about to be put between us. I had so lived—as I now found—in the hope of seeing him once again! not of speaking with him, for I dreaded an indifferent glance from the eyes that had looked such fond regard upon me—but one moment's sight of feature and form; one sound of the voice whose echoes wandered forever among the hills of my heart's background—what would I not risk and do to purchase these?

"They may be yours!" whispered a springing hope, wild as swift. "See him! There may yet be time."

I hunted eagerly for a morning's paper, and ran eye and finger down the closely-packed columns of marine advertisements. There was the name! the "Benjamin Franklin," advertised to start from the —— street pier that afternoon at four o'clock. I employed no artifice, and none was required. May kept her room; Mrs. Seaton was conversing with my aunt in the chamber of the latter, where I sat until the moment I had settled as best for my purpose drew near. Then I repaired to the dressing-closet where hat and veil were ready, donned them, and with no other protection from the heat, went out upon the burning streets whose pavements crisped my shoes, and glared fierce radiations into my eyes. Hot and still they were—still for city streets. The very booming of the ever-raging river sounded, from afar, sluggish and dull.

I knew where was the nearest hackney-coach stand, and stopping at an unpretending carriage before the door of the stable, asked if it were engaged. It was not; the horses were hastily attached; the driver was upon the box, and I within, safely hidden behind its Venetian blinds, rolling towards the bay and wharf. I concerted every part of the scheme before we were merged in the uproarious throng of vehicles and human beings, that trode, and fought, and pushed close to the water's edge. The driver alighted and opened the door. He was a civil, steady-looking man of middle age.

"—— street pier, ma'am—Benjamin Franklin!" he pronounced in a business manner.

I gave him some money, and requested him to drive as near as he could to the passage-way to the vessel, and halt there for further orders. He fulfilled the behest to the letter after a deal of trouble to himself, in which I took not the remotest concern. We had a most favorable position. From my loop-hole I examined every passenger that pressed along the straitened limits guarded by the cross policemen. The din was almost unbearable, but I set myself determinedly to endure it—nay, more—to analyze it. First, I understood the yells of the newsboys and confectionery-venders; then the shrill cry, "Matches! a penny a box—matches!" from old-faced children who dodged miraculously among heels and carriages; then the fragmentary sentences of those about to embark to others they were leaving behind. And then—so near to me that I could have touched him by thrusting out the fingers that held apart the slats of the shutter—came Herbert Wynne! His father was with him, and they moved at a slow rate. I should have been able to take a deliberate view of the taller and younger, even if they had not paused by my vehicle. An acquaintance accosted them at this spot. It was Mr. Dumont.

"Ha! Mr. Wynne! I was looking for you!" He spoke loudly, that he might be heard above the confusion. "I am here, sir, to say to you, bon voyage!"

"Thank you, sir. Sailors say that good wishes change to favorable winds. I shall be grateful for both or either."

The clear enunciation conveyed every word to me. To the echo among those shadowy hills they were committed, there to dwell with others that had emanated from the same source. He towered there, fully a head above the rest of the throng, except Mr. Dumont. But the latter lost immeasurably by comparison with him in other respects. The ingenuous expression of one countenance, the cynic smile of the other, I noted, brief as was my opportunity. They walked on towards the great, black hulk, rocking a few paces beyond us; mounted the inclined plane that connected it with the shore; were out of sight for a minute, and reappeared, a group that could not be mistaken—at least, not by me—upon the hurricane deck.

Faster rushed the tide of life past my hiding-place; louder, hoarser was the roar. I saw only those three figures, darkly distinct against the noon-bright sky; heard nothing but the echoes wandering, sobbing restlessly in my soul.

A bell clanged from the vessel, and a shout repeated its warning. The tide flowed back as boisterously as it had ebbed; the black sea-monster heaved his wet sides yet higher into the sun, laved them deeper in the wave. The deck group—my group—was broken. Heads bowed over clasped hands; two joined the shoreward bound; one remained in his place, motionless as a pillar of stone. The decks were soon filled with a tossing mass of forms, looking their last of land. He was alone—no friendly arm, no tone of affection was there to support him if he sorrowed for what he was quitting. Yet had I not vowed to follow him wherever he led?

"He does not want me now!" I said, sternly; and I was calmly observant again.

Once he raised his arm. It was to wave a salute to Mr. Dumont, who threw his handkerchief into the air, as the report of the signal cannon shook the earth, and the huge keel cut its first furrow in the water.

"Ready now, ma'am?" said the driver.

"No—wait!"

The wharf-throng thinned rapidly, urged as they were by the dust and heat. When, finally, my horses' heads were turned, mine was the only carriage there, and the way was unobstructed to where, through the gap in the forest of masts where the Franklin had lain, I could see her, a dwindling barque upon the horizon, and between us long swells of green water, like moving graves.

CHAPTER XXIII.

MAY was pale and said little during the evening, yet did not seem disposed to sleep when we were laid down for the night. I, too, was wakeful, but I manifested it by profound stillness, while she stirred frequently, as though her couch were set with prickles, and sighed, under the weight of physical or mental discomfort.

"Grace," she said, at length, "are you asleep?"

"No, dear May. Do you wish anything?"

"Your ear and your indulgence. I have a message for you from one to whom you were once—a friend."

"Well?" I waited for the rest, anticipating its purport.

"Do not accuse me of a lack of feeling or propriety, Grace, in venturing upon what is, by tacit consent, forbidden ground." She moved nearer to me. "Herbert Wynne was here to-day. I went out with him—I will be sincere with you—because I feared your questioning, particularly as you had seen that a gentleman was with me in the breakfast-room. Moreover, I was too much agitated to talk collectedly, and I did not wish to distress you. As to Herbert's visit, it was the only one he has made me in several weeks. He came to bid me farewell, for he sailed this afternoon upon a voyage—to California."

She listened for some expression of surprise, some comment, but I let her resume the story told so timidly.

"I did not tell you that he was here, because, from what you wrote to me the last time his name occurred in our letters; from your conduct in regard to him since, I supposed that the interview would be productive of unpleasant emotions to you."

"And to him also," I interrupted. "You were quite right."

"He charged me with a message to you," May continued. "I must assure you from him of his cordial esteem, his kindest wishes for your welfare; that neither time nor circumstance had detracted from his regard for your worth, his respect for the motives which actuated you in measures he deemed unreasonable, while the disappointment was fresh. 'And ask her,' he said, 'to remember me, to pray for me sometimes, as for a brother who is ever willing to serve her, whose principal regret is that the chances of doing this are so small.'"

"He was very kind," I answered. "A portion of your communication was already known to me; that he had been to see you, that you went out together, that he embarked this afternoon."

"How? who in the house"——

"No one in the house told me these things. Mrs. Wynne drove up as you left your door."

"Ah! she spoke of us—then? What more did she say on this interesting topic?—interesting, she evidently considers it."

"Nothing of consequence, nothing that was worthy of notice," I said.

But she was not to be put off in this style. "Grace!" raising herself up. "She is no mother to Herbert, no well-wisher to me. He has chagrined her, earned her implacable enmity by resisting her attempts to negotiate a marriage for him with a wealthy heiress, and upon me has fallen the rancor of her spleen. She undertakes to gainsay reports which no one ever breathed until her pretence of setting all right interrupted the ordinary course of affairs. Did she not hint to you that my friendship for Herbert was not what it seemed, and retail the 'they says,' she would have you think were current concerning us?"

I was silent.

"I knew that she would not spare you or me!" pursued May, with some bitterness. "Grace! sister! say that you disbelieve her charges; that her insidious whispers did not obtain a hearing from your heart!"

"Did I not declare my trust in you to-day, just after she had left me?" I said.

"Yet you do not speak quite naturally. Is there something yet unexplained? Have I displeased or wounded you?"

"No! no! the machinations of a thousand Mrs. Wynnes shall not engender a suspicion of your truth to me, your faith to your husband, May."

"My 'husband!' In heaven, as upon earth, he can never cease to be that," she said, solemnly. "A second marriage would be a sin in my case. When we stood at the altar together, my vow was for time and for eternity. 'There is neither marrying nor giving in marriage,' among the blessed, we are told; but I feel that his angel will attend my arrival in our upper home, that those who have loved best here, will not there forget their earthly ties. Do not misjudge me, sister, because I am outwardly like those who have not lost and mourned. The Father, in extinguishing the lamp in my breast, has instructed me to light up gloomy places in other hearts; bade me draw, from many rills, the refreshing for which I once applied to a single fountain. It is thus Frederic would have had me act—to love and do good to his kind, for him and for myself."

But I longed to have her add that her reputed lover had repaid her friendship in exact kind. How peacefully I could have slept if she had said, "I am no more than a sister to him!" It was not spoken, and my latest thought was a prayer for the wanderer upon the sea; a resolution that I would seek for strength to think of him as he had desired; as the brother, I so wished May to claim for herself, although a dearer place could never be mine.

I did not repay Mrs. Wynne's visit. If it had been my intention to do so, I must have economized time very savingly ; for my aunt's physician granted her leave to depart a week earlier than we had looked for his permission. He was undoubtedly moved to this by her longing for home.

"I am withering here!" she said to me, the evening she received the warrant of liberation. "I dream of Moss-side, of its groves and flowers, of my own room, and of Lilly, the dear babe! It is strange that I should dream so much, and every night!"

"It is a sign of rejuvenation, aunt," I remarked, jocosely. "Elderly people are less given to night-visions, and recall them less perfectly than do young ones."

"And you would assign this reason, also, for my many thoughts of my youth, which seems lately more a present reality, than this infirm old age."

"Old age, aunt!" repeated May, entering. "This from a handsome woman who has scarcely passed the meridian of life! I shall apprehend a relapse, if these symptoms of depression continue. Look at this!"

She held up one of the long, thick locks I was combing; black as night, with an occasional silver line stealing through it. Divested of her mourning-cap and nun-like attire, my aunt's appearance was indeed remarkably youthful, for one who had experienced sickness and care for so many years. She wore a white wrapper, and her hair, unbound, fell over her shoulders, and rounded, by shading, the decided outlines of her features. Our assiduity as nurses had won upon her gratitude, and her helplessness rendered her more accessible by making her dependent.

She met May's raillery kindly.

"I was forty-six, yesterday," she said. "I have lived almost half a century."

"And bid fair to see fourscore before you wear out," replied May.

"I was about to say, 'Heaven forbid!'" my aunt said, seriously; "but it would be sinful, were I not to wait patiently until my change comes. I trust I am not so rebellious of the tardy progress of time as I used to be. It is never too late to learn, and I am studying the goodness, instead of the judgment of God."

May gave me a glance over the invalid's head. She had never seen her so conversable before. I incited her to talk; partly in the idea that the healthy play of the mind might conduce to the good of the body; partly through pardonable curiosity to gather some reminiscences of the youth to which I now heard her allude for the second time in all the years we had lived together.

"I thought the flight of time was swifter, the further one advanced in life," I remarked.

"That depends upon the number and weight of the clogs upon the wheels," rejoined she. "If they have travelled through miry roads, they turn heavily. I can look back to a season—no short one either—when, to me, they moved without friction, and their way was over velvet turf. I was a happy child."

Her eyes were bright and soft, and although she chafed the lifeless hand when she spoke, it was from habit. She forgot its want of vitality in the scenes amid which Fancy was roving.

"It was a lovely homestead at which we lived—where I was born. I have never smelled such roses and jessamine anywhere else. There was one white jessamine that grew over the windows of my mother's room—much more luxuriant and fragrant than those your father planted at Moss-side in memory of that. The windows were large and long, and when I could just crawl so far, it was my delight to pull myself up by the lattice-work covering the lower part, and pluck my hands full of the star-blossoms. Then there were magnolia trees, under which my sister and myself built our baby-house ; for the summer showers glanced from the varnished leaves as from a tight roof ; and in the orange-grove, my mother's pride, we collected on fair evenings, when the day's sports and labors were done, and sang or talked until bed-time. It was a sunny home—a bower of pleasure."

"How many brothers and sisters had you ?" asked May.

"Two brothers, Archie and Frederic ; one sister—Maggie—older than myself by two years and a half. What a beauty she was ! Lilly reminds me of her sometimes ; but she has not her regularity of feature, nor her stature. We were precisely the same height ; in everything besides, each was the antipodes of the other. She was as mild as I was passionate, as docile to control as I was refractory. 'Day and night,' we were often called. My first grief was her marriage. I was ready to hate the bridegroom for rifling our nest of its most beautiful bird. She was hardly fit to quit it, for she had counted only seventeen summers ; but our parents were over-indulgent, and the young couple were ardently attached to one another. My father presented them with a pretty cottage in sight of our piazza, and they commenced housekeeping in a style that reminded one of the toy establishment under the magnolia. The mimicry did not last long. She died two years after she became a wife. Poor Maggie !"

The living hand still stroked its palsied fellow ; her eyes shone yet more softly, looking into what was to us, vacant space.

"I never think of her as ill or dying, although I saw her while she was both. To my eyes, to-day, she is dressed in her bridal-robes, blushing with love and bliss. I am glad this is so, for thus, I would believe, she looks in heaven—she cannot be lovelier. One little incident of her sickness I cherish very fondly. She had a hand of perfect beauty, tiny as a child's, but exquisitely moulded ; fair as a lily, except where the fingers were tipped with rose-color. My admiration of it was enthusiastic, and had caused her many a burst of amusement. It was not wasted by her illness, and on the morning of the death, she held it towards me with a smile—'I wish, Agnes, I could leave you this as a keepsake!' They made her grave in the orange-grove. Dear Maggie!"

"You were almost grown, then, were you not?" said I.

It was a luckless query. In one flash, the light in her eyes burned out; with one shudder, face and frame were inflexible.

"Yes—nearly. I am sitting up beyond my bed-time, and detaining you. As you will have a fatiguing day to-morrow, packing, you will wish to retire early."

The following evening, she went with us to the parlor after tea; an uncommon event, for since her affliction had laid so much infirmity upon her, she disliked to encounter strangers. May, to whom nothing human was unapproachable, settled herself, as of yore, upon the lowest seat in the apartment, and resting lightly against the knee, where I had never sat, even in childhood, chatted with her as unrestrainedly to all appearance, as she would have done with me. My father was near Mrs. Seaton, and Alfred and I were engrossed by the examination of a quantity of music he had purchased as a gift to Lilly. He was a warm-hearted fellow, and behaved to me with the loving respect he would have displayed to an elder sister.

"We shall miss you terribly when you are gone," he said. "I do not believe that your aunt is well enough to dismiss her physician. In my judgment, she would act more prudently in delaying her departure for some weeks longer."

"The wish is father to the thought—is it not?" I asked.

There was a stir in the hall. My aunt half-arose, but there was no room for retreat.

"The victorious Beautiful!" said Alfred, aside to me, as the door unclosed.

But it was not the subjugated "Useful" that attended her. Notwithstanding the disparity in their ages, Mr. Dumont certainly looked the more suitable mate for her. He had too just a taste to be dashing in apparel or carriage, but he could not fail to attract notice wherever he went. Now, he was most becomingly dressed, and had less the air of a made-over man than usual. He shook hands with Alfred, who met him near the entrance ; bowed, with his own eminent grace, to Mrs. Seaton, then to May, who introduced "My aunt, Miss Leigh," and in the same breath—"My father, Mr. Leigh, whom you have not met before, I think, Mr. Dumont."

My aunt fixed a startled gaze upon him—a glare, whose wildness insanity could not have heightened ; then, without any sign of salutation, sunk her head in her hand. May told us afterwards that she overheard a muttering—a convulsive sigh—"No ! no ! am I losing my reason ?"

My father recovered from a transitory confusion, into which the entrance of our visitors had cast him, and with his natural politeness, acknowledged his daughter-in-law's introduction. Mr. Dumont performed his share of the ceremony in haste, that might have been mistaken for disrespect. His discomposure was as apparent to us all, as its cause was unknown. Once, I thought him on the point of running away, instead of sitting down as he was invited to do. Then, rallying with a species of effrontery, he selected a seat by me. This scene transpired in a much shorter time than has been consumed in its description. Louise and May endeavored to restore ease to all parties, and Alfred supported them ably. Mr. Dumont would not speak of his own accord, and I addressed him with some trite nothings.

"Excuse me !" he said, under his breath. "What were you saying ? This visit is unexpected to me. Mr. Wilson requested me to take his wife to a party in his stead—he not being ready. I did not know that your relatives were with you. We cannot stay many minutes."

"Has he taken too much wine?" I marvelled, as he stumbled through the disconnected sentences. "Something has thrown him from his balance."

"You contemplate leaving us very soon, Mrs. Wilson informs me," Mr. Dumont went on.

His voice was almost a whisper; but my aunt dropped her hand and leaned forward. He did not see her, and I strove to engage him in our conversation that he might not be disturbed by her inspection. As he regained his presence of mind and his habitual manner, the agonized interest expressed in her starting orbs alarmed me. I was anxious and fluttered; rambled and hesitated in my speech, and at last, stopped short. His eyes, against his volition, it was evident, were carried by mine in the direction of her chair. She was rising—and in fear or amazement, he sprang to his feet.

Thus they confronted each other, for one instant—one only—and she walked unassisted, without tottering, across the floor. She laid her hand upon his bosom—it might have been to assure herself of his corporeal presence—but it seemed a caressing gesture. He did not move—his livid face looked down into hers—bloodless likewise, but in her eyes were burnings that mocked the chill of age, the mists of years.

"Can the grave give up its dead?" she said, in thrilling tones. "Julian! Julian!" and with a shriek, "It *is* he!" she fell forward into his arms.

It was but an impulse, the instinct of nature that stretched them to receive her form. It would have escaped them by its own weight had not my father relieved him of his burden.

There was a scene of utter confusion. My aunt was extended upon the sofa in a death-like swoon. Mrs. Seaton, May, and myself gathered around her; doors opened and shut; hurrying footsteps went to and fro. When I recovered my self-possession sufficiently to enable me to note others besides the inanimate cause of the commotion, neither Mr. Dumont nor Alfred were to be seen ; Louise stood aloof, steadfastly surveying us ; my father sat in an arm-chair on the further side of the room, his figure bowed together in speechless emotion. I touched him. He raised his head with such energy of action that I started back.

"What is it?" he demanded, huskily, shaking off his stupor and striving to appear a sane, collected man, while his disordered air terrified me.

"I am afraid that aunt has had another stroke," I said.

"My poor Agnes!" This was said more naturally. "It is enough to kill her!"

Alfred had gone for a physician, whose arrival afforded us only temporary tranquillity, for, by the light of another morning, his decision had gone forth, and its truth been ratified by our despairing hearts. There was no hope of her recovery ; a bare possibility that she would revive, even partially, from insensibility.

Insensibility, dull and dead it was, that benumbed every faculty and held dominion over the breathing corpsè. Hour after hour was marked by the sharpening of the features, the deepening of the greyish tinge about the mouth and eyes, and towards evening, by slower and shorter respirations. At sunset, these ceased. The last worn strand that bound the spirit to the clay, parted noiselessly ; the troublings of the wicked, the toil of the weary were forever ended.

Mrs. Seaton opened the shutters. The light flowed over the bed and my father's countenance, as he bent down to close the glazing eyes. Grief, not violent, but too mighty to find vent in tears or words, was depicted there. One gaze upon the changed face, and he turned away for the solitude of his chamber, which he did not quit until the day of the funeral. We buried her by the side of Frederic in the beautiful city of the dead, hundreds of miles away from her Southern home. No Magnolia or Orange blooms above her ; but in an ever-sunny Land she bears the palm-branch of victory, wears the white robe—for through much tribulation she entered the Kingdom.

CHAPTER XXIV.

OURS was a sorrowful return to Moss-side; yet my heart leaped within me, and a smile overspread my father's haggard visage, when we saw, from the bend of the road into the lane, the little maiden who watched in the porch for our coming. Her tears, silent and fast, bathed our cheeks, as we clasped her to our breasts. In mine, and, I doubt not, in her grandparent's, was a tide of thanksgiving that this, the sunbeam of our home, was still spared; a hopefulness that had not cheered our spirits since the moment of our bereavement.

We allowed a day or two for needed rest, and then addressed ourselves to the task of altering our indoor arrangements to suit the lessened number of our household, to conceal the external signs of the vacancy we could not forget. We chose a bright morning—Lilly and I—for our visit to the desolate chamber which had been our living-room of late years. The unpruned vines wandered over the casements, casting unwonted shadows through the place; the confined air was tomb-like in feeling and odor. First, we threw wide windows and doors; but the scented breath of Summer could not chase away the awe that induced us to tread on tiptoe around the bed, and the great old chair, ghostly in its spotless cover; to handle with reverence the contents of drawers and trunks, and whisper to each other over them. The utmost order and neatness prevailed through all. One thing I could not fail to observe incidentally—the absence of any souvenir, any relic whatever of her life prior to her domestication in our family. There was not a single dried flower; not a lock from "Maggie's" alabaster temples; none of darker hue and firmer curl; no jealously-treasured miniature—and what was especially remarkable, not one letter or even note. In her private life she had rigidly maintained the anchorite simplicity that characterized her conduct in her social relations. As she had lived, so had she died, leaving but floating threads upon which curiosity could fasten as possible clues to a history I felt was fraught with tragical interest. In one drawer—the only locked one—were a linen shroud and a burial-cap, yellow with time, deposited there, no one could say when, wrought by her hands and designed for herself. They were sprinkled by the salt drops that gushed up at the thought of her preparation, by strangers, for the dreamless rest in a stranger-grave. We packed everything away, as she would have wished to have it done; transferred some articles of furniture to other parts of the house, and made all practicable changes in the disposition of what remained in this apartment. My father would have no locked doors, no haunted chambers beneath his roof.

"Such spots, although sacred to the holiest of sorrows," he said to me, "and made the occasion of pious and loving pilgrimages, if dutifully frequented, often, in the end, lose their charm. If unvisited, they are too apt to be avoided, by and by, with superstitious dread, and come to be invested with all manner of foolish terrors. We need no appeals to our senses to keep alive the memory of her who is gone."

That afternoon, he sent for me to the honeysuckled arbor at the foot of the garden, and related the story of the skeleton in our home.

The introductory portions of the narration were known to me in part; the description of the abode in which he was born, where Maggie was married, the dissimilarity of the sisters, their tender affection, and the death of the elder.

"I was the oldest of the four," he proceeded, "and when

Maggie died, had been at the head of a family for several years. But as I was settled at a convenient distance from the homestead, the household bond seemed to remain intact. Agnes was a wild, undisciplined girl of sixteen, who gave promise of decided beauty of a certain order. Vivacious and high-spirited, she was my favorite sister, endearing as were Maggie's feminine virtues. She returned my partiality with all the warmth of her ardent temperament. My influence over her exceeded that of her parents, or even of the sister she well-nigh worshipped. We could not foresee how soon she would be obliged to depend upon me as her sole guardian, but our attachment grew stronger, as she neared womanhood. My brother, Frederic, was of a roving disposition, and obtained a commission in the navy. His going was the next severed link in our chain. A year later, our father died, and the grass was not rooted upon his grave, when our mother joined him. I removed to the old place, and Agnes lived with us. I have intimated that she was independent. She was more, proud and imperious, if her will was crossed ; impassioned in every feeling. To control her by severity was out of the question, but if love were the ruling power, she was all submission. She manifested a taste for learning unusual in one of her age and sex, and mine had long been the care of appointing her teachers, and to some extent, her studies. She had been a resident of my house but a little while when, in an evil hour, I was persuaded to send her to a seminary of note in New Orleans. Mine was the first false step."

He passed his hand over his brow, as if he felt the cloud that was gathering there.

" She was gay, romantic, susceptible, and was just completing her eighteenth year. She could not be considered a school-girl, and the accomplished French principal offered to admit her into the establishment with the privileges of a parlor boarder. To this I acceded, without a thought of what was implied by this ambiguous phrase, except that the spoiled child would not be subjected to the rigor of school-room government, and would have less reason to pine for the freedom of her country life. She was too brave and sanguine to mope in homesickness, or shun the labors and privations of a student's lot, and although she wept at our parting, there was sunshine mingled with the shower. Throughout the winter, her letters denoted more than contentment—active enjoyment in her situation. Her studies, her mates, the kindness of her instructors, the peeps at society Madame Duplanché sanctioned by her personal chaperonage, were prolific themes for her pen, while unabated love for the dear and distant ones ran through every epistle and attracted us the more nearly to her.

"Without warning, the other side of the picture was exhibited to me. It was during a brief but dangerous illness of your mother's that a letter came from Madame Duplanché, such an one as a Frenchwoman alone can write. With infinite caution and tact, and a multitude of apologies, she informed me of her misgivings with regard to my sister's acquaintance with a visitant at her house, Julian Darford by name, 'a young gentleman of unblemished character,' she said, 'if we may believe his credentials and the testimony of his demeanor since he has been an inhabitant of this city; well-bred, prepossessing in person and address. I do not marvel that he has captivated the imagination of Miss Agnes, whose tastes are highly cultivated, and whose appreciation of the beautiful and noble is so acute; yet I conceive it to be my duty to confide to you my views of the existing state of affairs, and leave it to you to interfere or not, as you may, in your superior judgment, think advisable.'

"Uncertain as was this information, for not an incident was mentioned as a support to her suspicions, save Mr. Darford's 'prepossessing' appearance and Agnes' lively imagination—it worked me up to an intolerable pitch of uneasiness. I could not go myself to tear my sister away from temptation, for my wife's condition forbade my absence from her sick-bed. Nor, for the same reason, could I confer with her who had ever proved herself my best counsellor. Had my measures been tempered by her judicious forbearance, the result might have varied widely from what I am about to tell you. Upon the spur of the moment, distracted by anxiety for the two, who equally, but from different causes, required my services; driven on by the emergency I had brought myself to believe was already upon us, I wrote to the principal and to Agnes. Madame, I thanked for her prompt notice to myself, while I animadverted as plainly as I dared speak to a lady, upon the laxity of rules which had made such a course necessary. I urged her not to intermit her watchfulness, and authorized her to break off the ominous intercourse without delay or explanation, other than that she had my warrant for the proceeding; promising to be in New Orleans so soon as the crisis of my wife's illness had passed, and release her from further responsibility by an examination of the case and corresponding action on my part. The communication to Agnes was more lengthy, and, I fear, more stern. It was a tone I had seldom employed towards her, and second thoughts would have convinced me that it was impolitic and dangerous now; but my excitement precluded mature deliberation. I told her of our love, it is true, but it was in reproach—to shame, not entice her back to the path of duty. I was harsh, Grace, but I meant well, my child, and I have been sorely punished."

"Few men would have adopted any other line of conduct, dear father!" I kissed his trembling hand, and again, crossing my arms upon his knee, as I sat at his feet, waited breathlessly for more.

"And you might add that there is no woman living deserving of the name, who would not have showed more mercy to a culprit so young and beloved; whose offence, for all the evidence I had to the contrary, was merely suppositional, and might prove eventually to be the figment of madame's brain. I concluded this letter as I had done the other, by a peremptory command for the dismissal of this Darford, let his pretensions be what they might, and a threat of removal from his vicinity, should I discover that she had, in opposition to my known wishes, in violation of her word, been so imprudent as to contract a clandestine engagement with him.

"No sooner were the intemperate missives posted, than I repented of my rashness. Through a sleepless night, merciful spirits were striving with my Spartan notions of duty. My heart yearned over the wayward creature, who, with all her faults, loved me, and in times past, would have laid down her life for me. What irritating goads would my angry words be to her! what was not to be feared from the effect of their wounds to her sensitive, haughty spirit? The next post bore an emollient for these; a retraction of all that was cruel in the preceding epistle. I represented the circumstances under which it was penned, and attributing my undue warmth to the depth of my affection for her, entreated her to trust implicitly in that; to unbosom herself to the brother who had always been an indulgent listener to her every plea, and who now pledged himself not to stand in the way of her happiness, if it should appear that this would be promoted by a union with the man of her choice. But we lived in the heart of the country, where mails were slow and unreliable. Before the answer to either of the letters came to hand, your mother had safely passed the turning-point of her malady, and was so far convalescent as to participate in my fears and hopes respecting the issue of this important matter. I was thankful that I was not with her when Madame Duplanché's reply arrived. My worst anticipations had not foreshadowed the whole extent of the affliction which, I learned from this, had befallen us. Alarmed into an approach to sincerity, the instructress wrote without circumlocution, of my sister's elopement with her lover, immediately after the receipt of my menacing letter. Not sorry to have an opportunity of retaliation for my strictures upon her faulty discipline, the lady introduced a regret that I had been so hasty; since dread of my anger had undoubtedly 'precipitated the dénouement she was sure might have been averted by dexterous manœuvering.'

"These reflections from her fell light as straws upon my writhing soul. My idolized sister was gone—I knew not whither; had fled from me to the embrace of an unprincipled stranger—for in what esteem must I regard the man who had tempted her from rectitude, had taught her forgetfulness of duty, gratitude, self-respect? Madame Duplanché was minute in her description of the 'melancholy event.' They had, according to her showing, outgeneralled her by consummate artifice; had escaped unchallenged and unsuspected, and succeeded in concealing every trace of their route. Consideration for the feelings of the unhappy girl's relatives, more than jealousy for the reputation of her school, had, she stated, induced her to circulate the report that the missing pupil had been withdrawn from the institution by her brother, and was now under his protection. 'No scandal has been excited by her disappearance,' she wrote. 'I flatter myself that my ruse will meet with your unqualified approbation.'

"Until definite intelligence of the wanderer's movements should be obtained, your mother agreed with me in thinking that we had best imitate the secrecy of the discreet teacher. There were days of suppressed mourning and weary waiting—and a lawyer's letter was forwarded from New Orleans, inclosing a copy of the marriage certificate of Agnes Leigh and Julian Darford, coupled with a legal demand for the surrender of the property I held in trust as the guardian of the said Agnes. The claim was presented by authority of her husband. It was lawful, and had there been room for quibbling, I would not have attempted resistance.

With considerable inconvenience and sacrifice of my own interests, I raised the just amount, every cent of my sister's patrimony, and made it over to the creditor, through his agent. I did not inquire where the wedded pair had fixed their residence; made no effort to renew my correspondence with one who had so easily renounced the ties of blood and feeling. The transaction was strictly one of business on both sides, and with it ceased my attempts to seek her—my hopes of reconciliation.

"One moonlight evening, six months after the elopement, your mother and myself were sitting in our chamber at the jessamine-covered window, of which you say your aunt talked to May and yourself. I was gloomy, and her pensiveness was in sympathy. We were thinking of the lost bird; our hearts aching for the sound of her voice in laughter or in song; the music that once was never wanting in the old mansion. We had not spoken for some time; her name had not been mentioned; yet when my wife laid her hand in mine, and lifted her eyes, so eloquent of grieving love, I divined what were her thoughts.

"'There is no hope of her return,' she said. 'What good can accrue from further concealment?'

"'What good can accrue from a gratuitous proclamation of our shame?' I returned, surlily.

"'Not "shame!" do not say that! We can never be disgraced but by guilt, and that our own. Our poor girl has been beguiled into error, but not such as would, in the eyes of the world, fix a stigma upon our name. Are we not incurring the risk we dread by not letting the truth be known? What would be said if it should become public by other means than our confession? I am tired of evasions. I would feel less degradation in declaring that our sister has married without our consent and —deserted us entirely.'

"Her voice trembled in pronouncing the closing words; but like the resolute woman she was, she had opened her mind when

Duty pointed out the impropriety of silence. I felt that she was in the right; still it was unpalatable counsel. I was tenacious of the family honor. It galled me to think how men would comment upon the marriage of a Leigh with an adventurer—a nobody—perhaps a scoundrel, else why this obstinate reserve now that marriage had made his prize secure? Of these, and a host of like wormwood ideas, I delivered myself aloud, as I paced the room, chafed and wounded. At the height of the fever, I was interrupted by a servant with a letter from the post-office. A light was procured, and I saw, with indescribable emotion, my sister's handwriting. The date was Havana (Cuba), and the characters were sometimes nearly illegible, as if dashed upon the sheet in the utmost agitation. Whence I drew the strength that sustained me to the conclusion, I never understood. It was a dark, terrible tale.

"Infatuated by an idolatrous devotion to her lover; terrified by the construction he put upon my misjudged harshness; in imminent peril from Madame Duplanché's immediate exercise of the power I had delegated to her—an authority that would cause a separation to which she would have preferred death—Agnes had escaped from confinement to the liberty of a love that was then worth more than all the world beside. The marriage ceremony was performed the hour she became free; the honeymoon was spent in a suburban village, until Mr. Darford could settle some business that detained him in the vicinity of New Orleans. During this month, she wrote repeatedly to me; at first, conjointly with her husband, and when these petitions for forgiveness and a return to favor were unnoticed—long letters with her own hand, blistered with tears and breathing the humblest penitence. They sailed for the island-home he had so often painted to her imagination; she, thoroughly converted to his representation that I had cast her off, and clinging, with all the fervor of her trusting, ardent nature to the only prop, the only shelter she had upon earth.

"The awakening from her rapt vision was gradual, for her love was too blind to discern trifles, too perfect for jealousy. She was chilled by absences that left her alone the greater part of the day and night; bewildered, and at times shocked, by the revelations chance and his carelessness made to her of bacchanalian orgies and infidel principles; but at one caress, one accent of fondness, she forgot whatever she could not understand, and relied upon him with the same unquestioning faith. He had an associate, inseparable as his shadow, who had assisted in his courtship and been a witness of his marriage; a bold swaggerer, from whom the young wife recoiled in disgust and wonder that a man of so much refinement of breeding, such nicety of sentiment as her lord, could tolerate, nay, encourage his familiarity. She was unused to concealing her dislikes, and this antipathy was obvious to its object as to his boon companion. The latter tried to laugh and argue her out of it; the former laid a subtle plot of revenge. Before it was quite ripe, its execution was hastened by a quarrel between the two men, over the card-table. Oaths, even blows were exchanged, and they were, with difficulty, parted. Darford's brain, in cooling and clearing, realized the danger in which he stood. He sought his sulky antagonist, apologized, and a hollow peace was patched up. That evening, while his *friend* and host was at a wine-party, the serpent craved an audience of the lonely wife, and betrayed the nefarious deception which had been practised upon her."

It was heart-rending to see my father's shrinking from what was now to be revealed; his lingering upon every petty incident; stopping to weigh each sentence, to put off the moment that would bring the utterance of what, after the lapse of so many years, it racked his soul to say.

"Dearest father!" I expostulated, "this is too heavy a trial. Do not tell me more, now at least. I cannot see you suffer so!"

"'Suffer!' I should have become inured to it by this. If the syllables were so many drops of life-blood, I ought not to stop here. You must know all. I owe it to you, my daughter."

"How 'owe' it?" I would have asked; but his pallid lips were regaining firmness to proceed.

"Grace! do you think it strange that she went mad at hearing—that I was frantic when I read that she was not the wife of the man she called husband?"

"Father!" I ejaculated in horror.

Globules of sweat rolled down his face; his fingers clenched my wrist until the flesh was blue beneath them. Yet he could speak with hoarse distinctness.

"Not his wife! To another, a deceived and deserted woman, dying of a broken heart in her native New England village, belonged that title. The name under which he had wooed and wedded this second victim, was false as his black heart. He was of Northern birth, and had, in boyhood, fallen into evil company and vicious habits; while at college had been guilty of a gross outrage upon the authorities and the community, and had run away to avoid punishment. Burnet, for this was the present *alias* to which his treacherous accomplice answered—was his comate in the scrape, and the partnership in crime had never been dissolved. Together they had led a roving career; living by various, generally disreputable means, but always contriving to maintain the style of gentlemen. A lottery-prize had furnished the funds for a luxurious summer sojourn in a picturesque town in Connecticut, where Darford laid suit and successfully to a provincial heiress, an orphan; married her with the approval of her friends, and set up a handsome establishment. But good fortune had not reformed him. He tired of his monotonous existence and the unpretending woman who had so generously linked her lot with his. Collecting, into a portable form, all of her property which he had not squandered, he abandoned her and his child, an infant a year old, and sailed Southward. In New Orleans, the confederates found a suitable theatre for the exhibition of their talents, and they selected that city as their head-quarters. The highest and the lowest phases of its society were alike known to them, and they were here, of all other places, least liable to exposure. An introduction to Madame Duplanché was employed by Darford as the key to her very select circle of parlor-visitors. Agnes' beauty pleased his eye, and an exaggerated report of her wealth tempted him to pay serious court to her.

"This was the story poured, like boiling lead, into the ears of the miserable girl by the wretch who exulted in her distraction. He heaped up the measure of his insults by proposing that she should fly with him from her betrayer, who, he more than hinted, was weary of her love, and meditating a re-commencement of his travels. She drove the brutal fellow from her presence with a torrent of fiery indignation, and while the fury still possessed her, began her letter to me. Burnet had told her of the manner in which the preceding ones had been intercepted and destroyed by Darford. A few burning lines of wild supplication—and she bethought herself of the character of the author of the recital that had maddened her. By his own confession, he was a lying hypocrite; his recent act proved him a traitor. Was he entitled to credit? She would ferret out other proof. Burnet had not overlooked the possibility of this reaction. A little while after he had been expelled from her apartment, he sent in to her a bundle of letters and other documents, abstracted from Darford's escritoir. They bore various addresses; the names she had heard as those by which the adventurer had passed in different places, and their contents were abundant confirmation of Burnet's disclosure. The most blasting sight was the certificate of marriage with his *real* wife, side by side with the worthless paper, whose duplicate had been used to obtain what was his end in espousing her—her money. She secreted the packet, and in the most fearful vigil that woman ever kept, finished her appeal to me, the brother she yet loved. Death or deliverance were the alternatives to her mind. A life of ignominy she could not support. She would not survive to see herself and be known of the world as his repudiated *wife.* In this deep of humiliation she would write no other term, although the italics imparted to it a terrible irony.

"'I am being stung to death by scorpions,' she said. 'If you have one spark of love or pity for the ruined thing I am, come and release me.'

"She engaged to join me at any time I should appoint, at a hotel in Havana; for I must not come in contact with Darford. This was reiterated most strongly. The letter she would intrust to a poor neighbor, her washerwoman, whose fidelity she had bought by some act of kindness, and to her care must my answer be directed.

"I did not wait for daylight. Midnight saw me on my journey, as bent upon vengeance as she was upon escape. My wife's tears were ineffectual to melt my purpose. I had not vowed it to her, but she knew me too well to pray with any hope, that it would suffice me to break the net of the captive. I returned no written reply to Agnes. I was in Havana sooner than it could have been delivered to her.. It was late in the afternoon when I landed, and going to a hotel, I engaged lodgings for myself and a lady. Armed to resist any violence, I stepped into a carriage and was rapidly whirled through the streets to the obscure dwelling of the humble friend whose address my sister had given me. She instructed me as to the locality of Mr. Darford's residence. It was a tasteful villa, the beauty of whose architecture and grounds was perceptible, dark as it was when I alighted at the gate. I gnashed my teeth when I thought who had purchased this luxury for its nominal proprietor, and at what cost—the wreck of happiness and honor. Threading the labyrinthine walks to the door, I rang and inquired of the footman if his mistress were at home. With unblushing assurance, he replied that she was not.

"'Very well! I will wait until she returns, and I pushed by him into the house.

"He stared, and would have grown abusive, but for a timely bribe which I slipped into his hand, as I repeated my inquiry. I was anxious to bear away the unhappy woman quietly, if possible. My entrance was effected; the next move was to see her alone. Scribbling a line upon my card, I asked the man to take it up to her chamber, and if he were correct in his belief of her absence, to bring it down again. The menial of such a master could not be incorruptible, and he departed with a knowing wink that was a harbinger of success.

"Flying feet came down the stairs and along the passages, and my poor, erring child was in my arms, panting and shivering like a hunted partridge. I should hardly have known her for the bright-winged warbler she had been in the parent nest. She was weak and thin, for neither food nor rest had been hers, since she had discovered how foully she had been wronged; and the large, black eyes were bloodshot and glaring as a maniac's. I could weep, but she had no tears. Their fount was dried for ever.

"'Take me away before he comes home!' was all her cry.

"'I will,' I said. 'What do you require to make you ready to go? a veil—a mantle?'

"She quitted me for a moment, and re-appeared, wrapped in a scarf.

"'Take nothing which you can leave,' I ordered. 'No trinkets! no money!"

"'I have none!' was her response.

"She wore a plain morning dress, with no ornaments, and thus apparelled, totally dependent upon me, she turned her back upon the habitation where she had quaffed Life's sweetest joys,

Sorrow's bitterest dregs. I conducted her to her chamber at the hotel, and told her that she was safe. Then, for the unsettled light of her eye, her fitful starts and incoherent mutterings made me uneasy for her reason, I pillowed her head upon my bosom and welcomed her to my love ; painted the reunion in prospect when we should once more see the dear home of us all. I would have bestowed the kiss and blessing your mother had sent to her. She avoided the salute. 'It is too pure !' said she, brokenly. 'She is your wife !'

"'Sister is as holy a name,' I returned.

"I have forfeited that from you !" she moaned. "Oh ! why do I not die ?"

"Affectionately I contended with these self-accusations. I showed her how, by a providential inspiration, as it were, we had refrained from divulging her secret to any one out of our household ; that to her schoolmates her flight was unknown ; her character was stainless to others as to us who were acquainted with the particulars of her misfortune. She was more composed as these consolations were applied. Her pride was spared—one of the ruling elements of her being. Despise herself as she might, the finger of public scorn would not point to a spotted fame, or pity, yet more humbling, grieve over her fall.

"'I will go with you wherever you please to carry me,' she consented ; 'only do not let us stay here a single hour The air of this place is killing me ! I cannot breathe in it !'

"I explained the impossibility of starting before the morrow, and begged her, for my sake, and if she desired to expedite our progress, to lie down and snatch a little sleep. She objected that she was too much excited to rest, but at last suffered me to place her upon the bed.

"'Now I must leave you,' I said.

"'Where are you going ? for what ?' She sprang up and seized me by the arm.

"'To my room, to get all ready for an early start,' I replied, in feigned surprise. 'Where else should I go at this hour? Moreover, I am fatigued, and if I am to journey again so soon'——

"She fell back, deceived, and ashamed of her fright. 'Go! go!' she said. 'It is all right. I am very foolish! Forgive me!'

"I did not require a second bidding."

CHAPTER XXV.

"THERE *was* much to be done by morning; but my plans were definite, and were prosecuted without delay. I went, as I had promised, to my chamber, though not to sleep. I had but one acquaintance in Havana, an American merchant, who had been a schoolfellow, and upon whose friendship and honor I could safely depend. To him, I wrote, asking him to call immediately at my lodgings, as the business in which I wished his aid involved life or death. If he were not in the city, it was my purpose to leave upon my table a letter to the United States consul, commending my sister to his care, with the means of defraying the expenses of her journey to Alabama. This would be attended with more publicity than was desirable, however much heed he might pay to my injunction of secrecy; therefore, was only to be entertained as a dernier ressort. The expediency of foregoing my sanguinary designs never presented itself to my thoughts. Blood alone was the bath for wounded honor, and while cherishing the full intent to wash out in Darford's, the blot upon our name, I was, to myself, and according to the code I had been trained to respect, a righteous avenger, bravely, lawfully defending the cause of the injured; helping to sustain the bulwarks of morality. If I left my wife a widow, my children orphans, upon his soul would rest the crime of having produced their desolation, as well as my murder. To them, I should bequeath an unsullied reputation and the memory of a death not less glorious than that of the soldier who dies fighting for liberty and truth.

"These ideas flitted before me as I folded my note; but I did not look forward to this result of the hostile meeting I had determined should take place. A superstition, borrowed from the feudal ages, nerved and balanced my mind as effectually as a principle of moral right would have done.

"'Heaven defends the right!' I said, unlocking the door, and setting my hat upon my head. 'I shall not die by a dastard hand.'

"I was in quest of a waiter who could be trusted with the instant delivery of my letter, and had to pass through the brilliantly-lighted saloon on the first floor. A number of loungers were there, smoking, drinking, and strolling about. I noticed none of them until a smart slap on my shoulder, and a voice, familiar as my own, turned me face to face with the last person I expected to meet there and then—my sailor-brother, Frederic! A greeting from the other world would not have astounded me more than did his hail:

"'Archie! old fellow! how goes it?'

"Without further ado, he dragged me after him up to his room, and slamming the door, hugged me with honest warmth, the water starting from his eyes. A handsome, rollicking fellow he was in his lieutenant's uniform. I could not look my fill while he piled questions upon exclamations, and, ever and anon, burst into fresh raptures.

"'The luckiest godsend that ever happened upon sea or land! How long have you been in this latitude? I came ashore myself scarce half an hour ago, and expect to lie-to until to-morrow afternoon. Who would have dreamed that the first fellow I should run into here would be you, my precious stay-at-home-brother? By Jove! it is too good to be true! Let me feel again whether you are real flesh, positive bone! What wind blew you into this port? and how did you leave that blessed little mate of yours—fortunate dog that you are! and the babies—how many of them are there? and Aggie—bless her black eyes and rosy cheeks! But man, you look white! What ails you?'

"I staggered to a chair as this flood of inquiries recalled me to a sense of the purpose of my visit to the island, the errand upon which I was bound when he diverted my thoughts into a channel so different. How could I tell him the stunning truth? and yet, had I the right to withhold it? Then another flash—was not he the very one whom I should have desired to meet? Agnes' brothers were the meet depositories of the fatal secret—the guardians of it and her. I communicated everything as guardedly as the confused state of my intellects would allow me to do. His bronzed face was paler, and his glance more fierce, as I forced my tongue to relate each incident. As the end approached, his breath became thick and loud, his fingers clutched at the dirk in his belt. When I ceased, he tore it from its sheath, and swore, as only an infuriated sailor can swear, that the betrayer should not curse the earth one minute longer than would bring him within reach of his steel. He rushed to the door in the thirst of this passion, but I prevented him, and prayed him to hear me.

"'Say on, quickly!' he said, savagely. 'My ears have heard enough, and too much already.'

"I sketched my intentions, and warned him in a spirit as determined as his, that I would not be defrauded of the right to avenge my sister.

"'She is mine, too!' he tried to say, roughly, but the tender heart almost broke with the recollection, and hiding his face in his brown hands, he sobbed heavily. 'Poor Aggie! that she should have come to this'——

"You are pale and sick, Grace, darling! I had better not go on!"

"No! no!" I murmured, "I will know the rest. This suspense is too horrible!"

He had not seen me for many minutes before this abrupt pause, so imbued was he with the spirit of the narration. It was but thinking aloud, and the fluctuations of his countenance evinced his perfect conception of the real and the visible in the drama he was depicting.

"We lay down towards morning, that we might be steady and cool in the scene that would test mental and physical courage. You will hardly believe that I slept thus ; my arm over him, as we had slumbered in his boyhood and my youth—that I slept soundly until he called to me that 'we ought to be up and at work.'

"That 'work !' His lowering brow reminded me what it was.

"'Mr. Darford was not up,' the sleepy negro grumbled. 'He would not be down before eleven o'clock—had been out all night'—and with this he offered to shut the door in our faces.

"'We must have him *now !* no more trifling !' retorted Frederic. 'When we have done with him, he may lie abed as late as he likes. Go ! say that two gentlemen want to see him, and that if he does not come down, we will pay him a visit in his chamber.'

"The man shuffled off, and we remained at the door. By mutual consent, we would not cross the threshold unless we should be forced to do it. Presently, we heard angry tones overhead, oaths at us and the servant who had disturbed his master's morning doze, and a man appeared on the landing of the stairs. A rude interrogatory as to our names and business met with silent contempt, and he descended to the hall. His exterior warranted Madame Duplanché's praises. Clad as he was, in dressing-gown and slippers, his hair dishevelled and eyes watery from his debauch, his bearing and features were some extenuation of poor Agnes' fault. Her image, haggard and forlorn, arose between him and me.

"'You call yourself Darford, I believe?' I said.

"'That is my *name*, sir,' he rejoined, superciliously.

"'And mine is Leigh!' I answered.

"A braver man might have showed fear at this announcement; but although his complexion grew very livid, his eye quailed for one second only, and he stood his ground, grasping, however, the back of a chair near him, that he might defend himself from bodily assault.

"'Well, sir!' he resumed, disdainfully as before, 'and what is the object of your—pardon my bluntness!—untimely visit?'

"'Untimely, I own it is,' said I. 'I should have introduced myself six months ago—the date'—speaking deliberately, that my feelings might not master reason—'of your illegal marriage with my sister.'

"He recovered coolness at this. 'Well sir!' he repeated.

"'As I design leaving the city and the island by noon to-day, you will oblige me by appointing an hour for the settlement of this affair, that will enable me to carry out my plan,' I said.

"He smiled sardonically. 'I will do my best to "oblige" you without damping your confidence in the certainty of your departure at the stated hour. You have chosen your friend?' bowing to Frederic.

"'My brother will be my second,' I replied.

"'And in the event of a result contrary to your anticipations, will step into your place,' he continued, with the same effrontery.

"'I will!' spoke out Frederic, unable to contain himself. 'And now, I am for putting an end to these absurdities. We waste time!'

"'Right, young gentleman! It would be advisable, however, for me to get a short nap before entering upon such hot work as I have ahead of me. What say you'—to me—'to ten o'clock? We shall not be detained more than half an hour at most. To me, as the challenged party, belongs the right to select weapons.

In most circumstances, it has been my practice to waive this, but you will excuse my seeming discourtesy if, on this occasion, I reserve to myself the trifling advantage. What say you to the pistol? Are you accustomed to its use?'

"I answered that I was, and signified my agreement to his proposition.

"'And the place?' he said. 'There is a fashionable rendezvous for friends bent upon these affairs;' and he named it. '*Au revoir*, gentlemen!'

"He partly closed the door, but opened it before we were off the piazza.

"'This is a malapropos season for speaking of ladies, but as you have, no doubt, been apprised, your sister, *Mrs. Darford*,' emphasizing the words with dignity, 'is now under my roof. Is it your wish to see her, or, to spare her needless agitation, had the interview better be postponed until after the *ceremony*?'

"Frederic's dirk was partly drawn, but I retained hold of his arm.

"'My sister has been, since last evening, in the charge of her lawful protectors,' I said.

"'Ah!' The start was unfeigned, his bow of acquiescence affected to conceal his surprise. 'Then all is right. Excuse my well-meant interference in family matters,' and we parted.

"I have been particular in detailing this conversation that you may have some imagination of what barred our hearts to all thoughts of forgiveness, blinded us to the enormity of the crime we contemplated. To rid the earth of this hardened villain, humanity of this disgrace, would be a meritorious deed. We both felt that foul play was to be expected, and to my merchant friend, I wrote a concise statement of the case, directing him what measures to adopt, should neither of us return alive. The letter was laid in a conspicuous situation in my room, and to ensure its delivery, I charged the clerk of the hotel to enter the apartment and dispatch it to its address, if I did not report myself by noon. Agnes was impatient to be gone, but I pacified her by showing the advertisement of the departure of the vessel in which we had engaged berths, and representing that I could not hasten its sailing. I said nothing of Frederic. He would not trust himself to meet her, nor would I hazard the derangement of our scheme by bringing them together ; sure, as I was, that he would be unmanned to a dangerous degree.

"We were punctual, and did not have to wait for the other party. Burnet attended his friend—his dupe in some respects ; a surgeon was in readiness."

The veins in the speaker's forehead pulsed into knotted cords, his face purpled, his fingers indented my wrist like iron talons.

"Father !" I entreated. "Say no more ! Why distress yourself with what is past and without remedy ? You did not kill him. Have not I seen him—talked with him ? You are not his murderer !"

"Thank God ! I am not !" He regained his calmness. "But, my child, for twenty-eight years, his blood was in my skirts; the brand of Cain upon my brow. Infinite goodness—undeserved mercy ! these claim my thanksgivings !"

He gazed upward, and his lips moved. I knew it was in prayer. His countenance was once more the serene soul-mirror I loved to look upon. No story of stormy guilt could deface it now.

"Yes ! he fell at the first fire—shot, the surgeon declared, through the lungs. We left him in the care of his second, and in less than two hours, we were upon the sea, in different vessels, with what dissimilar emotions ! The dart of remorse made of me an early victim. I heard from my brother after I reached home. His tone was one of stern exultation, and he congratulated me upon the success of my summary dealing with the caitiff. I did not read to the end of the letter. Every word was hot poison. The dying look, the contorted features of the wounded man were ever in my sight; his groan of pain and horror never left my ear. Blood cried against me from the ground. No man, innocent of blood-guiltiness, can enter into the awful meaning of that curse. From your mother, I could not hide the truth, and to her latest hour, the grief stamped upon her face was ineffaceable. In the midnight, I have awakened to find her gone from my side, and overheard from her closet, the 'strong crying,' with which she supplicated for the cleansing of my hands and heart. The answer was tardy, but it came in His own good time."

"And my aunt, sir?" I said, as he paused.

"My self-control, the equivocations with which I met her questions lulled her suspicions; but Burnet's malice was more than a match for my prudence. He wrote to her what purported to be a true account of the duel and its fatal termination to his principal, by whom I now suspect the letter was dictated. He was Darford's executor he said, and would willingly have made restitution of her property, but upon settlement of the estate, he had discovered its total insolvency. Darford had squandered everything, and died a fraudulent bankrupt. The cunningly contrived epistle concluded with a pretence of consolation, to the effect that the Cuban authorities had been negligent in the investigation of the affair, and that inquiry had now died out.

"This intelligence was transmitted while I was away from home. I was recalled by news of Agnes' illness, and returned to find her raving in a brain-fever that nearly cost her the life she ever after considered worthless. You know what she was from your infancy. The change was wrought during this sickness and her tedious convalescence. Your mother's health also declined perceptibly. By the advice of her physicians, and in accordance with my own inclinations, I disposed of the homestead and removed to this more northerly climate. I hoped that other scenes and associations might bring relief to us all, and indeed, the experiment was not wholly ineffectual. Your mother rallied partially, and lived to hail the dawn of the reign of Christian principles in my heart; to intrust you, her youngest daughter, our Virginia flower, to your aunt, confident that she would instill none other than these into your mind. Trials fell fast upon me at that period; the deaths of my wife and three children; the news of my brother's decease in a foreign port; the loss of property—until I was ready to say, '*All* Thy waves and Thy billows have gone over me.' Each affliction I strove to accept as the righteous chastisement of my great sin—never forgotten—no! not for an hour—borne about with me, as the ancients used to chain a corpse to a living body; ever loathsome, pulling me down to the dust. Then ensued many years of outward tranquillity. Frederic and yourself grew up under my eye, healthy, dutiful children, of whom any father might have been proud. Absorbed in love and cares for you, I felt my burden lighter. But my discipline was not at an end. Grace! my child! my best-beloved! the heaviest consequence of my guilt—heavier than the anguish of a wife; the remorseful, embittered life of a sister, the undying pang of my own soul—was the necessity thrust upon me of breaking your heart, of converting your joyous existence into a night of weeping. Darling! forgive me!"

His grey head sank, and big tears dropped upon my upturned face. He folded me to his bosom, and again besought my forgiveness.

"Mine! and for what?" I asked, in tearful amazement.

"Have you really never guessed the truth?" he said. "Could prejudice, however inveterate—could the maddest caprice have borne me out in my refusal to sanction your union with the man whom I acknowledge was, in everything, worthy of my favorite child? Herbert Wynne is, this day, as free from hereditary faults as he is ignorant of his father's name and character."

"You do not mean to say"—— I commenced, faintly; but, dizzy with the flood of thought, I could not go on.

"I mean to say that the Dumont you know, the Darford who I believed perished by my hand, the Mansfield who Herbert will tell you was the husband of his mother, and died when he, their only child, was but a babe—were one and the same person."

"It is so unreal!" I murmured, trying to collect my senses.

"It does indeed almost pass belief," said my father. "Yet we read constantly of like deceptions and like misery in our public journals. Of the truth of all that I have said we have abundant proof. You knew that Herbert was the adopted son of Mr. Wynne, the nephew of a former wife, to whom he was bequeathed by a dying sister?"

"Yes—he told me, and so did Louise."

"And that his real name was Mansfield?" he interrogated.

"Yes—yes! it was!"

"His birth-place—did he ever speak of that?"

Again I replied in the affirmative, naming the town.

"But he did not know—he never heard"——I stammered.

"My poor child! he was no wiser than you were upon certain points. For a short, blessed season, I did not dream whose son was the partaker of my hospitality, the suitor for my daughter's hand. Tell me truly, Grace—did Mr. Townley never throw any light upon this subject? never hint the reason of my opposition to your wishes?"

"I did not understand him then. It is more clear now, sir," I returned.

My father continued. "That man's genius for ferreting out hidden things is unparalleled; the coincidences that cast the clues to others' secrets into his hands, amount to a fatality. Do you recollect one morning in that eventful Christmas week, when he called by to accompany me to the Court House?"

Ah! did I not?

"Perfectly, sir!" I responded.

"His approach to his theme was extremely guarded. He began by extolling the talents and person of Mr. Wynne. Of the former and of his estimable social qualities, he had had an opportunity of judging in the course of a conversation with him at his (James Townley's) house, on Christmas evening. But on that occasion he had also obtained an insight of his history that produced uneasiness. Deliberate reflection had showed him that his palpable duty was to be frank with me. The ice thus broken, he went on to state more directly, that in his travels, the preceding summer, he had fallen in with a man, apparently a foreigner, who, on learning that he lived in this neighborhood, inquired about me, and by degrees, gave the acute lawyer a tolerably faithful description of my pursuit of, and duel with Darford, but glossed over the offence that provoked me to it, by a vile falsehood. Agnes was legally the wife of the murdered man, he said, his first partner being dead at the date of his later marriage. My vindictive attack he explained as the outburst of chagrin and rage that my sister's fortune had been wrested from my management. I had slain her peace with the husband she adored, and escaped the penalty of the misdeed by a flight to another state. If this blow was a shock, what think you, were my sufferings when he brought forward Herbert Wynne's name, and proved his connection with the tragedy? The stranger, who was doubtless Dumont or his coadjutor in wickedness, by innuendoes and desultory scraps of information, further instructed Townley that the son of the ill-fated Darford, or Mansfield, as he styled him, had been adopted by a New York merchant, in whose family my daughter was then a visitor. Townley would have had me believe that he had deemed the tale a fabrication, malicious or idle, until the aforesaid conversation with young Wynne had, by correspondence of names, dates and certain circumstances, alarmed him seriously for the consequences of the intimacy which was then the gossip of the day.

"I had the presence of mind to investigate his proofs. They were the death-blow to my hopes for, and in your happiness. If I was cruel in my denial of explanation, inexorable in my resolution, ask yourself, Grace, whether I could have bestowed you upon the man, whose father's blood had steeped my hands? Or, would your grief have been alleviated by the knowledge of this fact? Moreover, I was bound by a solemn promise to my sister not to divulge her disgrace while she lived. Pride was no longer dominant, but neither did it sleep in her bosom. Before she accepted my offer of an abode, she conjured me by my love for her, by my respect for the memory of our parents, to guard her secret. I would not ask absolution from my vow. It would have killed her to know that to you was unveiled the Past for which her spirit was clothed in sackcloth. This was my dilemma. How would you have had me act?"

"Just as you did!" I rejoined, firmly. "After all, yours was the greatest trial."

"Heaven never sent me one more grievous!" With what beautiful meekness was this spoken! "As by intuition, your aunt gathered that all was not right, and that the fault lay not with you or Herbert. She applied to me to solve what perplexed and troubled her. I was able to resist her entreaties and parry her inquiries, but pressed hard by her shrewd conjectures, I was forced to extricate myself by an admission which, I fancied, would create but a passing tumult and guard me from future persecutions. It was not like her, but she goaded me. The fester was too sore to bear the lightest touch. I summed up what I wished to impart in one sentence, declaring Herbert Wynne's relationship to her faithless lover. You witnessed the unlooked-for effect of the imprudent communication. That it was seared upon her soul you must believe with me, but it was never referred to again. The frost was black and killing upon my home; the pleasant garden, that had solaced me in my solitary woe. Then my gallant boy was taken, and ere the green wound in my heart closed, Townley aimed another blow. Robert Peyton was the innocent conductor of the stroke. A garbled version of the hateful story, perpetuated by its bloody stain, crept through the community—it must have been by Townley's means. Robert, enraged at the slander, appealed to me to contradict it. I refused, and without compromising my sister, allowed that the duel had occurred, and revealed to him the gloom flung by it along the track I had toiled over since. Abhorring the 'code of honor' as he does, his charity spread a cloak before my transgression. Too generous, too pitiful to upbraid the fallen, yet too conscientious to palliate the crime, he voluntarily proposed that the matter should be dropped at once and forever; and in his plea for pardon for his unfortunate interference, petitioned that I would suffer him to remain my friend. Here was one sun-ray. God knows I needed it! They are more abundant now. 'Light is sown' not 'for the righteous,' but for the penitent."

His eyes roved over the landscape, flooded by the mellow light of evening. The sinking sun touched the tree-tops, and Nature received, in happy silence, his parting benison. My unquiet heart surged and tossed—a brackish sea. Was there nowhere, in the wide world, a comforting gleam for me?

"Of what avail"—thus ran my selfish repinings—"is the tearing away of the veil that draped by-gone years; the end of doubt, and speculation, and anxiety? Can it restore the bloom of youth or re-unite me to *him*?"

My father's voice jarred unsympathizingly upon my feelings; yet he would talk. Unburdened of the load he had carried for near thirty years, he did not perceive my depression. He told me that he had not known Mr. Dumont on the evening of his call at Mrs. Seaton's, until my aunt's exclamation converted into certainty an indefinable impression he experienced, at their introduction, that the tower-like stature and marked physiognomy were not altogether unfamiliar. He had sought him the following day at his hotel, but he had left the city.

"He may never cross my path again," he said. "I hope fervently that I have seen him for the last time on earth. Alive and dead, he was, up to this providential meeting, the haunting demon of my life. This resurrection frees me from his power. I do not care to know more of the mystery of iniquity that enwraps him. The simplest theory is the most plausible. My shot was not mortal, but he secured his safety and a refinement of revenge by strengthening me in the belief that I had killed him The disguise of a different title and nativity, and the years, with which he has battled with wonderful success, would have been impenetrable to every eye but hers. I am thankful, since her death-hour was so near, that she did not revive after that look. In a woman's heart, there is always fire under the ashes, however coldly they may have thickened. A breath of Memory will oftentimes blow them away, and expose the glowing coal."

"Is this the burning in my bosom?" I asked inwardly.

A sad, lovely smile shone in the eyes that swept the landscape.

"God has left us much to bless Him for, my daughter," he said. "High above all else hangs the Prize. For it, shall we not forget the things that are behind?"

As by a straggling moonbeam, I had an indistinct, but how cheering a vision of Him, whose footsteps can still the billows of human passion, as of old, the turbulent lake subsided into smoothness at His coming. The cry of the drowning disciple was groaned up from my heart.

Then Lilly appeared, tripping through the garden walks towards us, singing in her young, clear tones—

"'His purposes will ripen fast,
  Unfolding every hour;
The bud may have a bitter taste,
  But sweet will be the flower.'"

"And if I am not to pluck it on this side Heaven, can I not wait in patience?" I thought. "It will be all the sweeter then!"

CHAPTER XXVI.

Three years had flown.

I do not like these leaps in a narrative more than you do, my good and patient reader; but they are preferable to a tramp, foot-sore and eye-weary, along a dull turnpike, where every mile is precisely similar to the one that comes before and that which follows it, except in the variation of the figures upon the stones sunken in the sand. Such a bore it would be to trace, step by step, the routine of Moss-side life through the period set down above. Three years, then, had flown, or slipped, or glided away. Choose whichever term most aptly describes the noiseless, easy revolutions of Time's machinery, and you have the most just conception of their eventless passage.

It was a cold December night. Our snug sitting-room was bright with fire and candles. Of the last there were two upon the stand between my father and myself. He was reading a letter, a lady's letter—for the under-sized sheets were three in number, the writing fine, and the paragraphs compact. It took him a long time to read each page. My work-basket was heaped with the week's mending, and I was darning a pair of lambswool socks. My corner was the same my aunt had occupied until her paralysis; my needle plodded in and out, under and over, as hers used to move. I was almost as grave, too, as she appeared to me in those days, for my father's attention was elsewhere than upon my face, and my thoughts were, with his, upon the paper he was perusing.

It was from our Lilly. I had received it at supper-time, bu

had just transferred it to him. She was with her aunt May. Our household fairy had not stood upon our hearth since the winter fires were kindled. She would be home by Christmas, however. Our small band must be complete then, if at no other season. I noticed my father's smile of satisfaction as he saw her positive promise that this should be so. My mental sight accompanied him, word for word, through what came next :—

"And now, dear Auntie, you may use your discretion as to the way in which you will share with grandpapa what I am going to say to you. Tell him yourself, or let him read the whole of my letter. It would be an uncomfortable novelty to us to keep anything from him. What a deal of preparation to pave the introduction of a trivial matter ! Diplomacy was never my forte, you know. Mr. Wynne has figured largely in my home-dispatches ; nor is this surprising, when we consider how constant has been his kindness to me—a bewildered rustic in this mighty Babel. Now, for the question—which Aunt May seconds by this same mail. May we bring him to Moss-side with us, Auntie ? Grandpapa ? He is not a stranger to you, says Aunt May—that he escorted her to Virginia, when she paid you her first visit, before she was married. She assures me, furthermore, that he will go upon her invitation, since he is aware that it will not be extended unless it will afford you pleasure to entertain him. I am hasty to conclude that he will be a welcome guest, if only because he is a friend of mine ; but she is more prudent, and understands the propriety of observing forms, even between relatives. So, too, she will abide by your decision, while, if I imagined, for a moment, that you could object, I would plead that you would humor your petted child in what lies so near to her heart. For my sake—to make your little Lilly happy, Auntie, write that you will be glad to see one who has so strong a claim upon my gratitude."

My father turned the leaf hurriedly, and glanced at me. I

was weaving the worsted network across a hole of discouraging dimensions. He read further, and I kept pace with him as before.

"To you, I must be open-hearted. Mr. Wynne is not an ordinary acquaintance; it will be no ordinary disappointment should you deny my request. This is my suit—do not say me nay!"

My father did not look at me as he refitted the sheets in their envelope. He would not have beheld a grave countenance, for I was prepared for examination. The corners of his mouth were slightly depressed, and more rigid than I liked to see them. Surely, he was not inimical to the child's petition! I interrupted his meditations.

"It is pleasant to think that we shall soon have her with us—is it not, sir?"

"Yes"—starting—"yet there are hints here," touching the letter, "which I must say I do not understand, nor do I quite relish so much of them as I can make out."

I laughed. "Ah, father! you are jealous of your place in Lilly's heart. You regard her anxiety that we should invite Mr. Wynne as an unfavorable portent—unfavorable for us—I mean."

"You have not hit it exactly"—with a dissatisfied air. "She is too young to dream of these things."

"What things?" inquired I, innocently.

"Why—courtship—and—and—marriage! Pshaw! she is our baby, Grace! what a silly notion! I wish we had not let her go!"

He walked up and down the floor, vexed or troubled.

"Do you know Lilly's age, father?"

"No—that is, not to a day, perhaps; but I have seen many a child of ten who was larger, and more of a woman in every way."

"She was a 'child of ten,' when she came to us. That was eight—almost nine years ago," I said.

He stopped. "Is it possible! The age at which your mother was married!"

"Yes, sir; and May was no older when she engaged herself to our Frederic."

His expression changed. He suppressed the words upon his tongue, and passing to the back of my chair, leaned down and kissed my forehead. His eyes and his heart too, I knew were full. May and I were the same age. The winter of her betrothment was that of her visit to Moss-side; to her, the sun of love arose, as it went down to me.

But I would not reflect upon this unavoidable suggestion; nor should he.

"Lilly, small in stature though she is, is verging upon womanhood," I said, cheerfully. "We ought to inure ourselves to this idea, and, as its consequence, to that of her being transplanted to another home. It is the most probable destiny of lovable women. We—you and I, father—are sensible of her charms. We are reminded now that there are others as discerning."

Dissatisfied yet! I tried again.

"It shocks us somewhat now. When she makes her choice, it will cost us a struggle to resign her. Yet is not this an interested love that would thwart her in the dearest hope she can ever have in this life?"

"I would not thwart her. No counter wish of mine shall run against hers. But this is unexpected."

"Not to me," I rejoined. "Her many allusions to Mr. Wynne, led me to anticipate something of the kind. She is too guileless to dissemble. He has filled her letters in proportion as he advanced in her affections."

I threaded my needle with steady fingers, as I spoke thus, and opened another roll of mending.

"These women! they surpass my comprehension!" muttered my father, continuing his strides across the apartment.

"They do not puzzle one another so much," I said. "It would be amusing, however, if this were a romance of our manufacture; if my patch-work, gathered up and pieced together from Lilly's letters, and some knowledge of the usual run of like affairs, and your disquiet were alike thrown away."

"I hope they are!" brightening up. "I cannot reconcile myself to it, Grace. I respect Mr. Wynne, as I have said frequently, I have a high regard and admiration for him; but this union would be unsuitable in point of age, if in nothing else."

"She is in her nineteenth year," I answered. "He is thirty-five, but, according to May and Lilly, does not appear nearly so old. His, a nature and constitution that will bear the wear and tear of time. At fifty, he will be younger than most men are at thirty."

There was a cruel pleasure in saying this. It was a salutary, and a merited lash which I inflicted upon myself. I could see that I had gained a slight advantage. However my father might construe, for himself, his repugnance to an alliance, he protested was too preposterous for discussion, something whispered to me that if I could disabuse his mind of all notion of wounded feeling and latent tenderness on my part, for Lilly's lover—could convince him that I was whole-hearted and sincere in my pleadings in his behalf—the main difficulty would be removed.

"Still, dear, I do not approve of such great disparity," he said. "Youth should wed with youth."

Another rapid turn of the room, and he brought out the next sentence, as if fearing my laughter, or ashamed of the confession.

"I detest match-making, but I was weak enough to hope—to think, that if Lilly ever married, Peyton Elliott would be the one to carry her off. They are very partial to each other's society, and Peyton talks of buying a place in this county, I was mistaken, it seems. I am sorry for Peyton and for ourselves. It would be pleasant to have her settled near to us. Is he attached to her, do you think? He is a fine young fellow—intelligent, and kind in disposition."

"They are fast friends, sir. Lilly has no coquetry in her composition. Rely upon it, there is an excellent understanding between them. Peyton is, as you say, a noble young man; but to her, as the person most concerned, we should leave the selection of a husband."

"Certainly! I mean to do it," he assented.

I braced myself to ask a leading question.

"You have no objection to Mr. Wynne, besides the difference in their ages, have you?"

The reply was not very ready, but had an emphasis of truth that atoned for its tardiness.

"Not the slightest, my daughter!"

"Thank you, sir!"

"*You* thank me!"—then, catching up his inconsiderate speech—"are you pleased at the prospect of losing our little one? You, of all her friends, will be most bereaved by her going."

"I do not forget this; yet if she will be happier with another—a life-long companion—than with us, I shall smile at her bridal. She is wholly dependent upon love for every earthly joy. Isolation, coldness would kill her. Some contend that singlehood is never the natural sphere of woman. I am not prepared to subscribe to, nor yet to refute this doctrine. Lilly certainly was not formed to walk alone. I am contented to remain as I am; but mine is one case in a thousand. Providence, in ordaining what shall be my position, has granted me blessings that compensate for its disadvantages, if any there are."

"And not the least is a cheerful, submissive spirit," said my father.

The cloud was clearing away. I laid my sewing in the basket and took his hand.

"Our conclusions, drawn from the evidence we possess in regard to the state of Lilly's affections, may be erroneous, father dear; but is it not expedient to form some? If Mr. Wynne come to us as our darling's declared lover, your answer should be ready, that both of them may be spared suspense. Edmund will not oppose anything which bears the stamp of your approval. If, on the other hand, we have been mistaken in our suppositions; if he is only the 'friend' she styles him; if her sentiment towards him is nothing warmer than the gratitude she avows, there is no harm done. We can keep our own counsel, and laugh in private, over our debate of this evening. But"—for he was going to interrupt me—"I must say, in sober earnest, that the pro-courtship scale far outweighs the con, in my estimation May expresses herself, as she always does, simply, yet with circumspection. One unused to her style would not detect any reserve in her manner of writing about this matter. There are several portions of her letter that I seize upon as circumstantial evidence of the correctness of my views. Now, may it please the counsel on the opposite side of the question—the night is waning; and since I cannot but observe that he is unprepared with further arguments, I move that the Court adjourn *sine die.*"

I brought the Bible, and our evening worship was rendered.

To his "good night" kiss, my father added his blessing—"Our Father in heaven keep you in perfect peace, my dear, *good* child!"

I hummed an evening hymn as I went about from room to room of the lower floor, locking and barring the outer openings. Then I put my head in at my father's chamber door, and said, "Good night again, and pleasant dreams!" blithely, before mounting to my dormitory.

The careful Martha had relaxed nothing in the assiduity of

her attention to my comfort and little, old-maidish fancies, during the years that had made her a wife, and the mother of four youngsters, noisy and troublesome enough to distract her thoughts from everything but themselves. The old lounge was wheeled diagonally across the front of the fireplace ; its dimity cover was whole and clean—otherwise, one might have doubted whether it were not the very one I made ten years ago, that the couch might be in its best trim for May's reception. The round-topped, spindle-legged and club-footed stand, bearing a candle and my Bible, stood guard by my pillow of the settee, for there it was my custom to sit and read before retiring. Over the mantel hung the pale girl-portrait—Louise's gift—the frame cracked and tarnished ; the sad, pure face still looking its mute prayer to heaven. The only change of note in the room was in myself.

I could not withstand the temptation to fall upon the lounge and weep heartily. It was a weak indulgence, and useless as weak ; but my strength had ebbed from me in the battle with my own heart and my father's scruples. I might well have exclaimed with Pyrrhus, "One more such victory will ruin me !" I was not envious of my child's good-fortune ; was not inclined to impute blame to her lover. The charge of fickleness was remote from my mind. I had freed him, weary ages since, and deigned no reply to his persevering suit. Whose fault was it that he had parted with the very remembrance of that far-off Christmas-time, while it had power left to master me ? I did not ask myself the cause of my emotion. Reason essayed once or twice to scourge me to self-examination—to shame me into composure. Great as was my awe of the beldame, whose despotism I seldom defied now-a-days, I did not attempt a feint of respect—only stopped my ears and wept on, until the sluices were dry. I sobbed tearlessly, while I undressed, and long after I was in bed, in hysterical exhaustion. The loneliness of desolation brooded in my heart. Duty stimulates to arduous endeavor ; supports her votary in the furnace and upon the scaffold ; but let him be surprised into captivity by Sorrow, and he finds in her the hard, unsympathizing task-mistress, requiring from her thrall the full tale of bricks, when he has not a stalk, even of stubble, wherewith to manufacture them.

I cried myself to sleep, and awoke at dawn, conscious that I had a week of labor ahead of me, yet so inert, so languid, corporeally and in spirit, that it was a sweeping draught upon my energy to arise and get ready for breakfast. My work that day was all toil ; so was that of every one of the seven that succeeded it.

The morning of the eighth, Peyton Elliot walked into the dining-room before breakfast was over, his eyes sparkling, and cheeks ruddy with health and pleasure.

"Why, Peyton! my lad, welcome!" cried my father, overturning his chair in the cordial haste of greeting. "I did not know you were in the neighborhood. When did you arrive?"

"Last night, sir, at Linden—this instant at Moss-side. Auntie dear, I am a breakfastless runaway. May I venture to pray for one tiny cup of coffee to melt the frost in my mouth?"

I loved the boy—for boy he was, in comparison with my maturity ; so I had his plate laid at the corner nearest me and the fire ; poured out for him the smoking hot beverage he craved, and pressed biscuit, rolls, ham and eggs upon him, until he sued for quarter.

"The best Aunt Grace that ever sat behind a tea-tray!" he said. "The best boy-spoiler in Christendom! You are the 'busy bee improving each shining hour,' just now, I suppose? I stumbled over a cake of wax and a scrubbing-brush in the entry, whose manifest destiny was the polishing of this neat hive, where the oldest inhabitant has never seen a grain of dust. Do you confidently expect your friends to-morrow?"

My father, sobered by the train of thought these queries set in motion, addressed himself, with instant diligence, to his breakfast.

"We do," I replied. "You will dine with us on Christmas-day, of course; but you will not put off your call to Lilly and our visitors until then, I trust."

There was a twinkling smile in his eye as he bowed, in mock decorum, to my invitation; a sort of roguish confidence that cut my heart. I would have escaped a tête-à-tête with him, but he out-manœuvred me by doubling upon me as I was retreating, and conducted me back to the breakfast-room.

"Why were you running away from me, Auntie?"

He had caught the pet-name from Lilly, and knew that it pleased me for him to use it.

"Running away!" he reiterated, "when I made my toilette by sunrise, before the fire was lighted in my room, and perilled my lungs by copious imbibations of the morning air, that smarts in one's respiratory tubes like stinging nettles, and for no other earthly purpose than to see you!"

"We housekeepers, my dear Peyton," I excused myself ——

"Are never non-plussed for apologies!" he interposed. "I will not detain you later than the proper hour for concocting that incomparable cake, those peerless pies, which are to shed new glories upon your name as the nonesuch of housewives. There is a time for all things; and this happens to be the season for hearing and talking to me. I want you to 'make a clane breast, out-and-out,' as Dr. Hamner says, of all this stuff concerning Lilly and the semi-centenarian, she is towing after her into this port."

"What a rattle you are!" I remonstrated, tempted to resent his levity. "State your inquiry in intelligible terms, and I may have some hope of answering you."

"There! there, Auntie dear!" laughing so that he could hardly articulate. "Don't bristle up so fiercely! I meant no disrespect to Miss Lilly and the staid gentleman whose grey hairs command my veneration. A tincture of asperity would be very pardonable in me, situated as I am, whereas I am a very lamb in my demeanor. What business has this antiquated cockney to be poaching upon our ground—yours and mine, Auntie? When I have been over head and ears in love with your Lilly ever since I discarded roundabouts! aye, and before that! 'Pharaoh's overthrow' was mine likewise. I ceased to be a free man from that day. And now, without so much as saying 'by your gracious leave and pleasure, Mr. Elliott,' or, 'after you, sir,' in steps this—this—organic fossil"——

"Peyton! I will hear no more nonsense. I believed that you knew better what is due from one gentleman to another. Courtesy to Lilly should, at all events, restrain you from applying such epithets to her friend."

"Is he truly her friend, then?" demanded the unabashed scapegrace.

His eager hanging upon my answer disconcerted me. I studied to frame one which should prepare him for the truth, yet not wound too deeply.

"She does not write that he is anything dearer. In the absence of direct proof, it is not altogether proper to express as opinion what is entirely clever guess-work. We shall ascertain how matters stand by the help of our own senses, before long. You must come over and judge for yourself."

"Isn't there an ice-pond in this vicinity?" was his most irrelevant query.

"Yes."

"A good, deep one, is it not? You were drowned there, once upon a time, if I recollect rightly."

"Almost," I replied. "When full, it measures six feet of water in the middle, where I went in."

"Six feet!" dubiously. "Mr. Peyton represents this ancient

wooer, this revered Mr. Wynne as a giant. What is the bottom of the pond—mire or quicksand?"

"I really cannot inform you."

"I might double him up and hold him under," he pondered aloud, with perfect seriousness. "Have you a personal regard for the gentleman, leaving Lilly out of the question?"

The foolish blood streamed hotly over my neck and face, and my voice as foolishly failed me in the effort to speak. I was angry with him for the abrupt inquiry, tenfold more angry with myself for the display of discomposure, greatly exceeding that which I felt.

"What is he like?" he pursued, without comment upon my silence. "You are acquainted with him. He has been to Moss-side, Mrs. Peyton tells me."

"He is strikingly handsome," I rallied desperately; "very intelligent, and possesses a heart as admirable as is his intellect."

"'Insatiate archer! would not once suffice?
Thrice flew thy dart, and thrice my peace was slain!'"

exclaimed Peyton, tragically. "Dear Auntie! pity me! Have you no compunction as you annihilate my air-castles! Cupid be my aid when I war with your Apollo! He has one vulnerable point, however. I will not go out and hang myself yet. He is *old*, Auntie! on the shady side of forty, I hear"——

"You are mistaken," I recommenced, but he did not stop to listen.

"Lilly is already well-supplied with fathers. One may have a superabundance of an excellent thing. Two of the first-class articles referred to are generally sufficient for one young lady. What will she do with three?"

"Peyton!" I said, decidedly. "If your intention is to offend me, you can persist in this tone. I do not say, mark me! that

Lilly will marry Mr. Wynne; do not know that he has addressed, or that he ever will address her ; but she could not select, for a husband, one more worthy of her love. The choice would call for and receive the congratulations of every disinterested friend."

"Intimating that I may be ranked with some other class," rejoined he, provokingly. "I plead guilty to the severe impeachment. Teach me, a poor, faulty, erring youth, this laudable disinterestedness, Auntie. You are the impersonation of its highest type, as you are of the rest of the cardinal virtues."

"Peyton !" I was wounded now.

"Forgive me ! It is nobody but your naughty nephew, dear Aunt Grace. He loves you as much as he delights, in a harmless way, to tease you."

"You have not teased me," I said. "Why should I be teased ?" for the word did not sound agreeably in my ears.

"Why, indeed ?" echoed he. "Now, as the French phrase it, 'return we to our muttons'—*i. e.*, Mr. Wynne. I will not back out ingloriously. I will fight him like a chivalric knight of the old cavalier stock ; will give him a fair field and no favor. If I am defeated, there is the ice-pond as a final resort to cool the flame of his love or drown my burning shame. An ally in the enemy's camp is a grand desideratum in a tough siege. May I depend upon you ? Which will you espouse ? the cause of which of the combatants, I should have said."

"I am neutral, and wish to remain so," I replied.

"That is contrary to nature and to art, and is, besides, ticklish ground for you. I am afraid you have been tampered with ; that you are enlisted in soul for the support of my adversary *Et tu, Brute !* And I am utterly friendless !"

My discomfort increased unaccountably.

"My dear boy," I said, "does it not strike you that this is a superlatively ridiculous conversation ?"

" 'Sport to you, but death to me'" he interrupted, ruefully. "Your defection caps the climax. The mode of tactics I had to propose was as follows: You were to captivate this son of Anak yourself. You could do it easily, with only half a trial of your strength. I am not the first, nor the tenth, nor the hundredth person who has told you of the power of your charms. You can be bewitching when you like—don't leave me, Auntie! I am in dead earnest! upon my word of honor, as a gentleman, I am! I will affirm the same upon that venerable and sacred folio of engravings in the bookcase yonder—the one with 'Pharaoh's overthrow' in it, if you distrust my veracity. You are superior to matrimony, I know. I don't want to force you to that extreme—but cannot your 'disinterestedness' sacrifice more agreeable pursuits, for a few days, to the occupation I have mentioned? Cannot you submit to temporary boredom to secure for me a lasting good?"

"The incomparable cake and peerless pies are suffering for my attention, Peyton."

"Burn them! I am agonizing, and I will have a declaration, defensive or offensive. Will you, or will you not take Mr. Wynne off Lilly's hands, and thereby keep my hands off of him?"

"I am sick of unseasonable jesting!" I answered.

"Just my case! I mean to settle your mind, and ease mine by one stroke. You shall help him you love best. Which is it?"

I snatched my hand from his grasp and ran out of the room. All the way up-stairs, I heard his laugh.

"He is surely demented!" I said to myself. "I will not go down again while he is here. I will teach him that he cannot worry me with impunity."

And from sheer worriment (what else could it have been?) I cried until I was tired. Age had not sweetened my temper, or why was I thus ruffled by the rambling bombast of a thoughtless youth?

CHAPTER XXVII.

I WAS a skillful housekeeper ; as skillful as a natural taste for, and experience in, the avocation could make me ; and I bestowed extraordinary pains upon the preparations for the holiday feastings ; worked as indefatigably as upon the last merry Christmas I had known—when May and Frederic danced, and rode, and rambled together, and I was not abandoned to loneliness, meanwhile. I accomplished more now, for mine was the principal responsibility, and I wrought with system and industry. "It is for Lilly !" was my invariable excuse to my father, who objected to my incessant toil. Never had my gift-daughter been so dear to me before. She was the centre and the bound of all my thoughts and schemes, and the reflection that I might be about to lose her, quickened every impulse of affection.

The trio of travellers was looked for in the evening, and I superintended the spreading of the supper-table before I dressed. It was a goodly show, although the more substantial viands were yet to fill up the empty spaces ; and I nodded complacence from the door, where the eyes of the destined partakers would be regaled, and their appetites sharpened by a view of the board. My keys jingled mutual gratulations in the basket on my arm, ceasing, with a united tingle of content, as I deposited them upon my dressing-table.

"Patience alive ! Miss Grace !" said Martha, in the height of fidgeting impatience ; "I'se been 'pon tender-hooks and broken bottles for bettern half an hour. You ain't got a millionth of a second to spar. I'm skeered to death for fear the folks should ketch you in that-are dingy Circassian. Please let me unhook it! We'll have it off, and something more decenter on, in a jiffy!"

The "more decenter" garment was a handsome dark silk, with broad satin stripes of a brighter hue, relieving the ground; my best winter robe. Martha's taste was commendable, for I had nothing more becoming. It was made open from the throat almost to the girdle, with flowing sleeves, and my judicious abigail had selected, from my drawers, a set of laces to wear with it. The gauzy chemisette was my favorite neck-gear; my arms would be plump and fair through the flattering veil of the sleeves—but there were other considerations of fitness.

"I shall not put that on, Martha," I said, shaking loose my hair.

"Miss Grace!"

"I shall not wear that dress," I repeated, as though I thought she had not heard me. "Get my stone-colored merino."

She took up the condemned apparel, but instead of replacing it in the wardrobe, began a parley.

"You think that solemn thing is fitter to war to-night! Miss May always dresses beautiful, if she *is* in mournin', and Miss Lilly, I'll be bound, is got more fine clothes than you can shake a stick at. It hurts my feelin's, Miss Grace, to see you look like poor white folks 'long side of 'em—so it does! Now, this"—rustling it ostentatiously—"is what I calls more respectabler—*gen*teel in fac'! Won't you put it on jest this once? To-morrow they won't be so companyfied. 'Twon't matter so mighty much then how you fix up."

I was obdurate, and with a bad grace, she produced the Quaker attire I ordered. It fitted me nicely, and was not obsolete in fashion; yet I looked prim and spinsterish, to myself, when the worked muslin collar finished my adorning.

Martha was lugubrious.

"If you would just stick some ribbon-bows about you somewhar, or war a sash with long ends, or put some flowers in your he-yar, 'twould help a little. Bless you, Miss Grace! it goes against the grain for me to 'low such a thing, but you *do* look old enough to be your own ma!"

"I have a grown daughter," I said, after she had taken herself and her bemoanings out of the way. "Has every vestige of youth then vanished? Let us see!"

I surveyed myself at length in the mirror, lighting another candle, that the obscurity might not befriend me.

"You might well pass for Lilly's mother, if not, as Martha asserts, for your own, Grace," was my judgment. "Bear this in mind, and you will not disgrace yourself by juvenile airs. Hold fast to your principles and your resolutions. In two months and a half you will be thirty—the age of discretion, or you will never attain to it. Do not delude yourself with any hope that Mr. Wynne's aspect will chronicle the years of your separation as truthfully as does yours. Time is proverbially partial to men. It is not often that he flatters women with these very acceptable tokens of favoritism. To you he has not vouchsafed a dispensation. You are a single woman of thirty! Do not forget this, and, as I remarked, you are comparatively safe."

"Cold comfort, this!" I hear some one observe.

It was just the harsh tonic I needed. It fortified me for the nonce, although it was not what supported me unto the end of the trying evening. I bolted my door, and knelt to pray for more enduring strength—for consolation. Only there, at the mercy-seat, did I confess my want of courage, my need of balm.

I have intimated that I bore up pretty well throughout the evening. I was not talkative. While we were at table I had not leisure and opportunity to engage freely in the general conversation. Lilly's never-flagging spirits enlivened the others to mirthfulness, and I smiled as readily as the gayest of them. I was glad to see my father treat Mr. Wynne with unreserved politeness; more glad at the gradual infusion of cordiality into his deportment, when they had talked together for a time. The massive centre-table maintained its place sturdily in the parlor, and, around it, as by a common centripetal attraction, we ranged our seats, supper having been dispatched.

"Your work-basket, Auntie!" exclaimed Lilly, who had found her way to her footstool at my knee. "I hoped you would do nothing except spoil me to-night."

"My fingers only will be busied with my work," said I. "Eyes, tongue, ears and thoughts are yours. The Christmas gifts for the servants are more backward than they should be. If you"—indicating a plural sense by my eye—"will excuse an appearance of neglect of your society, I will go on with those that are unfinished."

The desired permission was given, and my embarrassments were over. My downcast lids relieved me from the duty or chance of looking from face to face, and as I saw them not, I was beguiled into the fancy that I was myself unobserved. When my regards strayed, it was to Lilly. Lovely she had ever been in my sight; but now she had acquired an air of easy elegance, a confidence which was not of that species that degenerates into boldness. I had never possessed such a manner. If I had, the diffidence I did not pretend to conceal, when solicited to enter a higher, wider sphere, would never have existed, or if there had been a lurking misgiving, I would not have avowed it. Yet my "little daughter" had not outgrown her pethood. There was yet a child-like grace—an artless winningness about her that proclaimed the unsullied nature; the unchilled fount of affection. She sat at my feet as she did nine years ago; the smooth, open brow lay snowily within its frame of golden chestnut; the lustrous eyes, whether laughing or serious, were telling me, all the while, sweet stories of her love for me.

Wrapped up in admiration and maternal devotion for my darling, there was an enlargement of kindly feeling towards all whom she loved, and to whom she was dear. It was from the influence of this benevolent expansion that I was induced to accost Mr. Wynne, as we were dispersing for the night.

"Have you relinquished the idea of making California your home, Mr. Wynne?"

What a groundless apprehension had that been which had prevented me from encountering his gaze until this moment? It was gentle and brotherly, and reassured instead of confusing me.

"I had never an 'intention' of residing there," he replied. "The 'fever' did not attack me. My going was a cool speculation, with no attendant excitement, except a liking for adventure. I was tired of home, and I went. I became more tired of California, and here I am!"

"But a relapse—should that occur!" said I.

"There is, I trust, no danger of that. I regard my citizenship in the United States as perpetual; if one may call that perpetuity which endures as long as his life."

This was no idle talk, for Lilly stood beside him, and I intercepted a gleam of intelligent meaning in its progress from one to the other. Who would expatriate himself when his native land contained this treasure? who would not embrace patriotism, when this was her award to the staunch citizen?

"You have chosen wisely," I remarked, in default of a more original observation.

"I think so!" Another significant eye-messenger, while Lilly's cheeks dimpled witchingly. "It is a trite, but one of the truest of proverbs, that 'there is no place like home.'"

My heart *did* ache at the unexpected quotation, but I quelled the painful bound, soothed the smart by saying within myself—"I may be at ease as to what he remembers of the one passage that united our lives for a day. It is nothing—less than nothing to him. In loving Lilly, he is not haunted by the ghost of his youthful fancy for me—her maiden aunt."

I was not entirely prepared to listen to Lilly's history of their acquaintance and present relation, yet—so unreasonable are we—I was mortified, considered myself badly treated, inasmuch as she slept in my bosom all night, her hands joined there, as she did in childhood, when in my sleeplessness, I derived comfort from the fancy that the fingers, moving at intervals in her slumbers, were feeling for my heart-strings; I was wounded, I say, that she lay thus, and spoke of every other subject, never of this; that she followed me around through the house, in the day-time, loving, caressing, the image of frank innocence—yet never breathed a syllable implying that the chief, the highest niche in the heart temple had been occupied, and gloriously, since our parting; that the nestling was fledged and plumed for flight, although she tarried for a space in the covert where she had so long sheltered her head—the shade of my wing.

The Linden carriage drove over early on the morning after the arrival, and Peyton was the outrider. Lilly was at the window. She colored rosily; but as a shower of smiles fell upon her face, as she flew out to meet our friends, I concluded that there was nothing in her delight more complimentary to Peyton than to Annie and her husband. The audacious youth was helped by his vanity to a judgment more favorable to his pretensions; for he usurped Mr. Wynne's place at her side; conversed fluently and gaily with us, confidentially with her; had, in short, quite the mien of an accepted lover.

Mr. Wynne did not chafe as a younger man would have done in his situation. Indeed, he appeared to connive at the monopoly of Lilly, by her whilom playfellow. He coaxed little Mary Peyton to his knee, when she showed a disposition to cling too tenaciously to "cousin Lilly," and engrossed her father's attention, while May and I were chatting with Annie. I renewed my invitation to our neighbors to our Christmas dinner; our party was engaged for the second day to them, and they departed, leaving Peyton behind. Domestic cares obliged me, by and by, to absent myself from the parlor. When I returned, the incorrigible youngster was stationary as ever, in the luxurious height of what was, to all intents and purposes, a private interview, since Mr. Wynne and May were as far withdrawn as the walls of the apartment would permit.

May beckoned to me.

"With us, you are not *de trop*," she said, in an undertone. "With them, you might be."

Mr. Wynne smiled. He was very sure of his footing; fearless of rivalry, and he could afford to be magnanimous. I would reward his generous forbearance.

"They were playmates, you know," I observed; "and are on the most amicable terms."

"Or appearances belie them," answered Mr. Wynne, amused, perhaps at my bungling quietus to his jealousy. "Misery and dislike seldom deck themselves in such disguises as they are sporting."

"Lilly has no elder brother"—I plunged on, making myself more ridiculous at each step—"and Peyton seems very near to her."

Both my auditors laughed out here, and I, baffled in my search for anything diverting in what I had said, flushed up so redly that I feared they would believe me angered by their merriment. To avoid this, I joined in with them and laughed at I knew not what. I left the young couple alone after this unlucky explanatory measure by which I sought to account for the false appearance of the times; and there they were, talking as fast and as intently when the dinner-bell rang.

May, in the interim, reminded herself of a letter to be written to her mother, and Mr. Wynne had no resource against solitude except my society. How like, and yet how unlike was this to that dead, buried, forgotten Christmas! He was very kind. He could not have been kinder if he had cherished the memory of that lost time, and we had stood, hand in hand, beside its memorial-stone. He was more sedate; not so addicted to badinage as I remembered him; but the independence of thought; the manly earnestness of expression; the courteous deference to his fellow colloquist, particularly if she were a lady—deference that had a dignity of its own, and scorned the outermost verge of servility—were not all these known to me? spoke they not to me like the faint, delicious murmurings of the ocean-shell to the inland exile, who was born and reared beside the sea-waves? Precaution grew drowsy under the music; even the Argus eyes of my grim monitress, Dame Reason—than whom the "Old Man of the Sea," never clung more tightly to his hapless victim—even these were veiled in sleep, and I was happy with the happiness of my girlhood. It was one of those bright, rare days to my soul, such as the sun, in a prodigality of good nature sometimes in winter, pours upon the surprised natural world; when through the cold, bare bosom of Mother Earth run thrills of ecstatic summer rapture, as if her veins were throbbing with rich wines.

In my morning mood, I would have been seriously alarmed and offended at Peyton's conduct. He was utterly reckless of etiquette and conventional restrictions, regardless of another's just rights, in his behavior to Lilly. Not content with the four hours' conference of the forenoon, he fastened upon her when the repast was done, and conducted her back to the sofa in the parlor, which he only left, after the lapse of another hour, to advertise a ride they were to take in company. I was not so bereft of reason by the tropical breezes and perfumes I was inhaling, as not to oppose this motion.

"Is it not too cold, Lilly, dear?" I asked.

This question would, in other times, have been equivalent to a stringent prohibition, but she only bestowed on me one of her sunshiny smiles, and crying, "Oh, no, Auntie! I shall enjoy a gallop of all things in the world!" glanced out of the room like a veritable ray of light.

"I must see that she is warmly dressed," was my pretext for rising to follow her.

May pulled me down.

"Sit still, Grace! I am going to her." She subjoined a whisper. "There is no risk! Let the child enjoy herself!"

"No risk!" I repeated inly, comparing Peyton's glowing countenance and restless movements, attesting to what pinnacle of bliss he had climbed, with Mr. Wynne's contented air. "I believe we are all crazy or silly alike!"

Mr. Wynne, with an authority, modified by his graceful politeness, waved Peyton aside, as Lilly prepared to mount, and lifting the fairy figure dexterously, seated her in the saddle. He adjusted the reins also, and presented them to her, and while stroking the silky mane of her horse, said something lowly and rapidly, that made her blush and smile the most charming of the thousand that had chased one another over her face that day.

"May is nearer right than I am," I thought. "Yet no! there is danger to one of whom she does not think. Alas for the deluded Peyton!"

My heart fainted in pity for him, I imagined; but it came to surprisingly soon, for we elder pleasure-seekers walked out. May claimed my father's arm, and Mr. Wynne tendered his to me. May lagged in the rear; yet she was no despicable pedestrian, and my father's step was unlike that of age. We could distinguish her voice in animated narration, it seemed, by the inflections and infrequent breaks in the thread.

"What can she be discoursing about!" I said, curiously.

"Something intensely interesting to themselves—to her, at least," was the response. "We, for the sake of variety, will try a dialogue. I am not so complaisant as your father. I must have my turn."

The same rare, prodigal sunlight; the same coursing wine-veins, warming and exhilarating; the same Circe-song; the same weak and wicked intoxication—and the day departed and the night came—the twilight of reflection, with frost, not dew.

"What am I doing? what am I?" I said, in the depth of the dark hours.

Lilly was asleep on my breast. By the moonlight, I saw her calm fairness; felt, against my unholy heart the beatings of hers, trustful, free from doubt as from guilt; a rippleless lake, reflecting the heaven and stars of Love bent above it—and I, oh, what wrong of her was in my soul! Conscience and Reason blamed me for their negligence, and each zealously repaired her fault in exhibiting mine in its worst, vilest form. A wretched, mangled worm, I writhed till morning, when a retributive spirit took me by the hand, and bade me be guided by her through the devious paths where I had stumbled so sadly.

Fortune "or Providence," said my repentant heart, aided me. Mr. Wynne and my father rode out and were gone until dinner. I forced myself to think of the subject of their discussion. I had heard Mr. Wynne propose the jaunt, and detected the slight agitation, imperceptible except to such eyes and ears as mine, with which he proffered the request. I was with May and Lilly, playing the decent woman of the house, the whole forenoon, and presided with more propriety than on yesterday, at the table. Then, the flesh being unspeakably weary, I retired to my chamber, where I slept heavily, heavily—like a beaten, berated dumb creature.

When I awoke, the room was coldly dismal with the impending night shades. I had laid down without removing my dress

Half-dreaming, I shook and brushed the tumbled folds; twisted up my hair by the sense of touch alone, and groped my way down the steps. May's laugh sounded through the parlor door. My father's voice answered it, and without risk of disturbing Lilly and her lover, as I had thought I might do, if I went into that room, I entered. Candles were upon the centre-table; their blaze dazzled me; the merry hum of conversation bewildered me. At last, I made out to perceive that I was the only one wanting to fill up the family group. Wanting! was I wanting? had they missed me?

Mr. Wynne had been reading from a Magazine now shut upon his finger.

"We have wished for you, Grace," said May. "Lilly went to call you, but said you were sleeping so peacefully that it would be a pity to arouse you. Herbert has been reading a humorous sketch to us. You would have liked it."

"Liked it perhaps—but she is not over-friendly to professedly 'humorous' articles," rejoined Mr. Wynne. "I have a scrap of rhyme in my pocket-book, which will please you better, Miss Leigh, than a host of the wittiest *jeux d'esprit* Hood ever perpetrated. Written jests are not for me either. We once compared notes on this matter and agreed, I recollect, that they resembled re-bottled champagne. Yet neither of us are backward in our relish of spoken and acted fun."

He was *very* kind thus to remember and quote my tastes! I wished I could reply as this notice of me deserved; but I stammered an unintelligible assent, and sat down, protecting my blinking eyes with a hand-screen.

"The poem!" said May. "I love fun, written, printed, spoken or acted; yet my taste is not so vitiated that I have not some appreciation of a nice clever bit of poetry."

"This 'bit' is neither clever nor nice," returned Mr. Wynne, in a like strain. "It is *poetry*. The author is young, but I, for one of his admirers, shall never forgive him if he does not become the Tennyson of America."

"'Poeta nascitur, non fit,'" repeated my father.

"He is a born poet, sir," answered Mr. Wynne. "The sacred fire is within him. It remains with him to give it to the world as freely as he has received, or to make of himself a dark lantern. Will you hear his simple 'Legend?'"

It was mournfully musical as the wind-harp heard at midnight, tender and delicate as a maiden's thoughts of love. Hearts and breaths kept time to the rhythmic flow from the speaker's lips. The story was, as he had said, very simple. A lonely high-born maiden, pure and cold to others' sight as mountain snows, watched the sea from her castle-turrets, or wandered among the

"Ragged, jagged rocks
That tooth the dreadful beach;"

always looking from the land; straining her eyes across the waters, waiting, hoping, none knew for whom or what, until the deferred hope sickened into despair, and she died.

"She ever loved the sea,
God's half-uttered mystery,
With its million lips of shells,
Its never-ceasing roar;
And 'twas well that when she died,
They made Maud a grave beside
The blue pulses of the tide,
'Mong the crags of Elsinore.

One chill, red-leaf falling morn,
Many russet autumns gone,
A lone ship, with folded wings,
Lay dozing off the lea;
It came silently at night,
With its wings of murky white

Folded after weary flight—
  The worn nursling of the Sea!

Crowds of peasants flocked the sands;
There were tears and clasping hands;
And a sailor from the ship
  Passed through the church-yard gate.
Only '*Maud*,' the head-stone read;
Only 'Maud?' Was't all it said?
Then why did he bow his head
  Weeping, 'Late, alas! too late!'

And they called her cold! God knows.
Underneath the winter snows,
The invisible hearts of flowers
  Grow ripe for blossoming.
And the lives that look so cold,
If their stories could be told,
Would seem cast in gentler mould,
  Would seem full of love and spring."

I should not have been ashamed of the softness to whose influence others testified by trembling smiles and glistening eyes; yet I raised my screen high and nearer to my face. Their tears were the dew of sympathy; mine rained from the cloud of my own heart-grief. I, too, had had a watch of years, unremarked, because unknown by those around me; a wandering of fruitless expectation across a great, uncertain waste—the Hereafter of the monotonous Now; and to me, also, had come the end of waiting. The arms, erst flung in supplicating gesture towards the blank horizon, were folded upon my breast, the lids were fallen over the dimmed irids; but oh! not in "Maud's" peaceful rest! The "cold life," the "winter snows," heaped and hardened—these still remained to me.

Mr. Wynne came over and took a seat by me. I feared that he observed the drops I could not at once conceal, for there was compassion in his tone. I wanted to thank him for his goodness, and again, articulation played me false. I looked and behaved as any apathetic automaton might have done. Supper liberated him from the duty of entertaining me, and furnished me with work to do which became the inane, homespun maiden of thirty, a more comely partner for the tea-urn than for the suitor of her niece.

CHAPTER XXVIII.

Lilly was talkative after we retired to bed, and I did not dissuade her. My common sense showed me that the most effectual safe-guard against a return of the insane delirium of the previous day would be the reception of her confidence; to hear from herself what—nevertheless, I did not now doubt—that she was to be the wife of him whose betrothed I was at her age. So, I tuned my voice into better harmony with hers, and paid encouraging heed to whatever she said.

"To-morrow will be Christmas-Eve," she prattled, her hand on my heart, never dreaming how its strings were quivering! "It is nine years since papa gave me to you, Auntie dear. He might as well have brought you Pandora's box."

"You know that is not true, Miss Sauce-box!" I replied. "I will not humor you by contradiction. You bait too awkwardly to catch compliments from me."

"But, seriously, am I any comfort to? you have I recompensed you, in any degree, for the trouble I have given?" she asked.

"My darling! when you are my choicest treasure! The debt is mine, not yours, Lilly."

"You humble, you distress me by talking so, Auntie. I owe my life, and whatever makes life happy, to you. Mother! you *are* my mother!" putting back my hair and kissing the scarred temple.

How rough and old my skin felt, compared with the satin smoothness of hers! But my pained heart was easier for the beloved title she had applied to me; its bruised tendrils clasped her more tightly.

"It would seem hard, unkind, for us to be separated; would it not?" she resumed, thoughtfully.

"It is coming!" I whispered warningly to my spirit. Then I made answer bravely.

"Very hard for a while, love, until we were used to it. It is a thing that occurs every day. Daughters as dutiful and affectionate, leave doting mothers. It is one of the necessary trials of our existence."

"Is it"—hesitating—"is it *ungrateful*, Auntie?"

"You dear little goose! Ask Aunt May to-morrow, whether she ever suffers from remorse for having loved your uncle more than she did her mother. It is woman's nature, Lilly, the dictate of an instinct implanted by God himself. To contend with, or disobey this feeling is wrong, sometimes wicked."

She was playing with the ruffles of her sleeves, as if perturbed or restless, but I could see that she smiled meanwhile.

"I have always intended to live single, never to leave you and grandpapa," she said.

"Excuse me, dear, for correcting you. Whatever you may have believed were your intentions, you deceived yourself if you imagined they were to remain as you are, and where you are. Every girl—I do not believe there has ever been an exception—thinks of marriage, that is, a marriage of affection, as a desirable and probable event. This is not the language which others would use to you, but it is the truth. Nor is it an evidence of declining love for grandpapa and myself that you have had visions of another home, and another, a stronger feeling. Because you *are* dear to us, we would rejoice in your joy, were your heart overflowing with that ripe, all-satisfying happiness that only this reciprocal love can bestow. From the beginning, it has mastered parental and filial affection, and it is just that it should."

Her hand rested still upon my heart. Did she feel the leap of the blood through, and from it, at her reply?

"Yet, Auntie, you are not married, and seem happy—the happiest person I ever saw. When I was too young to understand these things, you told me that you were satisfied with your lot. Would the feeling you have mentioned contribute anything to your contentment? Are you ever conscious of its need?"

"Conscious of its need!" echoed the heart, with a sudden shriek of pain. "Would I not surrender the last forced breath of life to gain it?"

"I read a story once, Lilly," I said, "of a man who wished to enter a monastery or college of recluses, who called themselves 'silent philosophers.' There was no vacancy in their number; a blow to his hope, which they communicated by offering him a cup brimming with water. No more could be added without overrunning it. He comprehended the sign, and, bowing his submission, was about to retire, when he perceived upon the flags at his feet, a rose-leaf. He picked it up, and laid it so dexterously upon the surface of the water that not a particle was displaced. The happy conceit secured his unanimous election. Can you add the moral of my fable, darling?"

"I wish—how I wish that the rose-leaf of love were laid upon your heart, dearest Auntie!" she responded, raising herself upon her arm, that she might see my countenance.

"I have that which almost supplies its want," said I; "the belief that my daughter's cup is crowned with roses; that, to its very depths, it reflects their crimson."

She kissed me; then buried her face in my bosom.

"Our Father bless you both, dearest!" I uttered fervently, as I stroked the abundant, flossy curls. "Yours is a worthy choice. I can resign you without distrust to his keeping."

"I am such a child in everything!" she whispered. "So

young, so inexperienced! Indeed, Auntie, I fear he has been hasty."

"His is a mature judgment, Lilly, and not apt to hurry him into indiscretion. At your aunt's, he had uncommon facilities for reading your character. He knows and loves my precious one. He will wear the prize tenderly and proudly, as he should."

What ailed the child? Was it the involuntary reserve of her strange position as a woman and betrothed, or the start of shyness at her freedom of speech upon this topic, that made her draw away from my embrace, and speak so decidedly?

"We will not talk further of this to-night, dear aunt. To-morrow, or on Christmas-day, you shall have the story, from beginning to end. This is the only partial confidence I have ever showed you. It shall be the last. You will pardon me when you know the circumstances. It was not all my fault either"—faltering—"Aunt May, and—and"——

"Mr. Wynne," I supplied, composedly.

"Yes—advised me to wait until they considered it prudent to disclose the matter."

"You were right, dear, and so, doubtless, were they;" but at heart, I owned to a tinge of jealousy that they should have had the power to restrain the outgoings of her spirit towards me—they, who were the intimates of a day in comparison with my years of devotion.

I stifled the unworthy thought—unworthy of me and of them—in the birth, and while she slumbered, drew her hands, that yet felt like the baby-fingers I had pressed there nine years ago, to my breast, and my heart beat evenly beneath them, for I had gained a conquest over myself.

Once, during the following day, it stirred uneasily—only once. It was when passing the parlor door, which was slightly ajar, I beheld through it, a tableau within the room. Mr. Wynne stood near the fireplace, facing me, but his head was bent so that he did not see me—bent over another—girlish and rich in golden ringlets—which lay against his shoulder. His arm encircled the slender waist ; her face, averted in pretty coyness, was rosy as the morning ; his, smiling, proud, tender, with the look I had imaged, when I prophesied how he would wear his prize. 'Twas but a glance that I had, and neither of them were aware of my fleet step through the hall. I went to my father's room, where was May, sewing, on one side of his chair. I established myself on the other, and our needles and tongues were not idle until our father warned us that our eyes might be the sufferers from the failure of daylight.

I had to give out supper, and I sang from the dining-room to the pantry ; from the pantry, through the yard to the smoke-house ; sang, as I paused in the back porch, and gazed westward, at the streaks of pale flame, orange, and white, and red, shooting up into the wintry blue of the zenith. There, cloud flakes huddled motionless as if frozen ; and through the frosty stillness, fell down to earth the shrill, harsh cry of a flock of wild geese, darkly stringing southward.

"It will be bitter cold to-night !" I shivered, going into the house.

The redoubtable dandy butler opened the door, directed to me by my song.

"Miss Lilly 'squests the pleasure of your company to step into the parlor one half minute, Miss Grace," he delivered, pompously.

"What does she want, I wonder ?" I soliloquized. "She will not subject herself and me to a 'scene,' surely !"

The parlor would have been dusk, but for the crackling fire to which Joe had just added fresh fuel. First, I saw that Lilly was not there ; then, Mr. Wynne came forward and led me to a seat.

"Lilly sent for you, at my request," he said. "Can you spare me a little of your valuable time? Can you remain patient if I become prosy in what I am about to relate?"

"Certainly," I answered.

The time and the scene were here, and I borrowed nerve from the exigency. I set down my basket of keys upon the carpet, so carefully that they did not ring at all, and leaned back, with the civil equanimity of more than a resigned—of a willing listener. He stationed himself upon the same sofa, at a respectful distance from me, his back to the fire. It shone broadly into my eyes; yet I did not shirk this disadvantage. Why should I? *I* had nothing to divulge—nothing to conceal.

"Lilly says," he commenced, "that from some intimations you have made to her, she supposes you to be conscious that my visit here is not one of ordinary friendship. You have, perhaps, penetrated my design in escorting her home?"

"If he expects me to enact the sharp-sighted mother, elate with the prospect of her daughter's fortunate settlement, he will be disappointed," I determined; so I looked inquiringly after more light on the subject, and said nothing.

"She is very beautiful," he continued; "and trained as she has been, her graces of mind and character could hardly fail to match those of the exterior. You have perfected a good work in her."

"It was an easy and a delightful task," replied I, "and if I contributed anything towards its performance, it was an unconscious part. The seed was planted before she came to us. There was then a principle at work within the soil, which would have destroyed the weeds and brought the fruit to perfection."

"I am acquainted with the extent of her obligations to you," he returned, in the coolest manner imaginable. "I expected that you would deny it, yet I am none the less obstinate in my conviction that whoever is endowed with her heart and hand, will have to thank you for much of his happiness. To no other woman living would *I* so willingly owe the best blessing Earth has in its gift."

"Thank you!" I said, moved.

It was like distilling oil into my spirit to think that I had done something for his welfare; that he was mindful of, and grateful for it.

"Knowing you, as I did," proceeded he, "it was not possible that I should have been deceived in the likeness which I recognized when I met her in your sister's home. Her model was too faithfully copied."

"We are very unlike!" I corrected, hastily. "Your imagination created the resemblance, Mr. Wynne."

"Then I, alone, would have perceived it, whereas it is universally remarked by accurate observers. Those who have no perception for similitudes except those of complexion and the coloring of hair and eyes, do not see this, it is true. In tone and gesture; in certain peculiar forms of language; above all, in the beaming of the inner light and the modesty that would, but cannot obscure this; the forgetfulness of Self, and in love and thought for others—in these, I affirm, she is a copy of yourself. This is not fulsome compliment, Miss Leigh—my heart claims utterance this evening, and it shall have it!"

Should I tell him how painful such frankness was? Might he not misinterpret my reluctance to listen?

"Thank you!" I repeated, but in a different tone. "I am honored by your kind opinion of me, exaggerated as are your praises."

"Do me the justice to believe them sincere, nevertheless," he said, so dignifiedly that I felt rebuked for the chill incredulity of my reply. "May I inquire if you suspected that I was attached to your niece before I accompanied her hither?"

"I did—without sufficient cause, perhaps, but I certainly had such an idea."

" Or May is not the friend and correspondent I believe her to be," he answered. " Will you oblige me by stating candidly what were your sentiments on hearing of my suit to her ? what they are now ?"

I shook my head.

" One question at a time, if you please, sir !"

" For instance, then—did you think me presumptuous ?"

" By no means !" I said. " Lilly is very dear, very beautiful, very winning to us, but there are many who outshine her."

" Not in my estimation "—then smilingly—" we will pass that point, however. Does it appear selfish and unreasonable that I should covet the blossom you have nurtured ; in which your affections are bound up ?"

My voice was not so clear now ; but I answered readily, and it was firmer as I went on.

" Would it not be more unreasonably selfish in us to grudge you your possession of what we have enjoyed now so long ? Would it not be the height of unkindness to negative your offer, when her peace of mind hangs upon our decision ? True love does not think of, much less does it consult with Self."

" Yours does not !" emphatically. " Now for the grand difficulty ! Before I present it, I beg you to recollect that I am not sensitive touching it. Say out what you really feel. Is not the difference in our ages—fifteen years and some months, you know—incompatible with every theory of romantic affection ; at variance with your ideal of connubial bliss ? Do I look or act like a fitting bridegroom for your rose-bud ? Will not the world laugh at the oddly-matched pair ?"

" Do you regard the world's laugh !" I asked.

" For myself ? No ! But that is jumping the question. Your ideas are what I desire at this moment. Am I not too old for Lilly ?"

" If she has elected you of her own free will and choice, your hearts are the same age. The arbitrary divisions of Time into months and years are disallowed by them. What have you to do with these false data? Why mar your enjoyment by recapitulating them?"

He was silent and thoughtful.

Dreading a pause that would give me time for reflection, I pursued: "Look at our neighbors, Mr. and Mrs. Peyton! He is twenty years her senior, and no idealization of wedded bliss can be more charming than their real, every-day life."

"He was a widower, was he not?"

"Yes."

"Did he love his first wife?"

"Devotedly; and mourned her a long, long time. He has not forgotten her yet."

"There is, then, such a thing as second love?"

"Who doubts it?" was my reply.

I was not embarrassed, for I saw, each moment, how entire was the oblivion, to him, of our early attachment.

He reverted to the original topic, speaking softly, as in reverie. "She is younger than myself—much younger—a delicate, tender creature! It is the old tale of the ivy and the oak."

How thoroughly I understood, at these words, that he had parted with every memory of that love!

"The stalwart trunk, roughened by countless winters, and the frail creeper of one summer's growth. It loves the coarse bark upon which it fastens itself—does it not, Grace?"

I did not notice the slip of the tongue, although, up to this time, it had been "Miss Leigh," very rarely even "Miss Grace."

Indulging his mood, I said, "It prefers it to any other support."

"Can it live without a prop of some kind?"

"It was my impression that it could not," replied I, "until a year or two ago, I saw a clump of ivy bushes, stout and upright, which I learned had been forced into independence by refusing them any support. Since then, I have been told that the success of such trials is a familiar fact in the history of the plant."

I was getting very easy indeed, and quite surprised myself by the glibness of my tongue. It was a strange time for the recital of botanical phenomena, but if it pleased him to lead the way to them, it was my business to follow.

"The vine must have suffered intensely before the lesson was perfect," he said, interested. "Think of the vain reaching of the tendrils; their curling upon themselves in their hopelessness; their shrivelling away and dropping into dust! It was a cruel experiment."

"It was a hardy shrub," I answered—"green and vigorous."

"But not beautiful, I should imagine; a dwarfed, stubborn apology for a tree; when if left to Nature's guidance, and not repressed by untoward circumstances, it might have climbed almost to the clouds. It was a cruel thing!"

He could mean nothing except what was apparent on the surface of his speech. What weakness in my heart to trace an analogy between the life of the maltreated vine and my crossed, distorted, "dwarfed" existence! It was not so very wonderful, either, for I remembered, among the incidents which had slided forever—clear out of sight—through his time-glass, that he had once likened me to the ivy. "Let it be ivy to the last!" he had said, and I was—ivy that had been robbed of the support its branches implored; "not beautiful"—I allowed that, "but hardy!" I said, drawing in my breath, and sitting more erect. "He shall see how hardy!"

From this digression, he returned suddenly, as he had from speaking of Mr. Petyon's second marriage.

"Am I to understand, Miss Leigh, that you consent, without

reservation, to my marriage with your niece? Pardon my abruptness if it appears to you unseemly. This is a subject that vitally concerns my happiness."

My hands grew cold against one another; a premonition of ague ran over, and pinched up my flesh.

"I have already signified my approbation of your suit, it may be too plainly, Mr. Wynne. My father's consent is more essential."

"I have conferred with him, of course. He refers everything to you, as does Lilly."

Much effort was necessary to repress the visible signs of the iciness that pervaded every limb. The fire sang and leaped and roared up the chimney, and my teeth were beginning to chatter. An odd fancy entered my brain—odd, since it seemed an unapt association of the circumstances in which I was placed. I had read that, in some countries, criminals convicted of capital offences, were, on the day of execution, compelled to sit upon their coffins, clothed for the final scene, and hear a funeral sermon, preceded or closed by a reiteration, at length, of the formula of doom. I thought how much more terrible would be this ghastly, solemn mockery, if the dying wretch were required to read his own sentence.

But here was no criminal court, and the phrase I had to speak was the merest of forms. I was a referee by courtesy. The virtual authorities had sat and agreed upon the case. My daughter's declared and accepted admirer, armed with my father's endorsement of the compact, asked mine—not as a measure of additional surety, but to spare my feelings and compliment my vanity. I did not delay it one tenth of the time it has taken me to write down my sensations. Propriety would have recommended a pause of the length I made, ere I said, cautiously, lest my teeth should strike against each other and excite his wonderment.

"If my permission is all you wait for, it is yours, Mr. Wynne

I do not charge you to be kind to our precious Lilly. You cannot be otherwise."

He bowed in silent thanks, raising my hand to his lips. It was frozen, I knew, and I would have abridged this useless ceremony, but he retained it in his.

"Grace!"

It was not the voice that had conducted the previous conversation. It was a deeper tone; the music that had thrilled me upon the hill-side, that summer Christmas-week; that quieted my stormy grief at our farewell;—never heard since—but oh! how well remembered? I could not—I *dared* not stay! I struggled for freedom with the energy of expiring resolution.

"Grace!" he said again.

I drooped my head and abandoned myself to his will.

"Have you a practical faith in a second love?"

"No!" I said, recklessly.

"Nor have I! you have given me a bonny bride—young and lovely—almost as lovely as the one you pledged to me upon the hill-side yonder, that looked so bleak to me to-day. I have been there, Grace, and you should have gone with me. That day, stolen from Paradise, we lived eleven years ago, as I heard you remind May this noon. Lover and beloved have undergone some changes in that period; but what did you say, not ten minutes since? I am bent upon vanquishing you with your own weapons. 'The arbitrary divisions of time into months and years are disallowed by loving hearts.' Mine rejects them. My bride then is the queen of my affections this hour, as well."

Before I collected my senses, my head rested upon his breast, where he had laid it.

"If you will have it, this shall be your home—yours only—now and forever."

One instant—was I to blame?—for one instant, it reposed there, like a flower burdened with honey-dew—then recol lection revived; prudence sprang into the field, ready for battle.

"Lilly! Lilly!" I cried, wrenching myself loose from his grasp. "Oh! let me go to her! My poor child! this will be her death-blow!"

He pinioned me with one movement of his strong arm; and I resorted to entreaties.

"Oh! if you are an honorable man, unsay what you have told me! take it all back! say you were jesting, or wandering in mind, that you did not mean it!"

"Never!" he said resolutely, not sternly. "I can dissipate these alarms by three words, if you will hear me."

"No! no!" for I was wild with terror and remorse.

"You will! *Darling!*"

I was completely overcome. A torrent of tears gushed forth, and were wept out upon his shoulder. I could have died happily then and there.

"I do not love Lilly, except as a child sister. She leans upon me, trusts me as her elder brother; the confidant—are you hearing me, darling?—of Peyton Elliott's love for her, and hers for him—you may well stare! After your insinuation of wandering intellects, I am prepared to be charged with derangement as violent as yours was just now. Look at me—feel my pulse—am I a sane man?"

"I believe so," I said, so doubtfully, that he laughed. He was very serious a minute afterwards.

"I will trifle no more with you. Can you forgive the deception in which May, Lilly, Peyton, and more recently, your father, were accomplices, I being the instigator and ring-leader of the plot?"

"My father?" I uttered involuntarily, laying hold of his name as something I could not understand, in the clouded condition of my faculties.

"May enlightened him the afternoon of our ramble. Will you go and ask him if this is so? You are at liberty."

But he was smiling again, in violation of his promise, and my stupefaction, or some other equally cogent reason prevented me from availing myself of the offer.

"Tell me more!" I said.

"With all my heart, now that you have a lucid interval. How often must I say over to you that Peyton and Lilly are informally engaged; that the witch was thinking of him, and within an ace of spoiling our drama by speaking out, owning up repentantly to you last night, when you were advocating my cause? By the way"—the irrepressible mischief breaking out once more—"let me acknowledge the favor before I forget it. All my rhetoric and May's pleadings have been brought into action to hinder the truthful child from going to your confessional. Zealous as she was, from the beginning, in my behalf, she has been sorely buffeted by conscience on the score of your delusion. I had a hard-fought conflict with her here after dinner. 'It was wrong, and unkind, and needless to keep dear Auntie longer in the dark; I must expedite my declaration, or she would turn State's evidence, and betray the conspiracy.' I applied a sedative finally, by bantering her about the Simon Pure, and asking her how his courtship was to be conducted when the blind of mine was removed. What is it, love?" as I looked up in troubled inquiry.

"Those tedious years of absence—your silence! Why was I not spared them if you"——

"Loved you all the while?" he finished for me. "I wish to save us both one part of this story to-night. We have had enough of trial and mysterious suffering. Let us be happy—unmolested by unpleasant reminiscences. Suffice it to say that until the eve of my departure from California, I was ignorant of the removal of the obstacle between us, as I was of its character. I will relate to you some day, the manner of its discovery. In May's home, I found Lilly. We established a friendship, and in process of time a three-fold cord was formed : a league for the capture of the citadel that had proved impregnable to a host of 'irresistibles,' Mr. Townley included. Some of our manœuvres may have appeared heartless to you, but believe me, they were prosecuted with unwillingness, through a strict sense of their necessity. Peyton wrote an explicit definition of his sentiments to Lilly a month ago, unable, he protested, to languish in suspense until her return. May, the Napoleon of our cabal, seized upon this opportune engine, and Lilly, by her instructions, forwarded to the impatient Elliott a schedule of our policy, and commissioned him to spy out the ground in advance of our arrival. His kind heart would have defeated the plan, but for the spirit of fun which abetted his anxiety to obey the orders of his lady-love. Letters from May and Lilly opened our attack, and since we have been here, not an act or a word from any of us has been destitute of meaning and aim. All have had a bearing upon our object. If there remained a dormant regard for me in your heart, jealousy was the surest touchstone to bring forth some sign of it. My intention to wed another would strike the dart home more certainly than any other event. I doubt if death itself would be so powerful in arousing the sleeping emotion. You were stronger than we had anticipated. If there were indications of surrender the day before, your aspect yesterday and this morning dashed our rising spirits. Victory was not to be purchased by delay—that was evident. I resolved to hazard all upon one bold effort."

His pleasantry had produced the desired effect of banishing my agitation, and setting me at ease in his presence. Exchanging his jesting for earnest affection, he continued : "Be it my task to compensate to you for what I have made you endure to-night! Unselfish heroism ; love, refined from all impurities ;

a constant soul-cry to heaven for succor—these have supported you through the ordeal. Let me say, 'ordeal !' A squeamish coyness was never one of your traits, and we can afford to dispense with the affectation of reserve. You loved me, unknown, it may be, to yourself, while I feigned allegiance to another. Such abnegation of self, such fixedness of purpose to promote the happiness of a beloved one, I have never beheld before; I trust never to undergo so much in beholding its like again. When I drew out the reeking blade to plunge it anew into your heart, did you think I was the forgetful trifler I appeared; that I did not wince at every stroke I inflicted? could you believe that every incident, every word of our 'long ago,' was more dear to, more valued by, you than by me? Yours has been a thorny way since we parted last, beloved."

"It has had some flowers in it," I smiled through my tears.

"Because you set the roots, scattered the seed weepingly," he replied. "You will yet bind up from them more, and precious blossoms."

There was a fumbling at the lock of the door; a stick of wood was dropped upon the hall-floor, with deafening concussion. Joe, considering us by this time properly apprised of his contemplated intrusion, entered to replenish the fire, and inform us, in his peculiar style, that "tea awaited our demands." With all his gallant devotion to the fair sex, our beau-footman had passed twenty and neared his thirties, a bachelor. He was divided between a philanthropic wish to gratify all the ladies by his society, and a natural disposition to secure the greatest possible quantity of felicity for himself, which consummation, he maintained, in his orthodoxy, was attainable solely by marriage. A connoisseur in love-affairs, he forwarded them by whatever means lay in his power. I saw, at once, that we were upon his list and received under his benign protection. His address accorded with this benevolent patronage. It was compounded of approbation of our exemplary employment; regret that his duty to interrupt us was imperative, and a kind of general know-nothing and see-nothing air, that without approximation to stupidity was to compose our disordered wits and sustain us to confront the eyes of the rest of the world.

Peyton Elliott had a seat at the board, having come in noiselessly just after Lilly left the parlor. Even he was chary of significant glances, absolutely guiltless of spoken innuendoes. This evening also, the tall coffee and tea-urns were towers of refuge to me. Behind them, with the cups and saucers as resting-places for my eyes, my flushed cheeks cooled, and I was collected, if not staidly sensible, all through the meal, which I did not taste.

Peyton lagged behind the others on their way out.

"Auntie dear!" he whispered. "I wanted you to espouse the cause of him you loved most. You were set upon neutrality. Is this best preserved by espousing the *man*, instead? How I hate him for jilting poor, dear Lilly. Don't you?"

CHAPTER XXIX.

The smiling morning was looking in at my windows, when the rattling roar of the Christmas gun chased away my dreams. It did not startle Lilly, and turning over towards her, I went back (well-trodden, I found the path !) to my spring-time, to the shadowed valley, for which I left its light and bloom ; the narrow track that delivered me from the dank darkness.

"Does much of the dust of those years of travel soil me ?" I wondered. "Have I changed as little in his, as he has in my eyes ? Women show age sooner than men. Youth is very beautiful, very lovable, yet would I recall mine ?"

I weighed the question carefully.

"Flowers or fruits—April or September ?" Thus it resolved itself at length ; and the small, white fingers stirred upon my heart as their owner awoke to kiss me—"our merriest Christmas, dear Auntie !"

Our visitors came early ; Mrs. Bell, Annie, Mr. Peyton and the three children, with Peyton Elliott in the rear of the procession. And we *did* have the merriest Christmas that ever shook the floors and echoed from the walls of the old homestead ! Tables groaned, and we laughed unfeelingly over their agony ; there were romps and baby-games in the hall and dining-room ; Lilly and Peyton hunted up the identical battle-door and shuttle-cock with which they had fought away the shyness of their first day's intercourse ; and battered as was the one, frayed and moth-eaten as was the other, they did service still. They appeared to have caught the spirit of the times, as they beat and whizzed through the air past the ancient sentinel, whose rusty hands still journeyed by the hours we did not pretend to regard ; while from its roomy chest, wheel, lever, and hammer still grumbled their misery over the internal convulsions, regular and violent as ever, in their periodical attacks.

There was no parlor-company. We roamed from one apartment to another, as inclination and the children tempted us. My father and Mr. Peyton did not even remain stationary for their after-dinner smoke; but might be traced in entry, chamber and porch, by the circling incense and the cheerful murmur of their voices. Fires blazed in every room, for it was clearly, bitingly cold without ; a genuine old-fashioned Christmas holiday ; alive, from sun-rise to sun-down, with jollity, good-will and peace

I propitiated Martha by donning the "decenter" robe of her selection, and submitting to Lilly's hair-dressing ; freed from which, I reviewed myself in the glass, a youngish face and figure, after all, or, if elderly, tolerably well-preserved. My complexion was healthy, to say no more, and to-day was brighter than usual ; my hair luxuriant and glossy, my teeth unimpaired, my eyes unfaded. Not elate, but comfortable in this appreciation of my charms, I did not torment myself by a continuation of the queries of the morning while the festivity reigned.

It was when the Linden family, Peyton Elliott excepted, were gone, and the parlor was given up to our two selves and the fire-flashes, that I asked Herbert some plain, matter-of-fact questions.

"Did you never fear before you came South this time, that I had grown elderly and homely ? What would have been the effect of the transformation upon you ?"

"You have altered"—he rejoined, "altered greatly !"

My vanity folded its feathered train, and skulked precipitately into the dust-hole.

"I was prepared, however, to see you as you are. Lilly carried your daguerreotype to New York with her, and the sun is an unflattering artist."

Then I wished, with unavailing longing, for the vernal season and the flowers.

"And why!" I said, mentally, my heart rising at the thought. "My love is as fervent, and more thoroughly grounded than when he first sought it; my heart as unwithered. Impulse has ripened into principle; passion into fidelity. Is it, indeed, as I feared? Can he never again feel for me exactly as he did then?"

I said as much, when cross-examined, to him; eyes moist and voice quavering. He attempted no further sportiveness; but taking up the thought I had let slip, he proved to me how it wronged him and myself; how willful seemed my misconstruction of his language.

"There are alterations more material than the fading of the rose and the sallowness of the lily. Did I not say to you, when the glow of our former plighting was warmest, that you had faults? indicate, as one, your inability to bear sorrow? predict the wrestling of your undisciplined spirit with the storm, I did not think then, could so speedily overtake you? Was not this verified to the letter? Now—mark me! I neither suggest nor warn. Instead, I would learn of you"——

I put my hand before his mouth. "Please do not talk so!"

"I have done! Rest assured that you have lost nothing, and gained all you needed; that the wife must ever be dearer than the betrothed bride."

A blessed, soul-fraught pause to me, was that which ensued! He spoke again in a graver, yet still tender tone.

"We have been very happy to-day, dear Grace. Will you complain if I damp your joyfulness for a time—add a sprig of rue to the bouquet of your pleasures?"

I was pale with incertitude ; cowardly from past reverses.

" It is nothing of recent occurrence," he said, kindly ; " only a missing leaf from the volume of my history, which I refused to show you yesterday. Grace, May was faithful to the trust of the family secret you disclosed to her. It was not from her lips that I obtained the knowledge of my parentage."

I started. The skeleton again ! would it never, never be buried out of my sight !

" I had been trained to mourn a dead father. I have a deathless recollection of my mother's weeping over me, as her ' fatherless child ;' of her commending me to the orphan's God. That her husband died at a distance from her and home, and that the particulars of his end were transmitted to her by strangers ; how she pined into the grave, of a broken heart—these were among the lessons taught me by the aunt who had nursed her in her last sickness and who adopted me as her own son. Mr. Wynne, her husband, had never seen my father, and was gratified by my mother's dying request that I should assume the name of my generous guardians. I do not like to reflect upon this significant circumstance. It was not surprising to them ; yet I cannot but feel that if the sorrow that killed her had been regret for the untimely end of one she loved—alas ! too well—she would never have consented that his son should resign his title—all which now preserved his memory. How much of the truth she knew, is left to conjecture. Sure am I—too sure—that she realized how little reason I would ever have to value the discarded appellation ; that the grave was an inviting pillow, and the hope of the rest beyond the gate all that sustained her, during the season of her worse than widowhood. I bless God that Death was speedy and merciful !

" How I grew up in utter ignorance of the mystery that curtained my cradle, I cannot understand. No memory, no spirit-impression whispered to me of its gloom. I told my story, as I believed it, in a careless, straight-forward way to any who chanced to discover that I was not Mr. Wynne's son. My aunt's death strengthened the bond between me and this solitary friend of my boyhood. I described to you, long ago, his second wife's politic complaisance and my meagre affection for her. My sisters were very dear to me ; Louise, especially, was my chosen companion and intimate, while she continued to be a woman. Now "——

"Never mind! We will spare her!" I prevented the criticism foreshadowed in eye and lip.

He bowed, and went on. "Mrs. Wynne is uninformed on the subject of my antecedents ; or, I have confidence in her skill and economy to feel certain that she would never have suffered such material for my debasement to lie in disuse. My adopted father is prudent, and he hid his knowledge of the dangerous secret from her as sedulously and successfully as from me. Latterly, at my earnest solicitation, he has confessed that strange rumors reached him, prior and subsequent to my mother's decease ; stories, that begot in him a doubt of the correctness of the account she had received of her husband's life and its close. He reasoned prudently that no benefit to me could result from prosecuting inquiries on this head, and allowed the matter to rest there. You were cognizant of my introduction to Mr. Dumont, and the nature of our intercourse at that time. Six years later, I met him in the society to which Louise's favor was his passport. He fascinated me, as by magnetic attraction. I derived singular delight from his presence and conversation ; and he reciprocated, in every company and all seasons, the preference I manifested. I did not agree with him in many sentiments ; was averse to many of his habits of language and conduct ; I divined his want of deep feeling, his passion—if he had a passion—for novelty and excitement ; yet I admired him intellectually, and sought him, in spite of my better reason. His was the last hand I took, in sorrowful adieu, when I embarked for California ; his, the last signal waved me from the wharf. A month before I left that country—within the summer that has just gone—I was summoned, at the dead of night, to the bedside of a man who had been fatally stabbed in an affray at a gambling saloon. You may conceive what was my horror on finding in him, Mr. Dumont—no mortal can form any conception of the emotions with which I hearkened to the tale he insisted upon recounting.

"That death-bed! my *father's* death-bed, Grace! I cannot speak of it!"

It was now my place to be comforter. Trembling woman, though I was, I could support and console him. He thanked me when the strong shuddering was over.

"My angel of healing!" he said.

No peerage coronet could have won from me the title!

"You have had the wild, sad story in detail from your father," pursued Herbert. "The sketch given to me, while life flowed from the narrator with every breath, made my soul sick, my brain reel. That the sins of the father had been visited upon his offspring was nothing to the thought of the woe he had inflicted upon others; the desolated hearth-stones, the murdered happiness; the sacrifice of innocent victims to his cupidity and revenge—added up in the sum of his crimes. It was horrible! He had seen my attachment to you in the course of the day or two we travelled together, and then was laid the scheme to frustrate its end. His animosity against your father was unabated to the last; yet Remorse scourged him to a revelation of his agency in the destruction of our dream of love.

"It was an unpropitious fate for us, an auspicious one for his designs, that threw him, after he separated from our party, into the company of Mr. Townley. He did not scruple to use this contemptible instrument. Let our trying age of estrangement bear testimony to the efficacy of the means employed. He elicited, from Louise, information that notified him of his success

He talked with you of me, and exulted in the confusion which betokened a spirit wrung by anguish, and an undying interest in the lover of your happier days; for, darling—unoffending dove as you were, your father had been his foe! Towards me, he experienced some natural drawing of heart, something akin to affection, but it was not paternal tenderness. He had accidentally seen me in a public thoroughfare the day preceding his death, had inquired of an acquaintance where I was lodging, and determined to pay me a visit at an early opportunity. We met sooner than he expected.

"That is all, dear Grace. I do not lament the loss, to myself, of a parent who deserted me in my helpless infancy; who was the assassin of my mother; who, without relenting, crushed my dearest hope in life, to gratify his enmity of an innocent man. I *am* humbled, ashamed to look my fellow-creatures in the face, when I remember whose blood courses in my veins; I *do* mourn that his guilt was so great, and—my own beloved! you appreciate the unspeakable torture that attends upon the idea of his awfully sudden call to a world of judgment. Heaven knows what I suffered while I saw him die—what I have suffered since!"

"We will never speak—will never, if we can avoid it, think of this strange, dark history again," I said. "Let us rejoice in the light that almost 'at evening-time,' has visited us!"

His features settled peacefully, as I tried to comfort him, to exorcise the troubling spirit.

"At evening-time!" he said, by and by. "We are just entering upon a gladly bright morning."

Then we were still.

The fire sang a low, but merry strain, the embers changed from red to white, and back to red, with the consuming heat, and then tinkled into ashes. The quaint chairs danced in their several places, in the wickedly mischievous gleams of rising flame. Christmas fairies sported in every corner, tripped in the magic ring to the chirp of the cricket.

There were sprites, as active and as gay, at work in the long-closed chamber of my heart, sweeping away its dust and cobwebs; purifying the airless tomb with morning breezes and morning sunshine. Finally, they tore away the hatchment above the door, that proclaimed it desolate by the death of hope, and the room was ready for its master.

CHAPTER XXX.

I HAVE been a wife for one year, and again, I muse in the twilight.

But now it is summer weather, flowery June, as one might know from this purplish light; the love-souvenir, with which the sun endows his most favorite month, over which her nights dream, as her days rejoice. It should be perfumed light, for the air holds, not breathes, fragrance as pervasive and delicate as its blush. Through the windows, open to the floor, I overlook our cottage-garden, with its modest wealth of flowers; next, a quiet village street lined by trees, its white houses set back, each in a green covert of its own; and beyond, there are glimmerings like the shimmer of sun-darts upon a silver mirror. There rolls, in tranquil majesty, the monarch of Northern rivers, whose dignity they asperse, instead of extol, who name it "the Rhine of America;" its broad bosom heaving in the repose of conscious might, its waves breaking, like the ripples of an inland lake, against ramparts adamantine in strength, Titanic in proportions.

It is a cozy room in which I am sitting. The furniture, although not elaborate in quantity or style, would not correspond with the antique simplicity of Moss-side. Yet there is one thing which you, my reader-friend, have seen before. The pale girl, with prayerful eyes, gazes upward from the wall over that reading-chair, which will not be empty many minutes longer

The hands of the clock are nearing the most welcome hour of the day with me—that which declares that the day is done.

The wife of a year! The fairies are very busy as I think this sentence. It is a hint to them to draw forth and spread, in grand array, the treasures accumulated in the chamber they found so empty two winters agone. Brave riches they are which they disentomb from the coffers! Every day has there mementoes, more precious than diamonds; there are strings of pearls, linked hours of unbroken bliss; and the pure gold of affection knows neither flaw nor stain. My constant prayer is that the wondrous beauty of earthly gifts may not weaken the eye which would look beyond them, to the giver; would survey them as earnests of life and love and home, as far more excellent than this abundant happiness, as this transcends the most gloomy pass of my journey hitherto.

On the table there lies a daintily-shaped black glove, too small for my hand. May lost it here to-day, which she spent with me. I found it but a minute since, after she had gone. She will call for it again soon, for she is as often with us as in her home-proper. Loving, bright-tempered, deep in heart and thought, she is still my soul-sister, doubly beloved, that she aided in the establishment of what I now enjoy.

Last Christmas, we all assembled at Moss-side, as we shall continue to do, from year to year, while our father lives. His robust health gives no sign of failing, his mind is vigorous as ever, his heart overflows with love to God and to man, his faith is perfected, "so as by fire." He misses me yet, he says, and I love to believe it; knowing, as I do, that it is a want of the affections only, since in his outward estate, nothing is lacking that could conduce to his happiness. He has a gallant, trustworthy son, ever at hand, with whom to advise, upon whom tc lean. The generous, gay-spirited boy has learned many lessons in domestic virtue and piety from his wife.

I smile as I apply to Lilly the term, that sits well, with my thirty-second year, upon me. Her marriage was deferred for several months after mine took place, until Peyton was ready to take possession of Moss-side as part owner and sole manager of the plantation. This has been enlarged by the addition of a valuable adjoining tract ; a wedding-present from Mr. Peyton to his name-sake, and which was formerly attached to the Linden domain.

Mrs. Bell went to her rest last year. By her request, she was laid, not beside her husband, in the ground now owned by strangers ; nor yet, with the still-remembered "Mary," in the dutifully-tended "God's acre," of Linden, but upon the knoll above the spring, at the old brown cottage, close to two other mounds, marked by plain head-stones and inscribed with texts of Scripture. Over against the older and shorter is written, "Well done thou good and faithful servant !" over the other— "Mine eyes have seen Thy salvation." They were old Zack's dying words, as they had been his wife's. There, mistress and servants, they sleep, near where they labored in concert. United they were, in prosperity and adversity, here. In the changeless day of their everlasting home, they walk in company—friends and equals in the sight of angels and of Him who created and who redeemed them. Together, they bore the heat and burden of the day ; together, they reap their exceeding great reward.

The Townleys were at my marriage ; and from no other guest did I receive a more affable and elaborate congratulation than from the lawyer-brother. He had had his plans, and the day of their triumph. No principle of his nature or policy bade him trumpet their defeat by exposing his chagrin. He represented his county in the Legislature last winter; he will "run" for Senator of his District the coming Fall, and the opposition will be slight, for he is a "popular man."

I move my chair impatiently at thoughts, which my present happiness cannot quite teach me to discard. An aromatic sigh from a vase of flowers upon the stand I have jostled reminds me of their donor. Mr. Wilson brought them up to me, last evening, when he accompanied Herbert out of town to tea. He is often our guest, but visits nowhere else voluntarily, and without his lady.

She is true to the letter of her obligations to him, and the most approved moral code of appearances, in always requiring his escort in public. She furthermore defers to the law of the land and the general sentiment of the community by continuing to reside under his roof; to eat of his bread and dispose of his money; while she battles with pen and tongue, in print and in parlors, for "Woman's independence;" her "rights of property and suffrage," and "the sovereign, undisputed maintenance of her absolute individuality."

Her Howard's Gallic-Swiss governess is superseded by a foreign tutor of equally ambiguous nationality. The boy is a prodigy of genius and learning, Louise tells us. I would love him better if he had been taught to practise the fifth commandment. I question if he ever so much as read it; for in his mother's "Age of Progress," these primitive land-marks are left far behind.

She was disappointed in her brother's choice of a partner. Mrs. Wynne the elder took pains that I should not live and die in ignorance of this, which was no news to me. I am "antiquated in my tenets," my sister-in-law says—"utterly devoid of the progressive anima;" "content to live forever in my husband's shadow; to own him as authority for doctrine; dictator of action; liege of my person, possessions and will."

How proudly I plead "Guilty!" to each count of this indictment, let every loving wife reply. While the sap stirs in the heart of the princely oak, let the ivy cling and climb, closer and yet more close to its Heaven-lent support; drink of the showers that refresh it; flourish in its sunlight, and at last, in the Father's "own good time," lie down with it in the dust!

FINIS.

LIBRARY OF POPULAR TALES.

Ten Volumes, each volume with Colored Frontispiece. 12mo., Cloth, gilt back $1.

Perils of Fast Living. A Warning to Young Men, by Charles Burdett.

Lights and Shadows of a Pastor's Life, by S. H. Elliott.

The Young Lady at Home, by T. S. Arthur.

American Evening Entertainments, by J. C. Campbell.

The Orphan Boy; or, Lights and Shadows of Northern Life.

The Orphan Girls; or, Lights and Shadows of Southern Life.

The Beauty of Woman's Faith. A Tale of Southern Life.

The Joys and Sorrows of Home. An Autobiography, by Anna Leland.

New England Boys; or, The Three Apprentices, by A. L. Stimson.

Prose and Poetry of Rural Life, by H. Penciller.

NEW LIBRARY OF WIT AND HUMOR.

The Widow Bedott Papers, oy Francis M. Whitcher, with an introduction by Alice B. Neal, with eight spirited illustrations, 12mo. cloth, gilt back, ... 1 25

'Way Down East; or, Portraiture of Yankee Life, by Jack Downing (Seba Smith), 12mo., illustrated, ...Cloth, 1 00

The Life and Sayings of Mrs. Partington, by B. P. Shillaber, forty-three illustrations, 12mo......................Cloth, 1 25

The Sparrowgrass Papers, by F. S. Cozzens, illustrated by Darley, 12mo.......... .....Cloth, 1 00

The Puddleford Papers; or, Humors of the West, 12mo. illustrated,...........Cloth, 1 00

The Bunsby Papers; or, Irish Echoes, by John Brougham, 12mo. illustrated, ...Cloth, 1 00

Lord Chesterfield's Letters to his Son. With a portrait on steel, 12mo,...................... 1 25

Essays of Elia, by Charles Lamb, 12mo..................... 1 00

Addison's Spectator, complete in 2 volumes,............... 2 50

Foster's Essay on Decision of Character, and Gems of Thought, 12mo. ....Cloth, 1 00

Doddridge's Rise and Progress, 12mo.... .... 1 00

Baxter's Saints' Rest, 12mo. 1 00

Pen Pictures of the Bible, by Rev. Charles Beecher, 18mo. Cloth, gilt back, 50
Full gilt sides and edges, 75

Rhymes with Reason and without, by B. P. Shillaber (Mrs. Partington), 12mo. portrait, Neat cloth 1 00

Gerald Massey's Poems, 12mo...... ....Neat cloth, 75

The Balloon Travels of Robert Merry and his Young Friends over various Countries of Europe, by Peter Parley, with eight illustrations, 12mo. Cloth, gilt back, 1 00
Full gilt sides and edges, 1 50

Gilbert Go-Ahead's Adventures and Travels in Foreign Parts, by Peter Parley, eight illustrations, 12mo. Cloth, gilt back, 1 00
Full gilt sides and edges, 1 50

STANDARD HISTORICAL LIBRARY.

Twelve Volumes, 8vo., *Library Style* $2 *per volume*- *Half Calf Antique*, $3 *per volume*.

Rollins's Ancient History. The Ancient History of the Egyptians, Carthaginians, Assyrians, Babylonians, Medes and Persians, Grecians and Macedonians; including a History of the Arts and Sciences of the Ancients, with a Life of the Author, by James Bell. Only complete American edition, numerous Maps and Engravings, 2 vols.

Hallam's Middle Ages. State of Europe during the Middle Ages, by Henry Hallam.

Russell's Modern Europe. History of Modern Europe, with a View of the Progress of Society from the rise of Modern Kingdoms to the Peace of Paris in 1763, by W. Russell, with a Continuance of the History by William Jones. Engravings. 3 vols.

Fergusson's History of Rome. The History of the Progress and Termination of the Roman Republic, with a Notice of the Author by Lord Jeffrey, uniform with Gillies' History of Greece.

Gillies' History of Greece. Its Colonies and Conquests to the Division of the Macedonian Empire, including the History of Literature, Philosophy, and the Fine Arts, complete in one volume, illustrated.

Robertson's Discovery of America. History of the Discovery of America, by William Robertson, LL. D., with an Account of his Life and Writings, with Questions for the Examination of Students by John Frost, A. M. Engravings.

Robertson's Charles V. History of the Emperor Charles V., with a View of the Progress of Society in Europe to the beginning of the Sixteenth Century, with Questions for the Examination of Students by John Frost, A.M. Engravings.

Robertson's Scotland and Ancient India. History of Scotland and Ancient India. A History of Scotland during the Reigns of Queen Mary and King James VI., till his Accession to the Crown of England, with a Review of the Scottish History previous to that period. Included in the same volume is a Dissertation concerning Ancient India.

Plutarch's Lives, translated from the original Greek, with Notes and a Life of Plutarch, by John Langhorne, M. D., and William Langhorne, A. M. Portrait.

THE NEW CABINET LIBRARY SERIES.

With Steel Illustrations. Twelve Volumes 18mo., *Neat Cloth, Fifty Cents each.*

Johnson's Rasselas.

Dean Swift's Tale of a Tub.

Sterne's Sentimental Journey.

Hogg's Mountain Bard and Forest Minstrel.

Locke on the Understanding, and Bacon's Essays.

Christian Poets of England and America.

Gregory Chapone and Pennington on the Mind.

Beattie's Minstrel and Bloomfield's Farmer Boy.

The Sorrows of Werter.

Cowper's Olney Hymns.

Letters of Laurence Sterne.

Sabbath Poems and Holiday Recreations.

POPULAR BIOGRAPHY.

GENERALS OF THE REVOLUTION.

Six Vols., 12mo. Illustrated, $1 25 each.

Life of George Washington, by John Marshall.

Life of General Francis Marion, by W. Gilmore Simms.

Life of General Nathaniel Greene, by W. Gilmore Simms.

Life of General Lafayette, by Wm. Cutter.

Life of General Israel Putnam, by O. L. Holley.

Life of General Daniel Morgan, by James Graham.

Life of the Emperor Napoleon Bonaparte, by P. C. Headley, 12mo. ....Cloth 1 25

Life of the Empress Josephine Bonaparte, by P. C. Headley, 12mo. 1 25

Pictorial Life of Benjamin Franklin, including his Autobiography, 8vo. 2 00

Lives of the Discoverers and Pioneers of America, containing Columbus, Vespucius, De Soto, Raleigh, Hudson, Smith, Standish, Arabella Stuart, Elliott, and Penn, 1 elegant volume, illustrated, over 12mo.......Cloth, 1 00

Life of Gen. Sam Houston. The only Authentic Memoir of him ever published, illus., 12mo...Cloth, 1 00

Lives of Eminent Mechanics, together with a Collection of Anecdotes, Descriptions, &c., relating to the Mechanic Arts, illustrated with fifty Engravings, 12mo. Cloth, gilt back, 1 00

Lives of the Signers of the Declaration of American Independence, with a Sketch of the Leading Events connected with the Adoption of the Articles of Confederation, and the Federal Constitution, by B. J. Lossing, steel frontispiece, and fifty portraits, 12mo......................Cloth, 1 00

Life of General Andrew Jackson, including an Authentic History of the Memorable Achievements of the American Army, under General Jackson, before New Orleans, in the Winter of 1814–15, by Alexander Walker, with a frontispiece, 12mo.........Cloth, 1 25

Life of James Buchanan, by R. G. Horton, 12mo......Cloth, 1 00

Life of John C. Fremont, by John Bigelow, 12mo......Cloth, 1 00

Life of Patrick Henry, by William Wirt, with portraits on steel, 12mo. ....Cloth, 1 25

Life of Charles XII., King of Sweden, by Voltaire, 12mo. Cloth, 75

LIBRARY OF TRAVELS AND ADVENTURE.

Adventures of Gerard the Lion Killer, comprising a History of his Ten Years' Campaigns among the Wild Animals of Northern Africa, translated from the French, by Charles E. Whitehead, illustrated, 12mo............Cloth, 1 25

Travels and Adventures in the Far West, by S. L. Carvalho, illustrated, 12mo. ....Cloth, 1 00

The War in Kansas; or, a Rough Trip to the Border, among New Homes and a Strange People, by George Douglas Brewerton, author of "A Ride with Kit Carson," &c., illustrated, 12mo. Cloth, 1 00

Bell Smith's Travels Abroad, illustrated, 12mo. Cloth 1 00

Hunting Adventures in the Northern Wilds: or, a Tramp in the Chateauguay Woods, over Hills, Lakes, and Forest Streams, by S. H. Hammond, with 4 colored illustrations, 12mo...Cloth, 1 00

Indian Battles, Captivities, and Adventures, from the earliest periods to the present time, by John Frost, LL. D., with illustrations, 12mo. ....Cloth, 1 00

Cumming's Hunter's Life among Lions, Elephants and other Wild Animals, edited by Bayard Taylor, colored illustrations, thick 12mo...........Cloth, 1 00

Female Life Among the Mormons, with illustrations, 12mo......................Cloth, 1 00

Layard's Popular Discoveries at Nineveh, illustrated, 12mo...............Cloth, 1 00

The Green Mountain Traveller's Entertainment, by Josiah Barnes, Sen., colored frontispiece, 12mo. ....Cloth, 1 00

Travels in Greece and Turkey, by the late Stephen Olin, D.D., illustrated, 12mo. Cloth, 1 00

Humboldt's Travels in Cuba, with an Essay, by J. S. Thrasher, 12mo. ....Cloth, 1 25

MISCELLANEOUS.

Star Papers; or, Experiences of Art and Nature, by Henry Ward Beecher, 26th edition, 12mo..................Cloth, 1 25
Turkey morocco, antique, portrait, 3 50

Lectures to Young Men on various Important Subjects, by Henry Ward Beecher, 26th thousand, 12mo. Cloth 75

An Encyclopedia of Instruction on Man and Manners, by A. B. Johnson, author of "Physiology of the Senses," 12mo.................... 1 25

Physiology of the Senses; or, How and What we Hear, See, Taste, Feel and Smell, by A. B. Johnson, 12mo. 75

Webster's Family Encyclopædia of Useful Knowledge; or, Book of 7,223 Receipts and Facts. A whole library of subjects useful to every individual, illustrated with nearly one thousand engravings, 1,238 pages, 8vo. illuminated backs or sides in gilt, ... 3 00
This is a valuable and truly useful work, comprising everything needful to be known in domestic economy essential to the comfort, convenience, utility, and enjoyment of a family. In fact, there is nothing in the entire range of the domestic economy of a family that cannot be found in this book. It contains nearly 1250 pages, with a copious index, and is profusely illustrated. It is a work which every husband should buy for his wife, and every father for his daughter.

Wau Bun; or, The "Early Day" in the Northwest, by Mrs. John H. Kinzie, of Chicago, illustrated, 8vo.................... 2 25

Country Margins and Summer Rambles, by S. H. Hammond, and L. W. Mansfield, 12mo. Neat cloth, 1 00

Ewbank's Hydraulics and Mechanics, containing Descriptive and Historical Accounts of Hydraulic and other Machines for raising Water, with Observations on various subjects connected with the Mechanic Arts, illustrated by nearly 300 engravings, 8vo. Cloth, gilt back, 2 50

Spirit Rappings Unveiled, by Rev. H. Mattison, 12mo. Cloth, 75

The Enchanted Beauty; or, Tales, Essays and Sketches, by William Elder, 12mo.......................Cloth, 1 00

Camp Fires of the Red Men; or, A Hundred Years Ago, by J. R. Orton, illustrated 12mo. ....Cloth, 1 25

My Courtship and its Consequences, by Henry Wikoff. A true account of the Author's Adventures in England, Switzerland, and Italy, with Miss J. C. Gamble, of Portland Place, London, 12mo. Cloth, 1 25

The House I Live In; or, The Human Body, by Wm. A. Alcott, M.D., 1 vol. 18mo....... 63

The American Gift Book. A Perpetual Souvenir, with six elegant steel engravings, 12mo. Cloth, 1 00

The Sultan and His People, by C. Oscanyan, with numerous illustrations, 12mo......Cloth, 1 25

The American Revolution and Beauties of American History, 12mo.....Cloth, 1 00

The Husband in Utah, edited by Maria Ward, author of "Female Life among the Mormons," 12mo......................Cloth, 1 00

The Philosophy of Skepticism and Ultraism, by Rev. J. B. Walker, author of "The Philosophy of the Plan of Salvation," 12mo.................Cloth, 1 25

Buchan's Domestic Medicine and Family Physician, 12mo............Cloth, 1 25

Walker on Female Beauty, 12mo.......................Cloth, 1 00

Fox's Book of Martyrs, illustrated, 12mo................... 1 25

Captain Molly. The Story of a Brave Woman, by Thrace Talmon, 12mo. 1 00

The Prisoner of the Border, by P. Hamilton Myers, author of "The Last of the Hurons," &c., 12mo. 1 25